GRAB BAG

14

www.barbarianspy.com

This book is copyright © habu 2018
habu asserts his right to be known as the author of this work.
Published by BarbarianSpy in 2018
Cover design © S Bush 2018
Cover images: manipulated: © Wrangel | Dreamstime.com
ISBN: E-Book: 978-1-925568-33-2
Paperback: 978-1-925568-34-9
All rights reserved

BarbarianSpy
Australia

Grab Bag 14

Habu

Table of Contents

Introduction

Grab Bag 14 continues the varied mix of settings, themes, and fetishes provided by habu's eclectic gay male erotica Grab Bag collections. These fifteen short stories, written during the summer of 2017, are laid out in the order in which they were written and represent inspirations that hit habu during a relatively quiet season in which extensive travel didn't provide focused inspiration as his themed spring 2017 anthology, *On the Train*. did. Such "free to think" periods often provide expanded parameters for unusual stories, and this anthology certainly provide those.

Habu is known for historical settings. The two historicals in this collection explore settings and fetishes that habu has given emphasis in recent years. "The Golden Cord" covers lust in the Levant, involving Saracens and twelfth-century crusaders, and the other historical story, "When in Niamey," takes us to Africa in the 1950s to unfold a story of extreme fetish. Most of the stories are set in the United States, mostly in the New York–Boston area, but some also have locations as far south on the East Coast as Savannah, Georgia, and west to California. Three of the stories are set in the Caribbean ("Lottery Winner," "Fissure," and "In the Giant's Shadow"), three are set in Africa ("When in Niamey," "Shipwrecked," and "Hunting Dr. Weiss"), one in Japan ("Rainy Day in Tokyo") and one in New Zealand ("Is Capricious the Word?"). Together, they reflect how widely traveled habu has been.

Habu has signature topics, which are represented in this collection, as usual. Relationships figure high in theme, including here, "The Golden Cord," "Lottery Winner," "Fissure," "Good Neighbor," "Shipwrecked," "Is Capricious the Word?," "Rainy Day in Tokyo," "That's Why," and "Sunset Save." Two,

"Lottery Winner" and "Sunset Save," deal with older men. Writers are frequent protagonists in these stories, including in "Fissure, Pool Party," "Is Capricious the Word?," and "Hunting Dr. Weiss." Connections with universities and think tanks, in keeping with habu's "other" life, are included in "Pool Party," "Good Neighbor," "Is Capricious the Word?," "Rainy Day in Tokyo," "In the Giant's Shadow," and "That's Why." Habu is becoming increasingly bold in presenting extreme fetishes, and these can be found in "When in Niamey," "Hunting Dr. Weiss," and "Unlikely Obsession."

The anthology opens up with "The Golden Cord," a twelfth-century crusader story in which the commander of a besieged crusader fortress in the Holy Land attempts to offer a false son as a hostage to the Saracens to secure a retreat to the sea.

The anthology then moves to the present and the Caribbean. In "Lottery Winner," two mature men find each other on a Caribbean gay man's cruise amid young men throwing themselves at one of them, a lottery winner. In "Fissure," as an older-younger relationship cools off, the younger man, a novelist on the cusp of success, starts looking elsewhere for sexual satisfaction.

The fourth story, "Pool Party" also features a novelist as a protagonist, and it and the fifth story, "Good Neighbor," are contemporary stories set in an unidentified university town (just as habu lives in a major university town). In "Pool Party," a young novelist with a wife, who works at the university, is seen by his neighbor having sex with a truck driver in an edge-of-town tavern rendezvous room and is blackmailed into sex with the neighbor, leading to more. In "Good Neighbor," a university tennis coach seduces a shy gay neighbor who has recently lost his mother with what was meant to be a pity fuck but becomes something deeper.

The next two stories flip us over to Africa. "When in Niamey" is a 1950s stories set in Niger. In this extreme fetish story, men come to the capital of Niamey to avail themselves of the practice of fisting young men. The protagonist is there to please them, but he comes to the attention of the local strongman general, who also enjoys extreme fetish sex. In

"Shipwrecked," a young university student is shipwrecked on the coast of Africa and taken by a primitive ape man as his mate.

"Is Capricious the Word?" is another novelist/university story. It moves from New York to New Zealand in setting and gives us a young bisexual novelist in a marriage of convenience going on sabbatical to New Zealand with his university professor wife and finding a hedonist community there where everyone is doing everyone else.

In another story that starts in New York and, this time, moves to Malibu, California, "Cover Boy," university student and male model Russ finds that the road from being a photographer's model and a movie star goes through male prostitution. New York is also the starting point for "Hunting Dr. Weiss," in which an aspiring New York writer is sent off to help find and write a magazine article on a famous free clinic doctor who, not incidentally, is an extreme fetish sexual predator.

In a wistful story, "Rainy Day in Tokyo," a visiting theater arts professor enjoys rainy day sexual encounters with a young Japanese actor and an older Japanese professor in Tokyo.

Back in New York City, in "Unlikely Obsession," the assistant to and fetish lover of an Indian mystic conductor of a New York orchestra discovers that a man who had covered him with fetish sex in a gay cruising club and has become an obsession for him is his lover's car mechanic.

"In the Giant's Shadow," an MIT architecture student struggles to remain in an architect giant's stable and bed on an assignment in the Caribbean. In another story in which a young man is in the shadow of a lover, "That's Why," an ambitious and competitive Maryland think tank fellow works his mentor sexually while trying to keep a construction worker on the side.

As he usually tries to do, because his publisher prefers it, habu concludes the collection on a more romantic note. In "Sunset Save," a retired tennis pro struggles with whether there is sex life near the end of life.

And thus, in *Grab Bag 14*, habu provides surprises and a little bit of everything for the reader's pleasure.

The Golden Cord

"Tell the lad then to stay away from my table until he is well clear of the flux," Guy d'Castilon growled. He stood up from his table, where he had gotten the explanation on why his personal server and taster had not appeared. He walked over to the window in the high tower of the Heights of Bestal mesa fortress, one of the few Crusader-held fortresses in Outremer, the once extensive Crusader kingdom along the southeastern shores of the Mediterranean Sea, that still remained in Crusader hands in 1154. The forces of the Saracen general Amir Sharif invested the fortress, threatening even the chances of Castilon's dwindling forces to evacuate by sea, just as the greater Saracen commander, Salah-ad-Din, somewhat more loosely invested the nearby Crusader stronghold at the Heights of Hattin.

Primitive as the knowledge of medicine was in that time and place, Castilon did realize that he too could catch the flux from sharing space and cup with a sick table server. The commander of the Crusader garrison was a robust man, redheaded, hirsute, and fierce of countenance. He stood a head taller than any man under his command and was broader of shoulder and more muscular than any other. He ruled by natural as well as high-born right in the fortress.

His gaze first went toward the rolling hills of desert and scrub nearby and to the deployment of the tents of the Saracens. As usual, his mind went to working out a strategy for getting those in his charge to the sea. He could see the shore in the far-off distance and the Crusader enclave there as well as the hint of the sails of the vessels that were there to transport him and the remnants of his forces should he be able to reach the shore through the lines of the Saracens. As always, he concluded he could not make it militarily. He would have to try to make it by guile.

That's when he allowed his gaze to descend into the maze of courtyards below at the base of fortress. He looked around in the various nooks and crannies available to his view, watching men moving listlessly about their daily routines—an alarming decrease from mere days before in men, both in numbers and in stamina. At length, his observation went to a small side courtyard off the stables, where a golden-haired stable groom barely in his manhood was standing at a water trough and bathing himself. He was naked, and his body was beautifully proportioned.

Castilon's preferences went to young men. He moved a hand to his crotch and, unlacing his codpiece, found his horse-hung prick. He looked more intensely down into the small courtyard, catching the first view of one of his knights, Hugh Plantain, as swarthy as a Saracen, for which he could be mistaken, dark-haired and nearly as hunky as Castilon himself, emerge from the shadows. Plantain embraced the stable groom, most notable for the fine head of golden curls that brushed his shoulders, from behind, pulling the younger man into his chest.

The golden-hair groom did not resist. He leaned back into the chest of the knight, who he obviously knew and who had obviously previously known the young groom biblically, judging by their easy rapport and the yielding nature of the young man, and turned his face to the knight's searching lips. They kissed deeply, and, as Castilon watched, the knight reached down and unlaced his codpiece, releasing a thick, long erection, and then moved the hand around to grasp the young man's erection. The young man flinched and shuddered as he was raised and then set down on the knight's erection. The knight leaned back into a wooden column supporting a porch off the side of the stables, and the golden-haired groom spread his legs and raised his feet to press into the top edge of the water trough, as the knight began to pump his ass.

Castilon's seneschal entered the chamber, and not missing a beat in masturbating his cock, the fortress commander motioned the steward over to the window with his other hand. The seneschal didn't react at all in finding his master beating his

12

shaft. He was well aware of the man's appetites and sexual prowess.

"Look down below, Jacques, at the young man Hugh Plantain is riding in that courtyard by the stables."

Jacques LeClare looked as bade. "The young man? I do not know him. He is beautiful, though, is he not?" The steward had no illusions about where this was headed.

"I wish for you to know who he is. My cup bearer is ill. I wish for that young man to be brought up to serve at my meals as long as the cup bearer is ill—perhaps longer, if he pleases me."

"Yes, Sire, he will be at your next table—and anywhere else you wish him to be."

The seneschal backed out of the chamber and Castilon returned his attention to the tableau below. The young man was riding Plantain's cock well, rising and falling in a quickening rhythm, a look of ecstasy on his handsome, young face. Plantain was standing steady now, clutching the young man's hip with one hand and jacking his cock with the other. The golden-haired groom was using the leverage of his feet pressed into the rim of the water trough to rise and fall on the cock. One hand was gripping the hand the knight had on his hip and the other one was encasing the hand jacking his cock off. There was no reluctance in him for the plowing of his passage. His head was still turned, his lips open to the deep possession of the knight's tongue.

As Castilon watched, the golden-haired groom jerked and gave a little cry. Hugh Plantain tensed, momentarily took control, thrust hard and fast up into the young man's passage, and released, with a cry of his own. The groom collapsed, his cock again erupting cum. Castilon had shot his load as well.

Hours later, his meal complete, the fortress commander was having his dessert. The young groom, now cup bearer, Henri, was belly down on the surface of the supper table in Castilon's chamber, his head suspended out over the far side of the table, his mouth open, tongue hanging, out, eyes bugged out, white-knuckled hands gripping the rim of the tabletop to hold himself in place, and a pained-ecstasy expression on his face. Standing behind him, between his thighs, his strong hands

13

gripping the young man's hips, Guy d'Castilon was fucking Henri hard, deep, and fast with a cock appreciably thicker than Hugh Plantain had ridden him with earlier in the day.

Henri made all of the right sounds of glorious taking, moaning and groaning his way through putting his own pelvis into countermotion, taking his commander deep and causing his passage to ripple over the plowing cock, making love to it, and when the crisis came, pulling a series of shudders, jerks, and great gobs of cum out of the virile warrior.

Afterward, after Henri was dismissed and Jacques had come into the chamber, Castilon pronounced his judgment. "Yes, the lad will do very nicely. Clear the other one out of the chamber next to mine and install this Henri. But when I go abed tonight, bring him back to me—to my bed."

"I am pleased that he will serve for you," Jacques said, backing out of the chamber.

"Yes, he will serve nicely," Castilon muttered when he was alone. "And perhaps for more than my own immediate needs," he added. "Perhaps for all of us." Already his mind was racing ahead on how this golden beauty might serve his greater need—if, as his spy in the camp of Amir Sharif, Ahmed ibn-Ayyub, told him true about the proclivities of the Saracen general lurking out there in the darkness.

That night, lost to the charms of the young, golden-haired beauty and in deep lust, Guy pulled Henri up from the bed and strutted, bouncing the young man up and down on his cock, to the stone wall beside the window. There, Henri threw his arms around Guy's neck and hooked his knees on Guy's hips, as the virile, monstrously huge warrior chief thrust up inside him again and again. At a whisper from Henri, Guy reversed their position on the wall, pressing his back into the stones and gripping Henri's waist, as the young blond pressed his fists into the stone at either side of Guy's head and his feet into the wall on either side of Guy's chest and fucked himself in long, deep strokes on the older man's cock.

The young squire was wanton and he was good. He was very, very good. Henri was proving to be no innocent at coupling with a man, despite his young age and tender appearance, something that Castilon thought he would be able to use fully to the advantage of all of the men in his care.

Henri fucked on, pulling every ounce of pleasure and cum out of the virile fortress commander that was there to give.

* * * *

At the same moment, in the tent of the Saracen general, Amir Sharif, Castilon's spy, Ahmed ibn-Ayyub, like other retainers of the Saracen general, was peeking through rents in the tent walls at the general taking his sport with a Crusader captive.

The young, blond Crusader soldier had made the mistake of straying too far away from his scouting party from the Heights of Bestal fortress. He had been captured by the Saracens and, because he was a young, comely, and blond, he had been delivered to the tent of Amir Sharif alive. The young man had sustained a couple of wounds in the capture, but nothing life threatening. It would be left to Sharif to have sport with him and finish him off.

There was nothing that Ayyub could do for the young man. His fate was sealed and Ayyub could not reveal any sympathy for the Crusaders.

The young man was naked, on all fours on a carpet in the tent, his wrists and ankles bound, and the bindings at his wrists tied to a spike in the floor so that he was completely defenseless. Mounted on his ass, naked save for a golden cord belted around his waist, Sharif rode the young man's ass hard, fast, deep, and cruelly.

The young man, never before having been ridden by a man, was crying out the pain and indignity of the situation although, with a sniffle and deep moan, he settled down to taking the Saracen's cock as bravely as possible. As long as he was being fucked, he was still alive. Sharif was well versed in the art of prolonging a coupling and he fucked the captive for more than a half hour before he came with a prodigious gush and, with a groan, the young blond Crusader soldier collapsed under him.

After taking a few post-ejaculation thrusts as long as he was still hard, Amir Sharif untied his golden cord belt, wound it around the neck of his sobbing captive, cruelly bowed the young man's head back into his chest, and, as his victim gurgled his last, neatly garroted the young man into terminal silence.

With a sense of sorrow and frustration, the spy, Ahmed ibn-Ayyub, pulled away from his position at the tent wall. He would report this to Guy d'Castilon, of course—yet another testament to the Saracen chief's cruelty and fetish with young blond men, but it wasn't something the Heights of Bestal fortress commander didn't know all ready. He could only hope that this and the other intelligence he had to impart would help relieve the siege of the Crusader garrison. Ayyub longed to be able to set sail with the Crusaders and return to his family in Cyprus.

* * * *

The day was glorious. The small party of Crusaders that flowed out of the main gate of the Heights of Bestal and made its short way down the side of a ravine to a small stream below the walls made enough noise to attract the attention of the Saracens. The closest of these were held off from arrow distance by a manned defensive trench between the Saracen lines and the walls of the fortress. The armed party came down to the stream, where some went on watch and others stripped down and bathed in the stream. This was a normal routine, and, although the Saracens kept watch over the activity outside the walls of the fortress, unless they knew in advance it was happening, they didn't have time to launch an attack party before the bathers returned to the fortress—and the launch party would have to get across the defended trench before reaching the bathers anyway.

On this day, one bather, in particular, stood out. He was a young, comely blond with a cascade of curly golden-blond hair that came down to his shoulders. He stood on a rock at the stream's edge, like a young god, while other bathers sponged his perfectly formed body off. One of the knights broke away from those guarding the bathers and saddled up behind the young man. He was a big bruiser of a man, swarthy and dark haired.

The Saracens watching gasped almost to a man when the knight unlaced his codpiece, revealing a thick and long erection,

16

moved into position behind the naked blond, lifted the young man's body up, set him down on his cock, and began fucking him. The golden-haired young man yielded readily to the taking, reaching his arms back to fling them around the knight's neck, fisting his hands together, and raising his legs to hook the fronts of his ankles on the bulge of the knight's calves. The blond moved his core with the thrusts of the knight, fucking himself on the knight's staff.

The Saracen troops were well aware of their own general's sexual interests and proclivities, and it wasn't long before Amir Sharif appeared at the top of a hill to watch the young blond beauty being fucked. His eyesight was sharp, although he would wish that it was as sharp as the interest and arousal the young man raised in him. Standing nearby was one of his trusted advisers, the man who headed up his cadre of spies in the Crusaders' fortress, Ahmed ibn-Ayyub.

"That young man there, at the stream, being so willingly plowed. Can you find out who and what he is, Ahmed?"

"I need no help from spies for that, Sire," Ayyub answered, delighted that the Saracen general was taking the bait. "That is Henri, the son of Count Guy d'Castilon, the commander of the fortress."

"I want him," Amir Sharif growled, the hoarse sound coming up from deep in his gut. "Is there a way?"

"Perhaps," Ayyub said, with a tight smile. "Those in the fortress are approaching dire straits. They have already signaled that they will leave if they can be given safe conduct to the sea, where ships await them. Perhaps you can parley with them on that need they have."

"And that would give me access to the young man how?"

"It's customary to exchange noble hostages to provide surety for a parley," Ayyub said. "You could exchange your son for Castilon's as surety to negotiate the withdrawal of the infidels."

"I don't have a son here with me, and I have no intention of letting these jackals escape to the sea," Sharif responded with a growl.

"Neither would be necessary," Ayyub said. And he proceeded to tell the smiling Saracen commander why not.

* * * *

Neither Guy d'Castilon nor Amir Sharif rode to the initial parleys to set up a meeting to discuss terms for the peaceful withdrawal of the Crusaders. The Saracens left those two meetings in the no-man's-land between the fortress and the Saracens' tent city to Ahmed ibn-Ayyub, while grim and disapproving Sir Hugh Plantain represented the Crusaders at the first meeting. The first parley established what both sides wanted, the Crusaders saying they wanted safe passage to their ships on the Mediterranean and the Saracens saying they wanted the Crusaders gone. Both sides said they wanted this to happen without bloodshed. Neither side believed the other on this point. Both the Saracens and Crusaders reveled in war making and bloodshed.

They agreed to the exchange of royal hostages, Castilon pledging the son he didn't have and Sharif, in turn, pledging the same. The hostages would be held until the Crusaders had reached the safety of their ships and then they would be exchanged. The Saracens were a land force. There was little threat to the Crusaders once they had reached their ships.

The handing over of the hostages was the sole purpose of the second parley. Once again Ahmed ibn-Ayyub was there to deliver a frightened young man, a weapons cleaner who had never even been close to Sharif's tent and whose only sin was that he was barely in his majority and a beautiful young man who Lac would be pleased to exhibit as a son of his. Castilon's so-called son, Henri, equally frightened and white with fright, but threatened to an inch of his life not to reveal his true identity and fortified with numbing wine, wasn't turned over by Hugh Plantain. Another knight, eager to please his master, Castilon, did those honors. Plantain wasn't present for the turnover.

Castilon was in the first courtyard awaiting the return of his men, with Sharif's false son in tow, when the parley party returned. The commander of the Heights of Bestal effusively welcomed the young man to the fortress and spoke of the

18

comfortable conditions he would be maintained in while he was a guest of the crusaders. And then, when the young man was off his horse and beginning to feel more comfortable with his circumstance—and had turned his back on Castilon—the Crusader warrior ran the young man through with his sword.

This was all unfolding as Castilon had planned and enlisted Ahmed ibn-Ayyub to execute. He had known from the beginning that Sharif had no son to turn over as hostage—and no hostage was needed for Castilon's plan. Although he regretted the loss of Henri who was such a joy in bed, Castilon had no illusions that the Saracen chief would treat him any better than Castilon had treated the purported son Sharif had sent to him as surety. Castilon knew of Sharif's weakness for young blond men and also of his fetish of dispatching them with the golden cord. The loss of Henri was regrettable but necessary in putting Sharif off his guard.

Back in the Saracen general's tent, Henri's claim to be the son of Castilon was given no more regard than Castilon had given Sharif's claim of a son. The intent was the same, but the result was slightly different.

Henri was taken immediately to Sharif's tent. As Henri stood before him, stripped down by the two burly guards holding him at both sides, Sharif faced him and shrugged off his silken robes. Underneath he was in magnificent erection and naked save for the golden cord wrapped around his waist. It was obvious from his demeanor that he was overwhelmed at the beauty of the young blond god standing before him.

In desperate mode, with no delusions concerning the danger he was in, Henri brashly stepped forward, taking advantage of his guards' surprise that he would do any such thing, and knelt and took Sharif's erect cock in his mouth. Submerged in pleasure with what the young blond god was doing with his soft mouth, Sharif waved the guards away, placed his hands on the young man's head, and helped guide his pleasure giving.

At length, Sharif unwound the golden cord from his waist. The most dangerous moment at all for Henri had arrived. The cord didn't go around his neck, though. Sharif pushed Henri down on his back on the carpet by the center pole of the tent.

19

He forced Henri's arms over his head and tied the cord around his wrists, securing the young man, immobile, to the strong center pole.

He wishboned the young man's legs, knelt between Henri's thighs, and spent several minutes in devouring the young man's cock and puckered anal opening. Henri responded with sighs and moans and encouragement in broken Arabic. Overwhelmed with lust, Sharif covered the young man's body, holding his legs spread and raised, and thrust inside him with his cock.

Surprisingly the young man welcomed the cock with passion, drawing it inside him, and immediately starting to work it with the undulating muscles of his passage walls. Sharif realized this was not a first-time conquest, but a seasoned catamite, and he fucked Henri hard and long with full appreciation that Henri was fucking him back—expertly.

When Amir Sharif at last raised himself up from the body of the young blond Crusader hostage and wound the golden cord around his waist again, Henri, miraculously, had not been garroted. He had participated in the fuck so well and expertly that Sharif could not bring himself to dispatch the young man so quickly. There was no pressing need to do so. He would have the young man again and again before sending him to his infidel god.

The Saracen general, lost to the charms of what he understood to be a talented golden-maned catamite, summoned the guards to take Henri away and prepare him for more complete debauching later. He was determined to reach a cruelty of fucking that would break the young man. The ultimate garroting of the infidel with the golden cord could come as easily tomorrow or the day after as today. In the meantime Al-Bakr would feast on, bruise, and break the young man's body. He then summoned his commanders to discuss at what point in the journey of the Crusader forces to the sea it would be best to fall upon them and slaughter them all.

* * * *

Amir Sharif attended the face-to-face parley with Guy d'Castilon to negotiate the Crusaders' departure with senses dulled by the sexual charms of Henri, who, in each coupling, had given Sharif promise of even more pleasurable and inventive fucking to come as well as frustrating the warrior in his desire to break Henri to the point of not giving up until he had done so. So occupied with Henri had the Saracen general become that he hadn't planned for anything but the ambushing of the Crusader forces when they were traveling to the sea, supposedly under safe conduct ensured by the exchange of noble hostages.

Castilon had thought more deeply about this, though. Indeed, he had planned it all, including Sharif's actions and his mind-dulling obsession with Henri. Castilon made his move at the parley itself. His party pulled out concealed weapons and fell upon Sharif and his party before they could draw their own concealed weapons. As he did so, his forces inside the Heights of Bestal fortress, already prepared for a challenged forced march to the sea after dispatching the Saracen spies within their midst, as identified by Ahmed ibn-Ayyub, poured out of the fortress, joined with their leader in wiping out Sharif and his parley party and began their race to the Mediterranean. The Saracen forces, taken completely by surprise, were too late to muster forces and reach them before Castilon and his men gained the safety of the ships on the shore of the Mediterranean.

In the fight of the parley parties, Ahmed ibn-Ayyub somehow got run through with a Crusader sword as well. It wasn't really a mistake. Castilon didn't want the Saracens ever to get the full picture of the scheme he had brought off. And Ayyub was just another unbeliever no longer of much use to Castilon anyway. Castilon gave more thought of regret to the sweet young lay he had sacrificed to the plan. He assumed that Henri had been murdered as soon as he had reached the Saracen camp.

In this, he thought wrong. He also thought wrong that Sir Hugh Plantain was with the forces rushing to the sea.

Hugh Plantain had taken Castilon's use of Henri badly. He was more taken with the sexual charms of the young blond beauty than Castilon had been. He had refused to be part of turning Henri over to the Saracens, and when he fully knew

Castilon's plans and had also learned from Ahmed ibn-Ayyub that Henri was not yet dead—a fact that he convinced Ayyub not to apprise the Crusader general of—he made plans of his own.

As Castilon and his party rode to parley with Sharif, Plantain, dark and swarthy enough to disguise himself as a Saracen, stole into the camp of the Saracens. When the alarm was raised that their commander was under attack in the no-man's-land between the fortress and the camp and that the forces of the Crusaders were pouring out of the Heights of Bestal, chaos ensued in the camp. Under the cover of this chaos Plantain slit the back wall of Sharif's tent and found and unbound Henri.

"Come, you are going with me. Amir Sharif is undone and the Crusaders are on the move to the sea."

"Can we join them with the troops of the Saracens between us and them?"

"We're not going with them. Castilon thought so little of you and he was willing to sacrifice you to the Saracens. We ride in the other direction—away from both Saracens and Castilon. We go to the larger Crusader fortress at the Horns of Hattin."

"What can I do to thank you for saving me?"

"I'll think of something," Plantain said, with a grin. "I want to fuck you right here, but we need to get far enough away that it will be safe. I'll be hard as a rock the whole way, though."

Henri, the superb submissive, just laughed, folded himself into the strong knight's embrace, and began to think of some very special way he could thank his mentor knight—and to hang on to his protection into the future. Henri was well aware of the greatest weapon he possessed for his continued survival.

Lottery Winner

Gene jutted his buttocks out from the rim of the swimming pool on Deck 11 of the *Jewel of the Seas* as it steamed its way from Key West, Florida, toward Puerto Costa Maya, Mexico. Another young man was standing next to him in the pool in water that rose up to his and Gene's nipples. He was leaning on the rim of the pool on one elbow, the palm of one hand pressed against his cheek and smiling and chatting with Gene. He had his other hand buried down the back of Gene's Speedo, and he had two fingers up Gene's ass, the pad of one of them rubbing Gene's prostate.

You couldn't really tell that the twenty-something Julio was finger fucking the forty-eight-year-old Gene in the ship's pool because of how well they were disguising it under water. But it wouldn't have really mattered much anyway, because this was a chartered gay-men-only running of the cruise ship, and everyone here was cruising and on the make themselves.

Gene moved in closer to Julio and the two kissed, Gene moaned at the stroking of his prostate. He came in his own hand that had been pushed under the front of his Speedo and stroking his cock, and then the two pulled away from each other.

"How much? In my cabin?" Gene murmured.

"$200 for two. A quickie and then something slower," Julio answered.

"I'd like to dry off in the sun," Gene answered. "But I'll leave a pass key at the foot of my pool bed. If you're still interested in a half hour, come by and pick it up. There will be a twenty for what you just did."

The extra pass keys—giving room access but not the charging capability of the master door pass—was a special service for such cruises as this. All you had to do to get an extra key with door access only was sign a waiver and pay an extra fee.

Julio, who was a muscled-up Hispanic stud, laughed and swam off with impressive Australian crawl strokes to the other side of the pool. Gene moved over to the ladder and pulled himself up onto the pool decking. He was a pretty good looker himself, toned up nicely for a forty-eight-year-old man. You could tell that he spent time in the gym. He was more wiry than bulky, but there wasn't any fat on him. He was a runner, dark haired, some matting on him, with hazel eyes that attracted attention and a sultry smile. When he was in his twenties, he would have had to fight the guys off, if he had had any intention to. He'd been out of circulation for a while, though. Julio's advances in the pool had been a surprise, but then his travel agent apparently had transmitted the news to the people setting up the cruise and it had spread from there.

He'd thought his age would be a big problem on this voyage, but it hadn't been. Julio wasn't the only hunk buzzing around him.

He padded over to his pool bed. They were set close together and the pool area was crowded. There weren't that many swimmers, but the cruise being what it was, there were near-naked bodies on display from one end of the pool area to the other and everyone was ogling everyone else. The hunkier guys weren't staying long at the pool, though—whether tops or bottoms they quickly were leaving with someone for the cabin areas.

Gene could sense the assessing eyes and murmured comments as he passed from pool to lounge bed. Oh, yes, he thought, word was out. He didn't know whether to curse his travel agent or thank him.

"That was a beautiful young man feeling you up in the pool." The voice, a rich baritone, had come from the pool bed right next to Gene's. There was room beside his lounger on one side, but the other side directly abutted another bed. The man on that bed was even older than Gene was—probably in his late fifties. But he was very well put together. Very handsome and debonair even in his swimming trunks. He had a mane of salt-and-pepper hair, but the hair on his body, more a fuzz of tight

24

curls, was a reddish-auburn. He was built solid, heavy, but he carried it very well—barrel chested and tight, Zeus-like abs. He looked familiar. He also looked like he was fully in control—of whatever he wanted to control.

"Was it that obvious?" Gene asked, toweling off on the opposite side of his bed from the man who had spoken and then lying down on his back on the lounge bed. The man watched him towel off, both amusement and interest in his eyes.

"It was, because you give hope to someone like me. You are in terrific shape and very good looking, but it's still a surprise to see the young hunks like that Puerto Rican show such interest in you. Did you know you would be received so well when you came on this cruise? Are you a power top or something? Or do you own a gym in Key West all the men want to belong to? You look like you might own a gym."

Gene laughed. "I'm from Baltimore. And, no, I don't own a gym and I'm not a top."

"Nice," the man said, turning toward Gene on his pool bed. Gene could tell the man was hard.

"What's nice?" Gene asked.

The man smiled and said, "Would you believe I was referring to you being from Baltimore?"

"No, not really," Gene said, and laughed. "So, you're saying it's a good thing I'm not a top?"

"Yes, it would be a pity if we both were," the man said. "You have a nice smile and laugh. I find you very attractive."

"I find you very familiar looking—in a good way, of course," Gene responded. "Do many people tell you look like that movie star . . . what's his name?"

"Yes, I get that a lot. Do you find me attractive too?"

"Jock Kelso. That's the movie star. And he's very attractive, so, yes, I must find you attractive too."

"There's no reason for us not to make the most of this cruise. Turn your body to me. I wish to feel you up."

"Excuse me? Just like that?"

"Yes just like that. I think you know I'm hard. If I arouse you too, turn toward me, please. I'm going to feel you up; make you more aroused. You don't object to that on a cruise like this, do you? Or am I too old for you?"

25

Gene didn't know why he did—other than that the man was attractive and had a commanding voice—but he did turn on his side. "No, you're not too old for me. But the pool is crowded. We'll be—"

"Who gives a fuck what they see?" the man asked. He was already running his hand under Gene's waistband and taking possession of Gene's cock. Gene knew the man had now discovered that he'd gone hard too. He emitted a little moan. He did nothing to fend off the touch of the man's long, sensuous fingers. "Ah, yes, I do arouse you too. You may feel and stroke me off too, if you like," the man said. "I would like it if you do."

Gene slid his hand under the waistband of the man's trunks, glided his fingers through the man's bush, and sheathed the thick, hard cock he found in his hand. The two lay there, facing each other, panting lightly, their eyes locked on each others', and slowly stroked each other off.

"This is fine," the man said. "We can bring each other off like this. You would like to come, with me masturbating you, wouldn't you?"

"Yes," Gene murmured.

"I will enjoy coming for you too."

As they stroked, the man murmured sexy words to Gene in low tones, which flowed over Gene like a welcome breeze. It had been so long since a man had worked him like this.

"Your body is still so nice, your shaft so thick and long, that I'll bet you were a real firecracker when you were in your twenties."

"Yeah, I was bad to the bone," Gene whispered.

"Was there anything you wouldn't do?"

"Not much."

"Did you do doubles—let two men inside you at once?"

"Sometimes."

"Nice. You're so sexy. I'd like to be inside you. I want to fuck you. I'd like to share you with another man too—two hard cocks inside you, making love to you and to each other."

The unvarnished sexy talk was pushing Gene over the edge. They tensed, jerked, and came together, guided by the older man's whispered instructions on how close he was. He leaned his face into Gene's, and they shared a tender kiss.

"That was special. Do you mind me being that forward?" the man asked.

"No, not at all," Gene responded, and, strangely enough, he found that that was true. He moved his hand from the man's cock and up his torso, cupping his chin, and pulling his face in for another kiss. Gene had a fleeting thought to what all of the young men swirling about them would think of these two old codgers having "sort of" sex by the pool and then he didn't give a shit what they thought. His hand went back down to tease one of the man's nipples out of his chest hair and give it attention.

"My name is Jason. Jason Hurlock," the man said when they had both come inside their swim suits.

"Gene. Gene Dixon," Gene answered.

"Is this what you came on this cruise to get, Gene?" Jason asked. "But maybe from the younger men? Where are you in life that you have come on this cruise? Is there no one significant in your life to do this for you back in Baltimore?"

"There was," Gene answered. "There was for over twenty years, but he died recently. And then something else happened too."

"Twenty years? I've had a similar experience. Was he younger than you—or older than you, like I am?"

"Older."

"And were you submissive to him?"

"Yes."

"Was he hung? Did he fuck you with a big dick?"

"Yes."

"I am hung too."

"I notice." They both laughed.

"You mentioned another something that happened to you and prompted you to take this cruise."

"I won in the lottery. I suddenly could afford to get out of the rut—to get out and meet men again. But enough about me, Jason. What has brought you on this cruise?"

"I wanted to meet, seduce, and fuck younger men," he answered. They lay there for a moment, staring into each other's eyes. Their hands had retreated now, and they were just two mature men facing each other in adjacent lounge beds. The spell was broken, though, and Jason looked out toward the pool.

"Younger men? Younger than me?"

"At my age, nearly all desirable men are younger. You are younger than I am, Gene. I want to fuck you. Ah, there is your Hispanic stud walking this way now. Is he coming for you?"

"Shit," Gene said, and he reached into the small bag he had with him, scrounged around and found the extra pass card to his cabin and twenty dollars. He leaned over and deposited both of them on the foot of his lounge bed.

"Twenty dollars?" Jason said, with a low laugh. "Is he really that cheap?"

"I wish," Gene answered.

Julio strutted by their lounge beds, giving both men a sultry, knowing look. He picked up the pass card and the twenty and moved on toward the hatchway back into the interior of the cruise ship.

Gene sat up to watch Julio wiggle his butt as he moved away. He then turned and gave Jason a quizzical look.

"Go and have your fun," Jason said. "Enjoy spending some of your lottery winnings. We can fuck later."

Gene did have fun and enjoy spending the $200 he gave Julio.

* * * *

Julio had already helped himself to a shower and was coming out into the cabin, seemingly wearing only a towel around his waist, when Gene arrived.

"Are you alone in this cabin? This is a suite," the young man said, almost accusingly.

"Yes, I'm alone. And it's a junior suite, not a full one. I imagine you've heard I've won in a lottery."

"Yes, I have heard," Julio said. "I fuck you now. Put your cheek up against this wall by the door, please. First the quick one. We strip your swimsuit off, like this. Jut your ass out for me."

"Oh, shit. Oh, Fuck!" Gene exclaimed as Julio's fingers invaded his channel again, reaching for and finding his prostate. A few minutes later, when Julio had knelt behind him and opened him up more with his tongue, Gene found that the towel

28

wasn't the only thing the Hispanic young man was wearing. When he dropped that, he was revealed to be wearing a condom, which he put to immediate use, palming Gene's belly to keep the man's ass jutting out and pressing Gene's head to the wall with his other hand, as he worked his cock inside Gene and fucked him.

A bit later in the afternoon, the sultry young Hispanic fucked Gene more slowly and deeply in a missionary on the bed, with the older man on his back, his legs descending over the foot of the bed, and the soles of his feet pressed to the carpet. Julio stood between Gene's thighs, crouching over the older' man's chest, pressing his forehead into Gene's and staring into his eyes, as he held Gene's head to the bed with a choke hold on his throat with one hand and palmed the small of Gene's back with his other hand. His cock, sheathed in a fresh condom, was deep inside Gene's passage, held steady, with the stroking provided by Julio pulling Gene's pelvis to his and releasing it with his hand on the small of Gene's back and Gene counterthrusting his pelvis by leveraging off the soles of his feet.

They fucked in this position for nearly a half hour, both of them adept at holding off when the threat of coming loomed and then resuming the stroking when they regained control. Julio gave up the game first, and Gene came soon thereafter.

"You were very good," Julio said, coming out of the bathroom afterward in shorts and a T-shirt he'd brought to the room in a small bag. He was standing by the built-in desk unit, counting his $200.

"For an old man, you mean?" Gene said, still lying on this bed, naked, his legs dangling toward the floor.

"For any man," Julio said. "You're in great shape. And you are hung. I'd suck your cock for free."

"It isn't just because I won in the lottery and am willing to share it with you?"

"I wouldn't have thought of going with a man as old as you if you didn't have money—and pay me. As you must know, I'm a professional prostitute on the cruise to make money. But in the dark I wouldn't know the difference between you and a much younger man, and you've got better moves than most. Most can't get their gut muscles to squeeze my cock and milk it

29

like you can. Nobody else has sucked my balls like you did, either."

"You should try more older men," Gene said. "You would find they are more expert than young men—and more grateful."

"Will you be more grateful for this, then?" Julio asked, with a laugh. He sank down on his knees between Gene's thighs, took the older man's cock in his mouth, and gave him an expert blow job. He drove Gene wild and the older man had his pelvis going when Julio invaded his ass with his fingers while he was sucking Gene off and did a job on his prostate as well.

A moaning and gushing Gene was $50 more grateful.

Thank the gods for the Maryland Lottery, he was thinking. What a payoff this was.

As the young man got to the cabin door, Gene called out, "Julio, tell me honestly, was the sex good? Because, you know, as men get older . . ."

"The sex was very good," Julio answered. "If you had not paid me for the blow job, I would not have complained. I volunteered to do it. Of course, the money was good too."

Then he was gone. For some reason, Gene didn't feel fully euphoric. He had agonized about this when deciding whether or not to take this cruise. But he couldn't say he wasn't getting sex on the cruise. He wondered how many hopeful young men paid for the cruise but hadn't been fucked on the cruise yet. And not just fucked. The hand job he'd shared with Jason Hurlock, another old man, had been special.

Then it dawned on him that he'd come five times so far that day. It was a worthwhile cruising cruise after all. That hadn't happened since he'd been in his twenties—since he and Brad had taken up housekeeping together.

* * * *

Dinner in the Starlight Dining Room was strangely depressing for Gene. It wasn't just that he was sore from his afternoon fuckfest with Julio and was feeling his age. It also was this lottery win thing. If only they all knew. Of course, everyone seemed to think they knew. All of the young guys at his table were on the make for him and others would stop and press themselves up against him at the table and flirt while he was trying to eat.

Obviously, Julio had passed along some confirmations on the basis of Gene having a junior suite all to himself. Not only was it affirmation that he had the money for it, but also that he had the privacy for prolonged sex. He'd been additionally chagrined when one guy asked him if he and the other guy he had in tow could borrow the cabin while Gene was at dinner.

Thus, it was with thoughts that maybe this five-day cruise hadn't been such a good idea at all that he retreated to the Schooner Bar after dinner. He reasoned that this was where the older and quieter guys would go, as there was a transvestite show booked for the A Chorus Line lounge after dinner and the Casino Royale would like be teeming with young blood as well. There even was a nude pool party at the top of the ship on the schedule for later.

A piano player who played old standards was holding down the Schooner Bar after dinner. Before dinner there'd been an aerial act in the Centrum atrium, performed by scantily clad and muscular men. That had been invigorating, but the Centrum was featuring photo ops with the captain—who didn't seem all that happy doing photos with the passengers on this particular run—and a mariachi band. Gene could pass on that.

When he entered the Schooner Bar, his attention directed to an empty stool at the far end of the bar, a hand reached out from the area of low tables and swivel chairs by the bank of windows and stopped him.

"I was hoping you'd wind up here. Would you like to join us?"

The voice, of course, was that of Jason Hurlock. The "us" turned out to be one of the aerialist from earlier in the day, a muscular blond man in his late thirties by the name of Gustav. Gene sat, ordered a Rusty Navel, and tried not to feel too pleased that not only was Jason here, but he'd made the effort to invite Gene to sit with him. He already had a hunk in tow, although Gene wondered how much Gustav was in tow. He didn't strike Gene as being a submissive.

31

Gustav was wearing a form-fitting tan shirt that brought a safari guide to Gene's mind, tight white cargo shorts, tight mainly because the man's thighs were athletically muscular, and leather wristbands. He was something East Europe. He didn't join in the conversation much, but Gene had to pay close attention to what he did say to understand it.

"Gustav is a long acquaintance of mine," Jason said. "I recommended him and his group for the entertainment job on this voyage."

Gene and Jason engaged in some chit chat between songs from the piano—they were polite enough not to talk over the playing and Gene was pleased to see that Jason seemed to genuinely enjoy the music. Gustav tolerated it, but Gustav didn't have much to say. He did keep up with Jason on the wandering hands front. After Gene was half finished with his second Rusty Navel, he became aware that both men were touching him. He was wedged between them around a low coffee table, and both men were touching him—on his arm, on his chest, on his thighs, and, eventually, on his basket. Jason more than once cupped his head and pulled him in for a brief kiss. When Gustav did that too, while cupping and squeezing his basket, Gene fully realized where this encounter was going.

And he didn't care. He was on his third drink. He'd come in worrying about what the younger guys really thought of him. Jason was older than he was, and Gustav was older than most of the passengers on this vessel. They both seemed safe.

But then they weren't safe, and Gene was too mellow and sloshed to give what Jason suggested full thought.

The piano player was taking a fifteen-minute break. It was a natural time for conversations to blossom and get deeper and for there to be a changing of the guard of the passengers in the bar. There was a general hubbub in the room and men milling about. Jason leaned over and murmured to Gene, "I've been talking to Gustav about you. Gustav says he'd like to fuck you."

"Well, uh," Gene responded, looking at Gustav's hopeful smile and then down to where Gustav's hand was cupping Gene's basket.

"I want to fuck you too," Jason said. "This afternoon wasn't enough for me. I don't think it was enough for you either. We have a key for one of the owner's suites. It would be very nice."

"Um, well."

"Gustav and I want to fuck you together—together. Both. I told you we have known each other for some time. We enjoy sharing men. You really have done double penetration before, haven't you?"

"Not for some time," Gene squeaked. "Not since my twenties." It suddenly occurred to him that what Jason had been whispering to him about doing doubles when they were stroking each other off on the pool lounge beds hadn't been random or purposeless.

"But you have done it before? You've mentioned how wild you were before you settled down with your Brad. Gustav is very athletic. He's very good too. We talked about you. We want to share you."

"Well, um."

* * * *

It wasn't so much that Gustav was showing his athleticism on the bed in Owner's Suite cabin 1510 at the other end of the tenth deck from Gene's cabin 1586 junior suite as that he put Gene in athletic positions. The threesome fuck started off with Gustav breaking Gene in. Even before they got to the bed, Gene was doing the splits on the desk, hands pressed into the mirror on the wall behind the desk, with Gustav standing behind him, holding Gene's waist, and stroking his passage with a hard cock.

"Ja, you can do it," Gustav was murmuring, and, surprisingly enough, Gene found he could.

Then it was something called the crab on the bed, with Gustav on his back and Gene stretched over him, facing the ceiling, propped up on the feet of his bent legs placed on either side of the East European's thighs and on his hands on either side of the aerialist's biceps, and Gustav, again holding his waist, pulling him up and down on his shaft. Jason, naked, sat in a

33

chair facing the bed, watching and pulling on his cock for both of these positions.

Gene was riding the cock, Gustav on his back on the bed, his legs descending to the carpet at the foot of the bed, using the leverage of his feet to control the thrusts of his cock, while Gene sat on the cock, facing the foot of the bed, hands pressed into Gustav's knees, his passage rising and falling on the shaft. It was at this point that Jason pulled his chair over, took possession of Gene's bobbing cock with a hand and of Gene's mouth with his in possessive kisses.

Gustav turned Gene's body so that Gene was facing Gustav's head, and they moved into the main event. Gustav embraced Gene's chest, pulling the man down toward his chest and rolling Gene's pelvis up. Jason saddled up behind Gene and between Gustav's spread thighs, worked his cock inside Gene's passage above Gustav's buried shaft, and, to the tune of Gene's gasps, moans, and heavy breathing, the two men fucked Gene together. Gene's mind raced back to when he was in his early twenties, in the Navy, and doing doubles left and right—there were techniques for being open and staying open. He pulled these up to the surface and he found that he could take it. And he did take it.

Later, after Gustav had left them on the bed, showered, and was gone, Gene lay there with glazed eyes, still moaning softly and trying not to think about anything. Jason was lying beside him, on his back. Gene was turned on his side, facing away from Jason. The older man turned on his side toward Gene and pulled Gene's body into his. Gene shuddered and gave a little sob, which Jason didn't comment on. Instead, he kissed Gene on the back of his neck, placed a hand on one of Gene's breasts and stroked his nipple, and slowly invaded Gene's passage with his cock. He continued kissing Gene on the neck and slow fucking him.

"That was special," he whispered in Gene's ear. When Gene didn't answer, Jason repeated, "That was very special."

"It . . . it was overwhelming," Gene responded in a low voice.

"You don't want to do it again?"

"No. I'm too old for that now."

34

"Truth be known, so am I, but you are just too delicious not to have given it a go."

"I suppose."

"And me. What I'm doing now. Do you want me to stop?"

"No," Gene said with a low sob. "I don't want you to stop."

So he didn't.

* * * *

For the rest of the voyage, Jason and Gene were pretty much inseparable. This was to the chagrin of Julio and some other young men who had designs on Gene's lottery winnings, but, in the face of Jason's strength and command, they gave up.

Heeding Gene's reaction to the threesome, Jason didn't suggest any more of those. Rather, he saw to it that the two of them made love, not just randy sex. They cuddled and kissed, and prepared each other, so that when the long slide inside Gene came, he was open and begging for it—and it was slow and easy until they were both overcome by passion and giving as much as they were taking—and coming together.

The ship made one stop during the cruise, with one land excursion, Mexico's Puerto Costa Maya. The two men went together on the shore excursion to Mayan ruins, and they acted just like young, love struck, randy young men by finding a little-traveled path to the back of a Mayan pyramid, where Jason backed Gene up against a wall and Gene climbed the other man's hips with his legs and locked his hands behind Jason's neck, while the older man opened their flies and frotted their cocks. Taking on risk like youngsters, Gene stripped off his shorts and briefs, and Jason fucked him against the wall. They came to meet the other's release, giggling, and acting thirty years younger. The other young men on the excursion weren't fooled.

On the last day of the cruise as they neared the home port of Key West, the two men were sitting, facing each other, in the bathtub in Gene's junior suite. Jason had already frotted their cocks and stroked them, with Gene's hand on top of his, to a mutual ejaculation. They were paying no heed to the cloudiness of the water that they'd both participated in causing. They were drinking champagne that Jason had ordered to celebrate their homecoming, although he said he wished he could say it was celebrating something else.

Gene dared not hope what that was, and it certainly couldn't be with his living this lie.

"I have a confession to make," he said, his face taking a serious cast.

"You're not really from Baltimore," Jason quipped. His face hadn't turn serious.

"Yes, I'm afraid I am."

"Well, Baltimore is a good place to be *from*," Jason said, "but I pity you if you actually have to live there."

"It's worse than that," Gene said. "I'm not rich. I did have lottery winnings--$6,000. I decided to spend it all on this trip."

Jason contemplated that for a moment and said, "But you have some left, don't you? Haven't I saved you from spending it all on young male whores?"

"Yes, there's that," Gene said. "But a lot of it went to this cabin. I'm a telephone lineman. Nothing rich there."

"No, but that accounts for the flexibility and tone of your body at your age. I was wondering how you could manage all of the those positions Gustav put you in that first night."

"Not very well, I'm afraid," Gene said. "My body ached for two days. I'm glad you were gentle with me. What you did wasn't fucking, it was lovemaking. I thank you for that."

"If you have a cabin admission, so do I," Jason said.

"Oh?"

"That suite we were in. I didn't lie. I said that Gustav and I had access to it. But that's because it's my suite. And I'm the sponsor of this cruise. I told you I came on this cruise to seduce and fuck young men—and that's true. And before you object, you are a younger man than I am, so you count. But what I didn't say was that I came on this cruise because I am lonely and I hoped to find someone to be with. In addition to all of the other attractions I found in you, I thought that you similarly were lonely. We'd both recently lost long-term significant others."

36

"I hadn't thought about that much," Gene said, "but I think I was just avoiding thinking about it. But I guess it's true."

"One last confession and then I'm all out of secrets," Jason said. "When you said I looked like the movie actor Jock Kelso, and I side stepped that, I did so because I *am* Jock Kelso. I certainly don't admit that up front with a man I'm planning to seduce, though. I think you've found that having money isn't the most trustworthy way to shop for a mate. Jason Hurlock is my real name."

"Shopping for a mate?" Gene asked, brushing aside the other matter.

"Yes. Do you think we might get rid of the feeling of loneliness together? Can you bear not to live in Baltimore anymore or to climb telephone poles? I live in Key West—in a house much too big for one. I put this whole cruise together as a shopping spree. Can you be the treasure I found?"

"What do you think?" Gene said, as he splashed water in moving to Jason's side of the tub. "Can I say I feel like I've won the lottery?"

Fissure

"Have you had time to read my manuscript yet?"

No response. We were sitting by the pool of our house in George Town, capital of the Cayman Islands, both in our Speedos. We hadn't been in our Speedos for very long. We'd come out to the pool to cool off after sex, although the sex hadn't been that heated. Collin had lain on his back on the bed, and I'd ridden his cock, rising and falling and revolving in slow motion, coaxing the cum out of him. He'd seemed distracted. I'd had to do it all. He'd seemed distracted a lot lately. We'd burned up the bed with sex when we lived in our small apartment in Manhattan and he'd been training in as an international banker and I'd been finishing up my master of fine arts in fiction writing.

We'd been a sexy pair then, he a British hunk of twenty-eight and me a corn-fed Nebraskan of twenty-one. We had both been athletic and figuratively swung from the chandeliers in our inventive fuck positions.

Lately, here in the Caymans, where we had everything we could possibly want, including a sexy black majordomo from Jamaica, Thomas, who was forward enough to stand at the sliding doors into the bedroom from the pool and watch us fuck, I was having to do most of the work to bring us both off.

Having Thomas stand there had actually helped me. I could imagine him being with us in a threesome. I'm sure he would have been willing. He already was treating me like I was just another one of Collin's possessions, a sex toy, rather than anything close to his equal. That had been rubbing off on Collin. He was making a pile of money here in the Caymans with his British bank. I was still shipping manuscripts around to agents. I'd made money off of short stories, but nothing like Collin made from hiding other people's money. Collin was beginning to remark on that—on his view that I wasn't pulling my weight.

This seemed to have given Thomas the idea that I was just Collin's whore and that he, Thomas, could treat me that way too. He'd already cornered me a couple of times, embraced me, kissed me, and told me he planned to fuck me. I probably should have told Collin and had the Jamaican dismissed, but he had started coming on to me at the same time Collin was giving me less attention, and the Jamaican was a sexy black bull. The attention turned me on—as long as I could hold the stud in check. And if Collin didn't start showing more interest in our sex life, maybe I wouldn't play as hard to get with Thomas.

"I said, have you read my latest manuscript yet? I think this one has legs."

"Uh, no, I've really been tied up at the bank. Someone's got to pay the bills."

Of course, I thought. And we were living high on the hog now—a fancy house with a pool, each of us with a sports car, and a cook, cleaning lady—and Thomas, the hunky Jamaican man of all services. We were out of our element still in the Caribbean, so Thomas was earning his keep.

He came out on the patio at this point with drinks for both Collin and me. He was looking good. As was typical with him on this tropical island, he was only wearing baggy white cotton trousers and sandals without socks. He was tall—some six and a half feet, and muscular, an ebony god. The waistband of the trousers rode low on his hips. I loved the look of the line running down from each side below his six pack, pointing at the goods, when his trousers were dipping low enough to show the curls where his pubes started. Any false moves and the pants would cascade to the floor. He gave me a look and a wink, reminding me that he'd just watched me, naked, riding Collin's cock, and strutted back into the house.

"I've received a check from *Chicago Literary Journal*," I said. "Twelve hundred dollars."

"Great," Collin said without looking up from the papers he was sifting through. "We can fix the roof on the gazebo now."

That, of course, was a put down on my financial contribution here. He didn't really directly say I was sponging off him and was only here now as a sex toy—one he didn't make full use of—but there always were little jabs like this.

"Do you want to read the manuscript before I start sending it around? You always were a great help in pointing to plot holes and technical issues." That had been true in the past—when we lived in New York. Not so much here in the Caymans. He'd read a few, without commenting much and eventually stopping showing interest altogether. He once had been enthusiastic about my writing. It was a big reason I went with him to begin with. I hadn't gone with many older men before him.

"We'll see if I can free some time for it," he said, still not looking up.

That meant a "no," of course. Good thing I had other copies of the manuscript. He likely didn't even know where he'd last left the copy I'd given him. Time to ship other copies without his help.

"Should I tell the cook you'll be here for lunch?" I asked.

"No, I think not," he said, standing and stretching. "I have to go into the office. Dinner will have to be late too. I'd best get dressed and get out of here now." He was a handsome man—and he kept his body lean and muscular. I couldn't complain about his capabilities in bed—when he employed them. He hadn't changed his sleek form. We probably still could swing from the chandeliers during sex. It's just that we didn't. And I was too young and randy still not to want to.

I think for him, though, it had just become relieving the need to evacuate his balls regularly.

At the sliding glass doors to the bedroom, he turned and said, "Thanks for the nooner. You're still a sweet lay. I'm not sure I know where I put your manuscript. Do you have another copy?"

"Yes, sure," I said. "I'll put a copy on the nightstand on your side of the bed." We had separate sides of the bed now. In New York, we just had a twin bed. We both slept in the middle.

I waited until Collin had gone to his room and was changing into a suit. The bedroom opened onto the pool terrace,

40

so I knew everything he was doing in getting ready from the sounds. I didn't dare turn my head and look. I had been devastated by his indifference. He surely could have seen that—if he had looked at me. But he'd just prattled on about the weekend plans, which all sounded like business, and said he had to go into the bank—which I knew, as he was always going into the bank. This was especially so when we got anywhere close to talking about this fissure that was yawning and widening between us.

Thomas padded out with another drink. I couldn't look up at him because there were tears in my eyes. I wanted to wave him away. Another drink was the last thing I needed. He stood there briefly, looking oh so muscular and sexy, but then turned and went into the house.

When I knew Collin was gone, I stood and looked down at the drink. The last thing I needed at this moment was more alcohol. I picked the drink up and drained it in one go. I went into the bedroom—our bedroom—and sat at the vanity, looking at myself in the mirror. I could see the tears in my eyes, and that's not all I saw. I saw the fissure that was developing between Collin and me in all its yawning breadth. What had happened to us? We had been so happy in New York when we'd had practically nothing.

Here in the Caymans we had everything. But of course that was the problem. That was numbing each of us to the other.

I folded my arms on the top of the vanity and lay my head down and let the tears roll.

I don't know why I didn't jerk and move away when Thomas came close behind me and put his hands on my shoulders, or when he murmured that it would be all right, that he knew what I needed. Nor did I recoil from him when one of his hands glided down my chest and he palmed one of my pecs, worked his fingers into the light brush of curly hair there, and teased out a nipple. Nor did I pull back when he cupped my chin with his other hand and gently raised my head, turning my face up to his, and gave me a long, lingering look before he took my lips with his.

"Thomas, no, this isn't what we should be doing," I whispered.

41

"It's exactly what we should be doing," he answered. "You're not getting what you need."

I didn't resist when he pulled me up out of the chair, took me up in his arms, and carried me over to the bed. He laid me on the bed at the foot, my buttocks at the bottom edge, and slipped my Speedo off my legs. I was naked to him. He unbuttoned his trousers, dropped them, and kicked them away. And then he was naked to me. He was magnificently erect, his black cock thicker and longer than Collin's was. I was quickly hard too, expanding immediately as he wrapped his hand around my cock.

We both knew what we both wanted. But I made one more effort not to complicate the life here in paradise.

"Thomas, this isn't right. Collin—"

"You are Mr. Collin's mistress," Thomas said, with a laugh. "He treats you like his property. You are a whore to him. There's no reason you can't be a whore to me too. I don't have money, but I have a big black cock. I can take care of you better than his money can. He don't never need to know. I can make you happy with my cock, and then it will be easier for you to be happy with his money."

It's exactly what a man would say to a whore he felt the right to fuck. I couldn't argue with that. That, indeed, was what I'd become to Collins—his mistress—and not one that he paid a lot of attention to. Thomas could feel me surrender to him. He laughed.

I groaned as he disappeared onto his knees between my spread thighs and, first, took my cock in his mouth and then my balls and then was working my hole with his tongue. I opened wide to him, knowing I must if I was going to take him.

"If you're going to do it, fuck me good," I said, wearily.

"I always give good fuck," he said, with a low laugh.

Taking him wasn't easy, though. I lay on my belly on the bed, with Thomas covering me. He had worked three inches or so inside me, permitting him to reach up, grasp my wrists in his grip, and force my arms over my head.

His mouth was at one of my ears and he was whispering to me in that deep baritone Jamaican accent of his, "Just relax. Open to me, Mon. Let me inside. Let all of your worries go, just

42

for now. I will make you very, very satisfied with my cock. I will fuck fuck you real good, Mon."

I relaxed then. I wasn't a novice. I knew how to open to a man and what to do with the muscles of my passage when a man was inside me. Thomas was huge, but I could take him. I wanted to take him. I knew this was wrong—but it also was so right. I relaxed and he gave me another couple of inches.

I groaned and went up a bit on my knees, raising my hips more, spreading my thighs more, taking a couple of more inches of him. Surely he was all inside me now. But no, he urged me to relax more and when he did, I had it all in one glorious painful slide and felt the kinky black curls of his pubes on the tender skin of my buttocks.

"Breathe," he whispered in my ear. "You have it all now. Relax to it so that I give you a good fuck."

I hadn't realized I had been holding my breath in. I let it out and, although my breathing was ragged and panty, I felt myself open further to him.

It was then that I had second thoughts—when he fully possessed me and walls were stretched as they never had been before and the muscles of the walls were beginning to undulate over the velvet steel of his shaft. "Thomas, this isn't good. We shouldn't—" I started to struggle, but it was no use. He was stronger than I was and held me tight.

"You are fucked already," he growled. "You will take it until I am finished with you."

I surrendered to him and remained open to the cock. I was such a fraud. The time for saying that, for fending him off had long past. I should have said something weeks earlier, when he had taken me in his arms, kissed me, and told me he would fuck me. I knew then that he would—and now he was. My passage walls were rippling over his throbbing cock, making love to it. I was lost to him.

"It's what you need, Mon. Just a little attention. No harm in that. These are the islands. You can take your pleasures and your needs wherever you can find them. Mr. Collins has you here to pleasure himself. No reason you can't pleasure others as well."

And then his cock was returning the attention my walls had given it. He began to stroke. Using the leverage of his knees he was rising and falling on my ass, sliding his cock in deep and out, in deep and out. My pelvis was moving with him, rolling with the thrusts, taking all of him that my passage could get, the walls making love to cock. We were fucking.

"Yes, yes, you want it," he muttered. "You're a little whore for it."

Angered, I moved again to slip out from underneath him, but I no sooner turned then he slapped me twice in the face, with his palm in one direction and backhanded in the other and put me back in position. "Take it like the little whore you are."

I let out a sob, but I realized that the rough treatment was exciting me, arousing me. I was feeling the fuck, something I hadn't done with Collin for months. This demanding, masterful black bull excited me. I settled down with the fuck.

"Yes, please. Fuck me good. Give it all to me, deep," I whimpered, the acknowledgment that it was what I wanted being painfully pulled out of me.

"That's better," he growled. "You don't want me to have to beat it out of you. We're going to get down to business now. I'll fuck you great. We both know you want it."

And he was right. I did want it. I wanted it from him.

It went on forever and I cried out for it and submitted to everything he told me to do. All of my sensations were concentrated on that impossibly thick shaft stretching me, conquering me, working me, and I surrendered to the magic of it, never wanting the stroking to stop. He let loose of one of my wrists so that I could reach under and stroke my cock. He even covered my hand with his and we stroked together. I came on the bedspread with the realization that it would have to be washed before Collin came home—and then realizing that Thomas was the servant here. He would take care of that.

Just like he was taking care of me when he could see that Collin hadn't been attentive enough.

That's when I realized that I was going to continue to let Thomas fuck me when Collin wasn't there to do it or didn't show me enough attention—even if Collin fucked me too. Thomas was right. This was what I needed.

When Thomas came inside me, I realized that he had barebacked me. I didn't really give a shit.

We lay there, the big Jamaican having just rolled off to the side of me, both of us panting hard, bringing ourselves under control. We were both young—Thomas younger and more virile than I was. I fell back and grasped his cock, which came back to life and began to engorge again. But I released it as soon as I realized that he could harden right up again.

"We can't do this again, Thomas," I whispered. "This isn't right."

"Whatever you think, Mon," the Jamaican said. He was fingering my ass and even as he entered me with his middle finger and reached in for my prostate, I knew that he was smiling.

I rolled over on top of him, saddled myself on his pelvis, held his cock in position, slid my channel down on it, and began riding the cock. He'd already done me; there was little reason not to get all of the pleasure out of him that I could.

I'm fairly sure Thomas would have made that point himself to get on top of me again if I hadn't stolen a march on him.

We rested and then we swung from the chandeliers in wild sex, the sex of long-term lovers willing to give everything his partner wanted. And Thomas wanted a lot. He sat on the side of the bed, holding me cantilevered out from his body over the carpet, my legs streaming behind him, trapped under his armpits, his cock deep in my channel, his hands fisting my wrists, as my torso arched out in front of him over his thighs. Using the strength of his massive biceps and chest muscles, he pulled me on and off his cock. I hadn't been fucked in such a challenging position since Collin and I had left Manhattan. I suddenly was alive and firing on all cylinders for the first time in a long time.

It was nearly dark before he stopped, having shown that he could fire off again and again and again. "Mr. Collin will be home soon. We must straighten up," he said. He had the decency to saying it with regret in his voice. He could, instead,

45

have humiliated me by declaring that I was *his* property now, *his* mistress, *his* sex slave. I would not have demurred.

I felt guilty for several weeks after that, which, however, didn't stop me from riding Thomas's cock whenever I had a chance, although we did it in his room or in the pool so that Collin wouldn't see evidence of it. And he had a new, testing position each time. We swung from the chandeliers again and again and again. I spun on that big black bull cock. He reamed me so open that I was surprised that Collin didn't notice how loose I'd become during our much tamer sex sessions. Perhaps if he was giving me half the attention he was giving his bank and his money-hiding clients, he would have noticed.

The guilt stopped the day I came home earlier than expected from shopping in George Town and found Thomas on his back on a pool bed and Collin saddled on his pelvis, riding his cock. I knew that Collin was versatile and I also was fully aware of the power of Thomas's charisma and cock. I probably shouldn't have been surprised. Collin was paying less attention to me because Thomas was tiring him out.

The plot thickened and the fissure widened.

Having seen Thomas fucking Collin didn't stop me letting Thomas fuck me too. The first time he came upon me in the silver closet after I'd seen him with Collin as Collin's car was departing through the gate and I knew he wanted me, I tried to resist, struggling with him. But Thomas actually enjoyed that— and, in the end, so did I. With a laugh, he shoved me up against a cabinet, with one hand cupping my chin and forcing my head back against the cabinet door. His other hand pushed my shorts down to my knees and grabbed my cock. I otherwise was naked. I beat on his chest, ineffectively, with my fists. The man was bigger and stronger than I was, my strikes growing weaker and weaker as he worked my cock and came in to possess my lips with his.

Coming out of the kiss, he growled, "Step out of the shorts," and I kicked them away.

"Unzip me," he commanded. I went beyond that, taking his cock out. He was hard. So was I.

"Climb my hips with your knees."

With a whimper, I did so.

"Put it in yourself." When I had, he thrust up into me and started to stroke immediately. Snuffling and panting I moved with him. After that I didn't try to deny him ever again.

The day came, though, that Thomas was suddenly gone and Rondy was there—an older Jamaican, muscular, yes, but not like Thomas was. Not in a sexy, confident, overstepping way.

When I asked, Collin simply said that something had gone wrong in Thomas's family back in Jamaica, and he had to leave immediately. Collin said we were lucky that the family that had Rondy had shipped back to the UK and we were able to hire him on without a gap in help. That was certainly true. We had a cook and a cleaning woman, but we were still lost without a majordomo.

But the problem wasn't that we might have been without a majordomo—it was that we were without Thomas. I think that if Collin knew Thomas had been fucking me he either wouldn't care or he'd let me know he knew. There must have been some falling out between Collin and Thomas that had nothing to do with me.

Whatever it was, Collin must have felt a little bit guilty about it, because he paid me more attention from then and our life seemed to get back on track. He still was wrapped up in his own work, though, and didn't show that much interest in mine.

Rondy accepted both Collin and me as masters of the house and gave me every deference. Thomas had shown some deference to me when Collin was present but when he wasn't Thomas had treated me not only as Collin's sex toy—his property to be used as he wished—but as his, Thomas's, as well.

I missed Thomas—and swinging on the chandeliers.

* * * *

"They are all pigs, of course. Your Collin is a pig too, isn't he?"

"I wouldn't say so, no," I answered Bobby. We were sitting on the front porch of the Wharf Club, overlooking the George Town waterfront near the end of the city wharf. It was a gay club, not that anyone would admit to that. Sodomy was illegal in the Caymans, although, like most laws here, it was

47

ignored unless it became too obvious. It just was used socially in self-selection separating one strata of "us" from another of "them." Collin and I were somewhere in limbo socially. We were known to be a gay couple, but Collin had an important position in banking and I had an interesting background, as a novelist—a more successful one now that I'd sold one of my novels to G.P. Putnam. Being some form of "artist" gave me leave to be queer and even flighty, if I wished. The English had a tradition of celebrating, in a low-key way, the unconventional artist, and the Caymans were distinctly English in flavor. Thus far I hadn't wished to flighty, though. Still, we weren't being invited into the homes of the super wealthy or highbrow here.

"Oh, come on," Bobby persisted. "You've said that Collin hasn't given you the attention you needed."

I knew that was a mistake—telling Bobby that—as soon as I'd done it. But that was before I sold the novel and before Thomas left our services. Collin was a bit better now. A bit. I liked Bobby. I found him easy to talk to, both of us being young, in the arts, and essentially kept men on the island. His keeper was the owner of the club, Gordo Williams, a Jamaican much like Thomas had been—a big, strapping black bull. But where Thomas had been handsome, Gordo was ugly as sin. But he certainly had a magnificent body on him. Gordo owned this club. And he owned Bobby, who had been a dancer off Broadway, had signed on to a Royal Caribbean cruise line dance troupe, and had jumped ship here in the Caymans and was shacking up with Gordo. He danced for his supper now at the club. I also gravitated to Bobby because he was a sunny, funny, saucy, good-looking young man who I was studying to include as a character in a novel still in conception.

"He's better now," I said. We were here because Collin and Gordo had business—Collin was Gordo's banker—and I'd been invited along for a drink. I didn't get out much and was at a frustration point with my writing—what some called writer's block, although I didn't want to acknowledge it was that serious, so here I was. The writer's block would be gone by the time I got back to our house on Beach Drive. I had just needed to get out of the house and circulate a bit. Seeing Bobby again would get those juices going—and Gordo. I admit that, after Thomas had fucked me—my first black bull—and after Collin had become distant, I had gotten curious about Gordo. Before, I hadn't given him a second thought. Now I wondered if he was hung like Thomas had been.

"Well, Gordo is a pig. They are all," Bobby was saying. "But he has a redeeming quality."

"What's that?" I unwisely asked.

"He's got a dick to beat all dicks—I wonder if all the black men down here do—and he knows how to use it. What do you think, Sean? Do you think all of the black men down here are hung like bulls?"

"I doubt it," I said, with a laugh. "I haven't thought much about that." But I, of course was thinking that—I'd just been thinking it about Gordo. I was thinking maybe so, and ever since Thomas I most certainly had thought about it.

"*Gordo's* hung like a bull," Bobby continued. "I'll say that for him. Not much between the ears or much to look at in the daylight, but a regular baseball bat between the thighs. And that makes all of the difference. In the dark nothing is better than Gordo's cock—and dancing here at the club, I can tell you that I get a variety of cock."

"Lucky you," I said. And I meant that.

"Have you ever thought of another man while Collin was laying you—thought about someone else other than Collin being on top of you when Collin has his dick inside you and is pumping away?"

"No, of course not." I laughed, I hope not too nervously. Of course I'd thought about it—especially during the period Collin and I were in the darkest patch, the period in which Thomas was fucking me too. I thought about Thomas doing it when Collin was on top of me. And some other guys too, including Gordo. Not Bobby, of course. We were too much alike—and both submissives.

"If you did, who would it be? There's a Jamaican fisherman who comes out there on that dock every morning to take his boat out. I try to be here every morning to sip my coffee and watch him prepare the boat. He's big, like Gordo. And although Gordo is about as much as I can handle—even when he fucks around, which is OK with me. He's oversexed. But sometimes when Gordo is on top of me, I think of it being that fisherman. And I wonder if he's as hung as Gordo. I bet he is. I think they are all black bulls down here. Who would it be for you, Sean?"

Gordo, of course. But, not my first pick. A black bull dick isn't everything I wanted in a man who was covering me. That would be David Irwin, the society doctor, the champion tennis player who lived in the big mansion at the top of the hill, with his wife, Gail. A handsome devil in his forties, all smiles and robustness. An Aussie, I understood. Rich as hell. He and his wife were patrons of everything here. And they threw the most exclusive parties. Always in the society pages of the paper. I'd thought of him being on top of me when Collin was, although I didn't think of that until Bobby had mentioned it. And Thomas, of course. I always was thinking of Thomas being on top of me when Collin was—the two of us swinging from the chandeliers.

"No, I can't think of anyone," I said to Bobby.

"You know Gordo fancies you," Bobby said, laying his hand on my forearm. "He's told me more than once that he'd like to do you. If you're interested, I want you to know that I don't mind. Gordo needs variety. So, do I, and we have an understanding. He does me best when he's doing someone else too. I told him that you and Collin were having some difficulty—that Collin wasn't satisfying you. That's one thing Gordo does really, really well. He satisfies. So, if—"

"Thanks, Bobby, but Collin and I are doing just fine lately." Oh, shit, I thought. Another thing to worry about and to try not to give in to. Sure, I'd like to try Gordo out. "Is this why I was invited to come along today for a drink? You wanted to let me know that Gordo wants to fuck me?"

"Well, yes . . . except you know I'm always happy when you come along. You're the only one on this godforsaken pile of sand who I can let my hair down with. I wouldn't care if Gordo was doing us both, truly. I wouldn't mind if we did a threesome with him. Are you mad at me for telling you, though?"

I could see that he was unsure of himself now. That wasn't the way I liked to think of the character I was weaving from him. "No," I laughed, "I don't care. It's flattering to know that. The next time I need a big black cock, I'll be showing up here." We both laughed at that, but I couldn't help thinking that I could use a big black cock.

At that moment, Collin came out onto the porch and Gordo bellowed for Bobby to come inside. Collin, whose drink was only half finished, eased down into a rocking chair and Bobby stood and went inside. I had a line of sight into the barroom. Collin and I sat there, not saying anything, looking out at the activity in the small harbor at George Town, and pretending that we didn't hear the sound of sex from inside the club.

From where I sat, when I turned my gaze away from the sunshine brutalizing the harbor and into the dimness of the barroom, I could see that Gordo was fucking Bobby on top of one of the tables. All I could see was the muscular back of the black stud, his trousers and briefs off, standing, facing the table. Bobby's creamy, dancer's legs, were spread and raised, held up by big black hands gripping the young man's ankles. Gordo's plump buttocks were contracting and relaxing in a rhythm that harmonized with Bobby's grunts and groans.

My hand was shaking as I raised my glass to my lips. I hoped Collin didn't notice. He seemed to be trying not to notice that Bobby was getting fucked royally just forty feet from us. I couldn't help but wonder just how hung Gordo was. Bobby was a relatively small-bodied young man. So was I. How thick a cock could his passage take? How thick could mine take? Thomas had been thick and I, surprisingly, had been reamed to his needs— with difficulty, certainly, but with glorious difficulty. I wondered if Gordo was as big as Thomas was. Or bigger.

The fucking obviously hadn't escaped Collin. As soon as we got back to the house, he wanted me in the bedroom, on our bed. He covered me in a missionary, crouching above me, on his knees, between my spread thighs. He was hovering over me, his forehead touching mine, his eyes blazing as they stared into mine. I clutched him to me, drawing him inside me, my palms squeezing his butt cheeks in the rhythm of his thrusts. He was good. It was a good fuck. He was hitting all of the familiar spots. It was the best fuck we'd had for some time, fed, I'm sure, from the sounds of Gordo taking Bobby at the club. He pulled the

51

cum out of me and he came as well. It was a good, competent fuck.

But while he was fucking me, the images of Thomas and David Irwin . . . and Gordo were flipping up between his eyes and mine.

Afterward, as we sat by the pool, sipping drinks, mellow from the best fuck we'd managed in some time, Rondy padded out with a silver tray, with an envelope on it.

"Well, at last," Collin said, with a smile, when he'd read the note.

"What is it?" I asked.

"It's an invitation. From the Irwins. For a buffet dinner up at their house. We've arrived at last," Collin said. I could tell from the tone of his voice that this was the best thing that had happened to him all day—including the fuck we'd just had in our bedroom.

"That's great," I said, my mind going to wondering if David Irwin was hung. He certainly had a robust, strapping body. He looked like he had a bulging basket in those newspaper photos of his tennis matches. And how strong was his backswing; his ball delivery?

"Collin," I said. "You were unusually randy just now. Back there at the club . . . being able to hear and glimpse Gordo fucking Bobby . . ."

"You're wondering if I'd like to fuck Bobby too, like that, given the opportunity—and you not caring?"

"Well . . ."

"Sure, it makes me horny to think about fucking a cute little piece like that. It never hurts to think about the possibilities of variety."

OK, so I felt fine going back to thinking about Thomas and wondering about Gordo and David Irwin.

＊ ＊ ＊ ＊

David Irwin indeed was hung—and strong and charismatic. He fucked me in the garden of his house while fifty or more people, including Collin, were enjoying cocktails and a buffet in the Irwin house within our hearing. He had a hand over my mouth to keep me from crying out and alerting the other guests. The other hand was on my lower belly, holding my buttocks into his groin, as he leaned me over a railing behind a gazebo and fucked me from behind. He was long and thick and he knew how to work a passage. The muscles of my passage walls loved what he was doing and rippled over his pistoning cock in appreciation.

Still, I hadn't been totally a slut about it. I had struggled, surprised when he'd grabbed me and dragged me behind the gazebo. He'd told me in the house that he wanted to fuck me—that we'd been invited to his party because he wanted to fuck me—and I went into the garden with him alone. But I couldn't know he was serious and wanted to do it there and then when he was hosting a dinner party in the house. So I struggled against him, but to no avail. He was a strong, determined man, and he knew what he was doing. He had his hand over my mouth but his fingers were pinching my nose, controlling my breathing. He was efficient at stripping my trousers and briefs and unzipping and freeing himself. Once inside me, he took me strongly, having me panting at how thick he was. Once he was saddled, I surrendered to him—aided by my having wanted him to begin with.

I wouldn't have said this was consensual, but it was overwhelming and embarrassingly arousing. And then it obviously turned consensual, as I relaxed—he laughed when he felt me surrender to him—and I set myself and banged him back, pushing back with my hips as he thrust forward. Both of us concentrated on the fuck, both of us fully invested in it.

When he was done, he eased his grip on me, ran his tongue around in one of my ear cavities to check on whether I would moan for him, which I did, and whispered, "I'm going to let you go now. You can go into the house and announce that I've raped you in the garden or you can arrange your schedule to visit me here again Tuesday afternoon and I'll rape you again."

"What time Tuesday?" I murmured.

He laughed. I turned my face to him and we kissed passionately.

"Yeah, I was told that you were Collin's little whore and could be had."

I chose to ignore that. "So, do we go back in now? Separately, I assume," I said.

"No, unless you decide to start screaming 'rape,' I'm taking you upstairs and banging the hell out of you to give you another chance not to show up on Tuesday."

"Is that what you want me to think you did just now—rape me?" I asked.

"It's the feeling I like to have when I do it with a beautiful young man like you. And I suspect it gives you added arousal when you can feel that's being done to you, yes."

"Then take me upstairs and rape me again," I said.

That's what he did. He guided me upstairs by a back staircase to a bedroom that obvious was a servant's room, not the master bedroom or even a guest room. It had double locks on it like he didn't want anyone but himself to go in there. Once in the room, I knew why that was. There was a twin bed and nothing much else in the room, which had a dormer window on one wall. The rest of the room had various restraints in view. There were four on the opposite wall, two above and two below. There were restraints on all four corners of the bed.

"Is this where you bring young men to rape them?" I asked.

"Yes," he answered, with a smirk. "Take your clothes off."

He didn't use any of the restraints attached to the bed. He used connected double restraints to trap my wrists to my ankles on either side, trussing me up on my back, with my legs bent and spread and my genitals exposed. I didn't fight him. I didn't help him, either, I just sat or lay there, at his direction, docilely letting him truss me up, listening to the faraway music and hubbub of the party going on somewhere in the large house. He did tell me to let him know if I was resisting, but I remained mute, thinking only I wanted his cock moving inside me again and not caring that we might be missed from the party or that someone would come looking for us. This was his time with me to control. He could do anything to me that he wanted to.

He popped a ball gag into my mouth. Standing over me—he was a magnificent figure naked—he flicked my body all over with a riding crop as I jerked and writhed as best I was able

54

and screamed ineffectually through the ball gag until he got overly excited. Then he fell on me between my legs, thrust inside me, and fucked the shit out of me.

We were swinging on the chandeliers. I was climbing on the clouds. He was fucking the hell out of me and it was everything I ever could want. I just regretted that my mouth was gagged so I couldn't tell him how glorious it was while he was doing it.

When he pulled the gag out of my mouth, he leaned over me, his dick still inside me, and said, "So do you still want to come to me on Tuesday? We'll be using this room."

"You didn't tell me what time," I responded. "Tell me a time and I'll be here."

He laughed. "You are sweet prey and you take it like you really want it. We're going to have a great time, you and I, until I've used up every ounce of you. But this is your chance to pull away from what I have to give you. Do you wish me to let you be now?"

"No," I answered. "I'll be here Tuesday if you give me a time."

It all lasted for less than an hour between when I'd walked into the garden behind him and when we reentered the living room, he from upstairs and me from the garden. If anyone noticed we'd been gone, they didn't say anything about it. I found Collin and stood very close to him for the rest of the evening. He was glowing, talking with people he knew through business but only now was mingling with in a social setting. He obviously felt that he had arrived—and he also probably felt that the invitation had been all about him.

From the beginning, when we walked into the foyer of the house and reached the top of the reception line, I had known, from the looks Irwin gave me, that we got the invitation because of me, not Collin. I wouldn't have told him that in a million years, though. I wouldn't have burst that bubble.

The host, the doctor David Irwin, cut a magnificent, charismatic figure. His very presence lit up the room. He was quite tall and broad across the shoulders. He was in his late forties or early fifties, but he still had a wavy mane of reddish-gold hair. His ruddy complexion shrieked of robust health, vitality, and outdoor sports. I had known that he was a champion tennis player in his age category in the Caymans, but further research after we'd received the invitation revealed he had been a professional rugby player and was a horseman. He certainly knew how to ride me.

He was Australian. His wife, Gail, who obviously was some ten years older than he was but still well preserved, was from an old Cayman banking family. She probably had most of the money and nearly all of the social standing when he'd come onto the scene. His smile was broad, and when you talked with him, his concentration on you made you feel like he was fully invested in who you were and what you thought.

He spent enough time shaking Collin's hand that I'm sure Collin thought the man would call him in the morning to transfer all of his bank accounts to Collin's personal business even though his wife's family owned a bank. But quickly enough, he'd turned Collin over to Gail Irwin, and he had my hand in his. Collin, knowing where the family's money originated from, was happy to go off with Gail Irwin. The way David Irwin folded his thumb inside my palm and rubbed when we shook hands made me shudder, and I realized that this, coupled with the looks he'd sent my way, meant he understood that to be a homosexual top signal to a submissive. I left my hand there, signaling I would be submissive to him.

"So, you are Sean Walker," he said. "Haven't I just read in *Publisher's Weekly* that you sold a novel—something about the city—to Putnam's."

"Yes, sir, *Home from the City*," I said, not being able to stop beaming at him because he knew that about me. In just a mention of the novel, he'd shown more enthusiasm that I'd sold it than Collin had. Collin hadn't told me to send the $30,000 advance I got for it back, though.

"I've also read a short story of yours recently in the *Chicago Literary Journal*. I'd like to talk with you about that later . . . if there ever is an end to this tedious reception line."

It was only then that he let my hand go. I could still feel the tingling sensation of his thumb rubbing on my palm. I floated a few inches off the floor on my way to the drinks table.

In less than a half hour, he was at my side again. Collin had deserted me, choosing to take advantage of his evening at the top of the heap to try to make some connections that would help him in business. I was standing off to the side in the dining room, watching others graze at the groaning board, and nursing my drink. I obviously was too young for this crowd and possibly many of them knew my relationship with Collin and were politely shunning me.

"Are you enjoying yourself?" he said, sidling up beside me.

Before I fully realized who had spoken to me, I said, "Not really. A bit highbrow and much too British colonial for me, I'm afraid."

"That's right; you're an American, aren't you? But all of this is good for character research for novels, don't you think?"

I looked at him, realizing it was the host, David Irwin. "Oh, sorry, Mr. Irwin. I didn't realize it was you. I'm sure you have more important guests to talk with. But, yes, you're right. Observing your party is good research for characters in future novels."

"There's no one more important to me here tonight than you," he said. He placed a hand on the small of my back.

"That's flattering even if not true," I answered.

"Oh, it's true and I hope to help make your evening here more exciting." And then, before I could respond to that, he went on. "About that short story in the *Chicago Literary Journal*. Very interesting, but I don't think you were being fully honest in it."

"Oh, how so?"

"Your character, Joshua. He was so frustrated. I know that provided the tension for the story, but I don't think you revealed his true frustration—although I think you knew what it was. And I think Joshua represented you yourself."

"Oh?" I said. I, in fact, hadn't been fully satisfied with that story and I didn't know why. Maybe the man was on to something. "That's intriguing—that a story I managed to sell was dishonest."

"It was well written, I do think. And it works on one level. But on a deeper level, not on the level you were at when you wrote it—about yourself, your own emotions."

I didn't say anything, so he went on. "The story is about Joshua's unsatisfying relationship with the woman Maria."

"Yes," I said, wanting him to go on. His hand had slipped to palming my buttocks. I suddenly had an inkling where this was going, and the plot of that short story was racing through my brain, forcing doors of understanding open that had been closed when I'd written it and sent it off.

"I think the protagonist of your story wanted to go with men, not the woman Maria—and he wanted to be tested and manhandled by men. I know you are sleeping in Collin Destry's bed," he whispered in my ear. And then, off topic, he sniffed and said, "You smell nice. I know that Destry is fucking you. This story you have in the *Chicago Literary Journal*, though, tells me he isn't fucking you well, using you fully. I think you want to be used cruelly."

I was too much in shock to respond. I also was struggling with arousal. The hand on my butt cheek was squeezing it.

"I think you are a very passionate young man, Sean. It comes across in your writing. Your Joshua was unsatisfied with Maria because he wanted a man fucking him. That's what you want too. And you want to feel it when a man fucks you. You want it to be dangerous and taxing and to take you to the edge."

"Swinging on the chandeliers," I murmured.

"What was that you said?"

"Swinging on the chandeliers is what I call it. All-out sex."

"Yes, that's it. I think you want to swing on the chandeliers with a man."

"Yes, with a man. You've already said that you knew Collin fucked me. Did you invite Collin and me here so that you could fuck me?"

"Not entirely. I read your short story and then about your novel sale and that you lived here in George Town. Then I researched you and found that you were a beautiful, enticing young man. Only then did I invite you to this party—and, truth

58

be known the whole reason I'm having this party is to get you here. I could give you what Destry isn't giving you, Sean. I could swing you on the chandeliers. If you like big cocks, I can give you a big cock. Rumor has it that you liked your Jamaican servant's big cock. I want to fuck you like Destry hasn't fucked you. I want to fuck you like even your Jamaican black bull didn't fuck you. I can make you feel it—suffer for it. You'll write best-selling novels full of tension and challenge and satiation when I've done with you."

He had a finger pressing into my crack from behind, finding where my anus opened.

"Sir. We're at a party—your party. This isn't really—"

"You're not saying no."

"No."

He laughed. "That's ambiguous even if it sounds direct. What are you saying no to?"

"No, I'm not saying no. I want you to fuck me. I wanted that before I came to this party." God knows that when Bobby asked who I fantasized fucking me, David Irwin's name had popped out. And, no, Collin wasn't swinging me on the chandeliers. He did that back in New York when we had nothing, but he didn't do that here in the Caymans when we seemingly had everything.

"I am going out onto the patio and into the garden," he said. "Follow me."

And I had followed him.

So, truth be known, I knew exactly what would happen when I followed David Irwin into the garden and what it would lead to if he wanted me.

* * * *

Every Tuesday for weeks I was David's sex slave. He even called me that, took me to his secret sex nest, yoked my neck with a collar and chain when I was with him, and treated me as his slave. He took me in every sexual position he could think of, starting with him sitting on the side of the bed and me streaming down to the floor, my buttocks on his lap, he deep inside me, my ankles crossed behind the small of his back, my wrists bound above my head, my head bouncing off the floor, and him grasping my waist and pulling me on and off his cock.

I found out that the four restraints on the wall were for him to bind me there, either facing the wall or not, either my ankles also restrained or not, and lightly whipping me and then fucking me. The restraints on the pillars of the bed were to spread-eagle me for the attention of the lash and his cock. He took me out on his yacht and, when out in the Caribbean, down into his cabin. He bent me over a railing, bound my wrists to my ankles, and caned me with a stalk of thin bamboo until I begged for the cock—and he gave it to me.

I was his for whatever he wanted.

And he wanted to share me and did so with a black colleague and even with Collin. By the time he shared me with Collin, I knew the doctor was fucking my partner as well. Collin and David had a regular tennis date, but Collin wasn't that good of a tennis player. I saw his car parked at David's house and confronted him, and he didn't deny it. He told me it was just business—that he was cultivating the Irwins' money—but I knew that Collin was as much a sex slave to David Irwin as I was. What I resented was that, when Irwin called us to his house and said he wanted us both, together, Collin didn't bat an eye before agreeing to it.

The next Tuesday, when I was getting ready to leave for David's house, David appeared at our house. Collin was there too. He showed no surprise or rancor that I was there—that Irwin was fucking me too. I wondered how long he had known.

They tied my wrists over my head to the headboard and Collin went under me and speared me from below. He entwined his legs in mine and spread and lifted my legs, and David just came in between them, worked his cock inside me above David's, and they both stroked inside me, making love—no, sex, not love—with me and sex with each other. They kissed over my shoulder.

I was determined to leave them both then, but I lost David before I left Collin.

Before the next Tuesday, David was dead, shot by his wife, Gail. Officially, there was little given out and this being the Cayman Islands and Gail's family being as prominent as it was

60

here, it was written up as a gun-cleaning accident, with David, not Gail, holding the gun. The rumor mill, though, mentioned David's secret room and Gail finding it and finding David there with one of the family's young Jamaican serving men.

Within days, Collin had left for a meeting in London. I don't know if he really had a meeting scheduled there or not. And, frankly, I didn't care. I started packing the day his plane took off for the UK.

There was one last thing I wanted to do.

I walked into the Wharf Club when I knew Bobby was at the gym. Gordo was standing behind the bar.

"I hear that you want to do me," I said. "Just make it interesting, please. And if you aren't at least eight thick inches, don't bother."

He was more than eight thick inches. He stripped us and I knelt in front of him and took his cock in my mouth. He made it more interesting, though. He picked me up and twirled me around in front of him, so that I was off the ground and my feet pointed to the ceiling. My mouth was at the level of his cock. My anus was at the level of his mouth. We both licked and sucked until he couldn't take it anymore. He flipped me around, slammed me down on the top of a table, with my legs in the splits on the edge of the table top, and, as I yowled at the size of him, he worked his cock inside me, held my chest down on the table top with fists pressed into my back under the shoulder blades, and pounded me and pounded me and pounded me. My arms were raised over my head, grasping the far edge of the table.

After several minutes of this, he flipped me over, and as I panted hard, he sucked, squeezed, and stroked my dick and balls to my release. All the time he had a fat finger up my ass stroking my prostate. He crouched over me when I'd come, thrust inside me and missionary fucked me to his own ejaculation.

He was an ugly son of a gun, but he had the most divine black bull cock.

He wasn't finished with me. Hardening quickly, he hauled me off the table, hung me in front of him, my knees hooked on his hips and my fists locked behind his neck. He pushed my passage down on his cock again and strutted around the barroom bouncing me up and down on the shaft. I looked up at the ceiling not long before he and I came again, and I saw that the heaviness of his tread on the weak wooden floor was causing the chandeliers in the ceiling to bounce and swing back and forth.

Now *this* was a fuck.

* * * *

Months later I was in my apartment in Manhattan—one that was slightly larger than the one Collin and I had lived in, its small bedroom accommodating a double bed rather than a twin—when my bell was rung from the door down at the street. I'd been working on my latest—and I think, my greatest work. I'd sold another book, and my agent had written suggesting that I move back to New York to be accessible to publishers. She'd asked right at the time I'd been resolved to leave Collin and the Caymans. It had made my decision easier.

"Yes, who is it?" I spoke into the intercom.

"It's Collin. Please let me come up."

I guess I should have guessed he'd show up. He'd sent letters. My agent was an acquaintance of his and didn't know Collin and I ever were a couple let alone that we were estranged.

"Just a minute, please," I answered, looking around the apartment for any tell-tale signs for Collin to see, not being sure what they even would be. I spied my new manuscript, the one I was working on, the one I planned to call *Fissure*. It was the best one yet, although it wasn't for the mainstream. I'd have to publish it in some other distribution and under a pen name. I'd changed the main character's names also. They no longer would be who they really were. I had settled on name changes for the Collin, Thomas, David, Gordo, Bobby, and Sean characters. The problem, of course, is that there really were no likable characters in the book. The protagonist was needy, submissive, easy . . . flighty even. Certainly not noble. The rest were grasping. Well, the protagonist was grasping too. But the characters were honest in their dishonesty. I knew David would have given me that concession. I tucked it away behind some books on the bookshelf and then rang Collin in.

"Hi," he said at the door.

"Hi," I said back. It was no use asking him how he'd found me—or why he'd tried to.

"You're looking good," he said.

"Thanks," I answered. I know he wanted me to say that he looked great, which he did, but I wasn't going to give him that.

"I brought you this. I've read it and made a lot of notes, just like old times," he said. He was handing forth the manuscript I had given him to read all that time ago in the Caymans. I'd put that one aside. I flipped it open, and, good to his word, he'd covered it in notes. I'd have to take that back out and work on it—when the hurt stopped, if ever.

"Can I come in?" he asked.

"For a few minutes, I suppose." I stepped aside. "Do you want a beer or something?"

"What I want is that I want you back. I want us to start out at go again," he said. He was eying the room, looking for doors. His eyes stopped upon seeing the bedroom door. It was open and he could see the double bed beyond.

"That would be hard. I'm here now and you're in the Caymans," I said. "Despite what you thought, I have a career now. I make good money, here in New York." I'm sure that stung. I wanted it to.

"But you've missed me, haven't you?" he said. He was unbuttoning his shirt. He knew me too well.

"Yes, I've missed you."

He fucked me on the bed—gently, almost tenderly, until we both lost control and then frantically, passionately. I lay on my back, thighs spread, legs bent, feet flat on the mattress, and he lay between them, on top of me. He kissed all the way down my body and took my cock in his mouth and then my balls and then he grasped my thighs, pushed them up onto my chest, rolling my pelvis up, and ate my anus out. I gasped and sighed for him, giving him the moans and groans he wanted to hear.

I surrendered to him physically just as he wanted me too and, no doubt, believed he could easily make me do.

63

I was open to it, needing it, begging for it, as he slid inside me and, hovering over me, his forehead touching mine, his eyes capturing mine, began to pump me. If he noticed how easily I opened, he didn't mark it. It was a good fuck, a very nice fuck. I went with it, moving my pelvis with his strokes, gasping and groaning when he quickened the pace, filled out more, thrust deeper and harder. When we became frenzied, I flipped him, coming up off my back and putting him on his back—all without dislodging his cock. And then I was riding him hard, gyrating on his shaft, taking him to the root and rocking and revolving on the cock until, with a cry, we both came, simultaneous.

He wasn't getting all of my attention, though. From time to time I'd look up at the ceiling, at the dangling brass light fixture. It remained solidly in place, not shimmering, not swaying, and swinging . . . nothing.

We lay there, me stretched out on top of him.

"That was fantastic," he whispered.

"It was good," I responded.

"Do you think . . . maybe?"

"I think you'd best get up. There's time for a short shower, but then you'd best be on your way. It was fine . . . for old time's sake. Nothing more, though. My boyfriend's practice should be over soon. He'll come straight home, I imagine."

"Your boyfriend?" he said, instantly dejected.

"He's a real bruiser. I don't think you want to be here when he comes home." I had surrendered to him physically—I was weak that way. But I had not given in to him emotionally.

I stood at the window and watched Collin leave the building. He passed Terrence Jackson, a fullback with the New York Jets pro football team. I went back in the bedroom, pulled open the nightstand drawer, and took out the velvet-cuffed wrist restraints. Terrence was a 240-pound, all-muscle black bull. He had come to America from Jamaica. He had ten thick inches. When he fucked me the brass lighting fixture in the ceiling over the bed swayed, shimmered, and swung.

Pool Party

I lay on the bed in the cabin behind Hal's Tavern ten miles out of town and listened to the truck driver moving around in the bathroom. I had showered first, after I'd given him a blow job, and come to the bed and stretched out, naked, while he took his. He was going to fuck me when he came out of the bathroom. I was looking forward to it; he'd looked mean and lean at the bar. I wanted someone who made me feel it. I tried to remember what his name was—Ralph or Randy, or something like that. Although I suppose it didn't matter what his name was for why we were here. I hadn't told him my real name. All I knew is that I wanted him to fuck me good, to manhandle me. That was the mood I was in.

The bathroom door opened and he was standing there, a towel around his waist. I knew he'd be hairy and have tattoos. He was. I suppose the arousal for him was that I wasn't—that I was younger than he was and clean cut, a novelist, although I don't think he believed me when I told him that. A successful one too, but I hadn't bothered to tell him that; I could tell that he was only interested in whether I'd take his cock. It didn't matter. He might have asked me what the titles were of my books, and I couldn't have given those to him without revealing my real name. He didn't look like a writer.

He looked like what he'd said he was—a long-distance semitrailer driver—one who hit the gym wherever he stopped for the night. He was dark, maybe some Hispanic in him, with black hair—thick here and there—around his pecs and down into the rim of the towel at his waist. He was tall, broad in the shoulders and across the muscular chest, slimmer in the hips. He had the biceps of a bodybuilder and thighs of a rugby player. Other than that he was rangy and wiry, tattoos up his arm and down his chest. He looked mean, which had been what had drawn me to him in Hal's bar. I wanted to feel it. He'd already made me feel it and he hadn't been inside me yet.

He'd slapped me around a bit, forcing me to my knees to suck him off, him creaming my face with his cum, before he went to take a shower. I hadn't had or opportunity to see much of anything but his cock and balls as he showed me what he wanted me to do with them. He wanted to show me from the get go who was going to be boss. I had chosen him because I wanted to be bossed. When he went to the shower, he said the blow job was fine and if I didn't want to get the stuffing fucked out of me I should go before he got out of the bathroom. I stayed.

He dropped the towel at the bathroom door. He was in erection and thick, if not abnormally long, or maybe it just appeared that he wasn't long because his bush was so thick. He smiled at me. I tried to smile back. I had wanted someone like him. And here he was. I'd gone for nearly a year without it. I had tried to reform. It hadn't worked. I still craved cock.

"I forgot your name," I said.

"Vince. It's Vince," he answered. "That was a first-rate blow job."

He strode over to the bed and stood next to it. Getting the hint, I turned onto my side and took his cock into my mouth again. Yes, he was longer than I originally thought. I'd been nervous the first time and hadn't tried to take it all in my throat. He reached down and fisted my cock and we moved full throttle into the pre-fuck jacking.

I was on my back, my hands reaching over my head to grip the brass rungs of the headboard. My pelvis was lifted on pillows, my legs were spread and bent. I was leveraging off my feet to meet the rhythm of his thrusts.

"Yes, Yes. Like that. You're huge. Pump me. Fuck me! Pull the cum out of me!" My back was arched. So was my head, my eyes focused on the brass headboard. He was between my knees, in deep, pistoning me hard. It was a rough fuck. It was what I'd come to Hal's Tavern to get. Vince was giving me what I'd come here for.

He was laughing, clutching my hips, pulling me hard into him as he thrust forward. Pumping me fast and hard.

66

"You really want it," he muttered.

Yes, I really want it or I wouldn't be here went screaming through my brain. I'd come here in high heat. I'd needed it bad.

I moved a hand to my cock and stroked myself. "I'm going to come," I called out, as if he was interested. He was only interested in getting a big piece of me for himself, for his own needs from days on the road without it. He certainly hadn't gotten tail any easier than he was getting it from me. I laid right down and spread my legs for him. And he wasn't paying for it; I even paid for the cabin—and for his drink while he was feeling me up at the bar. The guys he was drinking with when we left to come back to the cabin were leering and rolling their eyes and popping their tongues in their cheeks.

And then I did come. I had both hands palming his chest, running my fingers through the swirls of hair around his pecs, thumbing his nipples. He continued to pump me, fast and furiously. I lay back in surrender, my hands moved to palming his buttocks, his buttocks contracting and releasing with his thrusts. I held him to me as he fucked and fucked and fucked.

It was worth every penny I paid for it.

We lay on the bed, side by side, him dozing, me going over the fuck again in my mind, picking out what would inform my writing. I quietly rolled out of the bed and went to the window at the back of the cabin. It overlooked the secluded parking lot, where the men who came to Hal's Tavern and cabins parked so their cars wouldn't be seen from the road. I lit up a cigarette, smoked it, and killed the butt on the window sill. I was standing at the window, naked, my arms raised and pressed into the corners of the frame at the top, looking out into the parking lot but not really thinking about anything in particular.

Vince came up behind me, wrapped his arms around me, and nuzzled the hollow of my throat with his hairy face. He was bearded, but it wasn't long or unruly. It looked sexy on him. He palmed my lower belly and pulled my feet up on my toes. He was hard again.

"You're a great lay," he said. "I'd like to bottle you and take you on the road with me."

"You're a great driver," I answered.

"You do want it rough."

"Yes, I do want it rough."

"I'm gonna drive you again. Jut your ass back at me," he commanded in a hoarse voice, and when I did so, he palmed my lower belly and pulled me up cruelly, jerking me back into his groin as he thrust his cock up into me, penetrating my ass several inches. He was inside me again, easier this time as he'd already reamed me to his size. I let out a cry of surprise and pain. Holding me tight, he pulled back and thrust up into me again and again, making each thrust a separate, "take all of it" act. It was the rough fuck I'd come here to get.

"Relax and take it, bitch. Be my little bitch," he said in my ear. "I'm gonna drive you like I drive my truck—hard and fast." Continuing to control and move me with a hand on my belly, he cupped my chin with the other hand and pulled my head into the hollow of his throat. I was completely at his mercy. And he didn't have much mercy to give.

He'd already driven me like his truck. I loved it. I was a whore for it. It had been too long. I'd tried to be good too long.

I relaxed and he continued to thrust up inside me but slower, more in a rhythm, with less intensity. I turned my face to him and we kissed. He gave me tongue. I was surprised that a truck driver would do that.

When I turned my face back around to the parking lot, I saw that there were two guys back there, leaning into a car. They were using the hood of my car, my Jaguar. I recognized the guy who had the other guy bent over the hood of the car too. They had been kissing, I was sure, but they must have heard me cry out when the truck driver thrust up into my passage. They were looking, startled, up at the window I was in. The guy I recognized was Jim Thornton, one of our neighbors. His wife and my wife were in a Saturday morning kaffee klatch together. The Thorntons had a nice swimming pool. We were going there for a pool party the next Saturday afternoon. I tried to pull away from the window, but Vince held me there, concentrated on his cock slow-fucking up into my channel, moving smoothly now that he'd reamed me to his size for the day.

Jim Thornton had turned and seen me—seen us, Vince and me—in the window of the cabin. He turned away, but at the moment so did Vince, pulling me back into the room and over

68

to the bed. He bent me over the bed, grabbed my wrists and forced my arms over my head, pressed to the surface of the bed. My chest was flat on the bed, as was my cheek. He started fucking me in earnest, in long, fast, deep, cruel strokes. It was what I'd wanted. It was why I'd come to Hal's Tavern and had brought a truck driver to this cabin.

I writhed under him. "Oh fuck! Oh, Shit. Do it, do it, do it. Fuck me to heaven!"

"Take it, take it, take it, bitch," the truck driver growled and fucked on.

He made me forget all about Jim Thornton—at least while the big bruiser had his dick inside me.

* * * *

There was no way I could go to the Thorntons' pool party on Saturday if Jim Thornton had seen me, naked, with another guy behind me, in the window of the cabin behind Hal's Tavern—and surely he must have seen us. And we needed to talk about this. I needed to get him to put it away. He'd been there too. I'd seen him kissing a guy in the parking lot. It wasn't good news for either of us.

I knew he didn't work days—he owned a couple of restaurants in town and rotated around at those at night. His wife, Bev, was a partner in a health spa and dermatology clinic across town, and she did work days. My wife, Ann, was a doctor in the oncology department at the university and worked days. I was a writer. I worked all of the time and, some thought, none of the time.

I decided I had to go over there and talk to him.

No one answered at the front door, so I walked around to the back, to the pool area—they had an extensive patio area in back with an oversized residential pool. The house rambled around in a curve between the pool and the street. A couple of additions had been added on as the family's wealth had increased. The restaurant business in this university town was lucrative. Thornton was barely thirty and quite probably was already a millionaire. A deck on the second floor of the additions extended out toward the pool area.

69

I stopped short of the patio, next to some foliage, which hid me from view of the pool area—or so I thought.

Jim Thornton was fucking a college-age guy on a pool bed. Both were naked. Two wet swim suits lay on the patio next to the pool bed. Thornton apparently had seduced the college kid in the pool—maybe fucked him there first—and then moved him to the pool bed. They were a beautiful couple, already moving in a coordinated rhythm in the throes of copulation, and my mind ran rampant on what had happened here already. The session with the truck driver had just made me hornier.

The college guy was tanned, but nothing like Jim Thornton was. He was slim hipped and broad chested, just as Jim was. They both were trim and nicely muscled. If anything, the young man was more muscular in the chest and thighs than Thornton was. His hole certainly was being stretched open by Thornton's cock, though. I was being given a good shot of the connection. I was mesmerized by the tan lines on Thornton. He was a deep brown except for where the edges of a skimpy Speedo would start, and then his groin triangle was much lighter in color. This contrast accentuated the slimness of his hips, the reddish-auburn of his pubic bush, the hairiness of his tight ball sac, and the length of his hard cock—which I only got a measure of when he pulled it nearly all of the way out of the college guy's hole before sliding it in to where his pubic hair was mingling with the curls of hair around the college kid's anal rim—then back out and back in in a steady cadence. By all accounts the college kid was melting to the steady deep penetrations.

The college guy was flat on his belly on the pool bed. His legs were off the sides of the bed, bent slightly, and the pads of his feet were pressed into the patio stone. His arms were dangling off the side of the bed as well, the knuckles of the hand I could see dragging on the stone. He was cheek to pool bed pad, his face turned toward me. There was a grimaced smile on his mouth and his eyes sparkled. He quite obviously was in ecstasy.

Jim was saddled on the young man's ass. His legs too were off the bed on either side, bent, the pads of his feet pressed into the patio stone, being used to provide leverage for his rise and fall on the young man's ass. He was leaning over the body

70

under him, with the palms of his hands pressing down on the young man's shoulder blades. He was fucking the college guy in long slides, where I could see him withdraw the cock almost to the rim of the cockhead and then glide in again, deep. Rise and fall; rise and fall. On the slide in, the college guy was pushing his pelvis up slightly to meet the thrust with a counterthrust, obviously welcoming the cock.

I couldn't stay there. This certainly was no time to have a conversation with Jim Thornton about sex with men and what we'd seen and hadn't. But I didn't leave. I stood, glued to the spot in the foliage on the path around the side of the house to the pool. I wasn't even aware of having unzipped myself, taking my cock out, and stroking it while I watched Thornton fucking the college kid.

I had thought that they wouldn't be able to see me. But Thornton turned his face toward me and smiled. He could see me; he could see what I was doing. I pulled back in horror and embarrassment, stuffed my cock back into my shorts, and hurried home. At home, behind a closed bathroom door, and sitting on the toilet, I completed masturbating myself to visions of Thornton fucking the college kid transitioning, when I got really heated, into Thornton fucking me in the position that he'd fucked the college kid.

Later, when the phone rang, I sat and stared at it until it stopped. No message was left on the answering machine. When it rang again, I picked it up on the second ring.

"Greg, this is Jim. Jim Thornton."

I knew it was Jim Thornton. We had caller ID.

"Greg, we have to talk."

"I . . . we can't come to your pool party," I stammered out. "I'm sure you understand. That's what I came over to say."

He snorted. "You could have called me to say that. That's not what you came over for. You came over to get what I was giving Randy. And I'm not sure how you will explain not coming to the pool party to Ann." He gave a low laugh. "You certainly will come to the pool party and we'll both act like nothing has happened—and, yes, I saw you in the window at Hal's. Then we'll have a private little conversation, just you and me, all alone. You'll like it. I'll like it with you, I'm sure. I'll bet you're a real sweet lay."

"I don't think so, Jim. It's just too close—in the same neighborhood."

"And if we weren't in the same neighborhood—would you like to get what I was giving Randy? Remember, we both were at Hal's Tavern. There's not much of a secret about that between us."

I hesitated, but what the hell. "Yes, if there weren't complications, I'd want your cock. But we do live in the same neighborhood. Our wives are good friends. We couldn't keep it secret. I couldn't hold off from you when our families were together."

"All that is important is that you want me to fuck you. I'd like to be your good friend too, Greg. You're a gorgeous man—great bod. Lots of the interesting stuff happens in this neighborhood, Greg. And I don't think you have a choice. Ann doesn't know about you, does she? I wouldn't want to have to tell her. Bev and I have an open marriage. She knows and doesn't care. See you at the pool party. Oh, and wear something nice in a swim suit. I bet you'll look stunning. You're the best-looking man in the neighborhood."

Other than you, I thought, as I disconnected.

* * * *

"Are you coming down?" Ann called up the stairs. "We're already late."

"I don't think I'll go," I called down. "Go on without me. I'm at a crucial point on writing this chapter."

"And it will be there when you get back," she called out. "You've always got that excuse. It doesn't wash. Come on down." And then when I did, she said, "There, you were ready to go anyway, weren't you? Is that a new swimsuit?"

"Yes."

"A little daring, but it looks good on you; you've got the body for it, I'm delighted to say. You'll make me the envy of all of the women there. Maybe we should just stay home." She winked at me.

It's not the women I want to impress, I thought—and I'll bet that it's Bev Thornton who is the envy of all the women who will be at the party.

"You looked dowdy in the other one—like most of the men who will be at the party," she prattled on. "I like my man to stand out. You and Jim Thornton are the only men around here who have an acquaintance with the number thirty."

She was right. All of the men at the party were dowdy and aged except for Jim Thornton and me—and later, a couple of college students who showed up. One of those, Randy Hill, was the son of one of the older couples here—Alex Hill was a history professor at the university and his wife was an editor at the university press. Randy was the young man I'd seen Jim Thornton fucking on the pool bed—the same pool bed I was standing in front of when Bev introduced him to me—two days previously. I had made the connection as soon as Jim had mentioned his name. He was going to the university here, but he also worked as a waiter in one of Jim's restaurants.

Our neighborhood was within walking distance of the university and was an upscale area, so we all were professionals of some sort or the other and most were connected with the university. Ted Collier was a retired minister who had worked in campus ministry; Bob Holland was a doctor, working with Bev Thornton on cancer patients at the university hospital; Jeff Stevens was a judge. Clarence DuPont, from a minor branch of the notable family but able to play on the family name, chaired a political think tank loosely connected with the university, and Zach Childs owned a consortium of auto dealerships in the town.

What brought us all together at the pool was our wives, all of whom had professional jobs of their own, but whose main connection was that they got together at the judge's house every Saturday morning for a kaffee klatch, where they ran over and ran down the national and state political situation and the neighbors who weren't involved in the Saturday morning coffees. I wasn't a morning person. I was sleeping every Saturday morning while they were sipping coffee and gossiping. But then I'd rarely been in bed before 3:00 a.m. any morning.

Except for Jim Thornton and me—and the college guys who showed up later, having pulled in a university soccer game earlier in the day—most of the other men were in their fifties through their seventies and were wrinkled, gray, and paunchy. That didn't mean they didn't come to use the pool, which was known as the best one in the neighborhood. They all were in droopy boxers, though, except Jim and I, who were in Speedos. Well, to be fair, Zach Childs didn't look too bad. He went on camera, trying to sell cars, so he worked out and wasn't in bad shape for someone on the dark side of forty. He had a good chest and biceps and his waistline wasn't that bad when he sucked his gut in, which he was doing all day during the pool party when he thought anyone was looking his way.

Jim spent most of the time before the food was laid out in the pool, playing with the younger children—all grandchildren visiting their grandparents. He had handed out water guns and they were chasing each other—and him—around the shallow end of the pool with arcs of water. I stayed out of the pool, sitting at the side in a white resin plastic chair, with my T-shirt on, chatting with those who passed by and drinking a beer, but regretting that I was there—and, mostly, that I had worn a Speedo.

From time to time, my eyes met with Jim Thornton's, and it was obvious that he was enjoying my discomfort. He'd smile knowingly at me, stand up in the water at the shallow end to give me a good look at his beautiful, tanned body, and then sink back down and send off a jet of water at a squealing kid, who was in ecstasy that one of the adults was playing with him.

At one point he drew a young boy into him, sitting him on his lap, under the water, hugging him and giving me a lustful look over the boy's shoulder. I shuddered at the thought of the sensuality of the man and couldn't understand why others couldn't see it too and weren't either disturbed or aroused by it. But, of course, maybe they were and were just trying to hide their reaction like I was doing. He bounced the boy up and down on his lap in the water and the boy squealed in innocent delight. I, however, went hard.

When we ate, I sat as far away from Jim as I could. All of the other men had put their shirts back on after getting out of the pool. Not Jim. He sat at the table, deeply tanned, muscular chested, and highly sexual, and acted like nothing about that was unusual or out of keeping with the rest. Of course he was getting interested looks from the women—and a few of the men too. I tried my best not to look.

I pulled out early, telling Ann I had to get back to my writing before I lost a plot twist that had developed my mind. That was actually the truth. The short story I was then working on came out of my encounter with the truck driver and my growing obsession with Jim Thornton. The story would never be published in the mainstream, but it was a scorcher. I'd titled it "Pool Party."

Ann nodded absently at me, in mid conversation with Madge Hill. It was a common excuse of mine, useful because it often, like now, was genuine. Story elements for "Pool Party" had been turning over in my mind while I was sitting there watching the action in and around the Thornton's pool—the looks going between Jim and Randy Hill were enough to light my fire—and I was hard and in heat. I needed to leave the party for that reason alone.

I made good money off my writing. Ann appreciated that and indulged my peculiarities that were connected with getting something written down that was publishable. I made the same excuse to Bev Thornton, who was accustomed to hearing it and not resenting it, hoping to make it out of there without encountering Jim.

No such luck, though. Jim was at my elbow. "I'll see Greg out," he said. "I want to check with him on something."

Around at the side of the house, in the bushes, Jim pulled me to him and into a kiss. I resisted, initially, but he was insistent and I opened my lips to his tongue. He reached down, took my hand, and ran it under the waistband of his Speedo, holding my hand on his cock, which was half hard and hardening.

"You know I'm going to fuck you, don't you? It's inevitable." he whispered when he released my mouth.

I said "yes" in my mind, but not openly to him.

"You enjoyed watching me fuck Randy, didn't you?"

This time I answered in a weak voice, "Yes."

75

"Maybe we could do a threesome."

I didn't respond to that.

"Tomorrow afternoon. Be here. In back, by the pool. We can talk then."

"I don't know. The wives . . ."

"Some of the women are going into New York to take in a Broadway play matinee—including Bev and Ann. They'll be gone until after dinner."

That wasn't what I meant in referencing the wives, but I didn't pursue the point. Of course I wouldn't show up the next day. We'd talk later, over the phone, at a safe distance from each other. This just wasn't something we should do with all of the close connections.

But, God, he was sexy as hell.

Then, and only then, did he release my hand from his cock. He was hard and thick and long now.

"Remember. 2:00 tomorrow. Here."

"I hear you," I threw over my shoulder as I escaped and started walking—no, staggering—back downhill to my own house. I left Ann the Jaguar. She had a food bowl to haul back when she left.

When I got home it was back into the bathroom, sitting on the toilet, and masturbating myself to a completion.

* * * *

At 2:00 p.m. the next day, I was walking around the side of the Thornton house to the pool area. I was in shorts, sandals, and a T-shirt. No way I was coming in the Speedo and swimming with Jim in the pool. This was a short meeting of the minds on stopping this silly business before it started. We were just too closely connected to get away with it. I was beyond pretending I didn't want it, but it had danger and tragedy written all over it.

He was swimming laps, seeming not to notice I'd come when he told me to. I stood, facing the pool, at the foot of the pool bed where he'd fucked the college kid—Randy Hill, the son of friends of the Thorntons—and of us.

76

But he had noticed me and, after half a dozen laps, stood up in the water at the shallow end of the pool, the end I was standing at, and walked up the steps in the pool to the patio. We stood there, facing each other, for the longest moment. He glistened in the sun, as the light bounced off the drips of water running down his tight abs. His body was magnificent. He gave me a teasing little smile and then slowly pushed his Speedo down and off his legs. He was in erection, the V at his pelvis that hadn't tanned as darkly as the rest of him highlighted the reddish-auburn bush, the long, thick cock, and the hairy balls. His body was even more magnificent and sexy naked.

"I came to talk, Jim," I said. "This isn't possible. We have too many connections. We'd be found out."

"You came to be fucked," Jim said. "We can get away with it. I always get away with it." And then, when I didn't have an answer for that, when I was just standing there, drunk on the sexiness of his body, trembling, he said, "Strip down, I want to see you naked. I didn't get the best view of you in the window at Hal's. Did the big bruiser holding you from behind in the window fuck you well?"

"Yes," I answered weakly—and honestly.

"Was he fucking you when I saw you?"

"Yes. He was a truck driver." I added that nonsensically, as if being a truck driver had anything to do with it. But of course it did, and Thornton picked up on why.

"So, you like it rough, impersonal . . . dirty?"

"Sometimes," I answered, again honestly.

"I can fuck you rough. Tell me how you like it and I'll give it to you that way. Do you want it here on the pool bed like I gave it to Randy Hill and then maybe in the pool?"

"Yes."

"You like being slapped around?"

"Sometimes."

"You want to be given orders?"

"Yes."

"Strip down for me."

I did so, and we stood there for a moment, both erect, eyeing each other. And then he moved to me, cupped the back of my head with one hand, pulling my face into his for a deep kiss, and frotting our hard cocks together with his other hand. He slow stroked them together with his fist. I moaned, already lost to him.

He pushed me at arms' length and slapped me across the face twice. I yelped and groaned in want. He pressed me down to sitting on the foot of the pool bed, and I pressed my cheek to his lower belly and reached around with both hands and palmed his buttocks, holding his pelvis to me. He rubbed his cock on my cheek and slapped it on my cheek a couple of times as well. Then he moved it down to my lips, which opened to it. I sucked on the cock, initially on the bulb, but then taking it deep in my throat. He held my head between his hands and moved his hips in a face fuck. I opened to the cock and took it all.

He laughed. "You know how to give blow jobs."

Yes, I knew. The truck driver had told me that too. I'd been doing it fairly regularly since my college days—up until a year previously. I had made sure not to go long without being serviced and servicing a man, but I'd never done it this close to home before—to the home I shared with Ann, and with a man whose wife I knew and played bridge with.

Pulling out of me before he came, he pushed on my chest and I lay back on the pool bed. He knelt at the foot of the bed, pushed my knees up into my chest, and rolled my pelvis up. I panted and moaned as he sucked my cock and ate out my hole.

Then he was turning me onto my stomach on the pool bed, in the same place the college kid had been several days previously. My legs were hanging off the side, the pads of my feet pressed into the stone patio surface, and my arms were dangling off the side of the bed, my knuckles dragging on the stone, while he ate out my hole some more and pulled my cock through between my legs and gave it attention too. He mounted my ass. I flinched and gasped as he entered me a couple of inches.

He leaned over and whispered in my ear, "Do you want me to stop?"

"No," I whispered back. "But would you stop if I said I wanted you to stop?"

"No," he answered and then laughed. "But if you said no to my cock, you'd be lying, wouldn't you?"

78

"Yes," I admitted, honestly, "I'd be lying. But you know that."

"Here it comes," he said. He lifted my hips up a bit with his hands, and I opened my eyes wide, and my mouth formed a deep, "Oh Shit!" as he plunged his cock up into me and immediately started pumping hard and deep.

"You said you liked it rough," he said.

I mouthed off a bit, trying to keep it down, as the lots here weren't that big and his eight-foot wooden fence closed off what we were doing from view, but it also gave us no clue what was going on in adjoining yards. I provided him assurances, though, as my huffing moved from "Oh, shit, you're big—you're too big. Slow down, you're killing me" transitioned into sounds of passion and "Yeah, yeah, like that. Fuck he hard. Harder. Yes, Yes! God, you're good!"

"So, this is the way you like it?" he murmured.

"I like it any way you give it," I answered, honestly.

For a few minutes I was able to get a hand under my raised pelvis and take care of my own need. After I'd shot my load on the pool pad, though, he grabbed my wrists, and pulled them back around his side, arching my torso up cruelly, burying his face in the hollow of my neck, when I wasn't turning my face to his for a kiss, and pounded my ass relentlessly to his ejaculation.

When he'd come, he let my body collapse on the pool bed. I heard him snap the condom off—I had no idea where the rubber had come from and how and when he'd gotten it on his cock—and he stretched out on top of me as we cooled down.

This had been a rougher fuck than I'd seen him give Randy Hill, the college kid, but maybe I'd left before the rough stuff started. But rough was fine with me—unfortunately. The fuck had been really fine. It just wasn't what I'd come here for, or so I told myself. Jim had told me differently.

I heard him snap anther condom on. "Come into the pool. I want you to fuck yourself on it in the pool. Randy did that too. Before you came and watched us."

Just as I had figured.

He stood at the wall, in water up to his nipples, and held my waist as I made like a crab in front of him, crouching over him, my arms stretched around his shoulders, my hands gripping the lip of the pool, and my legs raised and bent, my feet flat against the pool wall on either side of his chest—just like I was about to push off in the backstroke race. His cock was buried in my passage and, using the leverage of my hands and feet, I fucked myself on the shaft, moving slowly through the water. When I came, clouds of cum rose to the surface between us.

Thornton laughed. "Between you today and Randy the other day—and I don't know how many kids pissing in the pool, I'd better drain it and change the water," he said.

"Come upstairs with me," Jim whispered in my ear after he'd reversed our positions, put my back to the wall and my knees on his hips and fucked me again. "We've got all day. We won't do it in the family bedroom area, but there's a maid's room above the kitchen we don't use and Bev never goes in. We'll do it in there."

"We can't. We can't be doing this anymore, Jim," I said.

He fucked me on the floor of the maid's room as soon as we got up there. When we entered the room, he took me by surprise, backhanding me across the cheek and sending me to the floor. I rose back up to my feet, groggily, and he just pushed me down on all fours and I went down docilely, giving him no resistance whatsoever. He mounted me, high on my ass, and fucked me hard.

He fucked me on the bed an hour later and we dozed off in each other's arms. He woke me up as the light outside was fading by rolling over on top of me and slapping my thighs open. He fucked me in a missionary, with us in a close embrace, rocking back and forth, both of us concentrating on his cock moving inside me.

"How much of this can you take?" he murmured.

"How much can you give?"

"Forever," he answered.

"Since this is the last time, do your worst," I responded.

"We'll see about that," he countered. "I think you are in denial here."

We dozed again and woke to the sound of someone entering the house through the front door, which was just across the wall and downstairs from where we were in the bed, a bed that had been thumping against the wall to the tune of Jim's thrusts inside me just an hour before.

"She's home. Your wife is home," I said, panicked.

"Shush, it's fine," Jim answered, putting his hand over my mouth. "We brought our clothes up. There's a stairway down to the far side of the house from here. You can dress and go down that and through the bushes to the street. You didn't park the Jag out front, did you?"

"No, of course not."

"Well, you parked it at Hal's. That wasn't the best move."

"I know that now," I said.

"I'm going back to the patio and greet Bev coming out of the pool. I know how to do this. Don't panic. We can bring this off."

"We can't continue bringing this off, Jim. We've got to stop this."

"You can't give up the fucking," he said, with a laugh. "You can't give up the fuck from me."

I was so afraid that he was right.

When I got home, Ann had already returned.

"You weren't here when I got home," she said.

"I went for a walk," I answered without hesitation. I'd worked that out on the walk home. She bought it. I wondered how long she was going to continue buying it. Despite telling Jim it was over, I knew it wasn't.

∗ ∗ ∗ ∗

I was on my back at the foot of the bed in the cabin behind Hal's Tavern. Jim Thornton was standing at the foot, grabbing my ankles, and cruelly spreading them wide, as he fucked me in long, fast, deep slides of his cock. I was touching his lower belly, tracing the Speedo tan line, the sharp divide between dark and light flesh, with my thumbs, not only because the contrast in his coloring in the zone of his sex aroused me but also to maintain that contact with him. It must have turned him on too, because he was fucking me furiously. I was licking my lips and moving my head back and forth in pain-pleasure-

81

passion-agony as he ravished me. I shot my load and he shot his and then he collapsed on me, searching out my lips with his for a deep kiss.

Twenty minutes later, I was at the window on the back wall of the cabin, overlooking the hidden parking area. My Jaguar and Jim's Corvette were nestled next to each other. We shouldn't have done that, I was thinking. Jim was lying on the bed, having a smoke. I was having a smoke at the window. After the high heat of the meeting of our bodies, I, at least, needed some separation to dampen down the smoldering. I knew we weren't finished—that Jim and I would fuck again this afternoon. And I knew we'd come back to the cabin behind Hal's Tavern again and again—until we were caught. I was in the spider's web and I wasn't getting out alive.

I'd smoked the cigarette down to the filter and stubbed it out on the window sill as so many before me had done—indeed, as I had done myself on the "day of the truck driver." I raised and spread my arms, pressing my hands into the upper edges of the window frame and lay my forehead against the cool window. I needed to cool down. Jim had me in perpetual heat.

Jim came up behind me and took my hips between his hands. "Jut your ass back to me, I'm going to slow fuck you," he whispered in my ear. I did so and he slid up inside me and began to slow pump me. He was moving his tongue in my ear cavity.

"Is this what the truck driver was doing with you that day I saw you in the window here?" he asked.

"Yes, he was fucking me like this, from behind. He told me to jut my ass back too, and he thrust up into me too when I did that. You asked and I told you. He was fucking me like this when you saw us in the window."

"But not as good as I am, right?"

"No, not as good as you are."

I looked out of the window and froze. Zach Childs, the friend from the party, the car dealer, who was as close to Jim and my ages and to being in shape as any of the others in the pool party group got, was standing out there, looking at our cars—at the Jaguar and the Corvette, nested together as close as Jim and I were now. He was a car dealer, for christ sake. He knew who owned those cars.

He looked up at the window and saw me, naked, and he saw Jim's face over my shoulder.

I turned from the window, dragging Jim with me. "Take me to the bed," I murmured, "And fuck me into the next world."

Jim did just that, laying me out, fully open, totally surrendered to him—totally surrendered to the whole situation—and he ravished me, taking no prisoners.

I was sitting in the Jaguar, watching the Corvette pull away, giving it a ten-minute interval before getting on the road myself when my cell phone buzzed.

"Greg? This is Zach Childs. I'm in cabin 2. I think we need to talk about something I saw in a window."

I lay, belly down, at the foot of the bed, legs spread and feet on floor, my eyes popping wide open, grunting at the difficulty of taking him. Childs was hunched over me, between my legs, one hand palming my lower belly and the other one pressing down on the small of my back.

"Let me in. Open for me," he growled. He was grunting too at the difficulty of stuffing my ass. He wasn't long, but his was the thickest cock I'd ever had, what some referred to as a beer can cock. He'd already unhinged my jaw when I was sucking it off.

But then he was inside me—just. "Yes, relax," he muttered. "Relax and take it." He was in maybe an inch and a half, and, grudgingly, my sphincter let his bulb pop beyond it, and my channel began to stretch open to him.

"You're fucked now," he muttered. "Don't fight me. Open up. Give it to me. I'm going to take it. I've wanted to fuck you for ages."

He held there, the bulb beyond the sphincter, giving me time to adjust, and when he felt I had done so enough, he pressed in on my belly with his hand, pulling my buttocks into the cock, and I panted and groaned as he gave me the other four plus inches. I felt his short and curlies tickling my butt cheeks. He was all in. I felt relief and it helped. I opened further and was surprised when he had another half inch to give me—and did.

83

I relaxed and took it—he had given me no other choice, saying this would just be the first of many meetings—as, in as far as he was going to get, he began to pump my ass.

"So sweet, so tight," he murmured as he plowed me.

It wasn't that I was so tight; it was that he was so thick.

I groaned as he turned me on his cock and continued plowing me from behind, sucking in his gut and watching us in the mirror that had conveniently been placed over the headboard. I turned my face up to the mirror and saw that the expression on my face not only showed the pain of his size but also, in spite of myself and to my embarrassment, the ecstasy of being fucked by a man—any man. In truth, any dick would do.

He leaned over and whispered in my ear, "You gonna come for me, baby?"

Yes, to my shame, I was going to come for him. And I was going to open my legs to him if he wanted to fuck me again after that.

And he did.

* * * *

One night, two weeks later, in our bedroom, I sat on the side of the bed, in my silk sleeping shorts, and watched Ann, in her robe, sitting at the vanity, brushing her hair. She was a beautiful woman, with a natural beauty. I didn't have to watch her scrubbing off cosmetics. Everyone said we were a beautiful couple. Bev Thornton had said it at the pool party. Others had agreed. Jim Thornton, smiling, had agreed as well.

Then he fucked me. Repeatedly. I sat there, Ann counting each stroke of the brush in her hair out loud. Mentally, I was marking off an ejaculation under Jim Thornton's and Vince's and even Zach Childs's influence with each stroke she voiced. I included the times I jacked off the last time I was with Jim Thornton at the cabin behind Hal's Tavern and watched him fucking Randy Hill—and of course I included my ejaculation when I fucked Randy too. She reached the end of her count before I reached the end of mine. I was hard.

I said, "About that job offer you have on the West Coast, Ann."

84

"Yes, what about it?" she asked.

"I've thought about it. I think you should take it and we should move out there right away. They want you right away, don't they?"

"Yes, that was the idea killer, though, wasn't it? Going out there right away?"

"It's a good job. You'd be head doctor of the department. I think you should take it."

"But what about you? About your writing?"

"I can do that anywhere."

"Well, if you think so." She turned to me. Her robe opened to expose her right breast.

"Come to bed now," I said, my voice thick with need. I pulled my sleeping shorts down, and she could see my need. She, I'm sure, thought the erection was for her. That's what I wanted her to think.

Shucking her robe, she came to me. I lay on my back on the bed, as she straddled my hips and rode my cock, her head bent over me, her long, luxuriant hair brushing my chest as, hands on her still-thin waist, I slowly raised and lowered her on my hard cock—my cock not hard for her really, because my mind was thinking of me riding Jim Thornton's cock—or, now, Randy Hill riding my cock.

Something that couldn't continue. We inevitably would be caught and exposed.

Good Neighbor

I'd known he was interested in me even if he hadn't been making moon eyes at me at the neighbors' dinner on Sunday night. I was surprised the others at the gathering couldn't see it. He'd been watching me doing my daily swim for most of the summer. I hadn't realized the people who invited us even knew Dan.

It was the neighbors across the street from us, Gail and Chase, who we traded house checking and mail pickup with when either of us was on vacation, who had invited us over. They'd also invited Dan from around the corner. We lived in a neighborhood whose residents primarily were connected with the university in some way because we were only three blocks from the edge of the campus. My wife, Julie, was a medical researcher there. I'd been a pro tennis player and worked with the university's tennis squad. Gail was the university registrar, and her husband, who'd been a chemistry professor, had turned that life in in favor of landscaping gardens. Dan was a research librarian at the university library.

It turns out that Dan's mother had been a family friend of Gail's family. They didn't say so, but they'd invited him to dinner with us on their back screened porch to check up on him and to cheer him up. His mother had died that winter. The two of them had lived together in a split foyer house, where she had the upstairs, with three bedrooms, and he had the downstairs with two bedrooms and a home office. He was able to work at home a couple of days a week to help look after her as her health deteriorated. She'd taken over a year to die and that had taken a toll on her son.

He obviously was gay—in contrast to me—meaning it wasn't obvious, I didn't think, that I wasn't fully hetero. I don't think anyone would have guessed that I was bi and actually preferred men. Dan was good-looking, in his mid-thirties, with a slim body and a somewhat effeminate way of carrying himself. I think he'd had boyfriends before he and his mother moved in together, but that probably had been avoided from that point forward. His mother likely knew he was gay but, just as likely, they'd never discussed it. He probably hadn't been fucked for ten years. Even I could tell at the gathering that he was jittery and tense. Others, I'm sure, thought it was from the loss of his mother. I thought it more likely from not having been fucked good for a long time.

He kept up with the conversation at dinner, but he was reserved—except that I kept noticing him giving me a longing look when he thought no one—but maybe me—was looking. By the end of the evening, I was pretty sure he was signaling to me. He had every reason to know I was active with men even though the rest didn't. Guys of that persuasion have a radar for such things, but I had made it quite obvious to him.

I'd brought it on myself, I guess. His yard was connected to ours in back. In all, five yards abutted ours. His was the only one with a line of sight on our swimming pool, though, where I liked to swim laps every warm morning. We had a nice pool, and there had been gates between our back yard and the other five since before we lived there. Apparently, our pool was used by the whole neighborhood at one time. I'd retired from professional tennis at thirty with a pile of money—you can make very good money even though you never rose to the semifinals of a big tournament—so, other than dabbling in work with the university tennis team, I had little to do other than keep myself in shape.

I was narcissistic, I admit. I liked being in shape and I liked having a cut body—and an overall tan. Sometimes I swam with a pouch swim suit and sometimes I swam and sunned myself in the nude. I didn't think I had to worry about being seen. The only window in another house that had a good shot of our pool area was that second floor of the split foyer where Dan's mother was bed bound—on the other side of her house from my yard—and dying.

I hadn't kept track of when she died and hadn't thought that maybe Dan would move upstairs. Whether he did or not, he started coming to the upstairs window when I was swimming—and staying there as I lay out on a pool bed to dry off—either in a pouch bikini bathing suit or the altogether.

When I noticed that he was watching, I teased him, without revealing that I knew he was there. He initially hid behind the curtains, but as he became aware that I knew he was there and it didn't affect what I did, he increasingly came out from behind the curtains. Eventually, he made no pretense about watching me. I started masturbating sometimes while lying on the pool bed after swimming. So, I guess it was my fault that I added to the poor guy's frustration and to his loneliness after his mother had passed.

I wasn't even thinking of Dan being in the window, watching, the day that I brought Champhorn, a Thai sophomore tennis player, home for a swim in the pool with me and to suck off my cock as I sat on the rim of the pool and he stood in the shallow end, his arms around my waist and his mouth making love to my cock and balls. For the finish, I laid on my back on the pool bed and Champhorn, saddled on my hips, rode me in a cowboy. When I let my gaze drift around to the trees while I was holding the waist of the cute, lithe Thai tennis player as he was bouncing on my shaft, I saw Dan standing there, in his window, watching us.

That must have been when Dan realized that not only was I built and liked to walk around in the raw or nearly so and even jacked myself off on occasion on my back at the pool, I also got it on with men and topped them. I certainly made that clear to him that day, because, even knowing he was up there, watching, I put Champhorn under me on all fours, fucked the shit out of him, and went off to the shower, leaving him collapsed on the pool bed, arms and legs dangling off the side, a silly expression on his face, purring, and blowing bubbles.

So, at dinner that Sunday night, I tried to be very nice to Dan. He apparently saw that as interest and, yeah sure, he was about my age and very good-looking—and obviously a total submissive. So, yeah, I was interested.

And when Gail and Chase told us of the rough time Dan was having adjusting to his mother's death and coming back into society, I felt guilty too.

"I think I'll take a loaf of your homemade bread around to Dan," I said when Julie and I got home. "He's asked me to help with information on research he's doing on Arthur Ashe, the tennis player, so I might be over there for a while."

"Fine with me, Max," she said. "Remember that I'm off to Charleston in the morning for a few days to visit Beth. You'll have to batch it."

"I'll manage," I said.

Dan had his front door open when I came up the walk— it was like he expected me to show up. It made the next forty-five minutes easier. At that point, I considered that I was just on a guilt-ridden mission of mercy. It was only later that I appreciated what a sweet lay he was.

* * * *

I fucked him that first time on the floor of what would have been his living room in the downstairs of the split foyer house. We kissed just inside the door and the kissing, adjusting of clothes, and fondling continued on a downstairs sofa. I made sure the curtains to the outside windows were closed. I had my torso raised by stiff arming the arm of the sofa and suspending my pelvis over his face as he lay on the sofa under me and sucked my cock. I was surprised that he wanted to take my cock in his mouth so soon, but he begged to suck me, so I sank my cock between his lips. He had a soft, talented mouth. Some things about him I didn't particularly like. Others I did. It was a mercy fuck, though, so I didn't dwell on what I didn't like any more than I had to. Once we got going, he had a mouth and a hole and a warm passage, so it was all good.

Once we got started there was no shyness in him. He wanted our torsos and cocks exposed, he wanted his hands on my muscular torso, and he wanted his mouth on my cock. He wanted to deep-throat me, and he did a good job of it for not having been spiked for some time.

He wanted us to be completely naked when we fucked, which was fine with me. He had a nice body, and I knew I had a great body and didn't mind showing it off or using it. I wasn't a complete drone on the career front. I did commercials, and I

89

liked being in good shape for them. He couldn't get enough of me, running his hands over my body and telling me how beautiful it was. My concern was getting my dick in his hole. He gave me no fight in achieving that goal.

He begged for me to be inside him, and when we got there, we rolled off onto the floor, with Dan on his belly and, at first, me stretched out on him, covering him close and slowly giving him four thick inches, not knowing how much he could take, especially after some time of not getting any, but he urged me on, raising his tail to me, begging me, "Fuck me good; fuck me hard; make me feel it." I got my feet under me then, straddled his hips, gave him the other three inches, and rode his ass, pumping him deep. I fucked him good and hard, and he let me know he was feeling it. He squealed like a girl.

"Fuck, you're big!" he cried out. Yep, I was, thick and long. I was proud of that.

"Shit, I've never had it like this!"

Lucky you now, then I thought. You'd get it better from me, though, if you took it more like a man. Stop with the limp-wristed hand at my neck, fingers running through my hair, girlie begging for kisses crap.

And then when I turned him again, got my knees under his buttocks and an arm around his waist, he just lay, docilely in my arms, his torso arched back and his arms straight out in a sacrificial position, moaning softly, moving his pelvis almost imperceptibly with me, as I slow pumped him to a finish, giving him all of it in long, slow slides, and chewed on his nipples. He went all effeminate on me then, which I didn't like all that much, but I was too close to getting off for it to make much difference.

He took it. He wanted it. He wanted it again right after I'd come, and I carried him back to the bedroom area—he insisted we use a guest room rather than his bedroom. I laid him out on his back on the bed, slapped his thighs open, and came down hard between his legs. I fucked him hard and rough that second time and he took it like he'd been dreaming of it ever since he'd started watching me at the pool. And maybe he had.

"Yes, yes, rough. Harder. like that. I knew you'd fuck rough," he cried out. So, I did him even rougher, pounding him hard, giving him what he was saying he wanted from me.

I fucked him in a missionary, and he clutched me to him, his claws buried in my shoulder blades, his grip opening and closing to the rhythm of my thrusts, his face buried in the hollow of my shoulder and sobbing quietly as we rocked back and forth on each other, giving added motion to my cock inside him. I pulled it nearly all the way out and slammed it back in, again and again and again, trying to pull him out of the virgin girl being deflowered game. And he clutched at me and yelled. "Yes, yes, oh shit, yes!"

There didn't seem to be any suggestion I was taking liberties with him. He was sobbing, "Thank you, thank you, thank you."

As I was finishing him, he lay back, threw his arms to the side in a motion of total surrender to me, turned his cheek to the mattress, and took on the glazed look of someone who had been totally conquered. He had been tight at the beginning, but he opened up nicely too me and the muscles of his passage walls milked my cock deliciously. He was a sweet lay if you overlooked the girlie poses—far better than I had expected.

It was no chore at all. When I rose off him, I muttered that I was sorry and just went back to the living room, pulled my clothes back on, and left his house. He probably thought I was sorry for nearly raping him. What I was sorry for, though, was for cock teasing him and adding to his frustration at a bad time. I determined then to make it up to him. I didn't want him as my boy toy—he was a bit too effeminate for my long-term tastes, but I'd see what I could do to fix him up with someone else.

"Did he like the bread," Julie asked me when I got home.

"Sure did. He squealed like a girl," I answered.

"He *is* sort of obvious, isn't he?" she called back.

"More than sort of," I muttered and went right off to the shower so that she couldn't smell the cum I'd repeatedly pulled out of him on my body.

* * * *

The next day, all alone, I lay masturbating myself on the pool bed when Dan came to his window. I motioned him down, not knowing if the night before had been too overwhelming for

91

him to want more. But he did want more. In just a few minutes he was coming through the gate between our properties, in a Speedo, and was mincing his way across toward me. I could have done without the mincing walk, but his slim body was still as nice in the daylight as it had been the previous evening in the dark. He'd turned all of the lights off when he'd fully realized I'd come to fuck him and we'd copulated in the dark, as if he didn't want to shine any light on what we were doing.

I couldn't stay hard with the image of his effeminate ways as he moved toward me, so I got off the pool bed and dove into the pool. He came in after me and, as I started swimming laps, he did so, as well. He was a good swimmer, keeping up with me. When I thought of him more as an athlete than a limp-wristed librarian, my arousal increased and I went hard again. I pulled myself up to sitting on the rim of the pool and, seeing my hard on, Dan dog paddled over to me and took my cock in his mouth. I reclined back on my elbows and watched his head bobbing in my lap. He gave great head—he'd done so in the dark the previous night and he did so in the light today, as well. The sap rose in me and I pulled him out of the water, put him on my cock, facing me, and we rocked back and forth against each other.

He was plastered in front of me, like a monkey, and had his hands all over me, as my cock explored his passage seven inches deep. He wanted to kiss me everywhere and settled on nursing my nipples. I wasn't wild about the clinging aspect of this, but the cum was burbling up in me and took me to an ejaculation. He'd already come up my belly.

We embraced there, rocking back and forth. "I want you to do me like you did that Oriental guy the other day," he whispered.

So, I took him to the pool bed, put him down on his belly, mounted his ass, plugged him, and pounded him. When I left him to take a shower, I left him the same way I'd left Champhorn—flat on his belly, arms and legs dangling off the side of the bed, a silly expression on his face, and purring and blowing bubbles.

It hadn't been the same as with Champhorn, though. Champhorn was a man's man. His body was smaller than Dan's was, but he went with the fuck like a man would. He didn't get all deflowered virgin on me when I was finishing him, as Dan tended to do.

This wasn't going to go much further. I could keep it up thinking of a guy as fresh meat, a new challenge. But Dan gave it up too quickly and too much like a girl. I'd have to find some way to let him down and go easily.

The answer came with an invitation from Alec up the block from me, a university drama professor in his early fifties. He was having a party to watch the U.S. Tennis Open semifinals on TV at his house.

Alec was a gay top. He was gray and maybe a bit paunchy, while still pretty well muscled up for a guy his age. He was a little more effeminate than I normally liked to cruise with, so I didn't. But he was a top. He'd had one of his graduate students living with him, until the guy went out to California to try to break into movies. I didn't know how Alec did in bed, but his graduate student had always looked very satisfied when I saw him working in Alec's yard.

And I must admit that I felt a little guilty about Alec in a similar way to how I felt about Dan. I had done Alec wrong. Seeing the graduate student working in Alec's yard one hot day and looking like he was about ready to die with a heat stroke, I'd invited him back to take a cooling dip in my pool. I'd taken a dip in him in the pool, pushing him up against the side of the pool; barking for him to put his knees on my hips, which he did; and fucking the stuffing out of him. He'd come back for more a couple of times. Neither of us had told Alec I was sharing his graduate student with him.

I know, I wasn't being a very good neighbor with Alec. But here was a chance to make it up to him.

* * * *

Alec greeted me at the door with a "Well, who have you brought along, Max?" greeting. His eyes had gone directly to Dan, who was giving the host the glad eye too.

"This is one of our neighbors, Dan, from around the corner on Brevington," I said. "I hope you don't mind that I brought him along."

"No, not at all. Not at all. The men are gathered back in the den in front of the TV," he said, offering an arm to Dan rather than me. As we walked back, I had a little smile waft across my face. The two had gravitated toward each other like magnets.

As I suspected it would be, it was an all-male party—and all gay male at that. Alec wasn't a bit subtle. He was out, way out, his tenure secure at the university, nothing less expected of someone working in the theater. In no time, Alec and Dan were wrapped around each other in a corner and kissing and feeling each other up as it was an all-Swiss slug fest on the TV, Federer racketing it out with Wawrinka in the U.S. Tennis Open finals up in New York.

I wasn't bored because Alec had invited Champhorn for me. When I was coming back from one of the guest rooms early into the follow-on Murray-Djokovic match following Federer's surprise knockout of Wawrinka, where I had bent Champhorn over the bed and ravished his ass, I stopped, arrested by the sounds of sex, and looked into the master bedroom.

Alec was humping Dan on the bed in a missionary. Both of the men were naked, both of them were having a ball balling and being balled, and Alec was proving to be more than competent at the fuck. Dan was in what apparently was a favorite damsel-being-ravished pose, Alec's knees pushed under his buttocks, holding Dan arched back toward the bed, limbos all akimbo, a "Mom, the big bad man is fucking my snatch" expression on his face as he did the dying swan routine with his limp-wristed arms.

I left the house, without Dan, whistling and feeling fully free of a millstone that had been hanging around my neck.

To solidify the change of guard, I invited Alec, Dan, and Champhorn to a swim party at my house the day before Julie was to return from Charleston. Dan gravitated right to Alec, assuring me that the fuck at Alec's house had taken effect for both of them, and Alec fucked Dan in the pool while I fucked Champhorn on the pool bed.

A couple of weeks later, as I was driving home from the university tennis facilities, I drove by Dan's house and say the "For Sale" sign on the lawn in front of it.

"What gives with Dan selling his house?" I asked Julie when I walked into the house. She was part of a Saturday morning neighborhood kaffee klatch where everything—and I hope not simply everything—going on in the neighborhood was hashed over, so I assumed she'd know what was behind house sales.

"Oh," she said, giving me a little "scandalized, but not really" smile. "Dan is moving in with Alec up the street. He said his house was too big for him anyway and had sad memories since his mother had died there."

Yeah, I thought, but I think he found the view from a second-floor window there to his liking. Still, I was happy. My turn at being a good neighbor had panned out.

That didn't stop me, though, from having two fast-growing, tall funeral cypress trees planted in the back garden in just the right place to obscure the view of the pool area from the second floor of Dan's former house. Our friend across the street, chemistry professor-turned-landscaper Chase, put the trees in for me.

"This isn't the best place to put these," he had said.

"Yes, it is," I'd responded. And so he put them right where I wanted them. And then we went for a swim and I fucked him on the pool bed, riding his ass in a doggie until he came and collapsed flat on the bed under me and I fucked on. As I had for the years Gail and he had been our good neighbors, I left him with his arms and legs dangling off the sides of the bed, humming to himself, a dazed, satiated look in his eyes, and his mouth burbling bubbles.

I left them all that way. That was my specialty—my good-neighbor policy.

When in Niamey

"*Oui, Oui! Baise-moi! Baise-moi!*"—Yes, yes, fuck me!
"*Comme ça! Plus profound!*"—Like that. Deeper.

I lay on the plastic sheeting on the hotel room bed, my
hands gripping the brass rungs of the headboard overhead, my
eyes wide, focused on the suddenly cruel smile on the face of the
French businessman sitting next to me on the bed. The ceiling
fan in the hot Niamey hotel room was revolving lazily with a
grating whoop, whoop sound. A bright-colored bird briefly
alighted on the frond of a palm tree brushing against the frame
of the open window across the room, peeked in, apparently
wasn't comfortable with what it saw, and then flew away. I was
naked, my legs spread and bent, my feet flat on the bed, pushing
my pelvis slightly up. I was panting hard, moaning low.

Go loose, relax, go loose, I kept droning in my mind.

The Frenchman had a well-greased bunched hand up my
asshole to the knuckles. I was rocking my pelvis gently against
his hand, trying my best to be as open as possible to him. "*Oui,
oui, Fist moi. Fist moi*"—Yes, fist me, I repeatedly moaned,
assuring him he could do as he liked. "*Ce que vous voulez.*" He was
paying for it. Men came from Europe to Niamey expressly for
this fetish.

He hovered his face over mine, looking intently at my
reactions.

"*Prends-le. Prenez la fist*"—Take it. Take the fist—he
growled at me in an intense voice. He lowered his face to mine
and took my lips in a kiss. When he pulled away, I gasped and
groaned and arched my back. His hand had penetrated in, up to
the wrist.

"*Oui, oui, Fist moi*" I cried out as he opened his fingers
inside me and began to move the hand, in and out, in and out.

96

I panted even harder, concentrating everything I could muster to adjust to the greased hand.

"*Oui, oui! Baise-moi avec ta main*!"—yes, fuck me with your hand!

"*Prends-le. Prends-le.*"

He leaned his face of me again, but lower this time, taking my cock in his mouth and sucking it. After less than a minute of this, I came in a flood down his throat. He gagged a bit but took it all. His face appeared over mine again. He was still fucking me with his hand and I was moving my pelvis against it.

The expression on his face was a mix of cruelty, lust, affection, and want. He took my lips again and I opened to him. He was sharing my own cum with me in the kiss.

I groaned again, as I felt the hand pulling out of me.

"*Baise-moi. Baise-moi maintenant. Prends-moi. Défonce-moi. Donne-moi ta bite!*"—Fuck me now; take me; drill me; give me your cock, I pleaded. They liked it when you pleaded for the cock.

He was moving his body over me, coming down between my legs, entering me with his hard cock, penetrating me to the core.

"*Oui, oui! Oh fuck oui!*"

His hands glided up my arms, the right hand, the one that had been inside me, trailing grease up my arm. He grasped my wrists. he was on his knees between my legs, his cock buried deep inside me.

I wrapped my legs around him, hooking my ankles together underneath his buttocks.

He began to pump me in long, slow slides and I raised my pelvis up again, taking him as deep as I could, and moved my hips with him, making the most of the rhythm of the fuck. I set my passage wall muscles to squeezing, rippling over, and milking the Frenchman's throbbing cock, giving him his money's worth. He had come from Marseilles for this. He was moaning now too.

"*Vous êtes un taureau de l'élevage!*"—You are a breeding bull—"*Un éléphant de bull!*"—a bull elephant—I cried out, not only because men liked to hear this when they were inside me, but also because he was fucking me well.

97

I arched my head back and murmured, "Yes, yes! *oui, oui! Plus difficile!*"—harder—as he dove deep and flooded me deep with his cum.

Rising from me, he looked down into my eyes, a dreamy expression on his face. He gripped my thighs, high up with both hands, moved them to my inner thighs and glided them down to my knees. I spread my legs again, not knowing what he wanted from me now, but prepared to give him anything he wanted. My cock was hardening again—for him, if that was what he wanted. He briefly toyed with my passage opening with his fingers, murmuring how open I had spread to his needs.

I whispered *"Baise-moi encore"*—fuck me again—knowing they were words all men wanted to hear. *"Mettez-le en moi à nouveau"*—put it in me again. *"Fist moi encore une fois"*—fist me again. But he pulled them back, patted my knees, and rose from the bed.

"Alas, I have an appointment," he said. "But remember where we left off."

I watched him dress in his suit, waistcoat, and tie and all, primed to do what he came to Niger to do—if he hadn't just done what he had come to Niger to do.

He let several banknotes flutter onto my belly and murmured. "You are very good. I am not like this in France. I don't do this there." Both the extra money above contract and the almost apologetic excuse came as an expression of guilt, as if he could do in Africa what he couldn't do in France.

And then he was gone. It would be several more moments before I could feel like I could close my legs, that my passage, trained as it was could contract to normal.

* * * *

In 1955, Niamey, the capital of Africa's Niger, was a sleepy little French colonial town of some 27,000 inhabitants on the banks of the Niger River. I had been brought here—and abandoned—by a French plantation owner. I was making the best of what I had—which was a young, supple, blond body; an easy smile; and a willingness to open my legs to men and accommodate kinky sex for money that would help me get back to England.

I was sitting at an open-air café by the river and down the street from the small hotel where the French businessman was staying. We had met here after his appointment. He was paying for me for the weekend through the escort service I worked for in the Niger capital, so presumably after we had lunched he would take me up to the room and fist me again. It wasn't the first time I had been fisted. Niger was a collection point for all sorts of kinky fetish men who operated out of the mainstream.

I took what I had to take to continue paying for my rooms over a bakery, to put food on the table, and, I hoped, eventually to pay for a plane ticket back to London. I enjoyed some of what the men did to me to get themselves off.

I couldn't deny that the fisting got me off too—more the thought and emotions of it than the physical pain it caused, though.

The French businessman was a handsome man. He was in his late forties or early fifties. He was starting to go gray on his head, although, as I had found out, the curly hair on his chest and his bush were still an auburn color. He was a facetious man, impeccably dressed in tailored trousers and an open, long-sleeve white shirt here in the café—this being a weekend away from his job here, when, I was sure, he would be in a well-pressed tailored suit with a handkerchief in the pocket.

I was surprised that he'd worked on me with grease up onto his forearm, but his fetish must override his sense of cleanliness. He certainly worked with determination, a mad gleam in his eyes as he hunched over me, his hand up my ass and sliding it through the grease. He was a different man then than he was now, sitting across from me at the café table, sipping his tea, and chatting amiably with me as if I were a colleague or client rather than a prostitute he had been fist fucking earlier, a male prostitute he had had in bed, covering for half the day, a prostitute he planned to resume fist fucking that after he finished a pastry and a shot of cognac.

I couldn't help noticing another patron in the café, a large-built, ebony black man, in the uniform of an army officer, his jacket bristling with medals. He sat at another one of the café tables and was watching the Frenchman and me—or rather, not that I was noticing him, watching mainly me. Two other soldiers stood behind him at his table, as he tucked into enough food to feed a regiment, holding both knife and fork in his meaty hands, wolfing the food down, white teeth flashing, and scanning the landscape around him through blood-shot eyes.

As a waiter passed, the French businessman stopped him and asked who the black man at the table was.

"That's General Boulama. Assane Boulama," the waiter answered in a nervous whisper. "You'd best stay clear of him. He's head of the secret police in Niger. Nearly runs the country now. I've seen that he is looking at the young man with you. You might want to finish up and leave before he takes more notice."

Heeding the warning, the Frenchman downed his cognac and said it was time to return to the hotel room. As we were leaving, the general was calling the same waiter over to him. It was only a short walk down the street to the hotel, but I was well aware that one of the soldiers who had been standing behind the general's chair followed us at a distance.

In the room, the Frenchman pulled me gently to him and we kissed as he unbuttoned my shirt and then unbuttoned my shorts, and pulled my clothes off my body. He went down on his knees in front of me and took my cock in his mouth. One of his hands went behind me and slid into my crack, rubbing across my hole. Sighing, I opened my stance. The can of grease was on the foot of the bed, and he reached over, not losing the hold of my cock in his mouth, scooped up a handful of grease and returned his fingers to my hole.

I had my fingers dug into the wavy gray hair of his head, pulling at it, moaning deeply, my legs rubbery and held up only by his embrace around my legs with one arm, as he worked his fist into my ass with his other greased hand, when I exploded in an ejaculation.

He continued, however, breaching my sphincter with his wrist, and fist fucking me as I writhed in his grip, pulled at his hair, and gasped and moaned. I groaned as he pulled his hand out and pushed me down on the foot of the bed, on top of the plastic sheet that was still there from the earlier fuck.

I lay there, my back on the bed, my hand fisting and stroking my cock, as he stood over me and slowly undressed. He had a good, trim body. His cock was in erection. He leaned down, grabbed both of my ankles, and wishboned my legs. I moved my hands under me to my buttocks and used them to raise and roll my hips up to take the long slide of him inside me and focused my eyes on the slow-turning ceiling fan above my head that did little more than move the warm air around. I gave a little jerk and arched my back when he penetrated me with his shaft, but I settled right down as he grasped my hips in his hand and began to pump me.

"Fuck, fuck, fuck!" "*Vous êtes un taureau de l'*élevage!"— You are a breeding bull—"*Un éléphant de bull!*"—a bull elephant!

All thoughts of anything else happening in the sleepy town or of the gross, intimidating General Assane Boulama floated out of my brain as the trim Frenchmen fucked me expertly and I gave him his money's worth in vocal response and the countermovement of my pelvis.

* * * *

Wanting to be alone for a bit, I had left the French businessman in his hotel room that Sunday morning, saying I wanted to attend church. He wasn't interested in doing so. He lay there on the bed on his back, smoking a cigarette and, his legs spread and bent, playing with his cock as he watched me dress. Our morning had started with me riding his cock as he lay on his back on the bed and rubbed his thumbs on my nipples.

I didn't really want to go to a church. I only wanted a bit of time alone. My buttocks—my passage—was sore from his fist. He didn't seem to have gotten enough of being inside me that way. He said it wasn't something he normally could do with a young man when he was in France.

"There is something about central Africa," he'd said. "Something primitive and permissive here."

"When in Niamey," I had muttered.

When he'd asked for an explanation, I had said, "It was something that the man—the French plantation owner—said to me before he brought me here. In France he fucked me, but he didn't mistreat me. He hinted at 'when we were in Niger, in Niamey,' we could be freer with sex. I didn't know that, by freer with sex, he meant he could beat and whip me. When he did that here and I let him know I didn't want it, he threw me out."

"So, the men you go with here don't beat and whip you?" the Frenchman asked.

"They do sometimes," I answered.

"But—"

"I was here, alone, without funds," I answered. "It became a matter of 'when in Niamey.'"

"Interesting," he had said. "Freer here with sex," he said. And then he laid me out on the bed and fisted and fucked me again, not seemingly having any notion that this was in the category of beating and whipping and he himself said he would not subject a prostitute to in France.

"When in Niamey," he murmured.

Then, using my belt he tied my wrists behind my back and bent me over the bed and, with his belt, he strapped me on the thighs, buttocks, and back. In short order he splashed his cum on my back. It obviously was the first time he'd done this with a young man, and he found it arousing.

"I see," he said as he left me and went to take a shower, "only in Niamey. Freer with sex. Very invigorating." He went to his wallet and once more dropped banknotes that went beyond the contract on my reddened buttocks in acknowledgement that the kinkier sex went beyond the norm. Any guilt assuaged by extra banknotes, I supposed.

When I left him, telling me I wanted to attend a church service, I was walking on the street, deserted on a Sunday morning, toward the river, when a black van pulled up beside me and three black men in army uniforms jumped out, grabbed me, and pulled me in the van. They pulled a burlap sack over my head, bound my hands, pulled my trousers and briefs off my legs, and as the van drove around the city, the three black men fucked me in succession on the floor of the van. Rough hands grabbed my hips and three cocks of varying thickness and

102

lengths thrust up into my ass. Three cocks exploded inside me. Three flows of come were deposited in my ass.

During the whole time, not a word was spoken. Those at the escort agency had told me that this happened occasionally in Niamey. They used the phrase "When in Niamey." Central Africa wasn't like the rest of the world, they said. There were men in power here who lived only by their own rules. They said it was just the Army taking its cut of the street activity and that I should just endure it if it happened to me—that the thugs would return me to the street after they had taken what they wanted from me.

"Even if they take your life, it isn't any more than another man contracting you through our agency would take from you, if you are unlucky. They just won't be paying for it."

They didn't return me to the street after they were done with me, though.

I was exhausted and cowed when I was dragged from the van into a building and dropped into a chair under yet another lazily whoop, whoop, whooping ceiling fan. The bag was pulled off my head and I was sitting on the other side of a big wooden desk from General Assane Boulama.

"It has come to my attention that you are practicing prostitution in Niamey without paying the entertainment tax," he said, looking at me sternly. He was a massive man. The desk was a large one, but he made it look small as he leaned on his elbows, made small gestures with his massive hands, and gave me a half smile. He had taken his beribboned jacket off, which was hanging nearby on a clothes tree. His chest muscles bulged, straining the material of his white shirt, which was open down three buttons. His chest was tattooed in some sort of blue tribal design.

"I wasn't aware that there was an entertainment tax pay," I answered. "I am represented by a lawyer, who perhaps you should contact. He pays all of my fees." That's what the escort service had told me to answer in relationship to their role with me—they were my lawyer.

"You are responsible for your own fees," He said. "I claim the right to take the fee from you myself."

"I'm not sure what that means," I said, standing up from the chair. I was trembling all over, scared. The man was overwhelming. But I had to get out of there somehow. The only thing I could think of was a bluff—to move and to keep moving and to hope he was too slow to react before I was out on the street and running.

He wasn't too slow.

"I will tax you now," he said, standing and motioning to the men I hadn't realized were still behind me. They grabbed me and dragged me from the room.

* * * *

I was bound to some sort of platform in a windowless, concrete walled and ceilinged and floored chamber. The obligatory ceiling fan was slowly whoop, whoop, whooping overhead. I was lying on a wooden board and my arms were raised above my head and bent back and tied off at the wrists on the top edge of the board. My pelvis was elevated on a wooden block. My legs were raised and spread, manacled at the ankles and pulled up by chains hanging from the ceiling. My butt was suspended over the bottom edge of the board. I was uncomfortable, but I wasn't in the worst situation of some of the others around me.

Sweating; naked, except for loin cloths; ebony bodies were moving about in the chamber. Other ebony bodies were tied to other pieces of restraint equipment in the room. I was the only European here. The other trussed up bodies were naked, as I was. Most of them were writhing on whatever equipment they were tied to, crying out at the crack of whips or the prodding of clubs. One or two of the bodies were silent, just hanging on the boards they were tied to. The sounds of screams, moans, and groans permeated the room.

I found I was moaning and groaning too. General Assane Boulama was crouched over me, staring down into my face with a cruel smile on his lips. He was naked, massive, save for a loincloth. He had a paunch but he otherwise was muscular and glistening with sweat. The sheer definition of evil power.

I was moaning because he was stroking my cock with one beefy hand. He lifted the other hand so that I could see it, the fingers bunched up, the hand and forearm slathered with grease.

"Please, please. Mercy," I whimpered. "*Ayez pitié!*"— have mercy! Then the hand disappeared, dipping down between my legs, and I was nearly lifted off the table to the extent my bindings would permit, my howls floating across the other sounds in the room. His hand was bigger than the French businessman's had been, bigger than any hand that had been inside me before. He took his time working it into me up to the wrist, only laughing at my pleas for mercy. His other hand continued beating my cock off.

I shot my load toward the slowly revolving fan overhead and blacked out.

When I came to, he was below me, between my thighs, his hands gripping my knees, rocking back and forth against my buttocks, fucking me with his cock. His cock, like his hand had been, was the biggest one I'd ever had inside me, stretching me to the limit.

"*Vous êtes trop gros! Ayez pitié!*"—You are too big! Have mercy!

He laughed, taking it as a compliment.

Needless to say he showed me no mercy and that was the last time he was too big. He took me frequently after that and reamed me to his needs. By the end of his third fuck I fit him like a glove.

He came inside me in a gush and then held there, cooing at me and running his hands over my body. It wasn't long before I felt him hardening inside me again and he resumed pumping me, deep and thick.

* * * *

I was taken from what General Boulama said was the "examination chamber" up two flights, to a bedroom, with a lock on the door and bars on the window. This apparently was where General Boulama lived as well as worked.

I looked all around the room for a means of escape, but found none. I was naked anyway. I couldn't exactly run out into the street. If I did, I thought, the secret police would grab me. I realized that I was being hysterical. The secret police already had me. I did find that there was a bathroom, with a shower, off the bedroom. I took a long shower, dried myself off—there was a stack of clean towels on a table in the bathroom—and went back into the bedroom and laid down on the bed. There, in front of me, beyond the foot of the bed, I saw the hook in the ceiling and the chains hanging from it with wrist restraints at the end. I shuddered, shut my eyes, and soon was asleep.

Boulama woke me, coming in noisily, glowering at me, shutting the door and locking it, and disrobing.

"*Temps d'impôts*"—Tax time, he said, with a grin on his face.

It was the first time I had seen him completely naked. He'd been inside me in the "examination chamber," but I had not actually seen his cock. I almost swooned now that I could see what he'd already had inside me. He was both horrifying and magnificent at the same time. He was more than six and half feet tall and heavy. Most of the heaviness was muscle, but he had a beer belly on him too. What arrested the attention, though, was that he was hung like a bull, with a drooping ball sac—the sac of a fertile bull as well. He was ebony black, and glistening with a film of sweat. He also was covered in blue tribal tattooing.

He was all business, grabbing me, getting my wrists in the restraints of the hanging chains without a bit of trouble, as he was overwhelmingly powerful, and had authority on his side. I was putty in his hands, my mutterings of objections returned only by low grunts. My feet barely touched the floor even when I was standing on my toes.

And my feet didn't spend much time on the floor as I was swinging back and forth either under the strength of the lash of the whip or in trying to avoid it. He whipped me for an eternity, not putting the full strength of his arm into it, though. He more teased me with the whip than cut me. He raised welts but they didn't cut into the skin. What was most important was that it gave him a massive erection. I'm ashamed to say that he gave me an erection too. The planter who had brought me here

106

whipped me. Other men had flogged or caned me. I had never asked for it, but it had always made me hard and given me massive orgasms.

The whipping by Boulama did no less. When we were both hard, he dropped the whip, grabbed my thighs, wishboned my legs straight out to each side, set my hole on his cockhead, and pulled me down on him. Letting go of one of my legs he reached around me and stroked my cock to the rhythm of stroking inside me.

He was good, very good, both at fucking me and masturbating me, and when he put his cheek next to mine, I turned my face to him and let him take possession of my mouth.

"*Avez-vous aimé qui?*"—Did you enjoy that?—he asked after releasing the kiss.

"*Baise-moi encore. Fist moi encore*"—Fuck me again; fist me again, I whispered, not only for bravado. He was driving me wild sexually.

He did fuck me again then—on the bed—and he fisted me on the bed and then he fucked me again. I reasoned that this was his bedroom, because he stayed with me through the night, lying on top of me between my spread legs, possessing me with his massive cock.

The next morning when I woke, he was gone. The bars were still on the window and the door was still locked. And the chains with the restraints at the end were still dangling down between the foot of the bed and the locked door.

Not long after I woke up, the door opened and my breakfast was delivered by a hunky black bull young soldier, his chest bare, in camouflage pants and combat boots. He gave me a "don't even try bolting for the door" look, closed and locked the door behind him, put the breakfast tray down on a table by the door, and came over to the bed. He grabbed my ankles and pulled me to the end of the bed. He didn't crouch down or anything. He put me on my shoulder blades, my torso streaming up to him, my knees at first hooked on his hips, but later my ankles on his shoulders; he unbuttoned himself and took out a big, hard cock. He thrust it inside me, squeezed my buttocks in his hands, and he fucked me hard and furiously to a mutual ejaculation.

I writhed under him, glad to take a cocking from a young black bull any day of the week. I wondered if he was one of the three soldiers who had fucked me in the van before delivering me to Boulama. He left without a word when he was finished, leaving me lying there, panting and luxuriating in the fuck. My breakfast was cold, but I supposed it had been cold before he brought it.

At lunch it was yet a different black soldier hunk, bending me over the mattress, getting up on the bed on his knees, with me trapped between them, and having plenty of leverage behind his backswing as he fucked me in a power doggie position. He had grabbed my wrists and held my arms out in front of me while, covering me close, he fucked me hard. He put his mouth to my ear and gave me the explanation for all of this that I had anticipated. *"Considérer la pute"*—Take it whore, he muttered. "Give it to the foreign visitors, yes, but give the Nigers our cut."

So, I was just a whore paying my entertainment tax. When in Niamey . . .

Dinner brought the third young black bull hunk, convincing me that these were the same soldiers from the van and that this was how Boulama got them to do his bidding—by giving them privileges. He fucked me in a side split, standing on the floor at the foot of the bed, with my weight on my right hip and my right leg rising up his muscular torso, my ankle hooked on the back of his neck, me turned to him, my right arm extended to his muscular chest, palming one of his nipples, my tongue hanging out, my eyes giving him a *"Baise-moi"* look, and him pistoning my hole.

I startled them by crying out, *"Oui, me faire dur!"*—Yes, do me hard, to assure them I was the whore they accused me of being.

Later in the evening, Boulama himself reappeared to hang me from the chains and whip me and then take me to bed and fuck me, then fist me, then fuck me again. We showered together and he took me back to the bed and fucked me through half the night.

I was reamed to his requirements now. I enjoyed the fucking now.

I slept the sleep of the dead, to be awakened for the delivery of my lunch and a missionary fuck from young black bull soldier number one. I didn't really mind any of this. I even got used to the whipping, because he didn't lay his arm into it and it got me off. I'd taken four men in a day before, but they hadn't all been hard-bodied, big-cocked black-bull soldiers.

The pattern continued to the third day. At noon that day, though, after solider number two delivered my lunch and doggie fucked me and left, I'd eventually realized that he left the door open—not just unlocked, wide open. And, on the table by the door, instead of a lunch tray, he'd left a pile of the clothes I'd been wearing when I was snatched off the street. They were clean and neatly folded.

If this wasn't a sign I was free to go, I didn't know what would be such a sign. I hurriedly dressed—it had taken me several minutes of recovering from the glorious fuck to realize the door was open—and slithered out into the hallway. I cautiously went down the stairs, thinking that I'd be grabbed at any minute and that this was all a mistaken understanding on my part.

I heard someone in the hall below and I retreated back up the stairs and down the hall, pulling myself into a deep doorway niche. I peeked around the corner and saw two of my soldiers—I had come to think of them as "my" soldiers—dragging a young, naked European man between them. He was collapsed, probably unconscious, his head hanging over, his arms draped around the soldiers' shoulders, and his feet dragging along the floor as they carried him. They dragged him into "my" room. I didn't stay around to see any more. I scooted past that door and down the stairs and out into the street.

I first went to the French businessman's hotel to tell him why I hadn't come back to him on Sunday. But he had checked out. I then went to my own rooms above the bakery. I was surprised that no one had been there before me. What money I had was still there, where I put it. I hastily packed and went directly to the airport. I didn't have enough money to get me to Europe, but I did have enough to get me to Tangier, Morocco, on a flight leaving within the hour.

I found that "when in Tangier" was much more welcoming and accommodating to men who serviced men. I never went back to Niamey and its privileged few ways, but I never went back to London either. Tangier suited me and my lifestyle just fine. There even were some rich black bulls living there. I had been royally worked over by General Assane Boulama and his soldiers, but, in the process, I had become addicted to big black cock. And, after General Assane Boulama, there never again was a cock that was "*trop*"—too big, for me. So, I guess he did me a professional favor.

I found too that there were men in Tangier who had fists and liked to grease them up and use them.

Shipwrecked

It had come in my dream again—the dream of the hunky yacht captain between my spread and bent legs, his muscular, naked body heavy on me, pressing me into the thin mattress of the bunk in the tiny cabin. His hands were gripping my wrists, my hands gripping straps on the wall above the head of the bunk. His muscular, hirsute man's body was crushing my slim, young body. I was moaning, telling him I was scared and that he was heavy. He was shushing me, telling me it was all right, that he would make it all right, how pleased he was that I was taking him as my first.

He was inside me, thick, insistent, stretching me, causing me to pant hard. My grunts were loud, primeval. He was admonishing me to keep quiet, so that the Sylvesters, the couple I was traveling with on university break to see my parents in Cape Town, who were in their cabin just across the wall from the head of my bunk, wouldn't hear what the captain was doing to me.

I stopped grunting so loud. I didn't want the dream to stop. Always before it had stopped short of him penetrating me. I was frustrated that it hadn't happened before. It had happened now. I wanted him inside me. He was inside me. I didn't think I'd feel it in a dream, but I did feel it, filling me, stretching me, rubbing against my inner walls, sliding in and out, with difficulty at first, but more easily with each slide.

I tried to remain quiet, although I couldn't keep myself from whimpering and moaning as his pelvis rose and fell, sending his hard cock deep up into my guts and then pulling out only to slide in again, my passage taking him deeper than before. It was painful, but also so pleasuring, what I dreamed about ever since we'd left Marseilles for this journey down the west coast of

111

Africa to Cape Town. The dream, although I'd had it nearly nightly since we'd cleared the Rock of Gibraltar and the captain had seen the looks I was giving him, looks he returned, had come upon me more suddenly and more vividly than usual. I had struggled with him at first, and the feel of him forcing himself inside me, becoming one with me, had a realism and pain attached to it as never before. It seemed so real.

I didn't want it to stop. He was so big inside me. I was fully possessed by him. I was completely his, just as I had dreamed I'd be. I had dreamed of this before, and, since Marseilles, of the French captain, moving around with the crew on deck, wearing only a slip of a swim suit, muscular, hairy chested, tanned, and so handsome—always moving like a dancer, smiling, joking—and looking at me with lust.

When I stopped struggling—when the dream became real to me and I stopped wrestling against what I dreamed would be—and lay back, relaxed, and, as we both could feel, opened entirely to his churning cock, the captain of my dreams let loose of my wrists and grabbed my ankles, wishboning my legs.

"Good for you to surrender to it," he murmured. "It will go easier for you now. You are so sweet."

He pressed his knees under my buttocks, elevating my pelvis. He moved deeper inside me and started to pump rhythmically. I moved with his rhythm, using my grip on the straps overhead and the leverage of my feet flat on the mattress to thrust my pelvis up as he thrust his down, reaching deep inside me. We were one glorious, forbidden fucking machine.

"Good, good. You are fucked now," he murmured. "You are fully mine. Take my seed. I've got your cherry."

"Yes, yes, yes," I whispered in answer. I felt like crying, though. There was nothing romantic in his victory statement. There was no doubt I'd been had—that getting his cock inside me was the main event for him.

And then it no longer was a dream. Philippe really was on top of me, in the night, in a yacht off the coast of Africa—fucking me, a nineteen-year-old, never fucked before university student.

And, despite his crass characterization of what we'd done, I was loving it. I felt him tense and jerk—and give me his seed.

I heard the grinding noise and felt the lurch of the ship. The sickening sound of wood and metal being torn asunder brought me fully awake. Philippe was pulling out of me and leaving the bunk, racing for the door to the cabin. I heard the sounds of people screaming, having been abruptly awakened. I watched Philippe go, scrambling uphill on the decking because of the list of the yacht. I heard another crunch and was being drenched with water. I turned my head to see that there was a gaping hole in the side of the ship and water was rushing in and then, as the ship rolled in the other direction, rushing back out again—taking me with it.

I don't know how long I was out or how I got to the beach, but I slowly drifted into wakefulness, coming back through the same dream I had left, of Philippe on top of me and inside me, pumping. But then that turned out not to be a dream, didn't it? I reasoned. I certainly was sore enough in my gut for a man to have been there. Than what was this? He was inside me still, thicker and longer than ever, taxing the stretch of my passage, the muscles of which were spasming, rippling on his throbbing, insistent, possessing cock.

I opened my eyes. It was still night, but the moon was out. I could see the man on top of me. He wasn't tan. He was ebony black. He was muscular, but more so than Philippe—much more so. He was looking down into my eyes with primitive, primeval want. His probing cock was stretching me, reaching far up into my gut.

It wasn't Philippe. This wasn't a dream!

I came awake enough to struggle with him—but ineffectually. I was too weak. He was too strong. I beat on his chest with my fists, although "beat" was too strong a word for the energy I could muster. He laughed, grabbed my wrists, forced my arms over my head and picked up the pace of his massive thrusts inside me. When I surrendered to him and relaxed, collapsing back on the sand, he laughed again, shoved his knees under my buttocks, grabbed my ankles with his hands,

113

and wishboned my legs wide—just as Philippe had done earlier in the yacht.

Lost to him now, I arched my back and thrust my pelvis up as he thrust his down, fucking me deep in my core, my passage yielding to him, blossoming open for him, the muscles of my inner walls undulating over his throbbing, insistent shaft. I cried out when I felt the gush of his cum inside me. I had already come.

He laughed, pulled out of me, picked me up, and tossed me over his shoulder. He was a monster of a black man. I already knew that from feeling the size of him inside me. He was well over six and a half feet tall, sturdy and impossibly muscular. I hung bent over his shoulder, one of his massive hands palming my buttocks, his index finger buried in my anus as he sauntered up the beach and into the night-time dark jungle foliage.

I could feel his cum dripping out of my ass as he walked—no, strutted—into the jungle.

Exhausted, I blacked out.

I don't know how long I was down with the fever, drifting in and out, but I think it must have been three or more days. My system apparently didn't like swallowing a lot of seawater. I was on some sort of wooden platform high in the trees. There were other platforms off in other trees, connected to this one by a rope ladder-like walkway. I was lying on a pallet formed out of large palm branches. I was naked.

I woke up occasionally to having the black man—I came to know of him as Big, because he was big in every way—down on his haunches beside me, cooling off my brow with a wet cloth, the cloth looking suspiciously like a strip of material from the sleeping shorts I had been wearing when I was sucked out of the hull of the yacht. He wore a primitive loincloth, made out of a strip of material draped in front and back over a rope around his waist. His body was huge and magnificent in every way—and ebony black. Other times he was lifting my head up, helping me to sip water from a hollowed-out coconut shell.

Still other times, in the dark of night, he was between my legs on his knees, with his torso's weight supported on his hands, pressed on either side of the pallet by my arms, hunched over me like some sort of gorilla, making low, humming, snuffling sounds. His cock was inside me and he was fucking me in shallow strokes. He never went deep during these initial couplings, as if he had some regard for my feverish state. But he fucked me nonetheless, probably determined to get his rocks off while I was alive in case I didn't make it. I wasn't so far gone, though, that he wasn't able to pull a climax out of me and before exploding inside me with a series of prodigious blasts of warm cum before withdrawing.

That's how I figured I was weak with fever on the pallet for three days—the nighttime copulation. I would be awake long enough after he had lifted my head and ladled some sort of delicious soup between my lips and picked off chunks of meat from banana leaves along with bits of other fruit, putting them in my mouth for me to chew and swallow. For a time after that, I'd be more lucid than at other times. As it grew dark up in the eerie on the platforms under the heads of the towering jungle trees, he'd crouch on his haunches on the platform next to my pallet. His loincloth would be gone, and he'd be fisting an enormous erection. While I was still somewhat awake, he would reach over with his free hand and move in on my body, gliding around, paying attention to all of the curves and crevices there are on a young man's body.

Big would take my cock in his hand and stroke me as, involuntarily at first but hungrily by night three, I would engorge and then ejaculate for him. As I drifted, feverish, through the days, I increasingly looked forward to the intimacy of the nights, with Big holding me close, entering me, and becoming one with me. It wasn't like the sex had been with Philippe. Big was more intimate, entering me in peace rather than anger and expending more effort to take me with him to the heights of pleasure.

On the third night, he held my cock loose and, feeling stronger, I moved my hips, fucking up into the sheath he made with his cupped hand. He laughed and made a guttural sound I took to be some variation of "good" when I came. My response had assured him that he no longer was assaulting me—that we were now making love.

After I had come, he would move over on top of me, parting my thighs with his hands, coming down between them on his knees, his gigantic erection standing up proud out of his black-haired pubic bush. He'd cup my buttocks and raise and part them with his hands. I'd give a little cry as he forced his cock inside me, this being progressively less of an effort on his part and less pain on mine. On the third night he slid right in, my passage beginning to meet his requirements—me already becoming his. Then he fucked me in shallow slides to his finish.

He was training me to take all of his cock. I was assuring him that I wanted to take his cock.

By the third night, I was placing my hands on his plump buttocks as he stroked me, his buttocks tensing and releasing in the rhythm of his slide inside me. I was sighing and moaning rather than whimpering and sobbing as I had done on the first night. He fucked me deeper that night. From the size of him, I surmised that he could fuck me much deeper than he had as yet.

On the fourth day, I was up and off my palette and he was down on his haunches—in his loincloth—beside me, showing me some of the implements of his daily life. He had various fruits, roots, and seeds on a crudely woven tray. There were two other trays, and he was showing me, through sign language, grunts, and gestures, which were edible and which weren't. As he held them and let me try them out—or not—they went to either the "edible" tray or the "not edible" tray.

I followed this tentatively, still confused and not sure where I was and how and whether I was going to get away from here. It had been three nights, though, and I already was beginning to feel a willing slave to the huge cock Big had between his legs. I was beginning to fit him like a glove and to look forward to the next sheathing. Each time he took me, I willed him, in my mind, to take me deeper yet.

His training of me wasn't just physical; he was training me emotionally to be his mate. He was going to keep me.

It was late in the afternoon when I heard them, alerted first by Big giving a frightened expression and looking in every direction—and then up. He let out a deep grunt. I'm sure he didn't know what the sound was nor was he even sure where it came from precisely or what it portended. I knew what it was, though. I'd heard the sound of helicopter blades before. Instantly I knew the shipwreck had been found—and probably that everyone aboard but me was accounted for and had

116

conveyed I was missing. They were coming for me. I was being rescued. Instinctively, I stood, began waving my hands, and yelling as loud as I could.

Of course they couldn't see me through the foliage or hear me yelling above the sound of the helicopter blades. But I didn't think of that, and Big didn't know that.

He was up and had grabbed me in an instant. He manhandled me over to my pallet, dropped me down there on my back, and landed on top of me. His giant's body covered my slim, youthful body completely. He was heavy on me, making no effort to take any of his weight upon himself, and I was having trouble breathing. He pressed me to the pallet, his head raised, wildly looking through the foliage overhead, craning to see what manner of bird was up there, instinctively aware that it related to me and to someone looking for me.

His way of training me was with the fuck—controlling and subduing and then fully possessing me, working me until he knew I was responding with want and surrender. He reverted to that now.

He was in massive erection, his cock having slipped out of the side of his primitive loincloth covering. I slipped into heat and he knew it. He obviously was in heat as well. I involuntarily moved my body against his and he was moving on mine from above as well. I arched my back, he placed his big hand on the small of my back and his cock bulb was just breaching my hole and, then, suddenly, swiftly, he pulled my body into his, penetrating me deeper than he ever had before.

I started to scream as he thrust deep inside me. He was quick, though, covering my mouth with one hand, holding me to the pallet with his other arm encasing my neck. His hips rose high and then descended like a sword cutting through the air, his cock slicing into my passage hard and deep. The hips went up and thrust down again and again and again. Clutching at his shoulder blades and then his buttocks with my hands, I went with him.

He was fucking me hard and deep, giving me all of his cock, fucking the danger from overhead away, and I was going with him, the two of us rocking against each other and getting everything we could get from each other. For the first time, he lowered his face to mine, pressed on my lips with his tongue, and I opened to him, letting his tongue invade my mouth cavity and swab my inner cheeks, and stroke down into my throat. I sucked on his tongue, surrendering even that completely to him, as the black brute continued to fuck me. We fucked like animals and climaxed together like champions. Then we both lay there, still fused by his cock inside me, panting and listening—listening for the sounds of helicopter blades.

But the helicopter no longer was above us.

Big rolled off me onto his back and I turned my body, coming on top of his. With a moan of pleasure, understanding that I was going to perform the ultimate surrender to him, he held my chest suspended over his belly, as I took his cock in my mouth and he did the same to mine and we sucked each other off to another climax. He reversed me, pulled my body into his and we slept the rest of the afternoon that way. Until then, Big had slept on a different platform. After that he slept with me, holding me in his embrace, and sometimes waking during the night and slowly penetrating me with his cock and slow fucking me.

One thing was clear to me now. Big had no intention of letting me go. He was teaching me the ways of the jungle for me to remain here as his sexual slave.

That night when he came to me, he made his intentions completely clear. He ravished me totally, taking me in several taxing positions, leaving me with my legs spread and me unable to close them—and purring. The days of pandering to me because I had been feverish were over. In the morning he came to me again and repeated the ravishing. He then, gesturing for me to stay where I was, went off, down his rope ladder, on a foraging mission, leaving me moaning and smiling. I was still smiling when he returned and fucked me again.

We had reached a certain level of higher trust. The platform I had been sleeping on was higher in the trees than the main platform where Big had been sleeping and where he had been setting his pallet across the opening of the rope ladder from my platform to his. Only this platform, the one he guarded, as far as I knew, had a rope ladder down to the ground. It was too far down for me to safely drop to the ground. After the afternoon of the helicopter, though—of its first appearance—when I had so totally surrendered to Big sexually, he moved up to my platform and my pallet for the night. He came to me at dark and fucked me. We slept for a while and he woke and then woke me fucking me again. We dozed and then he fucked me again. We slept, and then it was light and he was gone. He was fucking me so much that my passage didn't really close back down now. I was reamed to his specifications. We didn't require much preparation now for him to slide inside me. We were a unit now when we were fused. I was trained to be his mate.

Any of the time he was sleeping, I might have made a break for it. I don't know if I didn't try it because he surely would have caught me and punished me or if I didn't want to leave him.

The trust broadened on the fifth and sixth days. On the fifth day, he took me down the ladder to the ground and we foraged together, him showing me what to put in the crudely woven basket and what not to. Then, when night fell, he fucked me on my pallet, we slept, he fucked me again, we slept, and he fucked me a third time. Exhausted, I slept late into the morning. He didn't. He did the same on the sixth day, taking me down to the ground in the early afternoon and standing off as I foraged for myself, showed him what I'd found, absorbed what I could from what he kept and what he tossed away, and then he let me go up the rope ladder myself to be assured that I could handle it alone.

Late that afternoon we were on the main platform when we heard the helicopter again. Big looked wildly about him, first trying to locate where the sound was coming from and then to see where I'd gone. He smiled when he saw that I had shrunk close to the tree trunk, under a branch heavy with leaves, and was looking up into the sky but not making a sound.

When the helicopter was gone, he came for me. His loincloth was off and he was in massive erection. He put me on all fours on the main platform, covered and mounted me, and fucked me like there was no tomorrow—like he knew and appreciated that I might be torn from him at any moment. He fucked me so long and hard that I thought he would not be able to do so in the night, but he did, three times again. And I can't say that I didn't love it. That night we remained fused, his cock never pulling out of me. We were a mated couple.

On the seventh day, Big sent me down the ladder on my own, while he crouched on his haunches at the top looking like he wasn't at all sure this was a good idea. Feeling a bit of freedom after so many days of being under the black giant's watchful eyes, I struck out in a different direction than we had taken the previous two days in my foraging expedition.

After a bit, I found that I was close to the ocean. I came close enough to the tree line above the beach to see that I was in the same spot where the yacht had shipwrecked. It was out there, on an outcropping of rocks. It was apparently that Philippe had been so taken with getting his cock inside a ripe young virgin's body that he hadn't taken proper precautions on how far off shore the yacht was sailing and he'd put it on the rocks.

There was another ship out there, though—a larger one. And there was a smaller boat pulled up onto the sands, and a group of men standing in a circle. One of them had a map and the men were looking at that and then in the directions in which he was pointing. One of the men was the yacht captain, Philippe. I sighed a sigh of relief. So, he had made it off the yacht. So, probably, had all the rest. That probably was why they were here so quickly to look for me. There must have been enough evidence left that I'd gotten to the beach when they'd gotten here to have hope that I was still nearby, somewhere in the jungle.

I hesitated for a moment when the men started fanning out, calling out to each other in French—and calling to me by my name too. But I hesitated only for a moment. I turned and moved as swiftly as the dense jungle permitted me, back to the platforms in the sky. Big was on the rope ladder to the ground, about a third of the way down. He had heard the men calling too. When he saw me, he stopped and gave me a confused look. I waved for him to go up the ladder again, putting my hands on the ropes at the bottom and my foot on the first rope rung.

Understanding—and trusting—he nodded and went up the rope. When I got to the top, he pulled the rope up and hustled me up the series of platforms to the very top one, where he went down on his haunches and pulled my body into his, holding me close. He had a hand tightly over my mouth, but when I gently pulled on it and looked into his eyes with mine, he released me and then gave a great sigh when I didn't call out to the men on the ground.

He was hugely erect, his cock running up the small of my back as we huddled there. But he didn't do anything about it until dark, when we hadn't heard anything from the rescue party for more than two hours and when everything was still in the jungle except for the sounds of the jungle that belonged there. One of those sounds was Big breathing heavily, though. Feeling safe now, he gave vent to his raging hard, laying me out on the deck of the wood platform, covering my body, and fucking the shit out of me. After he'd had an athletic go at me, I rolled over on top of him, straddled his pelvis and rode his cock. He fucked me and I fucked him back. His cock was inside me all night.

That night, once again it was him fucking me, the two of us sleeping, him waking me up fucking me, the two of us dozing, and him fucking me into the lightening of the sky above us through the foliage of the tall trees.

I woke in the morning, my legs spread and bent, my hole gaping open, cum dribbling out of my anus, feeling totally open and vulnerable and exhausted, but gloriously fucked and fully satiated. My passage was gaping open, ready to take him any time he wanted to be inside me. I heard humming coming up from the main platform below. In the light of day I realized I had made my decision. I was staying.

Is Capricious the Word?

Sandra had been doing a crossword puzzle as we waited for the visiting author from New Zealand to arrive at our Chelsea apartment.

"You're the prose man. What's a word for 'inconstant'?" she asked, stretching her long legs, in the turquoise pedal pushers, down the length of the white sofa. The tunic she wore over them, showing her cleavage almost all the way down to her navel, was the same white as the sofa. I assumed she'd stay on the sofa as much as possible while the New Zealand author was here—it highlighted her very nice set of tits. I also assumed that the author, invited by her English Department at Colombia, where she taught poetry, had impressed her with more than his best-seller status. Otherwise she'd have worn an Indian caftan. Before she'd wafted off to his lecture, she'd asked me if New Zealand was somewhere near India.

"Fickle? Vacillating? Spasmodic? Fluid?" I tossed out from the other side of the kitchen bar while I was tossing the salad. I did most of the cooking. Her friends tittered behind their fans that she had acquired me, when I had taken one of her classes as a graduate student, as a boy toy, but I knew that what she'd needed was a maid. No, more than that. What was a nine-letter word for a convenient husband? Camouflage. That was it. She liked men and women, a variety of them. I liked men, but for a room over my head and food on the table, I occasionally fucked Sandra. It had been a convenient—camouflage—marriage for both of us. "Does it give any clue?" I called out.

"It's ten letters," she answered.

"Oh, of course," I responded. "Capricious."

"Yes, that fits," she said.

It certainly would, I thought. And then the bell from the street rang and there was heavy trudging on the stairs, and the New Zealand best-selling author, Bram Overby, was in the frame of the entry door. The trudge wasn't because he was fat. It was because he was large, a hunk, in fact. He lit up the room with his smile and his ruddy rugby star looks, his broad shoulders, full chest, and biceps—and lips for that matter. He was carrying a large bouquet of flowers, which I knew weren't for me no matter how I ached that they would be. And from how outrageously Sandra was fawning over him, I knew that they would fuck.

The meal went well—better for Overby and Sandra than for me, but it appeared to be a winner all the way around. Sandra managed somehow to accept accolades for the food without outright lying about who had prepared it—which wasn't past her to do—and my reward was that, in the free-flowing conversation, it became clear that Overby, a best-selling novelist, was more on the beam with me, Aiden Macallum, a first-time literary novel writer, than he was with Sandra Gainsworth, the poetry professor. That was just on the professional level. I had no trouble understanding that the robust New Zealander was hard for Sandra.

I left them, wine glasses in hand, in the living area, looking out of a full wall of glass at the Manhattan skyline in the living area and retreated to doing the dishes and straightening up the kitchen clutter after we'd finished eating. Wes Montgomery was playing the romantic guitar loud enough on the stereo to overshadow their discussion. When I was done and moved back into the living area with full wine glass in hand, they were gone. They'd taken their wine glasses with them.

They were on Sandra's bed in her bedroom—she and I slept separately. She was on her back. Her turquoise pedal pushers were in a puddle on the floor by the bed. Poetically, his trousers overlay her pedal pushers and an opened condom packet crowned the pants. The two empty wine glasses were on the nightstand. Her white tunic was open and spread. The best-selling author lay between her long spread and bent legs, where he was doing groin pushups on her pelvis, they were kissing, and he was squeezing one of her ample tits and thumbing her nipple.

The decibels of her moaning told me that he was hung and doing a good job of her.

I turned, retrieved a jacket from my bedroom, and went out into the night. I didn't have far to go. I'd given up an invitation to hear the beat poet, Zach Taggert, perform his poetry to his own guitar music at a nearby bar we all frequented to help entertain the New Zealander. Obviously, my help wasn't needed any longer. The room was dark, save for the spotlight on Zach, where, dressed all in black, he sat on a black high stool on a black platform, backed by a black wall. The room was smoky, despite the obligatory no-smoking signs on the walls. It was that sort of bar.

I settled at a table near the back of a crowd of maybe thirty people. In a room this small, thirty constituted a crowd. It was hard to do a count in the smoky darkness. Still, Zach picked me out in the crowd, smiled his pleasure that I had come after all, and looked directly at me while he continued reciting his poetry and strumming his guitar. I didn't think it was specially performed for me, though. He was an intense man—all craggy angles and serious stare rangy and long-distance truck driverly, but with an intensity that made each and every one of us sure he was speaking directly to us—and not to the surface of us. He was slicing right into us and talking to our slow-beating hearts— mine, in particular.

He closed with a poem that was delivered directly to me and that I knew had been composed for me and about me when I last lay with him. It was his ticket to lay me again.

His room was in a nearby tenement.

He hovered over me on his bed in the dark, made darker by the black walls, floor and ceiling, relieved only by the single window looking out on a black fire escape and three letters of a frenetically flashing orangish-red neon sign advertising the pizza parlor on the ground floor.

I was naked, my arms raised over my head, my wrists tied together by a black leather cord. Zach was lying on me, between my spread legs. He was bare-chested—thin, tightly muscled, his torso covered in black curly hair that went down into an unruly black bush. His black jeans were unzipped and flared out from his groin. His face hovered over mine, his eyes intense, his mouth forming poetry that was nonsense to me in the circumstance, although I'd never tell him that, and he was deep inside me, moving his shaft in a slow pump.

He claimed to be in heaven with me, expressing himself in poetry, which, no matter how poetic, managed to emphasize dirty words. I was just happy to have a hard man between my thighs.

I panted, my back arched, my pelvis rolled up to him, all of my concentration on the cock inside me, not even trying to listen to his poetry. I shuddered as his cock pushed up into me, my walls shimmering, grabbing the shaft, and pulling it in deeper. I kept clinching on his cock. He'd groan and I'd moan. He stroked and stroked. Involuntarily my pelvis began to move with him, thrust up as he thrust down, gasping for him . . . and then coming for him in explosions, one after the other. And as the jerks of my ejaculations subsided, his started. This was always the forbidden thrill for me. A man of an earlier era, he barebacked—he checked often, but he refused to be sheathed. He had assured me he had just been checked. I had anticipated this from the time he told me he was clean as we walked to his building. I had no greater thrill than the release of his warm cum inside me. It may be the reason I came back to him again and again—that and how purely he was a man of an earlier, simpler era.

I lay there, totally laid out, panting slightly, as he tensed and jerked and tensed and jerked again, finishing me, reminding me of why when he held his hand out to me at the bar, I came here with him, laid down for him, and opened my legs to him. He pulled out to the surface this time, coming in spurts on my rim, my perineum, my balls, and then pushing inside me again, squishing through his warm cum, dragging it deep inside me. The feel of the warm cum breeding me deep had me sighing and moaning.

Later, he lay back in the bed, hard bodied, gnarly muscled, his shoulder blades raised on pillows, smoking a joint, but his eyes boring into me as I straddled his hips, my wrists still tied behind my back, and rode his cock languidly, moving forward and back and side to side, rubbing his hard shaft along my rippling passage walls, gliding through the lubricant of his earlier cum and of his newly releasing precum. He remained rigid, erect, and throbbing inside me, watching me with slitted eyes and puffing on his joint, as I literally rocked and rolled on his cock, using it to rub every inch of the surface of my inner walls, caressed me inside, pulled my cum out of me, and, as he jerked and grabbed my waist, released his cum inside me in strong, virile spurts.

Afterward, as I lay on the bed, recovering and panting slightly, he sat on a straight wooden chair facing the bed, strumming his guitar and composing a poem that, when polished, would make me almost cry when I sat and listened to it being performed at the club, knowing it was about me and that it would be his ticket to bringing me back here and fucking me again.

It was arguable who was using whom. It was certainly true that I had come to Zach after seeing the New Zealand stud, who I felt attracted to, fucking Sandra.

When I was dressing to leave early in the morning, he was sitting on the sill of the window, guitar in his lap, still in his black jeans, his right leg raised, his foot pressed into the side frame of the window. He was strumming his guitar and reciting poetry, a joint hanging out of the side of his mouth. He was backlit by the orangish-red neon lit, not as glaring in the morning light as it had been in the darkness of the previous night.

He watched me dress when I'd come from washing in the trickle of water his shower produced, and he watched me leave. I can't remember that he said anything at all—even when we left the bar the previous night, both of us knowing where we were going and what we'd be doing—beyond whispering his poetry. I don't think I said anything either.

When I returned to the apartment, the door to Sandra's bedroom was open. The New Zealand hunk was gone. She was on her back, legs spread, rubbing her nipples with one hand and playing with the folds of her cunt with the other. She gave me a little smile.

I stripped in front of her—I knew she liked that—and then walked, erect, to the bed. She slit a condom packet and handed the disk out to me. She dropped the empty packet on the floor by the bed, where it joined two other packets and two spent condoms. I climbed onto the bed and between her legs. I slid inside her and began to pump as she arched her back, threw her head back, laughed, slid her fingernails across my shoulder blades, and began to moan. This was the circumstance under which I usually fucked my wife—when she'd been with another man and wanted me as well afterward. And I always complied.

"Capricious." That was a ten-letter word for "inconstant." I knew a shorter word for it: "slut." The both of us.

At the breakfast table she told me of the change in our life.

"I have a year's sabbatical," she said. "Bram has offered his house and sponsorship, giving me that year to do nothing but compose poetry. I need to produce another book of poems to ensure I can get tenure at Colombia. He showed me a photo of the house. It perches on a cliff overlooking the sea near Wellington. It looks like a bird ready to take flight, raised wings and all."

"So, I'll have to be looking for other arrangements, another apartment," I said. I hadn't finished my doctorate yet. Money was coming in the first book, but nothing like I'd need to keep this apartment.

"No, I thought you'd come with me."

"Will Bram be there, in his house, during this year?"

"Yes, of course," she said.

"OK, I'll come with you." My thoughts went back to what I remembered the most of the New Zealand stud. When he was on top of Sandra, I'd seen his pull almost completely out of her before sliding in again. He had a thick cock that went on forever.

* * * *

Sandra was right about the impression that Bram Overby's house had, although you had to be out here in Cook Strait, off the North Island coast to the south of Wellington, to get the full effect of it. I had swum straight out to sea off the private beach below the cliff that Overby's house perched on. I was a strong swimmer, having been competitive when I was an

127

undergraduate. I had a swimmer's body. I wasn't tall, but my body was sleek: a very narrow twenty-eight inches at the hips, eight inches broader in the chest to accommodate breathing, and strong bicep and thigh muscles. I shaved myself smooth except for a tightly trimmed reddish-blond triangle at my bush, which aided in swimming as well. I had no trouble swimming a considerable distance out to sea and turning around and looking back at the top of the cliff.

The house did, indeed, look like a bird, wings spread, and about to fly off the top of the cliff. The central portion had a foyer on the land side, with kitchen at one side and a library at the other, with the foyer leading into a long dining room on the sea side. To the left from there was one of the wings of the bird house, soaring up two and a half stories in one large living area, glassed in on three sides. Opposite from this to the left of the central core was a matching wing, in two and a half stories, containing three bedrooms—two at the sea side—each with bath, and Bram's office on the lower floor, and the master bedroom above in a rising, glassed-in story and a half soaring to the west.

From here it looked like the sandy beach below the cliff was dedicated to Overby's house. There was a long, twisting wooden staircase coming from the back yard of the house, which was mostly taken up with a large infinity swimming pool, seemingly plunging over the cliff into the sea, and it's concrete-block terrace cascading in sections down to the sand. To add to the dramatic effect of that from the perspective from the sea, a waterfall did indeed send water down the cliffside at the end of the pool to a pool between terracing and the cliff wall down to the cliff's base. The water for that didn't really come from the swimming pool, though; it recirculated by pump from the pool below.

I could see the roofs of other houses on either side of Overby's, and I knew there were some houses on the land side of his, across a road. He'd said he lived in an artists' enclave and that there would be parties for us to go to, but so far we'd met no one else other than his house staff: a cook, a maid, and a houseman, the cook and houseman being wife and husband. These servants lived in a house across the road and were trained to be efficiently of service but rarely seen—and never seeing anything.

Overby's books had done him very well financially. The house was expensively, if sparsely, furnished. He had a very nice cabin cruiser bobbing around out here near to where I swam, and he had bought both privacy and everyone looking the other way rather than at his foibles.

We were only three days here, Sandra and I, and I'd already become a part of his foibles. I had come down to the beach, nude, just with a large towel, because of the frustration he'd already established in me. I had wanted him back in Chelsea, on the first night, when he'd come to dinner and we'd talked so passionately about writing novels, but then his passion had gone to Sandra, taking her to the bed and fucking her, leaving me, Sandra's husband, cleaning up the kitchen and sending me out into the night to seek my own sexual solace.

Sandra and I had been given separate bedrooms, the two guest rooms on the sea side of the bird house wing, but Sandra had spent more time in Overby's bed than in her own. That's where she was now. That's why I had come down to the beach and swum out to sea. That he was bedding her, supposedly my wife, was part of the frustration. But more of it was that he hadn't bedded me—not until the previous evening. And then it wasn't on a bed, but on the proverbial white bearskin rung in front of the soaring, smoldering fireplace in the far living room glass wall. It was trite and clichéd, but it was no less real, and, although it should have released tension, it only added to my frustration.

As with the first night here, we'd gathered in the living room after dinner, on a U-shaped sectional in the conversation pit facing the fireplace, which was burning despite the warm weather. Sandra was curled up in Overby's embrace on the section facing the fireplace and I was sitting in one of the wings. The two of them were cuddling as we drank our after-dinner wine. He was stroking her body, progressively opening up the kimono she was wearing to reveal the curviness of her naked body, the fullness of her breasts and nipples, and her silky blonde bush.

But he was speaking of the writing of Somerset Maugham in the South Pacific and he was discussing it with me. He too was in a robe—we all were, having swum in the pool nude before dinner and eaten in robes at the dining table afterward—and Sandra had his opened at the waist, had pulled his cock out, and was making it hard—and thick and long—with her hand. But he was speaking with me, looking at me. He obviously knew he was making out with Sandra, as he was thumbing her nipples and running his fingers into the folds of her cunt—and he was getting hard from her attentions. But he was talking with me on technical issues of Maugham's writing and was carrying on a perfectly erudite conversation with me.

I too, in watching them, had brushed my robe open and was stroking my cock. Overby obviously saw me doing so but went right on discussing Maugham with me and fondling Sandra.

It was maddening. We were operating on two different levels here. We supposedly were here to enrich Sandra's literary poetry efforts and yet every time I was with Overby he was concentrating on what enriched my prose writing. Which of us interested Overby enough to bring us here and sponsor us—Sandra or me? On the other hand, it was Sandra he was fucking, even though he looked at me with lust too. I didn't even know if he fucked men. Was he straight or bi? Did he just appreciate beauty wherever he saw it? Earlier in the evening, when I had emerged from the pool naked, he had remarked on the beauty of my body.

"Such beautiful proportions," he'd said. "Good definition in the chest and arms, but so willowy and trim below. I don't know if I've seen a young man with such slim hips—and the hollows between your buttocks and your thighs—so sexy. I think you are right to trim your pubes in a close-cropped curly V like that. But the slimness of your hips . . . I don't know how . . ."

He didn't complete the sentence because Sandra had chimed in with, "How about the wideness of my hips, love? The earth mother look. I could bear your triplets."

"Not unless we weren't careful and were being very foolish," he had answered, with a laugh, turning his attention from me, which quite evidently was what Sandra wanted.

130

"Although you bring such hot flashes and capriciousness upon me, that I could see us overlooking something important. And, yes, *your* hips give me no pause in your being able to take a bull like me. You do handle the thickness of me quite well. And I am a bull, am I not?"

He didn't say it, but he didn't have to. He was wondering if *my* passage, because of my unusually narrow waist and hips, could take the cock of a man bull—or at least he was alluding to his consideration of giving it a try.

"Yes, you a bull of a man," she'd said, pulling him on top of her on a pool bed. He proceeded to enter her and fuck her, leaving me to dry off and find a pool bed to stretch out on several empty beds from where Sandra had her face turned to me, making no effort to cover the flash in her eyes and grimaced smile on her lips each time he thrust up into her. Making a point, I'm sure, before he finished he had changed to fucking her in the ass channel, and Sandra took that in stride. I harbored the thought that that too was a signal to me of what he was contemplating doing with me.

What word had he used? Capricious? Yes, that was it. Which one of us was he most interested in? And was he really interested in me at all? He had been on the cusp of musing whether a slim-hipped man like me had a channel that could handle a cock like his—he was that close to declaring that he wanted to fuck me and yet he had capriciously veered away. Was he teasing me? Or was he just not really interested and was cruelly enjoying himself cuckolding me? Surely he knew that Sandra and I didn't care what each of us did with others sexually. Or was he challenging me on that point? It's true that some of our discussions on story themes had been wrapped around the concept of self-denial on sexual preferences and toleration. He, of course, was the hedonist in word and deed. But me? Did I even know what I really felt about these matters? Was that what he was trying to pull out of me?

The two left me for a while in the living room then. Overby picked Sandra up and carried her out of the living room. But he only took her as far as the dining room, which opened from the living room. He laid her on her back on the dining table, brushing her kimono full open. His robe remained on his back, but fluttering at his side, the two looking like some sort of gross bird of prey, while he hunched over her and fucked her in the ass again on the top of the table. As he fucked her, he grasped her flowing hair in his hand and jerked her head back into his chest, cruelly arched her back. This just made her laugh.

As Overby fucked Sandra, he turned his face from her. He was looking back into the living room, at me. The lust in his eyes was obvious. Was it for the woman he was fucking on the table or was it for the young man sprawled on the sectional in the living room, openly masturbating and watching him fuck the woman?

He wouldn't commit, which angered and frustrated me. Turning from them, not wanting to hear Sandra's exclamations on how big he was and how well he was fucking her, I picked up the novel that Overby had taken from the library after dinner and brought into the living room to discuss with me. It was Maugham's *Moon and Sixpence* treatment of Paul Gauguin escaping to Tahiti to paint. I stopped stroking myself off and became engrossed in the book, looking for points that Overby and I had discussed, and so lost knowledge of when the copulating on the dining table had ceased and the two had departed the living areas—or, indeed, how long it had been since Overby had returned to the living room, taken the book from my hands, stretched out on top of me on the sofa, taken my lips with his, and begun stroking my body inside my robe with his long, sensitive fingers.

He was stroking my hips with both hands. "Such slim hips," he murmured. "I wonder—"

"Do it," I hissed. "I've seen your cock. I can take your cock. I want to take your cock. Fucking do it."

He did it. He carried me over to the bearskin rug, murmuring, "Forgive the cliché," and stretched out over me in reverse. We sixty-nined each other throbbingly hard and then he moved me to my knees, my chest and cheek to the fur of the rug, my eyes staring into the smoldering, dying fire in the fireplace. Overby mounted high on my hips, finding he did indeed fit inside me, and fucked me to a mutual ejaculation. He fit inside me the perfect way—just, stretching me and rubbing every surface inside me as he stroked, causing my passage walls to ripple over his shaft and try to grasp it as it forced its way inside, pulling the cum out of me. My spirits soared as he kept mumbling that, "Yes, it fits fine. So sweet, so tight." He continued to be obsessed with the slimness of my hips, holding and stroking them with his hands as he fucked me.

He left me there without comment and presumably went to bed. Sandra wasn't in her bed when I went by her room. She presumably was upstairs in his bed. The capriciousness of it all was not lost on me.

Overby was in his office, working, when I got up. Sandra was on a pool bed at the pool, alternating between scribbling verse and filling in crossword puzzles. She had nothing unusual to say to me, either, although she did stare daggers at me as I passed by her on my way to diving into the pool, nude. So, she did know that Overby had fucked me as well as her the previous night. She still had the edge, though, because she slept in his bed.

After lunch, where Overby and I took up our discussion of Maugham where we'd left off the previous night and Sandra worked on a crossword puzzle as she ate, Overby took her to bed in his bedroom. The sound of him fucking her good was what sent me out of the house, naked, down to the beach, and far enough into the sea that I couldn't hear them.

When I had swum back to the surf line and rose from the sea, naked, I saw that it wasn't a totally private beach after all. Only from this perspective could I see that wooden stairs came down to the beach from the houses on either side of the soaring bird house. And I wasn't the only one on the beach either. Standing over my oversized beach towel was an Adonis. He was over six feet tall, several inches taller than I was. He wasn't much older than I was, probably in his mid-twenties. His body was magnificent, muscular, covered with fine, black curls. He had a close-cropped beard and loose, shoulder-length black hair. His eyes were a contrasting light color—pale blue or hazel—and his smile was sensual. He was tattooed, barbed-wire bands on his biceps, a swirl of a colorful design half buried in black curls on his left pec, and the head of a snake about to strike at his navel, its tail wrapped around an extraordinarily long, if not overly thick, erection. He was, of course, naked.

"I am Jarrod," he said in a melodic voice. "I saw you enter the sea from my deck, and I couldn't help but come down. You are a beautiful young man—very sexy. Bram tells me you take cock." He motioned for me to lie down on the towel. I was about to say no and head for the stairs to Overby's house when I saw Overby himself at the top of the wooden stairs to his house. He was naked and there was a towel over his arm. I reasoned that he was coming down to be on the beach with me.

I was hit with a flare of anger and frustration. His capriciousness was frustrating to me. He didn't declare himself or ask permission for anything. He just took what he wanted when he wanted it. I don't know what he wanted from me in relationship to what he took from Sandra. Yes, I was jealous. Yes, I wanted to strike out at Bram and make him choose me.

Jarrod was standing over me, hands on hips, completely open to me in his nakedness. He was smiling. "Do I look good to you?" He asked. "I am horny. Will you take my cock?"

Without voicing an answer, I went down on my knees in front of this Jarrod god, licked around the curl of the snake's tail, and took his cock inside my mouth. We lay stretched out side by side on towel, exploring each other's bodies with our hands, until Jarrod coaxed me onto my back, stroked my inner thighs until I spread them for him, rolled over on top of me, and pushed his knees under my buttocks.

I lay there, my buttocks elevated on his thighs, my torso reclining on the towel in front of him, my fingers buried in the curls on his chest, and my head arched back, watching Bram pause at the top of the cliff, while Jarrod slowly made the snake's tail disappear inside me. He stroked my narrow hips lightly with his fingers while he fucked me.

"Nice, very nice," he murmured. "And tight, but you took it all."

We rocked against each other and I moaned, as his shaft reached far, far up inside me, and he fucked me slowly—and totally.

When we'd both come, I looked again to the top of the cliff and Bram was gone. Jarrod was still here, though. Without withdrawing from me, he leaned his face down to mine and we kissed. I embraced him and stroked his shoulder blades with my fingers, until I felt the snake tail coming to life again. Then I moved my hands to his buttocks and grasped him close to me.

"There's more," he whispered.

"Yes, oh yes!" I cried out to the top of the cliff as I arched my back and he began to stroke inside me again. He turned me onto all fours, mounted my ass, and fucked me in doggie style, allowing him to push in to the root. It was then that I noticed we weren't alone.

Overby wasn't at the top of the stairs when I looked because he had come down to the sand and was sitting on his towel, watching Jarrod fuck me. He didn't sit there for long, though. He rose, positioned himself behind Jarrod and took over the control of thrusts, his thrusts inside Jarrod's ass determining Jarrod's thrusts inside me.

Damn him and his presumption of control over everything, I thought. Jarrod took his cock without objection or flinching. It was obvious that Bram had mastered Jarrod before and been given leave to do it at will.

After a while, Jarrod pulled out and disappeared and it was just Overby mounted on me, stroking my hips with his fingers, murmuring, "Such sweet, slim hips," and slow pumping my passage. He was huge inside me and I gasped and panted, willing my undulating channel walls to open for him and moaning deeply when they did.

∗ ∗ ∗ ∗

The mail had come when I regained the ability to move and went back up to the house. Jarrod had left after Bram had taken over the pumping of me down on the beach and Sandra was up in the master bedroom, taking a long bath. She called out to me as I came back into the house, pulled on a pair of shorts in my bedroom, and then roamed around the house locating everyone. The cook was in the kitchen, working on something. The back door to the laundry room and garage that jutted out on the land side of the house was open and I located the houseman covering the maid from behind over a rumbling washing machine and pulled away from that quickly. The mail was on a table in the foyer.

Included in the post was a letter from my agent, which only now was catching up with me. I'd sold a second book and the hefty—for me—advance check for $25,000 was included. I was ecstatic. With the money I still had from the advance on the first book, I now had some independence. The letter from the agent spoke of negotiations for a three additional books deal.

I went directly into Overby's office to tell him of my good news. His response was as self-centered as I could possibly imagine. While telling me how wonderful that was for me, he said we should celebrate. He pulled my face down to his for a kiss, grabbed my hand and moved it inside the robe he was wearing and onto his cock. "Kneel and suck me off," he murmured.

I barely heard him, though, spinning around and racing upstairs to inform Sandra. Her way of congratulating me was to pull me into the bath, lock lips with me, and grab my cock. We did fuck on occasion, and this was one of those occasions—if only as my reaction to Bram's assumption I was knuckling under to him whenever he wanted me to. Water sloshed around in the tub, as she raised her legs and hooked them on the side of the tub and I pushed my knees under her buttocks and spiked and fucked her.

Overby appeared at the bedroom door and watched me hump her and ejaculate. I then came out of the tub and raced to my room to compose a letter back to the agent. As I wrote, I heard the water sloshing around in the tub overhead again. Capricious Bram and my equally capricious wife were celebrating for me by having a go at each other. I paused for a moment to be frustrated by the uncertainty of the sexual tension in this bird-on-the-wing house—including, I now thought, the domestic staff. Somehow I'd thought the maid was the cook and houseman's daughter. But then again maybe she was. Everything was fickle and topsy-turvy here.

* * * *

My head was spinning—either from what I'd smoked or what I'd drunk or both. I was standing at the deck rail of Clea and Jarrod's house, next door to Bram's, and looking out to the

136

Cook Straits, up into the stars overhead in the clear night air, and north to the glow of Wellington, New Zealand, in the distance, across a bay. The man standing close to me and towering over me was an older French gentleman—although I strongly suspected he was no gentleman—who had told me his name was Georges and that he was a sculptor and that he wanted to fuck and sculpt me. I was standing, facing out at the rail. He was standing beside me, facing me. He had his left arm around my chest, his fingers stroking my side not far under my armpit—my arms were spread, my hands gripping the rail. The fingers of his right hand were stroking my right hip.

For some reason all I was wearing were bikini briefs. I was barefoot. He was in baggy shorts and an open godawful vivid colored Hawaiian shirt. He was hard; I could feel him pressing that to my waist on the left side. Why was I in bikini briefs? There was a party going on around me. Oh, yes, I thought. The striptease on Clea and Jarrod's dining room table when I was three sheets to the wind. I was celebrating my literary independence in style. One published novel could very well be a fluke. Two published novels and a contract offer for three more wasn't.

I'd thought I'd be alone in the bird house this evening. Overby was taking Sandra to a poetry reading at Massey University in Wellington. They were offering her a visiting scholar position for her sabbatical year here and he was introducing her to some of the faculty. I had not been invited. Yes, I was a bit ticked about that—until the letter and advance had come through, and then I was glad I wasn't going. I was jealous enough not to want to spend an evening where Sandra was the focal point when I'd just entered the professional novelist ranks.

They'd been gone three hours and it was getting on to 11:00 in the evening when Bram reappeared—without Sandra.

"I couldn't do it," he said. "I couldn't not be with you to celebrate your novel sale. I know exactly how you must feel."

I doubted he did know how I felt. It wasn't just the acknowledgment of my coming to life as a published novelist but also that he had chosen me over Sandra.

"Sandra?" I said, jubilant no matter how he answered.

"I left her in good hands. Stephanie is Massey's resident poet. How shall we celebrate?"

We could stay home and you could fuck me all night in front of the fire and on the clichéd bearskin rug, I thought. But he was already off on other plans.

"The Nelson's next door are having a party. It was in full swing, I could hear, when I arrived home. I can think of no way better to celebrate your manuscript sale than with other artists. The whole community out here will be there."

I could think of a better way of celebrating, but there was no contradicting Bram Overby.

The Nelsons turned out to be Clea and Jarrod, both fine artists. Jarrod was the same Jarrod who fucked me on the beach earlier that day.

"Ah, you made it to the party after all," Jarrod said in meeting us at the door. "And you brought him, I see. Wonderful."

"Did you bring wine, darling?" Clea bubbled out. "I'm afraid we'll run out of wine, and you have such good taste in wine."

"He brought his young house guest here, Clea," Jarrod said. "That's what he brought to the party for us to enjoy."

"Fine, you go and do your life of the party chores, you sweet little boy," Clea said, hanging onto my arm and leering at me in a way that indicated that she started drinking well before the party started. "Go. Mingle. Bring joy to the world. We'll be intimate later."

That was a sure clue that I was meant to be part of the entertainment tonight.

When we moved into the heart of the party, after giving me a glass of highly spiked punch, pulling a joint away from a passing guest and passing that to me too, Bram swirled off into the crowd. The glass of punch and joint were followed by others, not to mention a few lurid-colored pills, as I was passed from one interested little group to the next who had already heard of my book sale and were quite pleased to be quite pleased with me—and to offer me more to drink and to puff. Some had already heard that I was visiting Bram Overby, that I sometimes fucked women and more often took cock and that Bram Overby

138

had already had both my wife and me several times. That seemed to cut the ice in this artists' colony and to spice up the conversation.

The host, Jarrod Nelson, pulled me aside and into the butler's pantry, where he trapped me backed up to a counter, his arms extended around my sides, the heels of his hands pressed into the edges of the counter. One of his knees came up between my thighs, forcing them apart and nestled up under my balls, the knee pressed into the counter door behind me. I was effectively trapped there. The room was a bit dizzy and his handsome face filled my world. His hair was up in a ponytail.

He pressed his forehead to mine. "I enjoyed you this afternoon."

"It was special for me too," I answered. "That's quite a snake you've got."

"You mean my tattoo?" he asked.

"That too," I responded. We both laughed, a low guttural laugh of lustful remembrance. I raised one of my hands and took his hair out of the band that had it in a ponytail, letting it cascade down to his shoulders.

"Undressing me already?" he asked.

"Getting there," I said. "I like you better with your hair off."

"And my clothes off?"

"Maybe. Yes, probably."

"You know I'm going to fuck you again . . . tonight . . . at the party."

"You're the host. It's your party. You can call the party games," I said. I couldn't believe I was being this forward. But it *had* been a very nice fuck on the beach. And I was a bit more than half way looped.

He came in for a kiss and I opened my lips to him. The kiss deepened and he unbuttoned my shirt, spread it, and palmed my right pec. I sighed and the kiss went even deeper. He lifted me up and sat me on the counter. I heard and felt the zipper of my shorts being lowered.

I broke away from the kiss and his mouth went down to my nipple. His hand was inside my fly, cupping my cock through

139

the material of my bikini briefs. I pushed my package up into his hand.

"Are you going to fuck me right here, on this counter?"

"Nobody would notice," he murmured. "It's that kind of party." His hand was under the waistband of my briefs, on my cock, which was engorging for him.

The voice of the hostess cut through the din of the party in the house beyond the quietude of the butler's pantry save for heavy breathing. "Ice. We need more ice. Jarrod, where did you go? The iceman needeth to cometh."

"But maybe not just now," Jarrod said, taking his hand out of my fly and zipping me up. "But later; definitely later. They can't need ice forever."

I gave it a minute to cool down after he'd left the pantry, hopped down from the counter, and headed in the direction the party noise was coming from. Beyond the pantry, just inside the kitchen, was standing a tall, muscular black man dressed in a flowing white Arab robe. He was flashing a white-toothed smile. He projected a hand, palm up, in which there was a display of colored pills. I took two and popped them. Immediately my vision clicked into something I could only call elongated 3D.

And in that vision was the face of a black man, as he leaned down and kissed me on the lips. His tongue pressed on my lips and I let it in. When he pulled away, he whispered—or I thought he was whispering—"That will cost you, of course."

"Cost me what?" I replied.

"All in good time," he whispered and then was gone. I wandered into the dining room and to the punch bowl. Someone was changing the records on an old six-changer stereo cabinet.

Before I knew it, I was on the dining room table, dancing to "The Stripper" and stripping down to my bikini briefs. Then I was out on the deck being fondled by Georges, the sculptor, and being fed the line by him what a perfect model I'd be for him.

"You ask what I, a Frenchman, already famous for my sculptures in Europe, is doing out here in the South Pacific," Georges was saying.

Had I asked that? I didn't think so.

"Have you read that Maugham book, *Moon and Sixpence* . . ."

"Yes," I said, amused that everyone seemed to want to talk to me about Maugham these days. Maugham wasn't my style of writing at all.

". . . . about Gauguin finding his muse in Tahiti," he continued without taking a breath. "That's me, but there are more comforts of life in New Zealand. And I can be me freely, here. Who cares what my wife in Paris says or complains about with others there. I prefer men. I like to fuck young men."

"Yes," I said.

"I don't think I've ever seen such a perfect body on a young man before. Such slim hips." He was stroking my hip with his right hand.

"Yes," I said.

"My technique is that I must be intimate with every square inch of my model to be able to sculpt him honestly."

"Meaning you want to fuck me," I said.

"Of course I want to fuck you," he said, laughing heartily. "Bram has fucked you; Jarrod has fucked you. Both recommend that everyone fuck you. Everyone here wants to fuck you. Of course I want to fuck you too."

He was large of body, with a beer paunch. I could tell, though, by what he was pressing to my side that he was thick. He was gross and charismatic all at once. The clichéd artist. Only a fringe of gray hair on his head, but it was rampant on his beefy chest and paunch belly. It was the eyes, though. They bored right into you, undressed you, and you laid down for him and opened your legs.

"Yes," I said. "I keep saying that yes, you can fuck me. No more need to attempt seduction."

It was that moment, though, that the hostess, Clea, petite, dark haired and dark eyed, a pixie of a woman, with huge dark eyes, showed up at my elbow.

"You mustn't monopolize our prize guest, Georges," she was cooing. "Come, Aiden, I wish to show you something."

What she wished to show me was her bedroom and her bed and her cunt. She pulled me over on top of her, between her legs, her long skirt hiked up to her waist, at the foot of her bed, and maneuvered the bulb of my cock between her puffy labia.

My bikini briefs were on the floor beside my feet, and there were lipstick marks on my erection.

I was setting a good rhythm and she was writhing under me and babbling in French when Jarrod and Bram entered the room, arm in arm. Jarrod stripped and saddled up behind me. He thrust up into my ass and fucked me while I was fucking Clea. Bram watched for a bit but then he too stripped, saddled up behind Jarrod, and we had a chain going.

Later, in another bedroom and on another bed, Georges lay on his back like a beached whale, puffing on a lavender-colored filtered cigarette, while I swung my leg over his pelvis and positioned my hole on the head of an extraordinarily thick, but not long, cock. He took a puff on his cigarette, dropped it into an ashtray on the nightstand, and stroked my hips with his fingers.

"Such slim hips," he said in a hoarse whisper. "I must remember to memorialize those." And then, "Spike yourself slowly, please. I want to savor the thickness of me opening up that sweet, small hole of yours. I trust that, with such slim hips, you are lusciously tight."

I assumed I would easily be able to control him. That's not the way it went, though. I had taken only about three inches of him, when his eyes flashed, boring into mine. I moaned and then I gasped and cried out as his grip on my hips tightened and he lifted me and then slammed me down on his cock. My passage went into shock, trying to open to him, but not accommodating him fast enough. Shots of mixed pain and ecstasy shot through my body, as he lifted me and then slammed me down again. Lifted and slammed. Each time he was getting a little more of himself inside me; each time I was opening a bit more to him. It wasn't so much a fuck as a ravishment of a rag doll. I flopped around on his cock, my teeth rattling, and my eyes spinning around in my head. It was all for his finish and he took command and no prisoners.

I writhed on him until I collapsed on his mound of flesh, and just moaned and groaned as he took over in thrusting his cock up into me, still going on long after I'd shot my load.

Of course, even in my drunk and drugged state, I realized that Georges wasn't fucking me because he had to know every inch of me to sculpt me. I knew that he was fucking me because he wanted to get his rocks off with a young man—a man, as he said, who had slim hips and therefore, presumably, a tight channel that would delight a thick cock such as he had. And I wasn't so far gone on drink and drugs that I didn't realize that I was riding Georges's cock because he reputedly was a famous French sculptor who wanted me to ride his cock. That I also thought it would make Bram Overby jealous *was* a reflection that I was high on drugs and drink. Overby didn't give a shit who fucked me as long as he did too. The revelation to me, though, as I was royally screwed on Georges's thick cock was that I had no intention of being here in New Zealand long enough for him to sculpt me. Just long enough for him and anyone else Bram pointed to to screw me silly. It was my entrée into this artistic community.

I was in the first bedroom again, but not on the bed—draped over a footstool, belly down, arms dangling over the sides, legs dangling too, knees not quite touching the floor, toes pressed into the carpet. Colors of the rainbow danced before my eyes. I didn't know who it was. I don't remember being introduced to him. I don't remember telling him he could fuck me. I hardly mattered, as I'd taken plenty of cock tonight.

I couldn't see him, as he was mounted on my ass, behind me, his hands pressing down on my shoulder blades. I certainly knew he was inside me, fucking me with his cock. I could see his bent legs. They were ebony. I tried to remember what man at the party was black, but there were more than one of them. I saw the garment puddled on the floor beside the footstool. A white robe-like garment. The black man in the kitchen, the one who had given me the pills. Getting the payment for the pills that he said he'd collect on later. Still unknown beyond that, though. What I did know was that he had a godawful big cock.

Bram was kneeling beside me, his hand run into the hair at the back of my head. "Take it, take it, good, good," he was murmuring. He turned my head toward him and stood. His cock was out. He pressed the head of it to my lips and I opened my mouth, took him inside, and gave him suck. The unidentified man on top of me continued to pump—to pump thick and deep. He was stroking my hips with his thumbs.

143

Later, in another bedroom, on another bed, and even in another house, the bird house, my bedroom, my bed, it was Bram lying on his back on my bed, me straddling his pelvis, and him, gripping my waist and more gently raising and lowering me on his long, thick cock—lifting me up high, almost, but not quite, disconnected, and then bringing me down slowly on the cock to where his curlies merged with mine, smiling as I gasped and whispered, "Yes, yes, yes. Just like that." And then just like that again—long, thick, throbbing, perfectly satiating.

I just wished I could remember how it ended.

* * * *

I woke on the morning of day four in New Zealand to the maid, Christine, pulling the drapes on the window, opening to a new day. She'd brought a mug of steaming coffee and a tray with a little pile of aspirins on it. My head, of course, was splitting and I was beginning to remember only half of what had transpired the previous evening. I hoped it was the hedonist half.

She stood at the foot of the bed, looking at me, with a little smile on her face. She was a saucy little thing. I was naked, on the sheets, not under them. I was in erection.

"Is there anything else I can do for you, sir?" she asked. "Anything at all?"

"Yes, and quickly," I said. "That waste can over there."

She was very quick with it indeed and scurried out of the room as I took care of some of my overdoing it from the previous night.

Bram was in his office, whistling, when I dressed and dragged out of the bedroom. As a writer myself, I knew better than to disturb him while he was composing. I went into the kitchen and discovered, gratefully, that there was still coffee in the pot. I stood at the window, looking out toward the road, and thus managed to view the arrival of Sandra.

An old, classic MG sports car drove into the turning circle. A tall, thin man unfolded from the driver's seat. As the figure stood, though, I realized it wasn't a man at all. It was a woman dressed as a man—seemingly a woman trying to be a man. The Stephanie of Massey University who Bram said would

144

take care of Sandra, I decided. Sandra didn't mind being taken care of by a manly woman, she'd been out all night—because the passenger in the car that the manly woman was helping out of the MG was Sandra.

They walked to the front door hand in hand and kissed there. Sandra went straight to her bedroom, I heard the shower going as I sat at the desk in my bedroom, collecting my thoughts and holding my head in my hands. When I checked later she was in her bed, asleep, and softly snoring.

That afternoon Overby drove Sandra back into Wellington for a meeting on her possible visiting scholar position at Massey University. As soon as they were gone, I packed my bag. I realized that this was as far ahead of Sandra as I was going to get with Bram. He'd bring her back from Wellington, fuck her on the dining room table, I would pout, he'd fuck me on the bearskin rug, and then he'd take her into his bed. The next day he'd do the same. On some days, he turn me over to Clea or Jarrod or Georges or someone else to fuck. They'd fill me with drugs and drink and would all be amazed that, even with slim hips, I could take a big cock. They'd fuck me again just to be amazed again. And if I stayed here, I would let them. I would let them fuck me on their terms, capricious with their commitments.

I had the houseman call for a taxi and went to the airport. I took the first available flight out to the States, booking business class because I was still celebrating my rise to professional novelist.

I returned to New York in two flights, the first was to Los Angeles, the venue of the book I'd just sold. I checked into the 777 Motel at Seal Beach, a motel that had figured in my novel. I decided to celebrate the sale of my novel in my own way.

I called the hunky young Navy sailor, Harry Hobart, who I encountered in researching my book and who, under another name, had been a character in the book. I picked him up at the gate of the Seal Beach Naval Weapons Station in my rental car and took him to the 777 Motel, where, as he had done before during my research and also as the character I'd fashioned from him had done, perhaps a little less graphically, to my protagonist

145

in my novel, he fucked the stuffing out of me for two hours. He was young, virile, horny, long-lasting, and straightforward. He didn't care if my hips were slim or not; he already knew that he could get his big cock in my hole.

It was just before his climax—the hunky young sailor—the second time that I realized that this was the best for me that it would be. He had stopped stroking, but building to the climax and holding off as long as he could, wanting it to be sheer ecstasy, as short as a man's climax is. The cum was burbling up in him and he wanted it to be a big blow. He held me tightly, his lips pressed into the hollow of my neck, both of us holding our breaths, waiting for it, wanting it to be bigger than the first time. I realized this is the state I wanted to be in, a man holding me close, ready to blow, his cock deep inside me, filling me, throbbing.

Then he blasted the bulb of the condom, two, three times—virile and full of cum. He groaned and grunted, and then we both relaxed with a long sigh. He started to rise from me, to withdraw. But I held him close, gripping his buttocks and holding him inside me.

"No, please. Stay in me," I murmured. "Again. Do me again. Stay inside me until you can."

He gave a low laugh, but he did as I had pleaded he do. Exhausted, smiling, and purring, I sent him away in a taxi and slept the sleep of the dead until I had to appear for the flight to New York.

It was dark when I got back to the apartment in Chelsea. The neighbor across the hall had accumulated the mail of the last several days on the foyer table. She would have gathered it together at the end of the week and sent it to us in New Zealand in a prestamped envelope. She didn't have to do that now.

There was a flyer in the mail about another poetry and guitar performance at a local coffee house by Zach Taggert that evening. I'd been thinking of him on the flight from Los Angeles. I had taken out the letter from my agent and, for the first time, focused on the kind of novel the publishing house said it would like for me to write next. It fit with what had already been forming in my mind for months. The story of a hippie poet out of his time, still performing in smoky bars and coffee houses for tip jar contributions. Still making enough to satisfy him and to feed his wish to remain simple and in his chosen era. Satisfied too with what sex came his way. Uncomplicated. Not capricious by any means.

I'm sure that Bram Overby was assuming that my third novel would be about him. But he'd just have to wait for the next one.

When I entered the smoke-filled room after Zach's set had already begun and stood at the back of the room, his eyes focused on me, and he smiled, pausing for a nanosecond in his reciting of his poetry. His guitar playing was smooth—reminding me of Wes Montgomery. His eyes kept coming back to me. He wasn't looking at anyone else in the room like he was looking at me. When he started into his next poem, I realized it had been the one he'd started to formulate and polish the last time he and I had had sex.

I knew that it would be me he would be taking back to his room tonight. I sighed, content with that.

Holding motionless, tense, the seconds before exploding inside me, holding to get as much ecstasy out of the moment of orgasm that he could, I held him close, both of us sucking in our breath. He tensed and we both jerked as he, a man of the pre-AIDS era, was barebacking me again tonight, hit me once, twice, three times with blasts of his warm cum. I was an addict of feeling the cum released inside me. I let out a deep, long moan, lasting through his releases. Letting out a deep sigh, he made to withdraw from me, but I clutched at his buttocks, holding him in close.

"No, please. Stay in me," I murmured. "Again. Do me again. Stay inside me until you can."

With a low laugh Zach complied, and I sighed with contentment.

Cover Boy

"A shot, please, of Russ in front of Troy, with Troy palming Russ's belly." The two models moved into position. Troy was the big, brawny, blond football star-looking one wearing a Navy sailor's tunic. Russ was the smaller one with auburn hair with blond streaks in it who looked like the more sensitive, sultry one—more beautiful of face than handsome. He was bare-chested and muscular, but not to a "cut" extent. Troy's hand on his belly was big, manly, giving the impression of possession.

Click *Click*"Good," the photographer, Felix, tall, gaunt, sharp featured, with a long, black ponytail hanging down his back, said. "The hand lower, Troy, if you please. Suggestive of ownership." Tony dutifully moved the hand palming Russ's belly lower, three fingers disappearing under the waistband of Russ's trousers in front, clearly extending into the top of the smaller man's bush, indicative of intimate privilege.

"Very good," Felix said, "Now, Russ, turn your head up for a kiss, please and thank you. Yes, like that," *Click* *Click* "Now kiss." They did. *Click* *Click*

"Give Troy a look like you would happily open your thighs for him, Russ—because you are going to." Felix laughed. "Good, very good." *Click* *Click*

Felix was moving around them at different angles. The shooting session was to feed a photo site for erotica book cover images. Final rounds of shots—the carry through of the models—would be posted to a different kind of Web site. Felix was in worn jeans, barefooted, and bare-chested. His torso was lean, muscular, but in a tight, gnarly way. He had tattoos haphazardly placed around his body. Both Russ and Troy were clean of any tattooing, with smooth, hard bodies.

"Now the same shots without the tunic. Good." He did another round of shots. "Now something sexier. More embracing and looking lustfully into each other's eyes. Good." *Click* *Click* *Click* "Against the wall, I think. Russ's back to the wall, Troy forcing Russ's arms above his head, coming in for a kiss. Yes, like that. Perfect." *Click* *Click*

"Now, facing Russ to the wall, one of Troy's hands trapping the little guy's wrists above his head. A hint that the other one is doing something else—yes you can feel Russ up, if you want. These are just torso shots, so it's imagination time. You'll be given your chance to make it real. Russ's butt jutted out. A pained but passioned expression on his face. Troy is fucking Russ from behind. All to be imagined. Yes, good. Very, very good." *Click* *Click* *Click*

"Now on the bed, Troy on top, between Russ's legs, and . . . yes, OK, you're stripping Russ's briefs off, Troy. If you must, you must. We'll switch over to the video camera."

Troy, kneeling over Russ, pressing a hand down on Russ's sternum, the latter looking not so happy with where the shoot was going, but, with a nod from Felix, sighing and going with it. The sound of the snap of the condom Felix handed to Troy being put in place and then Troy took Russ's ankles in his hands, wishboned Russ's legs, and came down between the smaller man's thighs.

Whir, whir, whir went the video camera, as Russ arched his back, raised his pelvis, and was penetrated by Troy's cock. For the next fifteen minutes, the video camera did its thing in filming a scene of Troy doing pushups on the smaller young man and Russ exhibiting very interesting expressions on his face for the camera.

"And that's a wrap," Felix called out after Troy had shuddered through his ejaculation and the two models had kissed.

Felix was across the room attending to his camera, taking out the video camera, and adjusting the lighting around the bed, preparing for the next photo shoot job.

"Who knew that doing cover photo work could be so exhausting?" Troy said. The two of them were pulling their clothes back on.

"Yes, who knew?" Russ answered, his voice a little stiff, not warming to the conversation.

"But a lot sexier, don't you think?" Troy asked.

"Yeah, I guess."

"And it brings up a thirst. Shall we stop off at a bar to lift one before we go our separate ways?"

"Thanks, but no," Russ answered. Not a "not tonight"; a "no." "I've got to hit the books tonight." Russ was studying commercial communications at NYU and was about finished with his BA. He wanted to be in front of the camera in broadcasting. He had the looks for it. He'd managed to keep on schedule by selling himself with these cover image shoots—and more so for the videos made at the end of some of the shoots. He was gay, but not as public about it as the cover images implied. He colored his hair and wore different-hued contact lens for anything going beyond a cover-image shot.

He'd graduate before turning twenty-one. Not bad for a guy from a coal mining town in West Virginia. "And, uh" . . . just to pin it down . . . "I don't mix work with pleasure. Sorry, that's just too messy."

"Yeah, OK, but I think you're really sexy. I think we could get it on for real, not just for this camera work."

"Yeah, well . . ." It had been real enough for Russ, although he was trying to pretend it wasn't. Troy had been inside him. Troy had fucked him. It had been for pay and part of a job, though. Russ wanted to keep it that way with the other models. He could pretend it wasn't real then.

From across the room, Felix called out. "Could you stay a few minutes longer, Russ. I want to go over your release form again."

"Yeah sure," Russ called back. He looked back at Troy. "Look, I think you're hot too. It's just not a good idea going with a guy you have to work with."

"I think it would make our cover shots steamier," Troy said. "I just think it would be better for both of us if we didn't have to think about doing it for the camera and creating the best camera angles. But OK. If you don't want to now, you don't want to . . . yet." He picked up his duffle bag and headed for the door.

150

When he was gone, Felix turned and said. "OK, Russ, strip again. Now for some serious filming."

* * * *

"Now jack yourself. Good, like that. You're such a sexy slut, baby." *Whirrr*

Russ was on his back, on the bed, his legs bent and spread. He had a hand wrapped around his cock and was stroking it to the directions being given him. Felix, jeans unbuttoned and flared now, his hips barely keeping the jeans hanging on his legs, his erection pushing out from his curly black-haired bush, was moving around the bed with his video camera, taking it all in.

Felix was licking his lips, his eyes lustily drinking Russ's body in. He was going to fuck this sweet little piece. Soon.

The guys had been paid $300 each for the cover image shoot and another $300 for the sex extension video. Russ was getting $500 for this sex video. He hadn't done this often, but the closer he got to graduation, the more money he needed to get across the finish line. He'd do maybe two more of these and he'd be free. He'd have his BA, he'd get a job in broadcasting far away from here, and he wouldn't do this again. Felix had assured him this was for a very private, exclusive subscription site.

Felix attached the camera to a tripod set on a stand he'd rolled up to and over the bed, positioning it over Russ's thighs. His hands were unsteady, his motions jerky. He could hardly contain his need, his want, to cover this luscious little model, to penetrate him and pin him ass to the bed.

"Arch your back, look dreamy, and play with your nipples, while I eat you out," Felix commanded, "After a minute grab your cock again and stroke it until I brush it away."

Felix came in below Russ, stroked the young man's inner thighs, coaxing his legs to spread more. "Silky. Nice."

"Open your legs for me, baby," he said, and Russ did so.

He placed pillows under the small of Russ's back to lift his pelvis.

"Roll your ass up and show your sweet hole to the camera," Felix commanded, and Russ did so. He moaned as

151

Felix played with the rim with a finger, pushed it in, and then pulled it out. "Such a sweet, tight hole," Felix murmured. The hole tightened right back up. "Pucker it for the camera." Russ did so. Whir went the camera.

Felix struck his head between the young man's thighs and began to tongue his asshole. *Whirrr* The camera was placed directly overhead, set to pan from where Felix was eating Russ out up Russ's heaving torso to the young man's face to catch his expressions. Russ arched his back, moaned, and fingered his nipples. After a minute, he ran one of his hands down his torso, through the auburn hair of his trimmed bush, and onto his cock. He slowly masturbated himself, moaning and groaning in a low hum, while Felix ate him out, sucked his balls, and, eventually, brushed Russ's hand off his cock and covered the shaft with his mouth.

Whirr went the camera.

Felix rose from Russ, took the camera off the rolling stand, rolled it back off the bed, stripped off his jeans, and came back up on the bed between Russ's spread legs. He held the camera in one hand, taking in the shot of him deftly crowning himself with a condom with the other hand. And then the camera whirred, taking in every second of Felix's hard cock entering Russ's hole. Felix pushed in and pulled out. The camera panned up to Russ's face to catch the expression of his reaction to the penetration. "Priceless," Felix muttered. And it was, indeed, a priceless shot.

The whir of the camera caught the in and out of going into the root and then the fuck itself, Russ writhing and bucking against the pumping cock. It caught the verbalized, "Oh, shit. Oh, fuck. Yesss, fuck me good!" Felix's technique was to catch all of the natural sound, including his instructions. His clients' feedback indicated they liked that.

"Come for me, baby," Felix commanded, and Russ did.

"Yes, yes, yes," he cried out as Felix continued pumping. Then he too tensed, jerked, pulled quickly out, ripped the condom off, and squirted cum on Russ's balls and the base of his cock.

"Turn over and spread 'em," Felix said, in a shaky voice.

Russ did as commanded, spreading his butt cheeks and showing his reamed hole.

"Look at how open it is now," Felix said. "Daddy opened baby up real good, yes he did." Russ groaned as Felix showed he could easily push three fingers up in the passage now and the hole would remain gaping open when he pulled the fingers out.

Here came the only false part of the act, but the clients loved it, so Felix did it. He moved the camera to show him jerking on his cock over Russ's firm buttocks, spread cheeks, and open hole, and he squirted egg white on the hole from a syringe, faking another prodigious ejaculation on Russ's tail.

The camera stopped rolling, Felix said, "Good one, baby. You did good," and slapped Russ on the butt. "Go get a shower now and get out of here."

Blushing, not being able to look at the wall of mirrors on one side of the room as he escaped the bed, Russ went off to the attached bathroom, grabbing up his clothes on the way. He couldn't get out of there fast enough.

He walked the ten blocks to Otto's apartment in Manhattan. He felt too dirty to take the subway; he needed to be out in the cleansing fresh air—as well as cleansing as the air could get in downtown New York. Most embarrassing was that, when they got fully into the fuck, he'd been fully into it.

He lived with Otto, a fashion designer, older than Russ by some thirty years. The good part of that was that Otto didn't want it very often. He was a handsome, elegant man and he made Russ laugh, but, primarily, he provided a roof over Russ's head while Russ was finishing his college work. He couldn't have managed in New York without a sugar daddy of some sort. Otto, interested in sex and beautiful young men but rarely able to get it up, was the best of the opportunities Russ had had. The fringe benefit was that Otto had to have his young man well dressed, and he provided the dressing. It helped in the modeling Russ did on the side, with a good many of the gigs provided by Otto.

Lately their relationship had been strained. Lately Otto's brief opportunities to get it up had been expended as much elsewhere as with Russ and, as Russ's last year at NYU was

153

drawing to a close, both of them seemed to realize that so was their arrangement. Otto seemed already to be moving in that direction.

This impression was borne out to Russ when he entered the foyer of Otto's apartment and heard the sounds of sex from the living room. He went to the entrance to the living room and stood there for a moment, watching.

They were on the sofa, the back of which was toward the entrance into the living room from the foyer. Thus, all Russ saw was from their shoulders up. From their shoulders up was bare for both of them, though. Otto was sitting on the sofa, turned away from the doorway. Trevor, a young dancer on Broadway, not more than nineteen years old, who both Otto and Russ knew, was sitting in Otto's lap, facing him. What Russ could see were the naked soles of the dancer's feet, heels rubbing the top of the sofa back on either side of Otto's shoulders, Trevor's hands locked on the back of Otto's neck, a look of ecstasy, natural or faux, it didn't matter to Russ—on Trevor's face, and the young dancer bouncing up and down. The interlaced fingers of the young man's hands were opening and closing in rhythm to what obviously was the rise and fall of Trevor's passage on Otto's Viagra-aided cock.

Russ turned and quietly left the apartment.

* * * *

"So, is the studying done for the night?"

Troy pulled up the stool next to Russ in the gay bar Russ had gone to after leaving Otto's apartment, not knowing where to go until Otto was finished with Trevor and Russ could pretend not to know what they had been doing. He'd decided he needed a drink. Club 216 in Chelsea had been his first thought.

"No, I can't get to my books?"

"Building on fire?"

"No, my boyfriend is fucking a dancer on the sofa of his apartment and I'd have to walk right by them to get to my bedroom." Russ had drunk enough to be open and honest. Tory wanted him enough to take advantage of that.

"Ouch."

154

"Yes, ouch. We don't have an arrangement that permits us to bring anyone home to fuck under the other's eyes. I think my roommate is giving me notice."

"You need someplace to crash for the night?"

"No, thanks. I'll think of something."

"Come on back to my place. It's nearby."

"I'll be fine."

"Come on back to my place. My performance earlier today doesn't reflect what I can do in private. And we can just do nothing, if that's what you want. Your call. But you need somewhere to crash tonight on short notice."

Troy fucked Russ up against the wall of his living room, just inside the door. He had Russ cheek and chest against the wall, arms raised above his head, trapped there by Troy's hand gripping Russ's wrists. Troy's other hand was palming Russ's belly, pulling the young man's pelvis and legs back, away from the wall. He was thrusting up inside Russ's passage. "Shit this is good," he growled in Russ's ear. "I wanted to do it like this back where the photographer was positioning us for the cover shots."

"God you're big!"

"Yes, I am. But I'll bet you tell that to all the boys."

Troy was bigger than Felix was and definitely bigger than Otto ever had been, but Russ wasn't going to tell Troy about that. Russ was so upset with Otto that Troy didn't really have to pressure him to go into the clinch.

Troy fucked him on his couch, Russ's belly on the arm, Russ facing a large window overlooking the Manhattan skyline, Troy behind Russ, grabbing the young man's wrists and arching Russ's torso back toward him, as he crouched over Russ's buttocks and pounded away inside him.

And Russ rode Troy's cock in Troy's bedroom, again looking out onto a different view of Manhattan from the high-rise window wall behind Troy's headboard. Troy lay on his back on the bed with Russ straddling his pelvis, facing him, and Troy lifting and lowering Russ's passage on his thick, long, hard shaft. When they had both come, Russ just collapsed on top of Troy and they both drifted off into la-la-land.

Russ didn't notice until the morning when he lay in the bed, watching Troy at his bathroom sink through the open

155

bathroom door, shaving himself, that this was a really nice apartment. Troy was standing at the sink, naked, exhibiting why he made money as a model. But he couldn't make enough money as a model to afford a nice one-bedroom apartment like this.

"This is really is a nice apartment," Russ said as Troy came out of the bathroom and stood there, body magnificent, cock in half erection.

"Yes, it is, and you look really sexy lying there on your belly like that, with your sweet ass smiling at me. And sorry, last night you could stay, but the apartment's booked for tonight, so we'll have to think of something else for you."

"Booked? Think of something else?"

"You don't really want to go back to your boyfriend's apartment to live, do you?"

"No, of course not. But it's what is for a couple of more months. I need someplace to stay until I graduate from NYU and pin down a job somewhere else. But you said the apartment is booked for tomorrow night."

"Yes. You're right. I can't afford an apartment like this. The agency provides it for me."

"The agency?"

"The escort agency. They provide a place for me to bring clients. Men. This is my office as well as my home. I have to keep it looking nice. And I can't have my boyfriends staying here."

"Boyfriends?"

"Close enough; working on it, I hope." Troy climbed up on the bed and stretched out on top of Russ. There was no talking for a while—only moaning and groaning and grunting and loud exclamations of the taking, as Troy nudged Russ up on his knees, penetrated him, reached up to grab the young man's wrists and trap them over his head, and started to pump inside him.

Afterward, as they lay there, Troy still inside Russ, languidly moving his pelvis and Russ moving ever so slightly with him, Troy murmured, "You could get an apartment like this. You could earn more than enough to finish out your decree.

I can set you up with an appointment this afternoon. You could be out of your boyfriend's apartment by tonight."

"It's a thought," Russ whispered. "There, like that. Shit, you're hard again. You're huge. Oh, shit, fuck me!"

And Tory did.

* * * *

The big black bull, a Nigerian businessman visiting New York, was between Russ's legs, choking his throat with one beefy hand and slapping his face with the other. Russ's legs were waving in the air, his feet coming down to the Nigerian's hips every once in a while, trying to push the big man off him, but to no avail. The Nigerian was just too strong for him, and Russ was in shock and pain. His stomach hurt from where the john had punched him "to get his attention," the Nigerian had said and then laughed, and his left eye was puffing up and closing from the punch he'd taken to the face.

The Nigerian's shaft was inside him, the biggest Russ had ever taken, and was filling him and pounding away. The unopened condom wrappers were still on the nightstand beside the bed in the high-rise apartment building. The apartment the escort agency had provided Russ was in the same building and on the same floor as Troy's apartment.

"I don't use rubbers," the Nigerian had declared. And he didn't. He was barebacking Russ, stretching him to the limit, stroking hard, punishing the young man's channel walls.

Russ gave up and collapsed, lying there docilely and letting the john have his way with him. He concentrated on getting the next breath. Sensing he'd won, the Nigerian loosened his grip on Russ's throat, and Russ gasped with appreciation. The Nigerian stopped slapping him, but he used the hand to twist Russ's nipples and reach down and squeeze his balls. He jacked Russ's cock hard, painfully, but Russ hardened up and came in the Nigerian's hand. The black bull fucked on, while Russ moaned and groaned and writhed as best he could when his balls were squeezed and nipples twisted.

The Nigerian paused, holding briefly, tensed, withdrew his cock head to Russ's entrance, spouted cum, and then thrust

157

back in, sliding cruelly through the added lubricant of his prodigious semen.

He held there, suspended over Russ, staring down into the young man's face, a hand grasping Russ's throat, the other hand now roaming all over the young man's body, feeling, prodding, testing the firmness of him with controlled jabs of a closed fist.

Russ lay there, panting and moaning, mentally assessing the damage.

"Don't you even think of moving," the Nigerian hissed.

It hadn't been the thought uppermost in Russ's mind. Survival had been. Checking the damage had been next. A thought to the huge cock inside him, a thick slug even when flaccid.

But it wasn't fully flaccid and it was getting less so. "Oh, shit; oh, fuck," Russ whimpered as the giant black bull began to move inside him again. The long slide out, the longer slide in. Quickening in intensity until the bed was bouncing and groaning and the Nigerian was pounding away at him again.

He lay there, on his back, panting and still whimpering, as the Nigerian, out of the shower, moved around the room, dressing again in his impeccable pinstripe suit. Every once in a while he'd make a feint toward the bed, Russ would cower and moan, and the Nigerian would laugh and a big, white-toothed grin would float across his ebony face.

When the Nigerian was gone, closing the door to the apartment after himself, Russ rolled over in the bed, groaning deeply, to the nightstand. He called Troy, who was over in a few minutes and was dressing Russ's wounds as best he can.

"We'll get you to an ER," he said. "I'll call the escort agency and they'll take care of everything."

"No. They'll just toss me out of the apartment and I have another month until I graduate," Russ said. "Don't call them."

Troy called them. "This happens, Russ. Just don't tell them you plan on leaving soon anyway. They'll pay for everything and give you time off to heal."

"And then send me another Nigerian businessman."

"Probably. But, with luck you'll be gone then."

"Terrific."

Russ lay back on the bed.

"You're hard, though," Troy said. "What the Nigerian did turned you on, didn't it?"

"Yes," Russ admitted in a quiet voice.

"Someone should take care of that hard of yours," Troy said. Then he leaned his face over Russ's pelvis, took Russ's cock in his mouth, and took care of his need, while fingering Russ's hole, which had been reamed big enough that Troy could have gotten his fist in there.

* * * *

Russ's first week as a weatherman at a small TV station in Pomona, California, in the southern section of Los Angeles, had gone very well. The feedback from the station managers and the public had been good. He hadn't taken the highest-paying job he'd been offered, but he'd taken the one that was the farthest away from New York City.

As the station always did after the 11:00 news wrap-up on Friday night, they had drinks and crunchies in the break room, discussing how the week had gone. The second-ranking anchorman for the station, Hal Olson, pulled on Russ's sleeve.

"I have something to show you out at the anchor desk," he said.

Russ had been leery of Hal Olson. The man was in his forties, and, as was natural with a TV anchorman, was very facetious about his appearance. He wanted to look in his thirties, and he wanted to be California tanned. Russ thought that the man must spend all of his time away from the station either sunning himself or exercising in a gym. He was smooth, much too smooth, and Russ knew what was behind the looks the man gave him. Still he was solidly built and a looker, even if some of that had been from cosmetic surgery. And he was oh so sure of himself.

On the way out to the television studio, Hal put a hand on Russ's arm and said, "You had a great first week, Russ. I thought you might want to go out after this for a drink with me to celebrate."

159

"It's after midnight, Hal," Russ said.

"You're new to Los Angeles, kid," he said. "Midnight here is noon almost anywhere else. So, how about a drink?"

"Sorry, I don't think so, Hal. I try to make a point of not socializing with those I work with. It complicates things."

"I can see why you would avoid complications," the anchorman said, as they reached his desk and his computer, which was on. "Thought you'd want to see that," Hal said, pointing to the screen, where Felix was fucking Russ in a pretty-good quality video.

"Hal. Turn it off, please."

"Yeah, as soon as you say you'll go for that drink with me."

There was no drink. It was the Motel 6 in nearby—but not too nearby—Rowland Heights.

"A Motel 6?" Russ asked when they arrived. He didn't use the word "tacky," but it was there in the atmosphere and both of them knew it.

"I'm married. You think I'm going to take you home? This motel's beds don't creak when they are exercised. I've checked that out, and I always consider that when I take a man to a motel to fuck the stuffing out of him."

There wasn't much Russ could say about that. It wasn't hyperbole, though, Hal did fuck the stuffing out of him in that Motel 6 and the bed was up to the exercise.

Russ knelt on his knees on the bed, his cheek and chest pressed into the mattress, Hal crouched over him, holding Russ's wrists in his fists, and Hal, mounted on Russ's ass, fucking Russ with a perfectly adequate cock.

Once it had been done once, Russ was "what the hell" with it. He hadn't been fucked in weeks, and he missed it. Hal lay on his back on the bed, smoking a cigarette and drinking Russ's beautiful nude body in with his eyes. Fascinated by the micro bikini pattern contrast between what of Hal's body was tan and what wasn't, Russ traced the tan line with his fingers. Hall liked that. It kept him in erection. And the contrast between light and dark on his body emphasized how nice his erect cock was. After sucking on Hal's cock for several minutes, Hal had had enough of the play and rolled over on top of Russ, slapped the smaller man's thighs open, spiked him, and rode Russ's ass to heaven. He fucked him and fucked him and fucked him, until Russ's tongue was lolling out of his mouth and his eyeballs were swimming in cum.

He was good, very, very good, Russ thought, lying back on the bed, arms and legs stretched out in total submission after Hal had fucked him for the third time.

"You are good, very, very good," Hal whispered. "I've followed your career and you live up to your promise."

"My career?"

"Yes. I'm betting you lying there thinking you can stop this any time you want—that I have more to lose than you do."

Russ didn't contradict him, which was an admission that he was right.

"I don't. My wife doesn't give a shit what I do as long as I bring in money and don't bring the clap home. And the station managers know me—and they want to keep me. I have great ratings, which is all that they—and anyone else in Los Angeles—care about. I picked you out to hire, and they hired you."

"You picked me out?"

"Yes, as soon as your application arrived—along with a gazillion of other ones, I recognized you. I recognized you from the cover photos you did. You're a gay male e-book cover boy star. Then I found the private subscription sex vids. I wanted you and I wanted you to work here where I'd have access to you. But there's more than that, kid."

"What?" Russ asked.

"I recruit for a high-class escort service downtown. You perform. I think they'd love to have you in their stable."

"No can do," Russ said, rolling out of bed and gathering up his close. They'd driven there separately, so he could see his own way home. "It's been good—no, great—Hal, but I'm on my way out of all of that."

"OK for now," Hal said with an indulgent smile. "But it's big bucks. And you're already there. Think about it. You'll keep coming to me when I want you, though, that's for sure."

Russ suspended pulling on his cowboy boots. "Yes, I will," he said. "Because of you, not because of your offer or anything you're holding over my head."

"Appreciate it," Hal said. "See you on the set Monday night." There was a weekend crew at the station. Neither of them worked the weekend. "But, then, I could see you tomorrow night—not to fuck you, but there's a party. While you're thinking about it, you could get a taste of it."

"A party put on by the escort service."

"Yes. It's a big Hollywood thing. Men who like men out here don't hide it as much as they do on the East Coast. They're always looking for fresh meat. The escort service provides young men. You don't have to do anything but drink their drinks, eat their canapés, and look beautiful."

"Sorry, I'm busy washing my hair tomorrow night."

Hal laughed. "I've always wanted to be able to use that line too. Did I mention that they pay $500 just for you to stand around and drink their drinks, eat their canapés, and look beautiful?"

* * * *

The party was at a big house on the ocean in Malibu. The house was owned by a recent break-through heartthrob actor in his late twenties, Jeffry Howard. It didn't matter that he was known to be gay. That hadn't curbed his box office appeal at all. He was starting in action thriller movies at the rate of two a year. He did all of his own stunts. He was in such good shape that he could do so.

"Jeffry, I'd like you to meet the new weatherman at our station, Russ Gordon," Hal Olson said when he ushered Russ down the initial reception line before the party went into full swing. Only men attended the party. It wasn't long before the party got racy.

"Ah, yes, Hal has been telling me about you," Jeffry said, taking Russ's hand in his and not letting it go.

"He has?"

"Yes, I've seen your tapes."

"You watch the weather of the Pomona TV station?" Russ asked.

"Not those tapes."

162

The party was still in full swing when Jeffry guided Russ up to his bedroom and fucked him. The actor was very athletic and put Russ through his paces in a challenging way that Russ barely managed but that impressed Jeffry enough that he kept him.

He had Russ rocking on his belly on the edge of the foot of the bed, his legs streaming behind him, toes buried in the carpet, and Jeffry standing between his thighs, arching Russ's torso back toward him by bowing the young man's arms back, while Russ' channel rocked on Jeffry's long and thick cock. This was after Jeffry had strutted around the room holding Russ's reversed body on the front of him, with Russ sucking Jeffry's cock, Russ's legs stuck straight out from his body and Jeffry eating out Russ's asshole. More strutting around involved Russ plastered to the front of Jeffry, his knees hooked on the actor's hips and his arms encircling the actor's neck, while Jeffry bounced Russ's channel up and down on his cock.

Later, Jeffry said, "I don't want you just to let me do you. I want you to commit to me. Fuck yourself on it. But surprise me. Be inventive." Russ had him sit at the foot of the bed, legs spread, as Russ bent over between his legs, grabbed his ankles, backed onto the cock, took it deep, and rocked on it, while Jeffry held his waist. "Enough. Good enough," Jeffry pulled Russ into him, positioned the young man's legs over his thighs, embraced Russ's torso in his arms, and cupped his balls with one hand and stroked Russ's cock with the other as they rocked to a mutual ejaculation.

"You are all I've been waiting for," Jeffry whispered in Russ's ear.

"And you me. I didn't even realize I was seeking you until you found me."

Jeffry fucked Russ all night and Russ took it all. They came down for breakfast, surveyed the damage and the undulating bodies still here and there on the floors and couches and tables and went right back upstairs and fucked again while waiting for breakfast to be served to them in bed.

By the end of the week, the tabloids had photos of Jeffry Howard attending events with a beautiful young man, Russ Gordon, on his arm. Russ closed down his apartment and had all of his stuff delivered to the Howard house on Malibu beach. It was a long run to Pomona, but Russ insisted on keeping his job—at least for now.

Three weeks later, on a Friday night, Hal called Russ over to his desk. "I received an advance copy of this scandal sheet that goes on the newsstands tomorrow," he said. "I think you should see it."

Russ was a cover boy again. Two photos with him in it were on the cover of the magazine—he and Jeffry in tuxes attending a charity concert in Pasadena and he and Troy from one of the gay male e-book covers. The racier photos and a lurid version of Russ's past ran in a long article inside the covers.

"Jeffry knows about my past," he said.

"Not about all of it," Hal said. "And having a gay boyfriend is different from everyone knowing you have a boyfriend who was a hooker and who did porn films."

"Did you do this?" Russ asked. "You haven't fucked me since I moved in with Jeffry. Did you want to break us up?"

"No, kid. I'm the one who put you together—I thought it was the right fit for both of you. Call him and see what he thinks."

He wouldn't come to the phone. The butler said that "Mister Gordon" could find his possessions out by the garage when he wanted to come pick them up.

"What now?" Russ said.

"You can stay at the Motel 6 until you can find a new apartment," Hal said.

"Very funny," Russ said. "I suppose you're going to stay with me there."

He did at least that night, taking Russ to the Motel 6 and fucking him and fucking him and fucking him. Russ had to admit that it took his mind off Jeffry and his rejection. It also told Russ that it wouldn't have worked out with Jeffry anyway. The actor knew Russ had done porn—he couldn't be surprised to know that Russ had turned tricks too. It wasn't that he didn't want to fuck a hooker and porn actor; he just didn't want the public to know he did. He seemed to think there was a line there somewhere when someone came out.

After Hal had fucked him all night and had showered and was dressing—the two of them agreeing they'd arrive at the station separately, he turned and looked at Russ, lying on his back on the bed, legs spread, and fondling his cock.

"Don't do that. I've got to go to work, not jump your bones again," Hal said. "You asked 'What now?' This opportunity is still open. I have the escort service's card here—the one only I can give out to prospective escorts. Call them. They've already told me they want you."

"After the scandal sheet and Jeffry dropping me—"

"They want you even more now. This is tinsel town. You're more of a marketable celebrity now than when you were going with Jeffry. Think about it." He picked Russ's wallet off the dresser and tucked the card inside.

Later that day, a telephone call came in to Russ. He was packing up a box of his things from the office. The station was letting him go. He couldn't say he didn't understand why they would do so. Hal was sympathetic but reminded him of the escort service card in his wallet.

"Russ this is Felix. Remember me? I've relocated to Los Angeles and am putting together a stable of men for book cover images and vids. I've seen the article on you and figure you might be shopping for a new job."

Felix. Of course.

"It was you, wasn't it?" Russ said. "You're the one who provided the stuff for that article."

"You were my best boy," Felix said.

Russ hung up on him. He stood there, a "what now?" look on his face. And then he pulled his wallet out and extracted the escort service card.

Sometimes you go a great distance only to get back to where you started, he thought, as he punched in the numbers on his cell phone. He had started as a cover boy and had ended this phase of his life—and the chances of a straight career—as a cover boy—in this case being covered.

165

Hunting Dr. Weiss

The middle-aged man in the suit was crowding me at the bar at Harvey's in New York's Chelsea district and talking dirty to me. I was smiling and nodding, but my eyes kept drifting over to the table, where a guy a bit younger and far better looking and built was giving me the eye. If he'd just been a bit more definite in his signaling I'd have broken away from the suit and gone over to his table. It was the middle of the day, so traffic was light at Harvey's. If I was going to eat that night, though, I was going to have to attract some paying action. I wasn't really a pro at this, but there were a couple of days a month I was so stretched for cash that I had to turn a trick or two. This was one of those times. I needed to turn the freelance writing into something more steady if I was going to hang on for much longer in New York. I wasn't anxious to have to go back to New Orleans, where prospects weren't much better.

I looked down at the ten and five spots the suit was laying out on the bar. This—$15—and the beer was what he was offering for a blow job. I gave him another once over. He wasn't so bad—pushing fifty maybe and could stand to lose a couple of pounds, but his face wasn't too bad and his suit was clean and cut well. And he looked like he'd be easy to control.

"It will have to be here, in back," I said. "I'm not going anywhere with you for fifteen. And it will be quick."

"Sounds good to me," the suit said. I put my hand on the two bills, and the suit put a hand on top of mine. His nails looked like they'd been manicured. Maybe I was underestimating what it was worth to him. But a deal was a deal. I looked over to Craig, behind the bar, who I knew had one eye on us. He looked around the bar—you never knew when a vice cop would be sitting and watching, but the guy at the table didn't look like a vice cop to me, or to Craig either, apparently. He gave a slight nod and inclined his head toward a beaded curtain-covered doorway to the corridor of rooms behind the barroom. I knew that back corridor well, as Craig knew what I needed when I came in here in an afternoon—never at night, as the clientele at night tended to be rough and the pros staked out their territory here at night.

Craig and I had an understanding. Once a month I showed up here at closing and drank a complimentary beer while he closed up. Then he took me into a room in the back and doggie fucked me. Once a month. For that he looked the other way and aided and abetted me—and gave me protection—when I had to come in here a couple of times late in the month to turn a trick or two to make it through the month.

This wasn't a bar where blacks usually came—either bottom or top seeking—and thus I was a novelty here and probably attracted more favorable attention than the white rent-boys coming in here later in the day. But then I wasn't full black, more what they called coffee and cream—with as many French, Dutch, and native South American features as West African.

I pushed away from the bar—and out of the loose embrace the suit had me in, his hand on the arm around my back having dropped from my waist to my butt when I'd accepted the bills on the bar top. "Follow me through that door," I said, "the one with the beaded curtain."

The suit looked at Craig, who nodded at him.

As I moved toward the doorway, I looked over to the younger guy at the table. He was giving me a steady look, which I hoped meant "later." If there was a later with him, maybe I wouldn't have to come in here tomorrow. Maybe I'd make enough to see me to the receipt of the promised check from the *Plenitude* magazine. And if there was a later with the guy at the table, I wouldn't mind it being more than a blow job.

The suit positioned me crouching on my knees, back to the wall, in the dimly lit corridor beyond the beaded curtain. This wasn't my favorite position, as it gave the john more control over movement. I found it was the more experienced and demanding men who established this position rather than their back to the wall and me free to move in any direction I wanted or needed to anytime during the encounter. I had misjudged how easy this was going to be.

He established maximum control from the start, putting a hand against my bicep on either side, pressing me to the wall, while I unzipped him and took his half-hard cock out. He wasn't particularly large, but he wasn't small either. I did a double take, though, to find that he had a PA ring in his cut cock head. He was far from being a novice.

I cupped his balls and ran my tongue up and down the sides of his cock as it engorged and he whispered, "Yes, yes, take it. Good, good," in a breathy voice. "Swallow it. Deep-throat it," he growled.

I did, and everything was just fine for a while. I set up a rhythm of swallowing and then pulling back and sucking on the head, letting the PA ring click against my teeth so that we both could hear and appreciate the sound of it. But when he took his hands off my biceps and moved them to grab my head, I knew he was going to take this downtown—and he did.

We had about ten minutes of him face fucking me hard, him pulling my head into him as he thrust inside me, penetrating me deep and making me gag before he released. He only released when there was a danger of him coming; he wanted to get more than his money's worth. When he came, he creamed my face, let loose of my head, and let me just sort of collapse down at the base of the wall, as he zipped up, turned, and pushed back through the beaded curtain.

I remained there for a few minutes, breathing heavily, licking his cum from around my mouth, and moaning slightly. In some ways that had been enjoyable, in others not so much. I liked giving up all control, but I didn't like the back of my throat bruised quite that much. I counted my lucky stars that he hadn't been hung, but that wasn't a fifteen-dollar blow job. That was worth no less than twenty.

I went to the men's room and cleaned up my face and straightened my clothes. He'd pulled my T-shirt over my head as I went down on my knees. I'd unzipped my shorts myself—and I'd beat myself off while he face fucked me, coming before he did. I had a little cleanup work to do on the front of my shorts.

When I felt presentable, I reentered the barroom through the beaded curtain. There was no evidence of the suit. He'd gotten what he wanted and had left. The man was still sitting at the table, however, his eyes going to me as soon as I pushed through the curtain. I'll admit that my eyes had gone directly to his table too, hoping he'd still be there, and he was.

There were two beers on the table in front of him. I walked back to the bar, but before I got there, Craig gestured toward the room and said, "Guy at the table over there is buying you a beer if you'll go sit with him."

Bingo.

* * * *

"Jacques. You pronounce it just like J-A-C-K, but it's spelled J-A-C-Q-U-E-S." I didn't see why I shouldn't be open with him about my name—or anything else he wanted. He had a nice smile, and from what I could see of him, he had a good body. A great body if you took into account that he was probably in his mid-thirties. Although he was seated, I could tell that he'd be tall when he stood—big hands. He was starting to go bald, his forehead being quite high in the middle. But his honesty in not hiding that was fine with me. His face was good—his features rugged, but masculine. And, as I'd already noted, he had a nice smile—not predatory. Best of all, though, I had found that there was a fifty-dollar bill laying next to my beer glass when I sat down. That was worth me being open with him.

"I'm Phil. Jacques. That sounds French, but you don't—"

"It is. My family is from Martinique, which was Dutch and French. And I'm here by way of New Orleans—a couple of generations back."

"I could tell that you had some sort of accent. It sounds nice. Sexy."

"And you could tell that I'm black, but not completely so. My people came to Martinique as slaves from Senegal, but, once there, they mixed with the Dutch and French. So, I'm quite a mix."

169

"Quite a mix, indeed. The best of all the parts. You're a beautiful young man, Jacques. I'm from Iowa. I guess if you shared so can I. Scandinavian before that, I guess. What brings you to New York from New Orleans, Jacques? I like saying that name. I'd think you would be perfect in a New Orleans setting. Not that you aren't perfect right here too."

"Thanks. I'm a writer. Or trying to be. It's hard freelancing here in New York. I don't know how much longer I can hang on here."

"Fiction or nonfiction?"

"Newspaper and magazine features when I can."

"Financial problems? That's why you're doing what you are here, in this bar? Why you went in the back with that man?"

"Yes." He'd brought me back to earth and I was a bit irritated. "What is it you want, Phil? What do you want me to do for this fifty dollars laying here by my beer glass? Or did it just find its way on the table on its own?"

"You are quite direct, aren't you?"

"I don't have the time or privilege of being otherwise. There's dinner to be paid for."

"I'll take you to dinner. I'm interested in your writing. I edit for the *Gay City News*. No, really I do." I must have given him a disbelieving look. "We're always looking for writing talent. I'd like to see some of your work."

"Well, that's a new come-on line. You'll pay me fifty dollars to look at samples of my work?" There was a fifty-fifty chance he was shitting me about working for a newspaper just to get in my pants. If so, he was trying too hard. What I liked about him and that fifty-dollar bill was all he needed to fuck me.

"No, I'll pay you fifty dollars to lie on your back and take my cock—twice, if I like the first time. Is that direct enough for you? And if I like your writing, I might give you a job. If you're a good submissive, I might do both—give you a job—and fuck you regularly. Deal?"

"Yes. Take me to dinner and then I'll take you to my place, such as it is; show you samples of my writing; and let you fuck me."

* * * *

"We have until midnight," I said, as we reached the fourth landing of the old brownstone apartment house above a 29th Street Chinese restaurant. We were headed to the sixth floor. There was no elevator. "I have a roommate, but he's a dancer and in the chorus of *Hamilton*. There's a performance this evening and he won't be home until at least midnight."

Midnight was time enough for whatever we were going to do. I didn't usually bring men home, but my apartment was close to where we had dinner and Phil Ames—he'd told me his full name over dinner and I'd told him mine, Jacques Rostoland—didn't offer to take me to his place. So, he probably was married, I surmised. He told me he lived over in Brooklyn, close to the *Gay City News* office on Metrotech North and not close to where we were. He said he couldn't wait as long as it would take for us to get there. That sounded like a nice excuse, at least. Plus, if he was on the up and up about being a newspaper editor and wanted to see a sample of my work, that would have to be at my place, where my laptop was.

He looked around, which didn't take long, when we entered the studio apartment. It was essentially one room, with a bath, a kitchenette on one wall, and one window overlooking an alley and the brick wall of the building next door.

"There's only one bed. You said you had a roommate."

"Yes, one bed, and I have a roommate," I answered. "Do you have a problem with that?"

"No," he answered and then gave a little laugh to cover the question he wasn't asking. "You have samples of your writing to show me?"

"You want to do that first?" I asked, a bit incredulously. I already had pulled my T-shirt over my head and he'd given me a big smile. "OK," I said when he seemed not able to stop looking to answer me. "The laptop is on the table over there." I pointed to the small table with the two straight chairs pulled in under it. Other than that and the bed, we had a leather sofa and an easy chair. The large-screen TV was on the wall over the kitchenette appliances, the countertop refrigerator, stove, and the piece de resistance that justified the outrageous rent, a washer-dryer combination. "It's just sleeping. I have a work in

171

progress on it, but it's far enough along to give you an idea of my writing. I did go to college in journalism—Southern University."

"You went to college?" he asked, sounding a bit incredulous, as he sat down at the table, his attention away from me, and woke the laptop up.

"Yes, did I sound like I was a dummy?"

"No, you sound quite educated—with a kicky Louisiana accent. But you look like you are nineteen—at least I hoped you were. I was afraid to ask."

"I'm twenty-two," I said.

"Great genes then," he answered, but his voice sounded a little distant. He was engrossed in reading my article draft I was freelancing for the *Gay & Lesbian Literary Review*. He left me fidgeting there for several minutes while he read.

"Yes. Very good. You can write." He did some keying work on the computer and then said, "I'm serious when I say I edit for the *Gay City News*. Here's our masthead. You can see my name. I'm also serious in maybe you working for us. What do you think—?" But then he stopped as he'd turned and looked at me. I'd stripped down and was standing there, naked. "Holy shit, you're beautiful. And sexy as hell," he said.

He forgot all about the laptop then and rose from the chair, stripping off his shirt as he did so, was close to me in two strides, went down on his knees, and took my cock in his mouth. His hands went to cupping my buttocks, which was a good thing, because he was so good at sucking me off that my knees turned to rubber and all that was holding me up was his grip on my buttocks and my hands gripping his head.

When I warned him that I would come if he didn't let up, he let up and pulled his mouth off my dick. Then he stood as I went down on my knees; unbuckled and unzipped him; pulled his trousers and briefs down to his ankles, with him stepping out of them; and serviced his cock with my mouth. He was what you'd call a reddish blond on top, which got redder as the pattern of swirling tufts of hair covered his pecs and then descended in a line to his bush, which was a flaming red. His cock was long, at least seven inches, but not appreciably thick.

He was a considerate blow job subject, holding my head in his hands, crouching a bit to reduce his height to my convenience where I knelt, and moaning and whispering encouragement to me, letting me know what he liked and what he liked better, warning me when he might not be able to stem his coming and letting me back off and suck his balls until he signaled that I could swallow him again. I deep-throated him, but he let me control that completely, allowing me to pull off before I gagged on him.

He was attentive to me in the first fuck too. We were on the sofa, lengthwise, my back reclining against pillows jammed into the arm of the sofa, my ankles on his shoulders, as, on his knees on the sofa cushion, he worked his way inside me, his eyes capturing mine, speaking to me dirty in low tones, taking his time penetrating me to where his red pubic curlies mingled with my black ones.

Then, patiently, he held, fully sheathed inside me, more than seven throbbing inches of him, not seeming thick when I'd eyeballed his equipment, but feeling very thick inside me—and impossibly long, possessing me deep. We kissed deeply, and then he pulled his face away from mine, encircling my neck with his arms, holding me there in thrall, his cock throbbing deep inside me, as I built up the need for him. I writhed under him as much as his close embrace permitted, and, eventually begged him for the fuck. Then, with a low laugh, he started to pump me, with me primed to move my pelvis with him. He pumped me increasingly harder and faster, and I cried out in passion and went with him, my hand on my cock, stroking away to the same rhythm he was pumping me. With a cry I shot up his belly, and soon thereafter he stiffened, gave a low cry of his own, and filled the bulb of his condom.

"You're very good," he murmured afterward, still inside me, both of us concentrating on him going flaccid, but buried deep enough not to lose purchase. He was being considerate, bearing the weight of his solid six something frame on top of my slim five-foot-eight on his knees and with his forearms resting on the arm of the sofa on either side of my chest, inside my own arms, which I had encircling his chest.

173

"You're better," I answered before he locked his lips on mine and we went into a deep kiss session, during which I felt his cock engorge again.

"You said there would be a second if you approved of the first," I whispered as we came out of the kiss. "It feels like—"

"Yes, I want to fuck you again. Do you want it?"

"Yes,"

"Not just because I am offering you a job?"

"No, because your cock is magic and you make me explode."

He laughed, pulled out of me long enough to retrieve another condom from the pocket of his trousers and crown himself. I saw him pause and lift his eyebrows when he tossed the used condom in the wastebasket next to the bed and saw others there. But what did he expect? Neither Greg nor I were good at housekeeping. He returned quickly, turned me over so that my belly was over the sofa arm and my head and arms were hanging toward the floor, mounted me, and fucked the shit out of me. No long hold inside me to experience my buildup of need. He had his own need. He fucked me hard, fast, and deep, inclined like a board on top of me, the balls of his feet pressed into the sofa cushion, his hands gripping my waist, and fucking the hell out of me—making me explode.

"You want a beer?" I asked when we were done and he was back at the table, reading a finished article of mine on the laptop. We were both still naked.

"Do we have time?"

I looked at the clock on the nightstand, which showed that it nearly was 9:00 p.m. "We have time for that and more," I said.

He laughed, but he continued reading on the laptop. "This is good, really good," he said.

"Thanks." I didn't know what else to say, but then I did say, "You know I don't offer a beer to a john after he's fucked me unless I liked it."

"I'm glad you liked it," he said, but he continued reading for a while. I walked around the room, not being able to settle. I couldn't stand being right there while someone was reading my work. It wasn't like they were off somewhere else reading what already had been through editing, published, and paid for.

After several minutes, he turned and looked at me, and said, "You are so beautiful, and such a sweet lay. You want me to fuck you again? I want to fuck you again, but I wouldn't pay for it. I've offered you a job. That should be enough for me to have privileges."

I looked at the clock. 9:20 p.m. "Yeah, I want you to fuck me again. But shouldn't you be getting home? Don't you have a wife who's expecting you home?"

"She knows I work all hours at the newspaper. It's what newspapermen do; she's used to it."

No beating around the bush and pretending he wasn't married. For some reason that made it better for me.

"We could use the chair this time," Phil continued. "No mussing of the bed. Your roommate wouldn't even know I'd been here."

"I don't give a fuck whether my roommate knows it or not." If he didn't care about his wife, why should I care about Greg? We weren't married or anything.

He fucked me on the bed, more slowly and more sensually this time. I was stretched out on my belly and he was stretched out on top of me. He was fisting my wrists, holding my arms over my head, my fists wrapped around brass slats in the headboard. My legs were spread wide, held there by his. Both of us had our knees dug into the mattress, giving us leverage to move our hips. Our only moving parts were our pelvises, his rising and falling as he mined my ass deep, and me going with the rhythm he was setting. He had his mouth buried in the hollow of my throat and was whispering dirty words to me as he fucked me and fucked me and fucked me.

After we both had come, we relaxed and dozed, him still stretched out on top of me, our lips plastered together, and him still inside me, his hips slightly moving so that I could feel the full length of his penetration.

He didn't leave until 11:30. "The address is there on the screen," he said. "9:00 Monday morning. I'll leave it to personnel to tell you about the salary and benefits, but I'm sure it's better than you are managing now. You want the job, though, I have

175

free access to your ass. And you keep clean for me. No barebacking. I now own your ass."

"You can give out jobs just like that?" I asked.

"Yes. I do the hiring of the writers," he said. And then he was gone, and I had a job at last.

He probably passed Greg, who was home early, on the stairs. The actor was in an exuberant mood, the *Hamilton* performance having gone well. He fucked me for an hour, not even seeming to notice that the bed was already messed up or that there were three condoms in the wastebasket that weren't his brand.

* * * *

"What the hell sort of name is Rostoland?"

"No one I asked could tell me for sure, other than it's either French or Dutch," I answered. I'd let him think that I was Jack rather than Jacques. I didn't think he'd care that there was a difference. He seemed the dominating type, which I, in fact, found attractive—especially because he was massive, all muscle, and he was black, black, black.

We were at DeStefano's Steakhouse in Brooklyn. Phil had said there was someone he wanted me to meet, and Phil was still calling the shots between us—not so much during off hours as he spread his interests around a lot, but certainly while on the clock with *Gay City News*, where he'd come through in getting me a writing job that more than took care of my needs. I'd thanked him by doing a job that everyone above him thought was professional enough for me to merit the position without also letting him fuck me. He still did that well, when he did it. It's just that life got in the way for both of us and we cooled down the hot and heavy within a couple of weeks. That had been almost three months ago, after the first time his wife breezed through the newsroom, picking him up for lunch, and I found that I liked her.

"Funny name for a black guy—although you aren't that black. Black enough to be my kind of meat—dark meat, good enough for me to shoot one up your tailpipe."

Was that why Phil wanted me to meet this Andre Jackson, I wondered. He'd been introduced as a photojournalist for *People* magazine. Phil had said it almost in reverential tones. The man was a real bruiser. Not much more than thirty and in bodybuilder shape. Not someone you'd want to mess with, certainly not in an alley. But he dressed expensively—casual, but it was all expensive. The sweater shirt had to be cashmere. That it was white and pulled tight over his muscled chest enough that I could see the form of the bar piercings in his nipples and get a hint of a left arm and pec busy tattoo pattern, that just added mystery and danger to him.

The nipple piercings hinted at gay; the crack about sending something up my tailpipe more than hinted at it—and a top. It had made me go hard. He'd be a forceful and cruel dominator, I was sure.

Was Phil selling me to him for some sort of return favor? For Phil to get an article in *People* magazine? Did I care? I wondered if he was a black bull—hung like a bull. He certainly met the specifications in external looks.

And then, yep, he had his hand on my thigh under the table top. The finger spread was massive, the grip strong. I laid my hand on his thigh. No pressure in the grip, though, signaling I was a submissive—and, more important, willing.

"The island of Martinique," I explained. "My family came from there to New Orleans. Both the French and Dutch were prominent there—they messed around with their slaves sent over from Africa. I probably got the name the same way you got Jackson. Some white man laid your great-great-great slave grandmother. In my case, a Rostoland was the governor of Martinique when the slaves were all freed. Some family probably picked up the name in gratitude."

"Well, you're light skinned enough to almost pass—probably more than one plantation owner fucking his female slaves in your background."

"Sorry," I said, "that I can't be as pure black as you."

"No, no, on you it looks good." His hand went higher on my thigh.

"Ditto on you," I answered and did him one better. I was sure now that Phil was giving me to this guy for sex, and I

177

couldn't wait to find something out. I cupped his crotch. As I hoped, he was hung like a horse—and hard. He smiled and did the same with me.

Phil could hardly avoid knowing we were feeling each other up under the table. "Andre wanted to meet you, Jacques, because I'd mentioned to him that you were a good writer and he needs a writer to go on a *People* magazine assignment with him."

"A foreign assignment?" I asked, turning my attention to Phil, who was sitting across the table from Andre and me. "Where? What sort of assignment. I'm not wild about going into war zones. Not really into bravery or bullets."

"But you have a passport?"

"Yes. Still have family in the Caribbean."

"What are you into?" Andre asked. "Into what you are feeling up now?"

"I could be."

"Ever hear of Gunther Weiss?" Phil asked.

"The male Mother Theresa? The guy with all of the awards? The guy who gave up a cushy medical position in Europe to go to Africa to save the people?"

"Yes, the same. Ever hear of Tambacounda?"

"No, can't say that I have," I answered. "Was it on the menu here?" I'd taken my hand away from Andre's crotch, but he hadn't followed suit. I widened my stance and scooted my butt to the edge of the banquette bench seat, and he was doing a serious fondle of my package. I was hard for him, and if he went on with this another ten minutes or so, he'd rub one out of me.

"That's where Dr. Weiss's clinic is. It's in a very remote area of Senegal, on the West Coast of Africa. I think you told me your ancestors were from there—from where Senegal is now. I thought you might like to see where they came from. It pays six thousand for two months plus all expenses. The two of you, Andre and you. It's a 'hunting Dr. Weiss' piece for *People*. Something like the search for Dr. Livingstone or coverage of Albert Schweitzer when he went off to Africa to dedicate himself to caring for the natives. You wouldn't be losing your job with the paper; you can come back to us at the end of the assignment, and you can get credit for filing any side articles you write while you're gone."

"Just the two of us? Is it just because I'm a writer whose ancestors came from Senegal that you've gotten Andre interested in me?"

"Not at all," Andre said, with a grin. "It's because I have this medical problem. I'm oversexed and have to fuck someone daily. Phil here told me that you not only were a good writer and have ties with Senegal but also that you were a great lay. If I choose you to go with me, I'll fuck you every day."

"If you choose me?" I said. "So, it's not a done deal?"

"No, not without a sample. My hotel's nearby—the Brooklyn on Clark Street."

"I can show you a sample of my writing right here," I said. "I have my laptop with me."

"That's not the kind of sampling I want to do," Andre said.

"And if I don't want to go to Africa on this hunt for Dr. Weiss?" I asked.

"I'm still taking you to my hotel and fucking the stuffing out of you. Are you going to object to that?"

"No, not at all."

He had to be nine inches, thick and long. His muscles had muscles. There wasn't an ounce of fat on him. Phil sat in a chair across the room and watched the black bull with the jet-black monster cock lay me out and cock me for an hour and a half.

Andre sat on the side of the bed, feet on the floor, with me skewered on his cock, sitting in his lap, facing him, and pulled me on and off his. And he stood from the bed, with me draped on the front of him, and walked around the room, bouncing me up and down on his cock. And he fucked me on the dresser in the room, first with me supporting my torso with my fists gripping the front edge of the dresser and my back to the mirror, with my pelvis jutting out over the carpet, my ankles on his shoulders and Andre pulling me on and off the cock. And then with me doing the splits along the surface of the long dresser, facing into the mirror, my hands pressed on the dresser top in front of me to give me stability, while he stood behind me and fucked up into my passage.

Then, after a pause, he and Phil tag teamed me on the bed, me on my back, legs spread, and the two taking turns at me, crouched over me in a missionary fuck, while, exhausted, I lay there, docile, collapsed, panting, and moaning softly.

"So," Andre asked, the three of us stretched out on the bed along each other's bodies, me sandwiched in the middle, "Do you want to go to Africa with me?"

"Yes," I answered in a tired voice.

* * * *

Over the first two weeks of our assignment, Andre and I went both forward and backward in time. We didn't fly directly to Senegal. Andre wanted to establish the background on Dr. Weiss, so we went to where he was born, near Vienna, in Austria, and worked our way to London, where he initially worked, providing free clinics in slums, and then through Geneva, where he worked in UN programs, and Stockholm, where he had received international awards, and then, and only then, down to Africa, first to Tangier, and ultimately to Senegal, working our way from Dr. Weiss's birth to the present.

Andre didn't include me much in the research. Much of the reason I was along bore out why he said I mostly was along. Andre, indeed, wanted to fuck someone at least once a day. I was the sure once-a-day lay, but he also went out and cruised wherever we were, finding a rich pickup environment in the area of London where Weiss's clinic had been located and an even richer environment in Tangier, which proved to have quite an enclave of a gay community. Even I was picked up at an outdoor café by a hard-bodied, rich Arab and fucked in a backroom set up like a harem at the back of his shop in the bazaar.

Andre shared with me only a certain amount of the information he was building on Weiss. There was a file on his working life, which I could peruse at will and use to write the section on his professional background, but there was another building file in the laptop on Weiss's personal life that Andre wasn't showing me and had put behind a password.

We were moving forward in time in researching the doctor's background but backward in civilization from the doctor's privileged childhood and medical schooling in Austria, to the rougher and more primitive slums of London to where we finally tracked Weiss down—in the remote Tambacounda region in the arid east of Senegal.

Tambacounda was a small city of some 80,000 people as well as an eastern region of Senegal, but Tambacounda proved just to be a stopping place, where we changed from rail to sturdy Land Rovers for the trip into the even more rugged and remote region to the south of Tambacounda to a small village, Koukari, where Weiss had his free clinic. Such was his renown and the quality of his services that he drew patients from throughout the Tambacounda region.

I was to learn the lengths that the people of the region would go to receive his services.

The clinic compound was a small village in its own right. He had an international staff of half a dozen doctors who were at the clinic for periods of varying lengths, working for free or on grants, for the privilege of being able to put service with him on their CVs. There also was a larger staff of Senegalese nurses, orderlies, and administrators in permanent residence, all of whom had to be housed. And then, in addition to the medical wards and dining and social halls, there was temporary housing for patients and their families who had come from all over the region for health care for one of their family members. All of this was supported by charitable contributions gathered via the Internet, corporate sponsorship, and humanitarian aid. Dr. Weiss's fame was establish such that that the gravy train of contributions was thick and rich.

Publicity was the lifeline of the operation, and, although we weren't received for a formal interview immediately by the man himself, we were welcomed and given accommodation in a hut of our own. I should say I wasn't received by Dr. Weiss immediately. I did see him soon after we had been driven into the compound, and it became obvious that Andre Jackson and Gunther Weiss already knew each other. The doctor came out onto the front porch of his medical building as we were unloading our baggage from the Land Rover, and Andre went

181

up to the porch to talk to him, but I had been told to wait behind, near the Land Rover.

The two of them spoke at length and Andre gestured toward me. I could see that the doctor, a tall, gaunt, ruggedly built man with bushy gray hair and a ramrod straight back, looked at me with piercing grayish eyes, but I wasn't called forth for introductions.

That didn't bother me. My attention was taken with the bustle of activity around the compound and was accosted by, and lingered on, the figure of a chocolate-black man, in doctor's white, leaning languidly against a porch pillar, smoking a cigarette, and looking at me with a smile I well knew. One of interest and desire. I openly returned the look, because he was a beautiful man, a mixed-race man, like me, who had benefited from the beautiful genes of each race.

As we stood there, one of the local staff members came to the bottom of the porch stairs with a Senegalese family in tow. The patriarch of the family was being carried on a litter by other family members, Andre drew aside while Dr. Weiss briefly talked with the staff member and the older woman who appeared to be the sick man's wife. As they talked, they all turned to look at a young black man, no older than I was, who, looking down shyly, stepped away from the litter and turned full circle slowly. He was slim and perfectly proportioned, his only distinguishing feature being a strawberry birthmark under one of his eyes that was more interesting than off putting. He was only dressed in shorts and dirty sneakers. After a few moments of discussion, Dr. Weiss waved them away, and the local staff member escorted the family toward the patient housing sector of the compound. Weiss and Andre resumed their own short discussion.

My attention went back to the gorgeous man in white medical scrubs who was intently staring at me and smiling, and I was only pulled away from him by Andre's return, with an administrative officer who took us to our assigned hut. When he had left and we'd both washed as best we could from the sink in the room—the showers were communal showers in their own buildings, one for men and one for women, centrally located in the staff area—we settled down to rest. The senior staff support

182

buildings were separate from those used by the local staff, which, in turn, were separate from those used in the patient area. Our hut was in the senior staff area.

"It was a long ride and we've arrived during the midday sun retreat time. We might as well nap too before we start our work," Andre said.

Andre's idea of "nap" began with a fuck, meeting his daily need. We lay there on my cot, me on my back, him, crouched over me, above me, cupping my head in his hands, his cock some nine inches inside my channel and churning, as, moving my pelvis with him in the increasingly vigorous rhythm he was establishing, I closed my eyes and dreamed of the succession of men who had been inside me—or who I wanted to be inside me. The man I'd just seen, leaning against the porch post, smoking, and smiling meaningfully at me kept coming up in my visions.

Who was he? A doctor, it seemed. Where was he from? What was the mix of him? Was he as sensual as he was sexy?

I found some of that out when I left Andre snoozing on my cot and decided to take advantage of the compound being down during the height of the sun to go and take a shower. Not everyone was down. The patients' housing quarter was astir with families milling about. As I passed along the edge of the quadrangle on my way to the men's showers, which were walled off but open to the sky, I noticed something strange—several of the young men I saw had welts on their backs and chests. They didn't look like old wounds either. Some sort of coming-of-age ritual in this region, I wondered. All of the men were young and well formed.

I was still mulling this when I got to the showers, but I stopped mulling that as soon as I stepped, naked, into the communal shower. I wasn't alone. The mixed-race black doctor—or at least I had surmised he was a doctor—I'd seen earlier in the day leaning against a porch pillar and smoking a cigarette was in the shower as well. He was naked, and his body was magnificent—finely muscled, chocolate brown, perfectly proportioned—everything milk chocolate except that he had a jet-black cock and ball sac. He was nicely hung.

183

He was flaccid when I entered the shower, but as he turned and saw me there—and smiled—I discerned him getting harder. I couldn't very well just turn and leave. And I didn't want to turn and leave. So, I stayed. I stood under a shower spigot, and, when I was wetted down, I soaped up. Across the shower, the man did the same. It was like he was mimicking me—or that I was mimicking him. I don't know which. Our eyes were locked on each other, so I couldn't say who was taking the lead. All I can say is that I stayed there, soaping up and rinsing off, repeatedly, in consort with him. And I hardened up—also in consort to him.

There were two shower heads separating us. He was the first one to make a move, moving one showerhead closer to me. Smiling at me, welcoming me to move over as well—which I did.

I don't know who was the first one to touch the other, but before I was aware of how we progressed into it, he was soaping me up and I was soaping him up. Then he was fondling my cock and balls, and I his. He was pressing down on my shoulders and I was going to my knees, taking his cock in my throat, and worshipping it with my mouth. He was hard as a rock when he raised me with hands under my arm pits, turned me, gestured for me to bend over and grasp my ankles, knelt behind me, and expertly ate out my ass and pulled my cock and balls through my legs and sucked them.

I moaned and gave a little cry when he crouched over my back, mounted my hips, drove his cock up inside me, and fucked me in a primeval, raw, flesh on flesh, taking, holding me in place with strong hands gripping my waist.

He fucked me deep in various off-beat rhythms that had me groaning and moaning and trying to get into the rhythm with his cock, which fully possessed me and managed to kiss and caress every inch of my canal wall, which spasmed at the touch of his bulb and the steel hardness and thickness of his commanding cock. My channel walls shimmered as I'd never felt before and the muscles of my inner surfaces gripped and rippled along the surface of his shaft. My knees went to rubber, but he held me up with the strength of his grasp on my waist.

I came in my stroking hand, the cum washed away by the stream of water from the showerhead we were standing under, and then he came as well in a series of spasms. I felt the warmth of his cum deep inside me.

He put his lips to the hollow of my neck, kissed me, and whispered, "We'll have to arrange to meet tomorrow. There's something you need to know."

And then, as I let loose of his grip on my waist and sank to the concrete flooring of the shower, he was gone.

I hadn't even asked his name. Could I face him again? I had been so wanton—just going with the flow of sensuality.

* * * *

An hour later I *was* facing the man who had fucked me in the shower, and both of us were managing to keep a straight face and act like this was a first meeting. The senior staff had a custom of meeting for drinks and a review of the day for an hour before dinner. In the rainy season, they met in the commodious living room of Dr. Weiss's bungalow. In the dry season, as it now was, they met on folding lawn chairs on his front lawn around an open pit fire. This evening had been given over to Andre taking photos and starting with questions for the *People* magazine article. I was there to take notes.

My shower buddy turned out to be a surgeon, from France, Chase Clauson, who had only been in residence for three weeks. When I looked quizzical about him being French but also being some proportion of black, he volunteered, "Senegal was once a French colony. One of my great grandmothers was married to a French colonialist and went back to Paris with him. The French are egalitarian that way. Even the native-born people in French colonies were fully French citizens and welcomed in France proper. This is the first time I've set foot in Senegal, though."

Clauson was a beautiful man and, as I'd already found out, a real stud, but the man who was the most commanding presence here was Dr. Gunther Weiss himself. There was no doubt that he saw himself as totally in charge and that no one here challenged him for that position.

185

He had the aspect of the Grim Reaper. He was old, for starters, but there was no question of him being in control, vigorous, and sharp witted and tongued. He dominated the conversation. And he didn't permit me to fade into the background, either. He cast his piercing gaze on me as much as on anyone else, and I felt the need to give him both a concise and fully responsive answer to every question he posed to me.

"You are a bit young to be a magazine writer," he said at one point in a tone that seemed to question my right to exist—and, most important, to be here intruding on his work, but did so without sounding unreasonable.

Andre came to my defense. "Jacques is quite a talented young man," he said, "and he isn't as young as he looks. He's twenty-two. I think you'll be pleased with what he can do."

"I certainly hope so," Weiss answered.

I don't think I took that exchange as it was meant at the time.

Only young men were serving our drinks and the "sweet and savories" that went with them during this cocktail hour. They all were Senegalese and all were beautiful young men, clothed only in shorts. To my surprise, though, most of them had the welts on their chests and backs that I had noted earlier. It made me wonder again if such mutilation was part of a coming-of-age ritual in the local tribes. One young man wasn't wounded in this way, though, and after looking closely, I thought I recognized him.

I turned to Andre, who was sitting on my right and said, "Wasn't that young man with the family that arrived the same time we did today?" but it was Clauson, on my left, who answered, getting my attention by lightly touching my forearm with two fingers and sending a shudder of remembrance and want through my body.

"Yes, Amir just arrived today. His father is going to be treated—for free, of course—but other members of the family are asked to serve in some capacity, by Dr. Weiss's choice, while they are here to help compensate for the food and lodging we give them." I could tell that wasn't all that Clauson wanted to say to me, though, and shortly thereafter when Andre and Weiss were conversing, Clauson touched my arm again and spoke in sotto voce. "I do need to talk to you—and more. I have two surgeries after dinner, though, so it will have to be tomorrow. Meet me at the front gate, please, a half hour before the afternoon rest period starts. If anyone asks, I'll be showing you the nearby river. And that's what I'll do, but we also will have a chance to fuck."

With that, he turned his attention fully to the discussion Andre was leading now with his questions about Dr. Weiss's clinic and I went back to fulfilling my responsibility to take notes and to think of angles to approach the *People* article from.

After dinner, Andre said, "You can go back to the hut and enter your notes into the laptop. I have interviewing to do with Dr. Weiss, but I've clearly got the signal that he wants that done in private, just the two of us. I'll discern what he's willing to see in print and I'll give you those notes to use to adjust your notes in the laptop."

"I can do that tomorrow, during the rest period, in the administrative offices," I said before leaving the dining hall. "That way you can nap tomorrow afternoon without interruption."

Happily, Andre bought that. I went back to the hut and luxuriated in being alone for the evening so that I could dream of Chase Clauson's magnificent body and masturbate myself to sleep.

I slept, but I woke in the night. Andre was in the other cot and was snoring loudly, which is what must have awakened me. I wasn't going to go back to sleep until he turned on his side. I didn't want to go over and turn him on his side, because I wasn't in the mood for sex with him, and if he woke, that's what would happen.

I quietly rose from the bed, slipped on my shorts and sneakers, and went out into the compound to walk off the energy that was coursing through my body. The compound was quiet, asleep. There was a light on in Dr. Weiss's house and I heard sounds coming from the house. They sounded like moaning and some sort of snapping sound. I was drawn to it, and I walked to where I could look into the window of the room light was coming from.

I no sooner focused my eyes on the scene in the room when I too let out a moan and withdrew a few steps. But what the doctor was doing mesmerized me, and I was riveted to the spot for several minutes.

Dr. Weiss was naked and in upcurved erection. He was holding a multithonged whip in one hand. A small, naked, brown body was spread-eagled on a double bed, wrists and ankles restrained at the four corners of the bed. The young man was lying on his belly, but his face was turned to the window, and I recognized the young man by the birthmark under one of his eyes. It was the young Senegalese man who had arrived at the compound with his family at the same time that afternoon that Andre and I had arrived—the same young man who served drinks at the senior staff cocktail hour late the previous afternoon.

I had marked him at the time as the only young Senegalese man servicing who didn't have welt marks on his body. That no longer was the case. He had welt marks on his back and the backs of his thighs now. He was moaning and quietly sobbing.

As I watched, Weiss dropped the whip, climbed up on the bed, positioned himself between the young man's spread legs, fed his cock into the bound man's ass, and started to fuck him.

I pulled away then and stumbled back to my hut. This was more of the doctor's humanitarian operations than I had ever wanted to see.

* * * *

We were lying in an area of beaten-down grass stalks, Chase Clauson on top of me, his legs parting mine, when we paused at the sounds of the motors of vehicles and the sounds of loud voices yelling from the nearby clinic compound. We couldn't see the compound from this spot on the river bank in a field of tall grass, nor could we be seen from the compound. The depression we were in no doubt had been beaten down by wild animals coming to the side of the river to drink.

"What—?" I murmured.

"Shush. Think only of us, here, now. Me inside you," Chase whispered.

He, indeed, was inside me, having taken his time—our time—in foreplay of kissing and fondling and licking and sucking until, with sighs, I opened my legs to him and begged him to fuck me. For many moments after that, all I could think on was that black shaft of resilient steel moving up inside me, causing my channel to spread and shimmer, the muscles of my passage walls to undulate over his cock, drawing it deeper inside me, and my pelvis to move with the rhythm of his penetration. His weight was on his knees between my legs, which were bent, the heels of my feet rubbing on his flexing buttocks, and one of his arms ran under my neck, pillowing my head as he looked down into my eyes. The hand of his other arm was slow stroking my cock and fondling and squeezing my balls, coaxing up my ejaculation.

The sounds of commotion had arrested him when we were both close to climax and we had to retreat a bit to build up toward the sought mutual explosion. Neither of us regretted the need from a second buildup in arousal to reach mutual satisfaction.

Concentrating on the fuck, as he had bid me to do, I managed to push the sounds of commotion from the compound into the back of my mind until after we had both tensed; jerked, almost in synchronization; and shot our wads.

"Now, will you tell me why you weren't disturbed by the sounds from the compound?" I said. "It sounds like a raid of some sort. And will you get off me now? You're heavy."

"It *is* a raid. That's why I coaxed you out here—so you wouldn't be taken up in it. And, no I won't get off you. I plan to fuck you again."

"I don't understand."

"You turn me on. I want to fuck you again."

"No, not that. The raid. Why I needed to be brought out here. Why you aren't in there. Why there's a raid at all."

"I'm covering you close because I don't want you jumping up and going back there to get involved in what's going on. I'm a doctor, yes. But I'm more than that. I'm an investigator for Interpol," Chase said. "Interpol's been hunting Dr. Weiss

189

down for years—looking for evidence that he preys on young black men, not all of whom are ever seen again after he's used them. He's left questions and investigations from Vienna and London, on to Geneva and Tangier, and now to here. I've been here to document his activities enough for the Senegalese government to become alarmed and to move to close him down."

"But what does that have to do with me?"

"Do you have any idea what Dr. Weiss likes to do with beautiful young black men?"

Then I surprised him. "Yes, maybe. I went for a walk last night. I saw him whip and fuck one of the young men who had come in with a patient yesterday."

"Ah, yes, Amir. So you should know then. Families here will do anything to get proper medical care for one of their own—especially the seniors of the family unit. Weiss doesn't require money in exchange, but he requires something else. The young man you saw last night would have been providing the something else. Usually we couldn't touch Weiss for his sexual predatory ways. Most young men agree to it to get medical attention for their loved ones. But there have been times when Weiss has crossed that line and his prey has disappeared."

"I understand that. But, again, why did I have to be taken away? I'm just here to write a magazine article on the doctor and his clinic. If you thought I needed to be absent for the raid, why not my colleague, Andre Jackson, too?"

"I don't think you are making the probable connection between you, Andre Jackson, and Dr. Weiss's predilections."

"I don't see any—"

"Weiss preys on beautiful young black men. Some come to him willingly. Others are brought to him unwitting. You are a beautiful young black man. Dr. Weiss and Andre Jackson aren't strangers to each other. Jackson has brought young men to Weiss before—and all of those men have disappeared afterward. Are you seeing why I've done what I have now? It was for your protection."

"I see," I answered. And then I certainly did see, and I know now why it was evident that Weiss and Andre seemed to have been acquainted already when we arrived the other day.

190

And it explained why Andre was as interested in the sexual side of me as my writing ability when he recruited me in New York.

"I'll help you find your way back to New York," Clauson said. "Although you might like to come to Paris with me for a while before returning home."

"The Clinic."

"I've already arranged with Doctors Without Borders for a nonprofit to take over Weiss's clinic here. It's self-sustaining. It needed his name to get started, but now I think it will have enough backing to continue with the rest of the staff they have here. We can keep all of this quiet. Dr. Weiss can just drop out of sight and none of his sexual proclivities need be associated with the clinic's good work. Weiss was getting to the point where he would have had to retire from it anyway. I think he only was hanging on to maintain his procurement chain."

"Andre. What about—?"

"I didn't bring Jackson out of the compound during the raid because he has much to answer to, as well. I'll leave it to the Senegalese government to sort him out. All I want you to think about now is to concentrate on the fact that I'm hard inside you again."

"You did say you were going to fuck me again," I murmured.

And then he did.

I did make it back to New York six weeks later, right on time for when Andre had estimated the assignment would be finished. I'd gotten the six-thousand-dollar fee up front and neither Andre nor anyone else was in the position to ask for it back—and I figured I'd earned it—so I kept it. I wrote up an article on Dr. Weiss's work in Senegal, leaving out the extracurricular stuff, and sent it off the *People* magazine to do with it as they wished. They published extracts of it in an abbreviated side bar. On top of that, I'd sent several feature stories back to the *Gay City News* on the gay nightlife and lifestyle in Paris that I'd researched from a month of living with and being fucked by Chase Clauson in the City of Lights.

The publishers of the *Gay City News* were quite pleased with my articles and paid well for them. When I returned to New York, Phil was quite contrite for having introduced me to Andre.

I hit him for a raise and he eagerly granted that. He wanted to resume fucking me, but I said I'd moved on to other types of men. What I wanted now was a hung, black Frenchman. I had a standing invitation to visit one of those in Paris—or anywhere else in the world that Chase was working as either a doctor or an Interpol agent.

Rainy Day in Tokyo

There had been rain off and on all day, and it started up again as I was walking from the theater in Tokyo's Ni-chome district of Shinjuku, so I dipped into a small grocery store entered by a foyer in a small apartment building. The deluge, although heavy, hadn't lasted long, and I could use some snacks for the hotel, so I walked the aisles of the store in search of snacks I recognized and liked. I was feeling a bit out of sorts, caused I think by an aura of being isolated. I was so much into everything in New York City, where I was an assistant professor in theater arts at NYU. There were always Off Off Broadway experimental plays to work with and interesting people working in them. Everything in Tokyo was alien and isolating to me.

I'd just spent two hours, at the behest of Professor Gokyo, consulting at the Sudonobu Theater in the center of the Ni-come gay district on an interesting, to say the least, Japanese-language production of Ira Levin's play, *Deathtrap*. My specialty was set design and the producers of this production weren't sure they'd gotten the set right. The production itself was a gay sexual version of the hit Broadway play in which a fading playwright sells an idea for a new play big time but it is actually an idea of a young playwright he is mentoring and the play revolves around the older playwright's need to get rid of his protégé so he can claim ownership of the writing. The two men have a close relationship in the original play; the Japanese theater was doing an interpretation that brought the two men even closer. The protégé blows the older playwright and is fucked by his mentor on stage during the production. It was a clever interpretation to be staged in Tokyo's gay district but a bold move even there. The house would be sold out for every performance.

My problem had been a language barrier in the consultations. There was an interpreter, who wasn't too good, and there was considerable misunderstanding going both ways. I didn't know any Japanese and I'd felt isolated and incapable of my usual fast pace in formulating, sharing, and conveying ideas. It didn't help that the young Japanese men swirling around me were sexy and were giving me the eye. The set I was supposed to be consulting on was still being erected, they were working on the lighting, and the two actors were practicing on the stage. There was entirely too much activity going on, and I constantly felt like I was three steps behind grasping the "discussion" and contributing to it.

It was a feeling that I hadn't expected to have in coming here, and now that I was here, it was unavoidably closing in on me on all sides—language I couldn't understand, signs I couldn't read, and customs that were alien to me despite how understanding and sensitive the Japanese people were about trying to help. I wondered if Professor Gokyo had felt the same way when he was visiting New York, where the people aren't as solicitous of foreign people and sensibilities. But then Shotei Gokyo could speak good English. My basic problem was that I neither spoke nor understood a word of Japanese.

What was most frustrating was that they were trying for a refreshingly bold and uninhibited production and I would normally have been all over helping to create this, given the sanction and financial backing to do so.

But I wasn't in Tokyo to consult on a gay theater. I was part of an international consortium of theater academicians who were attending seminars around the world. Two months previously the seminars had been in New York. Now they were in Tokyo, starting with a reception this evening at the Tokyo University of the Arts in Senju, where Professor Gokyo taught production arts. I had met Gokyo in New York and we'd hit it off well—better than well. We were much the same age—he in his early thirties and me twenty-eight—among an appreciably older crowed. We were, of course, both actively gay, as were most involved in the discipline, and we were attracted to each other. A drink at his hotel had led to me fucking him in his hotel room. He had been an inventive and athletic sex partner and we

194

moved with each other in achieving mutual satiation as if we had been long-time lovers. Our physical and professional attraction to each other had then led to a continuing international correspondence that had been aflame both with the exchange of ideas about the theater and high heat of the orgiastic interactive movement of body parts.

When I'd arrived at my hotel in Tokyo this morning, there had been a note from him. "I have seen that you arrive today," the note said. "I regret I am tied up in preparation meetings for the seminar and could not meet you at the airport or see you before tonight's seminar, but I have taken the presumption of giving you to the Sudonobu Theater early in the afternoon to consult on what I think you will find is an inspired production of Ira Levin's *Deathtrap*. If you aren't too tired or haven't hooked up already, here is the address, in both English and Japanese—the Japanese for the hotel driver—to the theater. They will be expecting you at about 1:00 p.m.—if you are able to attend."

I had smiled at the hint that he was giving me busy work so that I wouldn't hook up with someone else before seeing him this evening.

I stopped in at what I hoped was a small grocery store in my hotel. The labels on the shelved packages were overwhelming to me as I moved down the narrow aisle in the store. I couldn't concentrate on the items and I constantly had my eye to the front window of the shop and the status of the raindrops outside. I traveled extensively in Europe and was used to the euro and dollar ruling everywhere. Japanese money was beyond me—as were Japanese Kanji symbols instead of an alphabet I knew and the exclusively Japanese chatter going on around me. Even the music wafting through the store in half tones was alien to my world. I could only pick out a few items and hope that I had enough money to cover them.

I was staring, blindly, at a shelf of snacks that looked like maybe an octopus was the origin of the chips when I noticed a young man standing at the end of the aisle with a basket of goods in his hand. He was familiar and when he looked at me, he showed a surprise of recognition and smiled, I realize that he had been the one directing the lighting work at the theater. He

195

had smiled at me like that then—a smile of interest that I was quite familiar with—and he smiled at me like that now.

He disappeared around the end of the aisle. In walking up and down the aisle, though, I encountered him twice more, and we nodded to each other and smiled each time. He appeared to be a few years younger than I was, in his early twenties. He was short but muscular—not in an overbuilt way, though. He was berry brown, had long, straight black hair that was bound up in a ponytail, and his eyes were dark and expressive. He wore a tight T-shirt sporting a Japanese sporting hero cartoon on the front; cargo shorts, with multiple pockets for the equipment he'd had to carry with him to work on the lights; and open-toed sandals. Tokyo was in a heat wave this summer, so I was lightly dressed too—a white, billowy, open cotton shirt over a tight red athletic T-shirt, white cotton trousers, and sneakers without socks.

Having gathered a few things that I hoped I was recognizing as something I could eat, I approached the checkout counter with trepidation. He was there, though, and helped me count out the right money for my purchases, which was quite a bit less than I had thought it would be.

He smiled at me, pointed to himself, and said, "Hoshikawa Niho." He then said just "Niho," signaling that that would be enough for me to attempt. He pointed to me.

I responded, "Timothy Lord," with a smile. And mimicking what he'd reduced that to, I added, "Tim." It was obvious that we weren't going to do much conversing with each other.

We both looked out of the store window and viewed the ongoing deluge. He shrugged, put a hand on my forearm to get my attention, pointed toward the ceiling, and gave me a questioning look. Then he pantomimed going up stairs with his fingers. I understood that he was offering me refuge until the rain stopped and that he had access to somewhere above to wait it out.

He was cute and had made me go hard, so I followed him up the stairs—up six flights of stairs to the building's attic.

His room was small. It was dominated by a sheet-covered mattress on a platform. A kitchen counter ran down the wall to the interior and two deeply recessed dormer windows were on the street-side wall. A doorway covered with a beaded curtain led to a small bathroom, with shower. Clothes were hanging on pegs on an opposite wall. They were of more than one size, so Niho didn't live here alone. The room was impeccably clean, though, and there was nothing here that wasn't both functional and esthetic. It would have made a good theater set for a trysting room.

That's what it became.

Motioning to the only chair in the room, a legless Zaisu chair, a classic Japanese design, he went into the bathroom and I squatted, cross-legged, on the chair, blessing all of the yoga classes I'd taken and how diligently I'd endeavored to remain flexible.

When Nihon came out of the bathroom, he was wearing only a fundoshi loincloth, the traditional Japanese one-piece garment to cover a man's privates. He walked over to me and stood in front of me, fingering the knot at the side of the fundoshi and giving me a question look.

I didn't have to know Japanese to know that he was offering himself to me, if I was interested. Of course I was interested. I reached up, untied the knot, let the fundoshi fall to the floor, pulled the young man to me, and opened my mouth to his cock.

He pulled my shirt and T-shirt off my torso as I was sucking him off and then he pulled away from me, went down on his knees, and pulled my sneakers off my feet and my trousers and briefs off my legs. He sat, yoga style, on my thighs, facing me. His legs crossed behind the small of my back and mine crossed behind his back. We kissed as he frotted our cocks together—mine appreciably thicker and longer than his. I sighed as he docked the cocks, bringing the bulbs together in a kiss, and pushing his foreskin over my cut bulb.

I reached around and pulled the band of his ponytail out, causing his straight, black hair to fall down to below his shoulder blades. He was more beautiful than handsome like this, and I cupped his chin, tipped his face up, and took possession of his lips. He opened them to my tongue, which he sucked on as I ran my fingers through his luxuriant hair.

197

For what we were engaging in, language was no barrier. The language of sex was universal.

He had brought a condom and lubrication from the bathroom when he'd come to me, and we sat, facing each other, our legs entwining each other, our foreheads together, both of us looking down, as he rolled the condom on my cock, smoothed it out, and rubbed both my cock and his opening with the lube. This all seemed so Oriental and exotic to me—something that must be a Japanese form of foreplay. I liked it; the almost ritual nature of it aroused me.

We both were panting lightly and groaning and moaning in low tones, as he lifted and rolled his buttocks up. He placed his hole against the bulb of my cock and slowly moved his hips forward, ever so slowly impaling himself on me, making me shudder with every millimeter of me that disappeared inside him. We embraced and kissed as we rocked against each other and he fucked himself on my cock.

Later, after I had come and he arched his back, his shoulder blades going to the matting of the floor, and I, still inside him, watched him masturbate himself to an ejaculation, we positioned ourselves in one of the deeply recessed window wells. There were no curtains on the window. I crouched down, my back pressed against one side of the well, my legs spread and my feet flat on the floor, the palms of my hands pressed into the opposite side of the well, while Niho, shoulder blades leveraged against that wall, and fists pressed into the hollow of my shoulders and feet leveraging on the wall beside my back, fucked himself on my cock.

My face was turned to the window, watching the raindrops hitting the glass and rolling down it. All was silence except for the sounds of our sex, which was universal. No Japanese chattering or half-toned music. Just the gentle sound of slow, sensual sex. I felt like I was in a foreign art film, where every move we made was deeply symbolic and a bit melancholic.

Niho, naked, was at the kitchen wall, making tea, when Utagama Roko, obviously his roommate and just as obviously the actor playing the playwright's protégé in the Levin play I'd consulted on at the Sudonobu Theater, arrived. I was sitting, naked, on the platform bed.

198

Nothing was said; nothing needed to be said. He'd come home in the rain—oblivious to it raining. My mind told me that he had come straight home, regardless of the weather, to be with Niho. His soaked clothes were plastered to his body. It was as if he weren't wearing any, and his body was beautiful. He, like Niho, was small of stature, but perfectly formed.

He immediately discerned, without trying to communicate in our disparate languages, that Niho and I had been fucking and intended to continue to fuck. He shucked his wet clothes, taking them to the bathroom, and returned naked. He brought another condom with him, approached me, and leaned down into me for our lips to meet as his hand worked my cock to hard again. He crowned me with the condom and sat in my lap, on my cock. Niho returned to the platform bed and snuggled in behind me, covering my pecs with the palms of my hands and working my nipples with his fingers. I turned my face back to Niho, and we kissed. I gripped Roko's thin waist between my hands, and, as he arched back to the floor and placed his palms on the floor board, I penetrated him and pulled the young actor's passage on and off my cock.

Roko didn't let me finish inside his passage. He knelt between my spread legs, pulled the condom off my cock, and while Niho continued running his hands over my torso and flanks, gave me a blow job that told me that the older actor was going to be very happy during every performance of the sexed-up *Deathtrap* to be receiving a blow job from his young man on stage.

Later, as Roko and I were back in the window well, with his back to the wall and the soles of his feet plastered to the well wall behind me, using them for leverage to fuck himself on my cock, I crouched between his legs, clutching his buttocks and pulling him on and off my cock.

I noticed, after I'd come, that it no longer was raining. The light was bright coming in through the window panes, still beaded with water droplets.

I knew it was time to leave. I left the two stretched out against each other on the bed, Niho holding Roko in his arms and Niho's cock slow pumping Roko's ass.

"I hope you didn't mind the consulting stint at the Sudonobu Theater today, Timothy," Professor Gokyo said as he came to me where I was standing by the window at the Tokyo University of the Arts Faculty Club window.

"No, it was quite stimulating," I answered, with a smile. I was reflecting that he seemed to have turned me in that direction to keep me from hooking up with someone before I could with him—and it had led to two quite satisfying hookups. "It was a very satisfying afternoon," I added.

"I thought you might be amused and inspired by the production slant they are taking with *Deathtrap*."

"Yes, that too," I answered. He gave me a quizzical look, but I just smiled a little smile—I would have purred if I could—and didn't elaborate.

"I hope you didn't have too much trouble with the language barrier."

"It didn't prevent me from achieving anything I wanted," I said. Which is true, despite the initial frustration and irritation of the isolating nature of the language barrier. Niho, Rico, and I hadn't been stymied by a language barrier; we'd all managed to get what we wanted—at least I had. I'd achieved an uncountable number of quite satisfactory ejaculations.

"I'm sorry about the rain," he said. "It usually isn't that persistent or dousing in Tokyo in the summer."

"I enjoyed that too," I answered. The image of Niho riding my cock in the window well with the rain beating on the windowpane and that of Roko arriving in the flat soaked to the skin, his clothes transparent and clinging to his sexy body—and, indeed, the whole scenario that had me ducking into the small grocery store and being taken up to Niho's room for an afternoon of very pleasant fucking floated across my mind. No, I didn't mind the rainy day in Tokyo at all.

"Oh, terrors," Gokyo said, looking out of the window we were standing by. "It's raining again, and it looks like it's settled in. You can't be going out into this after the reception. I'll have to drive you."

We both knew he wouldn't be taking me back to the hotel from here, though. "I think you mean that you want me to drive you," I said, giving him a grin.

"I think it's time we left the reception. We've been here long enough for politeness sake." He said this as he reached out for my half-full glass of scotch. It was good scotch, but, after taking a generous slug of it, I handed the glass to him without regret.

An hour later, we were on the platform bed in his traditional-style wood-frame house, with the tiled roof and the shoji screens marking off the room separations. He was as inventive and athletic as he'd been in his hotel room in New York City. I was lying on my back on the bed and he was suspended over me, facing up at the ceiling, in the position of a crab. He was leveraging off his hands, his arms on either side of my shoulders and on his feet, his legs bent and planted on either side of my knees. And he was raising and lowering his buttocks on my cock, as I held his waist in my arms.

I knew we'd be going on like this for a couple of hours, Gokyo employing increasingly inventive and athletic ways to ride my cock. As he fucked himself on me surrounded by the muffled sounds of satisfying and totally immersed sex, I became aware that the sound of the rain beating on the roof tiles was whipping up into a frenzy of a storm—just as eventually our taking and giving would become a frenzied race to a shared orgasm—or two or three. Gokyo and I were a perfect fit, sexually.

As I became increasingly aware of the sound of the rain on the tile roof I also became more attuned to the changing of the pattern in Gokyo's rise and fall on my cock. I realized that he was hearing the rain as music and was melding the fuck to the patterns of this music. When I'd realized this, I started going with him in the effort until we were moving as one perfect fucking machine merging with the rain, becoming one with the elements.

And, no, I didn't mind at all that it had been a rainy day in Tokyo.

201

Unlikely Obsession

I'm not sure what I said while I was in the garage. I was in shock. He certainly didn't say anything or let on about anything. Of course that might be because his boss was standing in the doorway to the office behind me and listening to what was being said.

The mechanic was dressed in loose-fitting coveralls—and maybe just that and the boots, because he didn't have a shirt on underneath them. The armhole slits of the coveralls went midway down his hips and it was clear he wasn't wearing anything underneath. He was tall and sort of gangly here in the garage of the custom car repair shop. He looked sort of like a stork or a ferret in the light of day. He was something over thirty—maybe closer to forty than twenty. Nothing about him was that attractive, and yet he was sexy to me in ways I couldn't explain but I certainly would feel and reacted to.

"It's the oil pan," he was saying. "The rattle is because it came loose from its screws . . ."

I think I blushed when he said "screws." I know I had every reason to. He was drying oil off his hands while he talked with a rag that was oilier than his hands were. The hands were big, the fingers long and slender. They almost made me hyperventilate. But then I knew where those hands had been, what they had done.

". . . but you have another problem. While the pan was loose and hanging . . ." there was a provocative word again ". . . you ran over something that put a dent in it. I've tightened the screws, but you really need to have a new pan put in. Where it's dented is likely to give and then you'll have a mess on your hands. We can replace that, but for a baby like this, we'll have to order it. Say, maybe you bring it back around 4:00 p.m. next

Thursday? Drive it as little as possible between now and then."
Even the world "drive" cut into me like a knife.

The baby he was talking about was a classic 1956
Thunderbird convertible. Vijay had bought it for me for when
we were stateside. Vijay bought me just about everything I
owned—and he didn't stint on cost or style.

"Uh, OK, I think I can do that," I managed to say. He
was giving me a noncommittal look. No smile or knowing sneer
or anything. Maybe he didn't recognize me.

"Come on into the office, and we'll write it up and make
a note of the next appointment," the office manager was saying.

"Uh, sure. Right." I turned to follow the office manager
out of the garage bay and then turned and smiled wanly at the
mechanic and said, "Uh, thanks. That wasn't as serious as I
thought."

"Good," the mechanic said. "It's a sweet ride."

That made me almost hyperventilate yet again, but I
looked sharply at him, and there didn't seem to be any double
entendre in his voice, even though that was the second time he'd
said that to me. Indeed, he didn't really look smart enough to be
engaging in word play.

Still he had me hard. I turned and fled into the office.

When I was finished paying the bill for today's work, the
baby blue Thunderbird was out on the concrete apron in front
of the garage and the mechanic was nowhere to be seen. I drove
off and traveled—gingerly, looking for potholes to avoid—to
the new symphony hall that had been built for Vijay's orchestra
next to the Bronx Zoo. Although I'd been trembling, I managed
to maneuver into the parking garage under the building and
parked in my slot, next to Vijay's, which was empty because I'd
driven him in from New Rochelle that morning. I'd have to
switch cars we used until Thursday.

I put my head down on the steering wheel, closed my
eyes, and conjured up the scene from two Saturday's ago—when
Vijay was here, conducting one of Alan Horanhess's mystical
Armenian symphonies and I was slumming across the river in
Chelsea.

Somewhat frustrated at the aloofness of Vijay and him
being consumed with pulling together the symphony's new

203

season program, I'd searched until I had found a leather bar. I stuck out like a sore thumb there in my preppy button-down shirt, khaki's, and loafers, without socks, on top of my all-American junior accountant looks, which pretty much was what I was for Vijay at the symphony in addition to being his bed partner.

I'm in good shape and enjoy blond good looks and haven't hit thirty yet, so I drew some interest in the smoke- and obscenities-filled air with a slim guy in tight black leather pants and not very much else doing a bump and grind to loud music on a pole on a small platform jutting out from the side of the bar. I guess that's why I went in the bar—to assure myself that I could still draw men's attention and cat calls. There were cat calls aplenty. The pole dancer was getting a few more than I was, but he was working harder for them than I was.

One guy, leaning into the bar stood out in looking at me like he was looking through me, like he had no interest in me at all. Of course that meant I was interested in him. He certainly wasn't a looker. He was thin and tall and rather gawkish, with a face that was all sharp angles and a mop of greasy black hair. Still, I'd say he was muscular, in a tight, sinewy way, in that there were knots of muscles in all the right places and he was hard bodied, without an ounce of fat on him. His veins stood out in a pattern that made me want to follow them with my tongue and that had me going hard for him even though there shouldn't have been anything about him that was appealing.

It was a biker's leather bar. He was in black leather—tight black leather pants, biker boots, nothing on top except for a black leather harness. He had a funny thing around his waist for a belt, and I shuddered when I realized that it was the strands of a black leather hand whip, with the handle dangling down one of his slim hips. He was covered in crude tattoos that looked like he might have burned them in himself when he was drunk, and there were silver bars pierced in his nipples. His chest was covered with a matting of curly black hair, which ran down into the front of his low-rise trousers in a line that radiated in a way that emphasized his tight six pack as it descended.

He was repulsive and compulsive at the same time. Clearly a bad boy. And wasn't that what I'd come to a leather bar to find?

He was smoking a cigarette and hefting a beer bottle, and he was covering the ground of both looking past me in contrast to most of the other men in the room ogling and trying to make me and lasering me with his eyes when I glanced his way.

I saw him push himself off the bar, give me a piercing look, and then slowly back to the rear wall of the room and push through a doorway covered with a wooden beaded curtain. Telepathy told me that he commanded me to follow, and so I did.

He went into a small bathroom off a dimly lit corridor. The bathrooms obviously were for assignations, as there were four of them, two on either side of the hall, all one-holers, all with locks inside the doors, and none with a gender designation on them. They obviously were meant to be private and to be tied up for longer than it took to take a piss.

The leather guy went into one of these and when I followed, he pulled me past him. The door didn't lead directly into the stall with a toilet and sink but there was a short corridor little wider than the doorway you had to go through to get there. We never fully got into the bathroom stall. He propelled me abruptly past him and down toward the broken-vinyl tile floor, and I sank to my knees. He kept me there with one hand, while he locked the door with the other and then unbuttoned what was a square codpiece at his crotch on the black leather pants.

He did that slowly, smirking at me, letting me know I was going to suck his cock. And then, when he was free, showing a god-awful-long nine incher—not particularly thick, but particularly long—he pushed it between my lips and into the back of my throat, and I gagged as I serviced him in what he wanted to be a deep-throat experience.

When he was hard as a rock, he pulled me up to my feet, pushing me against the wall of the narrow corridor into the stall, undid my belt and unzipped me, pushed my trousers and briefs down to my knees, and commanded me to kick them off my legs, which I did. There was no kissing. He stiff armed me on the throat with one forearm while staring menacingly into my

205

eyes, while the other one felt me up. I went hard for him. His hand went up the back of my shirt, which he had unbuttoned before feeling up my chest, and I saw his eyes narrow and his mouth form a leery little smile.

He had felt the welts on my back. He knew why I'd come into a leather bar. He probably knew why I had zeroed in on him. It certainly wasn't his looks. It mostly was that hand whip he was using as a belt.

He pulled my shirt off my back, leaving me naked down to my loafers; turned me facing the wall in the passage; forced my arms over my head, palms on the wall, and to leave them there, which I did. The space was so narrow that he leaned his back on the opposite wall, pressed his knees on my thighs under my buttocks.

Then he pulled his "belt" out and gave me a taste of the whip on my back and arms and buttocks. The space was too confining for him to get much of a backswing and they weren't hard lashes, but enough to sting—enough to make me anticipate something more taxing. Trembling and writhing a bit, I moaned for him.

"Like that, do you?" he growled.

"Yes," I admitted in a small, "can't help it" voice.

It was just a taste. He quickly went for the fuck, in a crouching position, his shoulder blades against one wall, his knees pressed into the opposite wall, and me sitting on his thighs. When I'd raised my arms, I found there was a towel bar high up on the passage wall. I grasped that with my hands, my back was pressed against the opposite wall from his, my legs were spread and bent, passing by his chest on either side, and my feet were pressed into the far wall on either side of his chest. He had a choke hold on my throat with one hand and he was flicking my chest and thighs with the whip with the other, while he fucked me with his long, long cock, going deep, taking long slides. I helped by moving to his rhythm, using the leverage of my feet on the wall behind him.

It didn't last for long. I was keyed up, and the taste of the whip was just right. Still we were at it through two banging attempts to let someone in the bathroom, which we ignored. Our intensity was for each other. I wasn't looking for beauty; I was looking for nasty, and he was giving that to me. Our eyes were locked throughout the fuck.

I stroked my own cock to completion while we were fucking in that taxing position. When he'd come in his condom, he pulled back, let me sink to the floor, buttoned up his codpiece, unlocked the door, and, with the growled comment, "That was a sweet ride," was gone, leaving me panting in a puddle on the floor. Later I kept running over in my mind that "sweet" was not a word I'd employ for the ride that had been. But I couldn't claim that "satisfying" wasn't a good word for it.

He'd left the door open and a pair of guys started to enter the bathroom, probably to use it the same way the leather guy and I had, but, upon seeing me on the floor, panting and moaning, they just grinned and went into one of the other johns.

I didn't think I'd ever see the leather guy again, although both the nine-incher and the whip were exactly what I had been looking for that Saturday night.

And I *didn't* see him again—the mechanic who serviced my Thunderbird—until today at the custom car garage just off Westchester Avenue in the Bronx.

* * * *

When I was able to compose myself, I went up to the concert hall, where Vijay was conducting a practice of Gustav Holst's *The Planets* for a concert the next weekend. Vijay Kohli, considered a musical genius now at forty, had been the conductor of the Ahmedabad Symphony—and, indeed, still was—when he was plucked up and offered the position of the conductor of the New York Symphony. This symphony had once been a competitor for the New York Philharmonic, but was subsumed by that orchestra in the 1920s. Now, a consortium of well-heeled music aficionados who weren't being given traction with the New York Philharmonic had decided that there was enough musical talent and interest in New York City to justify another symphony. The investors had built a new hall in the Bronx and looked for a conductor who would provide symphony music to both compete with and be compatible with the Philharmonic. Vijay Kohli, a mystical Parsee from the

207

Gujariti region of India, who specialized in the mystical music of such composers as Horanhess, Messian, Saint-Saëns, Holst, and Sibelius, fit their bill.

I had studied such music and combined that with entertainment management in graduate school. The symphony backers had hired me, subject to Kohli's approval, to be his management assistant. Kohli had vetted me in symphony management and in his bed and now I lived with him. We spent half the year in New York and half in Ahmedabad. I preferred New York, as Kohli lived like a sovereign prince in Gujarat, which means his fetishes weren't reined in there as much as they were here. I was the only one in his bed here. In Ahmedabad he had a harem of young men in his palace—and I was confined to the boredom of an imprisoning harem. He'd had an established harem and a stable of young men there when he came to New York. If customs permitted here, I wouldn't be surprised if he would have a harem here too—and would indulge more in his sexual interests.

Regardless of where he was, it was clear in our relationship that I was there to serve him solely, but not as his one and only.

I went into the hall and sat about half way up and watched him at work. There was no mistaking that he was Indian. He was dark both of skin and hair and, although not a thin man, he moved with grace, like a dancer. He was an animated conductor, connecting with all of the musicians at the same time. They loved him and the connection he maintained with them with his dark, long-eyelashed eyes. As with me, he was clear with them that it was all about him, and, like me, they gave him all that he demanded of them. The only difference was that they totally worshipped him in the process and I was using him as a means to an end no less than he used me. I enjoyed being fucked by him—and almost as much being used cruelly by him—but I didn't worship him for the privilege of serving under him.

He dressed exotically—what would be called a Nehru suit, with a long-sleeved, form-fitting shirt with a Mandarin collar, but with the front open several buttons down to let his black chest hair cascade out. The suit was of a white silk

material. The trousers were tight across the crotch and wider at the hem. He wore sandals without socks, the tops of his feet, with their long, sensuous toes, were covered in curly black hair. The complete package was pure animalistic sex, and it was impossible to watch him work and not get the impression that he was having sex with the music—and the musicians. The audience couldn't be blamed for feeling they were being stroked as well.

The symphony had been an immediate success in New York, given the combination of the mystic material, the excellent musicians, and the sexy, animated conductor.

I was as mesmerized as all of the rest were—when I was with him. When I wasn't, he scared me a bit. I had not enjoyed what he enjoyed in sex before we met. He had brought me along, but I was afraid of where he'd taken me—and how much further we might go. I'd been with him in Ahmedabad for one season. My management presence wasn't as pronounced there, as I knew how to get things done in New York but it wasn´t the same in Ahmadabad, and Vijay had a staff there that efficiently served his every whim. In Ahmadabad I was more another young man in his harem than his administrative assistant, and in Ahmadabad he took more liberties in sex and release using than he did in New York.

The effect of the harem was that, being only one of several who might be selected, and otherwise being left for extended times with nothing but anticipation of having some attention given me, when he did call me to his bed, I was willing to give him anything. He, in turn, took everything before sending me back to the harem to pine for the next time. The next time usually was long in coming as a night with him left me with welts and evidence of beating that he would want healed before he used me again.

Thus, I had mixed feelings after I drove him back to New Rochelle that evening and saw that he was packing and learned that he was leaving for India earlier than planned but didn't need me to come out there early. He didn't ask me what I thought about it, and I knew that his mind was still in the concert hall, going over that weekend's program. He could go through an entire symphony in his mind, individual instrument note by note, and not miss a dynamic or a nuance.

His possession by the current musical work didn't stop him from taking me hard and totally that night, though. His bedroom was more mystical temple than bed chamber. Vijay was a combination of an ascetic and an aesthetic. His furnishings were sparse, but those he had had to be beautiful and sumptuous. His bedroom was dominated by a wall of cascading waterfall spilling down behind a trench of open-flame, flickering fire, fire and water being agents of ritual purity in his Zoroastrian religion, and by a gigantic four-poster bed with thick, carved posts at the four corners. The strength of the posts was functional, because they supported restraints.

That evening, Vijay "sexed" me up by laying me, naked, on my stomach and kneeling over me, in his white silk robe and loincloth and sucking and tonguing on my hole until I was begging for his cock even though I knew what he needed to prepare himself to fuck me—and that his preparation of himself necessitated bringing out raw pain in me.

When I was fully wanting it, he made me kneel at the foot of the bed, my arms extended and bound to the posts at the foot of the bed and there, in the dark other than the fire in the trench playing on the cascading water and the sound of my moans and groans mixing with the sound of the waterfall and a recording of Orff's *Carmina Burana* permeating the room, he strapped me on the back and legs with a wide strap of leather until he had hardened up enough to saddle up behind me, strip off his loincloth, and fuck me hard, fast, and deep. His cock was unusually long, reaching into the core of me and working me there with his magic. He was training me to the need for a long cock and the sting of the whip.

Usually, he used the strap lightly, but on this night he laid into me as he would have when unfettered and uncontrolled in Ahmedabad, knowing, probably, that it would be some time before he bedded me the next time, leaving me long enough to heal before he was at me again so that I could offer him pure, unblemished skin the next time we copulated. Conversely, he fucked me more totally than he usually did, and, to my shame, I had come to the point of welcoming the harder beatings to get the more satiating sex.

He was thick and long. His upcurved cock reached far into me, and the curve of his shaft had his cockhead caressing me at every point inside me had me panting hard and hyperventilating for him. He was hirsute and dark skinned and strong. He embraced me close from behind as he worked my channel, and the rubbing of his silky and curly chest hair against the welts he'd raised on my back brought me a pain-pleasure that was as sensual as it was unexplainable.

"Yes, yes, yes!" I cried out, not being able to help myself. His fetish had touched me at my most sensitive, sensual point.

I hardened and came for him more profusely than any man I'd had before—except, now that I thought of it, perhaps for the mechanic I'd just unexpectedly run into when I took the Thunderbird in for the problem of the loose oil pan.

Vijay didn't touch me again, allowing me to heal, for the next week as he prepared to leave for Ahmedabad and then did so, with the understanding that I would fly out in two more weeks.

I don't know if it was fortuitous or not that I would be taking the Thunderbird back to the car garage—and to the mechanic—before it was time for me to leave for India.

* * * *

The garage was closed when I arrived at the appointed time to have a new oil pan put on the Thunderbird, but the mechanic was there and he had the part. Again he appeared only to be wearing coveralls. When I pulled up in front of the garage doors, expecting them to open even though I saw no lights inside, the driver's door opened and he was standing there beside the Thunderbird, his hand possessively palming the hood of the car just as confidently as the hand had possessed me in the bathroom of the leather bar.

"Get out of the car and go over there and stay out of the way," he said.

When I was slow getting out of the car, he opened the driver's door, grabbed my forearm and pulled me out of the car.

211

The physicality of him made me go immediately docile and submissive. Vijay had trained me well. It was clear now that the mechanic remembered me from the bar.

"Are you going to—?" I said with a whimper.

"Shut the fuck up and go over there and be quiet until I finish this job," he growled.

I went off to the side, crouched down on my haunches, and watched him work. I was clear that we were alone at the garage. It was pretty clear too, that he was going to manhandle and fuck me when he finished fixing the Thunderbird. It was equally clear that I would let him.

He worked quickly and efficiently. There'd been no place for me to go, for me to find to sit, and that seemed to be his plan—to keep me off center.

When the pan had been put in place, he opened the driver's door again, took the keys out of the ignition, and turned to give me a long look. Then he started walking away. He held his hand out, with my keys dangling from his middle finger. He held me dangling the same possessive way from his cock.

I got it and followed him. He walked back to Westchester Avenue, turned right, walked a couple of blocks, and entered the Pelham Bay Baths. It was a gay hookup club; I'd been there once or twice when I was slumming. I'd gotten gang fucked in there each time. He never looked back to see if I was following him, but of course I was. When I got to the desk where you checked in and showed your membership or paid for a day pass, the attendant said, "No need to pay. You are Adrik's guest."

So, his name was Adrik. I followed him to the locker room, where he banged a locker open and I assumed, rightly apparently, that it was mine. I stopped there. He moved farther down the bench to another locker. We watched either other closely as we stripped down. I went to naked; all Adrik was wearing was the whip he wore around his waist as a belt. I followed him out to a dimly lit, cinder-block walled room that was sectioned off into wire cages. He slipped into one of the cages and to the far side of it, and I followed him in. Three naked young men followed us in. I don't know if that was by prearrangement or not.

I would have gone to him then, but two of the men embraced me in their arms, while the third went to Adrik, who had backed up to the wire cage wall and posed there, his arms raised over his head, the whip in his hand. The young man who went to him knelt in front of him and took Adrik's long, long cock in his mouth. Adrik's arm came down and he played the whip on the young man's back. Adrik's eyes were on me, though.

The two young, muscular men holding onto me prevented me from going to Adrik. One stood in front of me and the other behind. They ran their hands over my body and alternated between taking my lips with theirs. The one behind me lifted my arms and, too late, I found that there was a chain with wrist restraints coming down from the ceiling where I was standing. My wrists were bound. The two men went down on the their knees, the one in front taking my cock in his mouth and the one behind pressing his face with my crack and tonguing my ass.

The young man sucking off Adrik rose; climbed onto the front of the mechanic, like a monkey; and hung there in front of him, his thighs hooked on Adrik's hips, feet hanging on the wire, and his hands grabbing the wire wall of the cage behind Adrik's chest, and he fucked himself on Adrik's nine inches of meat, as Adrik kept his eyes on me and flicked his whip on the young man's buttocks and back.

The men using me stood. The one in back encircled my waist with a beefy arm and raised my body and pulled me back down on his cock. He tilted my hips up, and the one in front of me entered me with his cock as well, and the two fucked me together. I took the double attention of the two thugs silently. Vijay had trained me to the double penetration, and this wasn't too punishing—the two men weren't overly thick. I wanted Adrik to know that I would take it—and that I would take him again when he was ready to use me.

I don't know if Adrik came with the monkey man or not, I suspect not, because it wasn't too long before all three of the men pulled away from us and Adrik came over, flicking his whip, and gave me some attention with it, and when we both were hard as rocks, he released my wrists, guided me into the sauna chamber and settled me on a towel on the top shelf. He crouched over me, spreading my legs and hooking them on his hips, and, entered me slowly and deeply with his nine incher. Panting hard, I begged for all of it. He laughed, buried his cock inside me and rocked against me, working me deep. He fucked me to his completion. The other three men were in the sauna as well, and the two men who had shared me double penetrated the monkey man.

When he had come—I had already shot my load up his belly—he pressed his forehead to mine, and said, simply, "I am Adrik Aspidov. Your car registration says your name is Logan Gaines. We fit well."

"Yes," I answered, simply. All it took to possess me was to know my name and to state the obvious—that we were an unlikely, but perfectly matched, pair. I had been bred to crave long cock and pain and he dispensed both.

He left me and went to the showers. I followed. We stood under separate showerhead. Two men were in the shower, one fucking the other against a wall, but Adrik and I watched each other, not them.

I followed him back to the garage. He was sitting in the driver's seat of the Thunderbird when I got there, the key in the ignition. I climbed into the passenger seat. He drove me around the block and into an alley, driving up to a garage door.

"Get out and open it," he said. I did so, and he drove the Thunderbird into a single garage with tools covering the walls.

"Close the garage door," he said, and I did.

There was a door at the back of the garage, which opened into a stairwell. I followed him up two flights to a one-bedroom apartment that was simply furnished but clean. The bed was a four-poster bristling with restraints in various places. He put me on my belly, naked and spread-eagled, tied off at the four corners.

He whipped me on the back and thighs lightly, enough to show welts but not enough for the effect to last for more than a few days. I cried out, "Yes, yes, yes!" and he laid harder into me, whipping me until he was fully erect. Then he climbed up on the bed, mounted my ass, ran his nine inches up into to the hilt, and fucked the shit out of me.

214

Afterward, he lay stretched out on top of me, running his fingers over the welts he had raised, and kissing me in the hollow of my throat. Putting his mouth to me ear, he wished, "The thing is that we fit."

"Yes," I answered.

"I'm going to use you up," he said, "and you want it so bad you're going to let me do it."

"Yes," I answered, and I knew that I wouldn't be following Vijay Kohli to Ahmedabad.

In the Giant's Shadow

"Yes, I suppose you could add in a work semester, but—
"

"And not lose too much of the time if I continue to take and turn in assignments?"

"Yes, but . . . this is hardly the time to . . . oh shit, oh fuck, do that again."

Mark Carlson, who had stopped rising and falling on his professors' cock in a cowboy ride to ask the questions, moved his hips from side to side and then forward and back, caressing every surface of Sydney's buried cock. The twenty-three-year-old graduate architecture student at the Massachusetts Institute of Technology was having an evening session with the famous modernist architect Sydney Stone in the latter's Boston pied-à-terre on the penthouse floor of the controversial almost-completely glass-walled high-rise building he'd designed. Stone's apartment, where he lived when he was giving lectures at MIT, was totally glass walled, giving the two men fucking on his platform bed the sense they were suspended in space over Boston Harbor.

"Oh, Christ, Mark, I can't deal with these questions now. Take my cock; take it deep. Pull the cum out of me just like that."

Mark did as the fifty-four-year-old famous architect at the peak of his profession bid, concentrating on giving his faculty adviser at MIT a good ride. Good rides for good grades. Stone laid back and surrendered to him, watching the young, perfectly formed, dark-haired, sultry young man palm his chest and rise and fall and revolve on his cock, the young man's eyes slitted, both of them panting and moaning, suspended in time and space over Boston Harbor as Stone's orgasm started and

216

rolled on and on, the young man pulling every droplet of cum out of him.

Very few of Stone's students could make the sap rise in him and drain from him as Mark Carlson could—and Stone had much experience in the comparisons of his male students' sexiness.

Later, when Mark was standing in the shower stall—visible from the rest of the apartment through glass walls—and Stone was standing in the doorway, already showered, clad in a robe that was open in front and pulling on his cock as it protruded from his gray thatch of pubic hair, they resumed the interrupted conversation.

"You want the time away because he's down there, because Jemal Seljik is in Charlotte Amelie, working on a resort design, don't you?" Stone tried not to let his jealousy show. He was at the pinnacle of success as a modern architect. Seljik was rising above that pinnacle and still soaring.

"He has sent for me. I have to go."

"You still have work to do for this semester," Stone said. "I could arrange a work sabbatical for next semester but not this soon." He obviously didn't want Mark to go.

"There's just the paper on Frank Lloyd Wright's Midway Gardens in Chicago to turn in, and I've about finished that and can turn it in before I go. I've started the earth house design project. I can send that to you from the Virgin Islands."

"I can't condone shoddy work just because you want to go panting after being a junior draftsman for Seljik on a hotel project."

"When have you known me to do shoddy work?" Mark asked. "Was that shoddy work just now back on the bed?" He was smiling, but there were times when he had to remind Stone of everything Mark was doing for him to get this graduate degree. He had prostituted himself for this degree. This was one of those times.

"Is this perspective shoddy?" He turned to the far glass wall of the shower stall, palmed the wall and jutted his buttocks back at Stone. The older architect took in a heavy breath. He moved forward, grasped Mark's hips between his hands, put himself in position, thrust his hard cock up into Mark's ass, and

217

"went downtown" with the young man for another round. No one could make him go hard multiple times as Mark could. No one could pull the cum out of him like the beautiful, young, sensual student could.

And, he would never admit it to Mark, but Stone had never had as gifted a student as Mark was. It would kill him to give him up to Jemal Seljik.

For several minutes the two were lost in the resumed fuck. Mark was giving Stone all the right sounds and exclamations to keep an older man engaged and going at it. After he had ejaculated again, Stone pulled back to the doorway into the bathroom, if a glass cage could be called a room, and Mark stood under the shower again.

"If you can get those two projects in, I guess I can let you go." Mark couldn't possibly understand how painful it was for the professor to let him go, Stone was thinking. "But," he added, "You do realize the real reason Seljik has removed himself down to the Caribbean, don't you?"

Mark didn't answer. He was turned away from Stone and soaping himself up again. But Stone knew the young man had heard and understood him. He could see the concerned expression on Mark's face in the reflection of the glass wall.

"You know that he's left his family—that he's taken Philip Brandon down there with him—and not just as his assistant. Seljik has gone down there to escape the scandal. If he wants you down there just to—"

"He just wants me down there to be his draftsman," Mark said, having rinsed off again. "As you yourself say, he has Philip Brandon with him down there." He shut off the water, quickly ran a towel over his body, and brushed by Stone and into the living area. He hadn't looked at Stone as he passed. The invitation had only mentioned the need for a draftsman. But, in fact, Mark was hoping for much more. The presence of Philip Brandon, of course, was a problem.

"You'll finish both projects before you leave?" Stone asked?

"If I stay the night, can I send the earth house design in from the Virgin Islands before the end of the semester?"

"Can I tie you up and we play rape?" Stone asked.

218

"Yes."

"Then I think I can arrange that."

* * * *

As prestigious as MIT was for graduate-level architecture studies, it wasn't as prestigious as the program of the nearby Harvard University was. That Sydney Stone taught classes at MIT and Jemal Seljik taught them at Harvard was probably what stuck in Stone's craw in his sense of competition with Seljik for honors as a modernist architect. For that reason Mark hadn't told Stone that he was working part time in Seljik's Boston offices as a draftsman even while he was studying at MIT. Somehow Stone had heard this, though, and he'd heard about "the incident," even though it was the only time it had happened.

"You are certainly staying late," Seljik had said that snowy night when he was preparing to leave the office and found only Mark out on the drafting floor.

"My father once told me that a dedicated employee never leaves before the boss does," Mark had answered. The architect had turned off most of the lights in the room before discovering that someone was still there. The only light was the one illuminating Mark's work surface. It provided somewhat of a halo around the young man, accentuating his sultry sexiness. Mark knew he had a look that attracted men who sought out men, and he hadn't been shy about using the attraction to his advantage. He already was being fucked by Sydney Stone, with favorable effect on his grades and on the opportunities that were accorded him in the MIT program.

He also was attracted to Seljik. He worshiped the man for his unique architectural talent, his specialty being floating pavilions with a delicate Oriental flare. Beyond that there was the man himself. He was a handsome, muscular Turk, with an aura of authority, drama, sexiness, and danger. Mark's mother was Greek and had tried to instill in him a wariness of and animosity toward Turks, but, in the rebelliousness of his youth, finally encountering a Turk in the form of Seljik just imbued the man with mystery and attraction.

219

Thus, Mark surrendered easily to Seljik's seduction and to being fucked by him on his work table that snowy evening.

With a seductive smile—the first that the man had bestowed on the graduate student who was temporarily working there to cover Christmas leaves of some of the permanent draftsmen and to keep projects on schedule—Seljik had swept the room with an arm. "That work ethic doesn't seem to have caught on with the others here," he said.

"It's Christmas Eve and it's snowing out," Mark said. "And I'm only working here a few more days and want to finish this project. Besides, I don't have to go as far as the others do in this snow. I can walk back."

"To a dormitory?" Seljik asked.

"Yes," Mark said.

"I'm just up the street at the Hilton," Seljik provided. "It's where I stay when I'm in Boston. So, the two of us alone on Christmas Eve in the snow. That doesn't mean all that much to me. I'm a Moslem. But you——?"

"I'm Greek Orthodox or Anglican depending on which side of my family is present," Mark said, with a laugh. "But I don't really practice either," he added.

"Ah, a Greek," the architect said. He was standing close behind where Mark was sitting, facing the blueprint he was working on on his table. Seljik put his hands on Mark's shoulders and leaned over him to look at the blueprint on the table. "Ah, the Parson's building."

"Yes," Mark whispered, the touch of the master on his shoulders and the man's cheek next to his like an electric current running through his body.

"Good job."

"Thanks," Mark murmured. "Mr. Seljik . . ." He had no idea what he intended to say. He knew his voice was shaking. In any event, he didn't have to ask the architect anything.

Seljik took a breath in and whispered, "Your smile is nice. Young and vital. So sexy. I've never conquered a Greek before. I hear that you take cock."

"Yes," Mark responded in a low, thick voice. He had thought being a Greek would be a disadvantage with Seljik, a

Turk, but it seemed that a Turk conquering a Greek was a come-on for the man.

"Will you take mine?"

"Yes."

"So, I do not need to romance you?"

"No. All you need do is tell me what you want, and I will give it to you."

That was all Seljik needed. He leaned over and swept the blueprint off the side of the table and onto the floor. Mark was turned, and set down on the edge of the table, as Seljik unzipped himself, pulled out his cock, and brought Mark's mouth down to take it in. After a few minutes, he laid Mark on his back on the table. Mark was panting hard and looking at Seljik with "I surrender" eyes.

"You will let me fuck you—here, like this?"

"Yes," Mark answered.

The Turk manipulated the young man's body as he wished. Seljik pulled his trousers and briefs off, sat in the chair, and spread Mark's legs with his hands as the man's tongue and mouth went to the student's cock, balls, and hole.

Crouching over Mark and holding the young man's arms to the surface of the table over his head and looking commandingly down into Mark's face with an expression of challenge and dominance that was met with a look of surrender, the man, who was some twenty-five years Mark's senior but a commanding god in his profession, worked a thick, long cock inside the student's channel and fucked him in long, deep, hard, prolonged strokes.

After they both had come, Mark first and then the Turk, they remained in position for several minutes, panting and cooling down.

"I wish to fuck you again, to take my time with you. My hotel room is nearby," Seljik murmured.

"Yes," Mark responded.

The Turk fucked the adoring graduate student into Christmas morning on his hotel room bed.

The two were never alone together in the office through the next week of Mark's temporary employment at Seljik's Boston office and they didn't speak again in that week, nor did

221

Mark meet with the architect when his stay was up. By then he'd learned that Seljik had a family in Chicago and that he was spiking his assistant, Philip Brandon, a saucy blond not more than a year older than Mark but also finished with his masters in architecture. Philip's family lived in Philadelphia, and he'd had Christmas Eve and Day off to see his family. Other than that, one of the draftsmen whispered to Mark, Philip was in Seljik's bed when the master architect wasn't in Chicago.

The next time Mark had any contact at all with Seljik's firm was when he received the invitation to work for a semester on the hotel project in the Virgin Islands—and that invitation had come from Brandon, not Seljik.

But Mark was so smitten with Jemal Seljik that he gave no thought to turning the offer down. He would have pulled out of his MIT course if Sydney Stone had not agreed to the sabbatical. Somehow Stone probably had understood that and accommodated the young man with the hope of not losing him. He was one sweet fuck—and he showed more promise as an architect than any student Stone had had—or had fucked—before.

* * * *

Philip Brandon met Mark when his Virgin Airways flight landed at St. Thomas' Cyril E. King airport. There was no reason why Mark would expect Jemal Seljik himself to meet the flight, but he was disappointed that hadn't happened. He was even more disappointed on the drive in a Land Rover down to Magens Bay, where the resort hotel was being built and where the trailers were located that were being used for offices and housing for Seljik's staff, when Brandon disabused him of the circumstances of his invitation.

"I am honored that Mr. Seljik thought to hire me for this project," Mark had said.

Brandon's response had been deflating. "I doubt Jemal knows. He has so much on his mind that he leaves staffing details to me. We needed another draftsman—he's making sometimes major changes on a daily basis that have to be redrafted overnight—and we used you at Christmas time. I just

222

went down the list of those who would be available and who were familiar with our routines."

"Oh."

The young man must have caught the disappointment in Mark's voice, because he quickly added, "Of course the list only includes those Jemal has found acceptable. It means something to be on his list."

"Oh, yes, thanks," Mark had said a bit more happily. "So, you say the plans are still being changed?"

"Yes, you'll have plenty of night work to do. I've put you in with three others who are working as site supervisors. You'll probably be getting most of your sleep during the day and they at night, so, although the trailers are tight on space, you shouldn't get into each other's way."

"I guess if you've endured it—"

"Oh, I'm not staying in one of the trailers. Jemal and I are in hotels."

"Hotels?" Not the same one? Mark wondered. He was quite aware that Seljik was bedding Brandon.

"Jemal's at Frenchmen's Cove and I'm at the Mafolie," the young man said, his tone clipped. It was obvious that no more was going to be said about that, but it lifted Mark's spirits a bit. And then they were there, at the resort construction site. The main structure was starting to go up, and there he was, the man god himself, Jemal Seljik, standing in a group of men, holding blueprints in his hands, and giving direction. The men were closely attentive to him, as Mark thought was justified. The man was truly a god to Mark in both talent and authority.

"This way. The trailer you'll bed down in is over here; then I'll show you where your drafting table is." Philip Brandon was pulling Mark away in the direction of a small collection of dusty construction trailers. Mark kept glancing back at Seljik as they walked toward the trailers, but the architect was focused on giving directions and didn't look in his direction—as far as Mark could tell.

Four days later, Mark hadn't spoken to Seljik, let alone been in his presence. There was no indication that the great man even knew Mark was there and on the job. He did have work to do most nights, though, but it was either Philip or a Virgin

Islands native, a young black man named Terrence, who would bring him the instructions on how to amend the blueprints for the next day's work. It would have been so much easier, Mark thought, if Seljik told Mark directly what he wanted, but Philip and Terrence must be understanding the architect's intent well enough, as nothing came back to be redone for lack of understanding of what was wanted.

What Mark did gather, though, was that there was tension between Philip and Terrence. On the one evening that no changes came for him to redraft, Mark found out why. He was free for the first time in an evening. And he couldn't take it any longer that he hadn't connected with Seljik yet. The last time they had been together Jemal had been fucking him in his hotel bed half the night. There was no reason for Mark to believe that the great man had not been satisfied with him in bed. Surely it hadn't been just for that night. If only Mark could establish with Jemal that he was here—and available. Seljik and Brandon weren't at the same hotels, and Mark had checked—the hotels weren't that near to each other. If they were sharing a bed, there was no reason to have separate hotels.

Mark went to the Frenchmen's Cove resort. He had no plan other than somehow to run into Seljik "accidentally"—to at least establish with the man that Mark was here.

All that Mark established was the reason for the tension between Philip and Terrence. Seljik and Terrence had taken an after-dinner swim at the resort pool. Mark saw them, kissing as they sat, facing each other, on side-by-side lounge beds by the pool before rising and walking together to the bank of elevators.

So, Philip wasn't staying in the same hotel room Jemal was because Terrence was being bedded by the Turk now. Dejected, Mark decided to walk the two miles back to the resort construction site on a path along the Magens Bay shoreline. On the outskirts of Charlotte Amalie along a somewhat seedy-looking dock area, he stopped in a dive named Almondo's, which turned out to be a gay bar, and sucked on a beer bottle at the bar while watching young men, natives of St. Thomas—most of them black—dancing to noise from scratchy records.

A couple of them were white, though, including a good-looking gray-haired guy who had chiseled features who looked younger than his gray hair suggested. He, was expensively dressed and was obviously putting the make on the young mixed-breed guy sitting at his table, but who also was giving Mark the eye from across the room.

Almondo himself, a big, strapping black in his forties, with a wide grin and no end of advice to everyone at the bar, was helping to attend bar.

An hour later, Mark was lying on his back on a bed in a room behind the bar, panting hard, moaning, and striving to keep his legs spread and raised, as Almondo crouched over him, all glistening ebony muscle and gleaming white teeth, and grinned down into the young man's face. Mark clutched the black bull's bulbous buttocks in his hands, as the black giant pumped him hard and deep with a thick, long, black cock. In exchange, Mark's bar bill was being wiped out whenever he came to the bar for the remainder of his time in the Virgin Islands—with the assumption that Almondo had free access to his ass during this time too.

It was exactly what Mark needed at that moment—a half hour of getting it from a big-cocked man when he couldn't be getting it from Jemal Seljik. Of course all of the time Almondo was pumping him, Mark could pretend that it was the Turk who was on top of him.

* * * *

Late the next afternoon Mark came to his drafting table fairly humming. He'd been laid, and laid quite proficiently. It hadn't been Seljik, granted, but Almondo had done a really good job on pinning him to the bed. His good mood only added to his confusion, though, when Jemal Seljik showed up at his desk, all smiles and conversation as if they'd talked earlier that day—and, added to that, had with him the handsome gray-haired man Mark had seen in Almondo's the previous night.

"There you are, Mark," Seljik said. "I'd heard you'd arrived and already were at work. I'm sorry I've been too busy to talk with you before. I'm glad we were able to get you to come down to help us out. I'd told Philip that you were just who we needed and to get you down here. I remember how you'd been

225

willing to work under me on Christmas Eve when everyone else had deserted me."

Mark nearly dropped his jaw. That stream of statements was so full of surprises that he hardly knew what to say: Seljik acting like he'd been looking for him when it seemed to Mark that Seljik had been avoiding him; that Seljik was saying it was his idea to hire Mark when Philip claimed that the decision had been Philip's; that Seljik would refer to Christmas Eve night and in terms that Mark would know that Seljik had fucked him that night.

He was still formulating how to respond when the Turkish architect steamed right on to the other surprise Mark was being hit with.

"This is Chaz Winston, Mark," Seljik said, gesturing to the handsome gray-haired guy at his side, who was smiling—maybe a bit knowingly and with familiarity—at Mark. "He's the founder of the WorldTalk Internet social media network. He wants to build a house down here in the mountains overlooking the bay and is interested in me designing the house for him. If he hires us, you no doubt will be doing the drafting."

"Mark, is it?" Winston said, taking Mark's hand in his and flashing him a gorgeous smile. "And are you an architect too, Mark?"

"I'm a graduate student in architecture—at MIT," Mark said shyly, barely able to look into the man's face. Everything about him was gorgeous. He was a regular Paul Newman type.

"Any of these designs yours?" Winston asked. He picked up a scrolled design that was on Mark's desk and opened it up. "This one's interesting."

"That's just an assignment I'm doing for one of my courses and have to send it back."

"Is this vegetation on the roof?"

"Yes. The assignment is for an earth house—set into a ridge line."

"Very nice. Perhaps we'll be working together. I'm an admirer of the signature pavilion-style homes of the Seljik designs."

"Come back to my office and we'll talk about your ideas of what you want in a house," Seljik said, ushering Winston out of the trailer. As they were leaving, though, Seljik turned and said, "Would you be free for dinner tonight, Mark? We could eat at my hotel. I'm at Frenchmen's Cove."

"Yes, I'd like that," Mark answered in what was barely a squeak. It was the first time he'd had a chance to say anything to the architect he worshipped since he arrived in the Virgin Islands.

* * * *

Seljik pushed Mark down on all fours on the carpet of his hotel room just inside the door, jerked Mark's trousers and briefs down to his knees, stripped off his own trousers, mounted Mark's ass, and fucked him right there. Before finishing him, Seljik pulled the young man up, stripped him and himself down, and hustled him over to the sliding glass door out onto his balcony. Mark leaned against the glass, palms on the door, butt jutted back, and legs in a wide stance as the Turk took a time out to kneel behind him and eat his ass out, pull Mark's cock between his legs and stroke it, and finger his ass. Then the Turk stood up, covered the young man from behind, thrust his thick, long cock up into Mark's passage and fucked him some more.

Still, although Mark came, Seljik held off. He swung Mark over onto the bed, on his belly, covered him from above. He held Mark's wrists captive, with the young man's arms over his head, penetrated his channel again, and did pushups on Mark's back, stretched the full length of him and covered him close until, this time, he finally shot his load. He preceded to go to sleep there, stretched out on top of Mark and covering him close.

This would be one night that neither Terrence nor Philip were in Seljik's bed.

The next afternoon, when Mark entered the trailer, expecting either Philip or Terrence to deliver him some work to do overnight, one of the other men brought the list of changes Seljik wanted to have worked into the plans for execution on the main resort building the next day.

"Where are Philip and Terrence?" he asked. "I haven't seen them today."

227

"Mr. Seljik sent Philip up to Boston for some paperwork and Terrence has gone to his village for a couple of days," the man answered.

So, Mark thought, that's why Jemal suddenly had time for him. His usual pokes weren't here and Mark was. He wouldn't complain, though. He would take the man any way he could get him.

His cellphone rang. He was surprised when he answered it to be talking to the gorgeous Chaz Winston.

"I keep thinking of your earth house design, Mark," Winston said. "I want to take my yacht out late tomorrow morning and I thought you might like to go out with me. I'd like to talk to you about that concept."

"Are you sure that's why you want to take me sailing, Mr. Winston?" Mark asked.

"No, not really. You caught me. I saw you at Almondo's the other night. And I saw that you went in the back with Almondo. Jemal tells me that men fuck you and I did see you at a gay bar. I asked Almondo about you and he tells me you are a sweet lay. Jemal said I could have you if we do business together. I will, of course, let you decide that for yourself. But what I'd like to do is to sail you out into international waters and work your body over good. Am I being too forward? I am honestly interested in your earth house concepts too."

"No, I appreciate your honesty," Mark said.

"Then, would—?"

"Yes," Mark answered. Yes, he resented Seljik giving him to another man, like this. But, yes, going with Chaz Winston was just fine with Mark—and Seljik could jolly well sleep alone tomorrow.

* * * *

He had such a soft mouth and a tantalizing tongue and he knew just when to heighten the need and pleasure and then to back off in time for Mark to recover and to move to the next level of sexual ecstasy before Chaz started working on making him erupt. For his part, Mark was trying to hold up his end of the sixty-nine position. They were lying on towels, stretched out

228

in reverse on each other, Chaz on top, in control, on the roof of the cabin of Chaz Winston's yacht hovering beyond the northern coast of St. Thomas Island.

"Oh, shit, I think I can't hold out any longer. I'm going to come," Mark hissed through the lips he'd just pulled off the hunky Chaz's eight incher.

"Suck my balls. Bite the side of my cock. I want to come with you," Chaz commanded.

There was nothing but heavy breathing and deep moans for the next fifteen seconds, and then they both tensed, jerked their bodies in spasms together, and pumped out cum. Chaz took Mark's deep in his throat. Mark took Chaz's on his face. Chaz quickly reversed on Mark's body, taking the younger man in his arms and, after licking his own cum off Mark's face, took his mouth in a deep kiss. Holding him close, Chaz's hand went under Mark's balls and he penetrated the younger man's channel with a finger and worked Mark's prostate until Mark gave him a secondary ejaculation.

That was one of Mark's quirks—capability to have a second orgasm. Jemal knew that; Almondo knew that. There was no reason for Chaz to know that unless one of those two had told him.

"How did you know that—?"

"Shush. Don't intrude on the pleasure of coming down off the mountain."

"Coming down from the mountain?"

"Yes. That's what good sex is for me," Winston murmured. "That's why I'm building on top of the mountain here—the mountaintop experience. Building up to it is dancing on the mountaintop. The afterglow is a long glide down off the mountain. That's as important to me as the dance. And it was really good for me this time—I hope for you too. I want to give it to you hard now."

"Oh, god, yes," Mark exclaimed. The blow job had been good—very good—but that's as far as it had gone for over an hour out here off the St. Thomas coast. One blow job after the other. And he had such a nice cock, Chaz did. So long. Not overly thick, but long. Mark couldn't wait until he got it inside him.

As if anticipating Mark's anxiousness, Winston gave a low laugh and said, "Not for a while, though. I'm not a young man. We rest first."

They both drifted off, but Mark woke up with Chaz having moved over his body. He already was buried a couple of inches inside the younger man.

"Oh, fuck, yes. Yes!" Mark exclaimed, spreading his legs further, rubbing the heels of his feet on Chaz's bubble butt, and arching his head back and panting as Chaz entered, entered, entered him and started to pump in earnest. Every fiber of Mark's attention focused on that long, long cock working its way up inside him, caressing every inch of his channel as it invaded and then started to work him, slowly at first, but then faster, faster, and faster, until Mark was writhing under the older, gorgeous man, his cries of taking echoing across the water, and him dancing now on Chaz's mountaintop.

Chaz laid him good and proper, Mark begged for it again, and Chaz laid him out again. Afterward Mark sprawled there, limbs akimbo, blowing bubbles, and moaning in low tones, as Chaz propped himself up on an elbow and looked down, smiling, into the young man's face.

"You seem to have enjoyed that. I know I did," Chaz murmured.

"I'm such a slut," Mark whimpered.

"Yes, you are. I like you that way, though."

"Is that what all the talk was about concerning wanting to talk to me about my earth house design? Did you just want to get me out here and on my back?"

"That had priority, of course—getting you out here and under me—but, no, I do want to talk to you about your design."

"So talk," Mark said, sitting up with a groan.

"I don't want to build Seljik's signature open pavilions on the top of the mountain. I want the mountaintop clear for dancing. I want to build one of your earth houses just below the peak, strung out along the ridge. I want it to be invisible from below. I want it to be part of the mountain."

"I work for Jemal Seljik. It will have to be worked through him."

"I don't want to access you through Jemal. I want to possess you fully for myself. You can't get from Seljik what you can get from me. He's just using you when he isn't getting it from others. I want you to come work for—and under—me."

"I don't know," Mark answered.

"I've watched you. I have researched Seljik's operations. With Seljik, it's just him, the great man. Everyone around him is just there to serve him and his genius. Yes, it's genius, but he's not the only one who can think and create. You can live in his shadow as a draftsman, or you can come with me and be an architect—standing in no one's shadow in your creation. My creativity is in other directions altogether. I won't cover you with my shadow. You deserve to stand in the sunlight. Building this house for me will make your reputation. I can get it publicized."

"I'm just a graduate student. Working under Jemal Seljik will make my reputation too—more safely," Mark said.

"Mark my words. Working under Jemal Seljik with burnish his reputation, not yours. But just think about it for now. For now, I want—"

"I can see what you want," Mark said, with a low laugh.

"What I want," Winston said, as he reclined on his back, his long erection pointing to the sky, "is for you to ride me."

It was what Mark wanted to do too, so he did.

* * * *

Chest flat on bed, knees digging into the foot of the bed, tail in the air, Mark was concentrating on taking Almondo's thick, long, black dick deep inside. He'd told himself that he'd come to the bar to look for Chaz Winston, not knowing where he was staying and not seeing his yacht in Magens Bay harbor, to tell him that he'd be his architect. But he hadn't found Chaz here, and when he got here, he realized that he wasn't really looking for the man or prepared to give himself to him—either as an employee or a lover. The only thing he could think of all the time he was searching the area for Winston was that he still had so much to learn—that he was lucky to be living in Jemal Seljik's shadow.

231

When Almondo had tilted his head and smiled, Mark had gone with him willingly. It was the escape he needed from thinking about his options. But was Seljik even an option? The man hadn't made any commitments to him—certainly nothing beyond the current project and even his status in that was uncertain. Who had brought him here? Philip? Jemal? Who was to be believed? When did Jemal call for him? Only when Philip or Terrence wasn't available?

But then Almondo was pumping him hard—and good—and he lost all thought of Jemal and Chaz and architecture, which is exactly what he came to Almondo's to get.

When Mark got back to his trailer office, there was a telephone message from Jemal. He was to appear for dinner with Seljik at the Frenchmen's Cove resort dining room in two hours.

"Chaz Winston tells me he doesn't want to build a Seljik design for his house on the mountain," Seljik said, when they were seated at the table.

"I'm sorry to hear that," Mark said.

"He wants to build a design he saw on your worktable—a house built into the mountain just below the ridge, with vegetation-covered roofing that visually disappears into the mountain scape."

"Yes, I'm sorry. I didn't show it to him. It's an assignment I'm doing for my MIT courses. He just saw it and asked about it. I didn't work on it on my office time, but certainly, if the firm wants to use that concept for Winston—"

"The firm doesn't want to use any concept but a Seljik concept," Jemal answered, his voice not actually a growl, but the inference was there, just below the surface. His tone became more relaxed then, though. "We won't build that house for Winston, but you could, if you wanted. You could sign up with another firm, or you could start up your own firm with the Winston house. He's worth a fortune in PR as a client."

"I'm still a student," Mark said. "I'm still learning." And that was, in fact, the bottom line. It was only a school assignment that had caught Winston's fancy. Mark wasn't ready to go out on his own yet. And he didn't want to anyway. He wanted to work under Seljik—and what Seljik wanted from him

232

beyond that was also what Mark wanted from the Turkish genius in the world of architecture.

"I'm not going to build that house for Winston," Seljik said. "I will give you a contract to work with me at the end of your graduate studies, but it will be on my designs. Is that what you want?"

"Yes."

"Is there something else that you want, Mark?"

"What is important is whether there's something else you want, Mr. Seljik. Some other reason why you asked me to your hotel for dinner. Are Philip and Terrence not here?"

"No, neither one is available tonight," Seljik said. "Does it make a difference with you that I fuck them if I ask you to come up to my room now? I'm a man with daily needs."

"No, it doesn't matter at all," Mark answered. And he was content that it didn't matter. He felt privileged at this time of his life to be standing here in Jemal Seljik's shadow.

Seljik laughed then. "I guess I should have believed you on Christmas Eve when you told me your loyalty was complete," he said. "I can see that your loyalty would be complete. But it wouldn't be fair to take full advantage of that, especially such a special young man as you are, and I'm not talking only about your architectural design talent. I did send both Philip and Terrence away—because of you, and I don't need to fuck either one of them if I can have you. And my firm won't build your design for Winston, but I'll financially back a firm in your name to build anything you want for anyone, including Winston. So, here, I'm laying my cards on the table. Do you have any questions?"

"Just one," Mark said. "Can we go up to your room now."

The Turkish giant laughed, his eyes sparkling.

That's Why

Brad Besson caught on that he was the only one speaking—all other conversation in the high-flown witty debate on politics and economics had burbled down to nothing but what he was saying. They were gathered poolside on the terrace behind Frederick Gates's residence in the housing compound of the Baker Institute on the banks of the Chesapeake Bay, just to the south of the mouth of the Severn River at Annapolis, Maryland. Brad looked across the oval of open meadow at the rear of the houses on Reagan Circle to the parking apron at his own house, seven similarly designed buildings from Gate's dominating residence. Tom was getting out of his beat-up Nissan pickup there, bare-chested and in drooping, worn jeans, and entering the house through the garage, moving around Brad's Porsche Boxster. Brad wasn't the only one watching Tom move into the house.

Tom obviously was the sticking point here. Tom was the blemish on the peach. Tom clearly didn't belong here.

To this point, all of the conversations around the pool and barbeque stations had focused on the business of the Baker Institute, a self-contained think tank on conservative public policy, with direct links to the Naval Institute Press up in Annapolis, which published the institute's studies. The institute took studying, writing, speaking, and consulting on public policy on to the point of forming its own closed world in which to pursue its beliefs and pronouncements. The institute included a graduate student center, providing certificates of vetting as conservative pundits, and its own closed living environment. Those connected with the institute worked here and lived here in their own closed, protected bubble. As with any community, there was an inner circle, the one at the Baker Institute, strangely enough, not being based on a hierarchy of conservative pundits but on a small group of institute fellows, led by Frederick Gates, who also wrote political fiction.

Just outside the gates of the Institute grounds, a chapel they all were recorded members of and gave lip service to was located on one side of the entrance and a museum dedicated to American patriotism was on the other side.

Tom was an alien presence in their world.

Before Tom had been seen driving up to Brad's house, Brad, who was an assistant professor in the institute's graduate studies program and who also wrote political fiction, had maneuvered himself into a heady discussion circle that included Gates, Evan Peterson, Betty Tau, Tucker Coryn, and Maryam Noor, all members of the inner group. Brad, young and ambitious and a recent arrival at the Baker Institute, was dying to be included in this inner circle. He had worked hard to work his way into being comfortably accepted, even informally, in a discussion group like this.

Realizing that the discussion had paused and all of the rest were watching Tom walk into the garage at Brad's house made Brad realize for the first time what the sticking point had been on his acceptance in this group, despite the lengths he'd gone to to fit in. It was Tom's presence.

As if to bring this home, Betty Lau broke the silence by saying, "Your brother has been with you for several months, Brad. Is he settling in?" Brad understood that this was her way of asking when they were going to be rid of the alien presence of Tom.

Evan Peterson chimed in with, "Doesn't he work in the Baltimore area? That's rather a long commute from here, isn't it?"

Brad's eyes went to Frederick Gates. All of the acceptable behavior at the Baker Institute centered on the views of Frederick Gates, and it had been Gates who had brought Brad here and who Brad had completely subordinated himself to. The institute president was looking at Brad, his demeanor neutral. That wasn't neutral at all, though. He wasn't reigning in Tau or Peterson. They obviously were expressing his view, as well.

Gates cut an imposing figure. He was a tall, substantial-figured man, who was able to look collectively elegant, formal, and commanding even in a setting like this backyard barbeque. He wasn't a good-looking man, but his features were strong, robust, and dominating. It would be clear to any stranger, if a stranger were permitted to enter this environment at all, that he was the man in charge.

"He's doing more work around Annapolis now," Brad said. "There's a building boom in the region and a high demand for experienced construction workers."

Betty sniffed, and Brad blushed a bit at not being able to establish more about Tom in this community of high-level brain power than that he was experienced in house construction. But, although he now understood where the lines were being drawn on this and the danger he was in, he wasn't ready to give in yet. He still had some leverage. He turned his focus on Frederick.

"Where are Louise and the children, Fred?" he asked Gates. "I haven't seen them around this afternoon."

"Louise has taken the children to Harrisburg for the weekend," Gates said. Louise's father was a Pennsylvania congressmen. Frederick and Louise made sure he saw his grandchildren regularly and that he would remember he had them generously covered in his will. And Frederick made sure that Louise was happy with married life and was willing to share in family expenses from her trust fund. On the surface, at least, they were the perfect family. Brad knew that there was more to it—and to his question—than was to be seen on the surface. He had played the card on purpose, and Gates understood and accepted the play.

"I'll miss them, but it gives us time to go over that feature you are putting together for the *Wall Street Journal*, Brad. Perhaps you could stay back after the others have gone this afternoon and we can work on that."

"Of course, Fred. Whatever you want." Brad answered. The "whatever you want" was spoken with purpose as well. He cast a level and expectant look at Frederick, who delivered, as wanted. "We of course welcome having your brother here, Brad. It can be quite an advantage having someone who could help with building malfunctions close to hand."

236

Evan Peterson, who was about to express another concern about the presence of Tom, got the message and clamped his mouth shut, although he looked a little confused, which served to confirm in Brad's mind that Frederick had said something entirely different than that about Tom in a conversation with Evan.

Frederick turned to Betty and deflected her maneuver on her competition for advancement at the Baker Institute against Brad, by saying, "I expected the evaluation of Kenneth Peltz's progress on my desk on Friday, Betty. When can I expect to see that?" He already knew that she had done nothing on that yet. Frederick had an excellent network of informants among the institute support staff.

"It's done," Betty said. "I don't know why it wasn't sent over to you. I'll make sure it's on your desk when you arrive for work on Monday."

That would take care of Betty. She'd be busy all day Sunday putting that evaluation together.

Frederick turned to Evan Peterson, but he'd already separated from the group and moved to another one. He and Betty had obviously coordinated an attack on Brad's position with Frederick, neither liking how much in favor the "new man" had become with the institute president since he'd arrived, and the arrival of that redneck interloper brother of Brad had given them an opening. But in the face of Brad's successful parry, Evan was adept at realizing what had worked and he too had papers late in arriving on Frederick's desk. He was smart enough to withdraw from the fray for now.

That left Frederick and Brad, who nodded to each other and each peeled away to join separate discussion groups.

* * * *

Brad stood by the staircase as Frederick glad-handed the last of the guests away. It was after 7:00 p.m. and the party had been for lunchtime, so it could be racked up to be a success. By 7:00, though, everyone was more than tired of trying to jockey for position on their Saturday in the isolated and insular community. They had all run out of brilliant and witty political

237

observations and of equally brilliant and witty put downs of what their colleagues had to say in attempts to upstage them.

"Glad that's over," Frederick said, turning and moving to Brad. The strain of presiding over the soap opera showed on him. When he got to Brad, he put an arm around the younger, smaller, sultry, dark-haired twenty-six-year-old, and Brad turned his face up to his mentor's. They moved into a deep kiss. Frederick ran his hand down Brad's chest and cupped the young man's package. Frederick sighed and Brad groaned.

"I thought they'd never leave," Brad whispered.

"I, as well. Shall we go upstairs?"

Brad waited dutifully in the upper hall, while Frederick went around the second story and closed the doors to the master bedroom and to his children's room until only the door into the guest room remained open. He had already firmly locked all doors on the first floor with access from the outside. The guest room was on the east side of the house and thus the light was dim. The windows were open and an early evening breeze ruffled the curtains. For the following three-quarters-of-an hour, the initial sounds were of the curtains moving and the low panting of the two men slowly developed into heavy breathing, mutual praise and encouragement, and the cries of orgiastic release.

They initially stood in the center of the room, kissing and slowly slipping the clothes of each other off their bodies and moving their hands over each other's curves, crevices, and stiff cocks. Brad's body was lithe, lightly muscled, almost perfection. Frederick was taller, thicker, having thickened out and moved toward obesity, without having reached that yet. He had been in better shape when he'd been a senior scholar at Johns Hopkins University's Paul H. Nitze School of Advanced International Studies in Baltimore and Brad Besson had arrived there as a graduate student intern. Brad had been a handsome man at any age; Frederick had grown into looking distinguished but had bypassed any hope of beauty.

Frederick had had the privilege of coaxing Brad's legs open and fucking him while the two were at Johns Hopkins for over two years before Frederick brought Brad here to the Baker Institute.

238

Neither of them had ever said a thing about how Frederick could reconcile his hardline conservative views with not only adultery but also gay sex. On Brad's part, all he was interested in was advancement in his field and Frederick was his ticket to that. Of course he didn't say anything like that to Frederick. He gave nothing to Frederick but complete submission and the impression that he'd do anything to have Frederick's cock, which was nothing to write home about, inside him.

Although Frederick did not realize it and was too arrogant to entertain the concept, it had been Brad who had seduced him that first time.

Brad's ambition put him on his knees in front of Frederick in the guest room of the Baker Institute's president's home when they were both naked and that put his mouth on Frederick's cock. And it was ambition more than want or attraction to Frederick that put Brad on his back on the foot of the guest bed, his legs spread and raised and Frederick crouched between them as the sounds in the room became that of heavier breathing, Frederick's occasionally muttered "Oh, baby, oh baby," and Brad's answering of "Yes, yes, yes, like that" at ever increasing decibel levels as Frederick moved an almost adequate cock inside the younger man's channel.

To enhance Frederick's pleasure so that he could bring a handsome young man to a satisfactory climax, Brad cried out his "Oh, shit, you're going to make me come," while vigorously stroking his own cock, and Frederick managed a weak ejaculation a bit later.

Twenty minutes after that, going for the rare seconds, as meetings were usually furtive and fast, taking advantage of the overnight absence of Frederick's family and the satiation of contact with each other of the other inmates of the Baker Institute community, Frederick and Brad were stretched out beside each other on the guest bed. Frederick was doing what he best loved doing with Brad, reliving what he had thought had been his masterful seduction of the young man the first time. He was kissing Brad in the hollow of his neck and on his ear and whispering how fine the young man's body was. Simultaneously, Frederick, assuming Brad wasn't fully aware he was doing so,

239

had the fingers of one of his hands were caressing the young man's naked body. The hand went to Brad's closed thighs and he slowly coaxed them open to where, pressing the heel of his hand under Brad's balls, his index finger was able to reach, rim, and then penetrate Brad's ass. Brad was moaning and giving him little gasps of experiencing heavenly violation he could not resist.

Brad was breathing heavily for him and panting hard. "Yes, yes," he murmured.

Frederick whispered those memorable words of seduction he'd used the first time, "Your body is so fine. I must have you. I must fuck you."

"Yes, yes, fuck me," Brad responded and rolled over onto his side, allowing Frederick to pull Brad's ass into his pelvis and for his cock to slide inside and start to move. Frederick never tired of reliving this first taking and how masterful he'd been—of Brad's inability to defend himself from Frederick's masterful expertise.

As Frederick fucked him this second time in the day, Brad counted the ceiling tiles in the room while murmuring, "Yes, Daddy, fuck me. Fuck me just like that."

It was with deep pleasure that Frederick managed some semblance of a second coming.

Frederick saw Brad off at the top of the stairs, Frederick in a robe, ready to go off to the shower and then sit and smoke a celebratory cigar and drink a snifter of brandy and Brad, dressed, a portfolio of papers the two supposedly had spent the last hour working on in the crook of his arm as he prepared to leave and walk around the circle to his house. No doubt his colleagues would come to the window to watch him progress toward his house, all knowing he had spent an hour with "the man," further solidifying their relationship, but none having an inkling of just how close that relationship was or exactly how they were solidifying it.

"Your brother . . ." Frederick said. "I don't know why . . ."

"Tom, yes," Brad said. Then he said, "I wish we could meet more often than this, you and I." He didn't, of course, unless it moved his career faster than it was doing. "You do me so well, you know. I think you get better and better."

"Yes, well," Frederick said, clearly pleased and forgetting his original line of thought, which, of course, was Brad's intent that he do. "Now that it's summer and the children are older, I think they will be going to Harrisburg with Louise more often."

"We'll need to have more projects we must work on together. The seminar at Harvard next month. You'll need to take someone with you and whoever you take will need to coordinate a good bit before then."

"Yes, that's a thought," Frederick said.

Brad knew that both Betty Tau and Evan Peterson were vying for that trip as well. It suddenly seemed like this afternoon had been a good investment.

"Yes, that's something to think about," Frederick said, as Brad slipped out of the door before the man could again bring up the presence of the construction worker, Tom, in the pristine and high-brow Baker Institute community.

* * * *

"Was that another 'claws out' pool party you all were having up at the top egg head's house when I got home?"

Tom was sprawled on the sofa in front of the TV in just cut-off jeans, swigging a beer and watching a baseball game in the near dark. The light coming in through the windows was waning, but he hadn't bothered to turn on any interior lights yet. In contrast to Brad, Tom was thin and angular. He was hard-bodied, his muscles well-defined, his body deeply tanned from working outside in construction. His hair was a dirty blond, long and held back in a ponytail. Streaks of sun-bleached strands ran through it. He was good looking, but he looked like he'd led a hard life, like he spent time on a Harley, buzzing around the country with a gang. He looked like he'd break you in two if your crossed him.

He had piercings, which would shock the Baker Institute community if they got close enough to him to see them—a diamond stud earring, a bar through one of his nipples, and another one where very few got to see. And a few tattoos, including a barbed-wire band around his right bicep, a blue

241

starburst surrounding and highlighting his "inny" navel, and, most prominent of all, angel wings spanning his shoulder blades.

In all, Tom was a stark contrast with Brad's sensual, but clean-cut, dark look, and the angel wings in no way represented his overall look. If Brad's neighbors in the tight-knit "live where you work" Baker Institute community hadn't known he was a guest at Brad's house and they saw the man walking down any street in the compound, they would have been reaching for their cell phones to call 911.

"Yes, it was another 'I can top' that review and challenge of the pecking order session, combined with a scrutiny of who is in top mental shape and who isn't," Brad answered.

"And you came out ahead on both counts, didn't you?" Tom said. It was said as if it was a given. "You're in even better graces now than before you went?"

"I like to hope so," Brad answered. "I think I landed the trip with Gates to Harvard next month."

"That's good," was the answer. But then Tom yelled at a pitcher on the TV who had walked someone—obviously someone on the team Tom wasn't cheering for. He didn't pursue the question of what Brad had to do to gain favor with Gates.

"Do you need me to fix you some dinner?" Brad asked. "I had enough at the pool party."

"Naw, I got something when I got home."

"Did you have to go all the way to Baltimore for work?"

"Further. They're opening a new section in Colombia."

"So, you're tired?"

"Naw, I caught a nap before the game. It looked like the pool party broke up a long time before you came home."

"Gates had me stay late."

Tom cursed at another walk on the TV set. He didn't ask Brad what had caused him to stay late.

"I'm going to get a shower. I need to clean off what I have to do to get ahead here." Brad stood in the doorway to the living room for a minute as if maybe his statement would evoke an exchange between him and Tom that went more than a second or two in depth, but nothing came back. That was one of Brad's frustrations—standing between two worlds, the institute world, where everything was scrutinized for hidden or deep meaning and then analyzed and discussed and argued to death, and life with Tom, which was all shallow surface. He turned and went upstairs to the bedroom, stripped down, and went to the shower.

Brad turned in the shower and saw Tom in the bathroom door, leaning against the frame of the door, watching him lather himself up, and pulling on his cock. That was Tom's most distinctive feature—his nearly nine-inch cock and the piercing that few others ever saw, the thick Prince Albert ring in the cockhead. All of this was accentuated by the man's tan line, his midsection that usually was covered at least by the short jean cutoffs white, with his torso and legs deeply tanned. The whiteness of his pelvis focused attention on what he was swinging between his thighs.

The man was smirking. When he saw that Brad had noticed him, he strutted over to the shower, opened the door, climbed in, and pressed his hands to Brand's shoulders. Brad sank to his knees and took the monster cock in his mouth, the PA ring clicking against his teeth as he serviced the hardening shaft. When Tom was hard as hard could be, he pulled Brad back up, palmed Brad's buttocks, and lifted his body, sliding Brad's back up the slick tile wall of the shower. Brad cried out in pain-passion as Tom lowered his channel on the long, long cock. Brad hooked his knees on Tom's hips and locked his fists behind Tom's neck. He groaned and moaned—deeper and more genuinely than he had ever done for Frederick—as Tom held there, his cock deep up inside Brad, waiting for Brad's channel to adjust to him. When it had, he started a long, hard pumping, while Brad writhed under him, his cries of pain-pleasure echoing around the bathroom.

When they had both ejaculated, Tom, much stronger than Brad, threw Brad over his shoulder and took him out to the bedroom to the king-sized bed—their bed—and tossed him down on the bedspread on his back. Climbing over Brad in the reverse then, the two men sixty-nined until Tom was hard again. He reversed, held Brad's legs spread and raised, and gave him all nine inches again, as Brad arched his back, groaned, and begged for both mercy and everything that Tom had to give him.

Once again Tom held when he was in to the hilt. He whispered, "Is this better than Gates can give you?"

"Yes, oh yes," Brad exclaimed.

"They want you to get rid of me, don't they?"

"Yes, but you are here for as long as you want—as long as I'm here—as long as you give this cock to me. Fuck me. Fuck me now!"

"Can Gates get it up again this quick?" Tom growled.

"Shit no!"

"Can Gates fuck you this good?"

"Fuck no!"

And Tom began to plow him again, gloriously punishing his channel walls with the thick PA ring.

This. This is why I let him stay here, Brad screamed in his mind, at last answering the lingering question that he had deflected earlier in the day from Frederick Gates. I ignore everything you people say and hint about him because he has a nine-inch cock with a ring in it and knows what to do with it.

And of course Tom wasn't Brad's brother. He was just a big-cocked construction worker Brad had picked up in a bar in Baltimore. Everyone had just assumed and, in their self-anointed cleverness asserted that Tom must be his brother to tolerate the lazy redneck staying with him. Brad never had said he was; he just hadn't said he wasn't. Most of those in the Baker Institute didn't listen to anyone but themselves anyway.

Sunset Save

"You seem a million miles away. What has your attention—that newspaper or that Japanese maple out there? The tree is new, isn't it? Wasn't something else there?" The questions came from Walker Sharp, the novelist, and Maxwell Ackerman's neighbor in the row of small, but very expensive, townhouses on Drayton Street, facing Savannah's thirty-acre Forsyth Park.

Max turned his eyes on the man sitting beside him on the terrace behind his townhouse. The two had been taking turns hosting each other for 5:00 p.m. drinks for two years. Both were alone now. They came from two different worlds—Sharp wrote literary novels and Maxwell was a sportsman, having been a professional tennis player when young and a sports commentator and sports gear representative in middle age—with the difference between them even more pronounced. In his fifties, Walker Sharp was still turning out a best-selling novel every year. The public life of Maxwell, now in his late sixties, had been over for nearly a decade and his private world had collapsed two years previously. Walker was about Maxwell's only day-to-day contact now other than Dinah and her husband, Horace, who took care of Maxwell's minimal needs.

"Sorry, I'm just being morose," Maxwell responded. "I see in today's paper that Stan Murphy has died. He was entered at Wimbledon for the first time the last year I played there. I looked through the rest of the obits, and all the other men reported to have died are younger than I am."

"It happens, Max," Walker said. "That's just today's paper."

"I know, but I looked at their ages and you know the first thing I thought? I thought that they didn't die so young that

245

I'd say they died too young. No one can say they didn't get a full crack at life. And I'm older than they were when they died. I'll bet that's what others think too when they read those obits. That's what they'll think when they read mine. No one will say 'He died too young.'"

"I like to look at it more like my mother did when she was in a nursing home at the last," Walker responded. He wasn't going to try to talk Maxwell out of his morose attitude toward this. He had too much respect for Maxwell to try to sugarcoat life for him. "Although I'm sure she regretted the loss of friends, she admitted to me once that her first thought when someone else died was that she had outlived another one."

"And the tree out there," Maxwell said, "I put that in to balance the other Japanese maple, but I won't live to see it large enough to do that."

"There was something else there before, wasn't there?" Walker asked, trying to change the subject to something that would depress his friend less—but unsuccessfully, as it turned out.

"Yes. There was a white birch tree. Neal put it in, wanting something there with interesting bark. I told him that white birches don't thrive here, but he said this one would for him. But it died . . . just like Neal did."

"It's been two years, Max," Walker said. "Neal wouldn't like for you to withdraw from the world that long. I'm thinking of going to Club One this evening. Why don't you go with me?"

Club One was a gay bar and entertainment venue in downtown Savannah, known for its drag queen shows and as a good pickup venue. Walker and Maxwell both were gay. That was the main reason they were comfortable with each other, although they'd never gone with each other in that way. Maxwell had very definitely been partnered with Neal Jordan, the Savannah native who had brought Maxwell to town after a career on the road internationally.

"You aren't asking me out on a date, are you Walker?" Maxwell asked, a slight smile on his face. His eyes were still turned to the new Japanese maple, but what they were seeing was Neal planting the white birch. Since he wasn't looking at Walker, though, the novelist didn't hide what Walker, in fact, would like to see happen. And maybe, just maybe, Maxwell didn't look directly at Walker when he said that because he didn't want to see rejection in Walker's eyes.

"No, of course not," Walker quickly answered.

"No, thanks, not tonight. But do go ahead and go. You need to get out more."

As do you, Walker thought, as he pulled himself up from the lawn chair. "Maybe another night then," he said, as he moved toward the gate they'd put in the fence between their properties. Both of them knew that "maybe" was the operable word. "You need to get out as much as I do." If not more, he added in his mind.

* * * *

Max sat and watched Walker move off toward his own side of the fence. He knew what his neighbor was suggesting. He even suspected that Walker would go with him if he indicated that was what he wanted. There was a time, when Neal was still alive and Walker still had his wife, Alice, that they were attracted to each other and both realized it and suppressed it because they both had partners they didn't want to betray.

But that ship had sailed, hadn't it? Walker was still an attractive man at fifty-five. He had grayed but done so without losing his male model looks or his trim figure. And as far as Max knew, Walker was still healthy without any serious debilitations. Max couldn't say the same. He took eleven pills a day—for high blood pressure, diabetes, atrial fibrillation, and now there were arthritic pains cropping up here and there. He supposed he should be lucky to have reached his late sixties. He'd had some injuries in his pro tennis days, ones that built up to forcing him off the court before he was thirty-five. Of course, thirty-five is old for a professional singles tennis player, so he got no sympathy when injuries forced him into retirement from that. Yes, he'd kept himself in shape with gym work and club tennis, motivated to continue to look good and fit on camera, but in the last year—no, the last two years, since Neal's death—he felt like he was going to pot.

The only good thing he could say about his condition other than still looking presentable was that he still could get it up and still could produce cum. But he was driving it with his own hands these days. He knew that was by choice, but at the same time he was wary of being rejected if he tried to take his need for a spin with younger men.

It was too late to contemplate Walker. He couldn't even say whether they would be a good fit. Max had done some flip-flopping in his wild and sexy tennis days, but he'd been an exclusive top with Neal. He and Walker had never gotten around to determining whether they'd be a fit. After Alice had left Walker, there had been a procession of young men next door, but their preferences other than gay hadn't been something that Max had discerned. He had still been content with Neal.

No, it was too late for Max, he was convinced. And he was a nonperson now. He was just waiting around for the end, it seemed, reading the obituaries and regretting what he wouldn't be around to do and see—the trip to New Zealand would never happen now; he should have done that one of the years he played in the Australian Open. Nor would he be doing the around-the-world ocean cruise—or the ski village retreat in Aspen that one of his early boyfriends, Serge, and he had dreamed of. Neal was a beach bum; he had had no interest in snow.

What to do tonight? Max wondered. He could have taken Walker up on the evening at Club One. Maybe that would have stirred his juices. He hadn't had sex since six months before Neal died—since Neal had grown too weak for it. He didn't even know if he could keep it up now when faced with having sex with a stranger. He could get it up; he took care of himself. But with all the pills he took, could he keep it up with another man to deliver a mutually satisfying ejaculation? Wasn't he afraid he couldn't? Wasn't that why he was holding Walker at arms' length now and why he felt a bit threatened by the suggestion that they go to Club One together? Did he want to know that he couldn't get it up when watching a sex act on stage or in going into a back room with a stranger? And was he afraid of a stranger laughing at the suggestion of going with a sixty-

248

seven-year-old man, not willing even to go far enough to find out that Max was gloriously hung?

Max would walk into town, go through a couple of the famous squares, go to a steak house—maybe one of Paula Dean's restaurants—this evening and maybe pretend he wished he could have taken the risk to try out Club One.

But first he'd go across the street and into Forsyth Park. This is where he'd first picked up Neal, and where he'd asked Neal to partner with him—and where Neal had broken the news of his terminal illness. All on the same bench in an isolated part of the park.

Max, sitting on a bench—his bench—in Forsyth Park, barely noticed the young man with the tennis racket under his arm pass the first time. On the second pass, he did notice him, especially because the young man—looking a bit scruffy for tennis but otherwise quite good looking, slim and with a sultry look, a lock of hair flopping over into his eyes—paused and gave Max a scrutinizing look. On the third pass, Max watched the young man approach and stop, and stand in front of him.

"Excuse me, but aren't you Max Ackerman? The tennis player?" the young man asked.

"You recognize me?" Max asked. The young man— maybe twenty, maybe not quite—was a real looker, but both his cutoff jeans and his T-shirt were the worse for wear. He was wearing scuffed-up tennis shoes, but no socks.

"Yeah, I heard you lived somewhere around here. I play pick-up tennis on the courts at the southern end of the park when I can. We talk about you there."

"You talk about me?"

"Yeah. You're gay, aren't you? We are too—the guys who meet for tennis. We heard you had a younger guy living with you here—and that you were quite a rake when you were playing tennis. Sort of an open secret. Like the male Martina Navratilova or Billy Jean King."

"Which dates me, doesn't it?" Max said, with a little laugh.

"Hey, you look great to me," the young man. "Can I sit with you a bit? I mean, you're not expecting anyone, are you? The younger guy you're living with?"

"No, the bench is a public one. Sit, by all means, if you want. And there's no waiting for my partner. He died—some time ago, actually. His name was Neal. Do you have a name, young man?"

"You can call me Jamie. I'm sorry about your partner."

"That's OK. I guess news travels slow in Savannah."

"So, you waitin' for someone else? You got someone else?"

"No, I'm not waiting for anyone else. You must play a rough game of tennis with these friends of yours," Max said, wanting to change the subject. "You look like you've gotten the worst part of a rough game."

"Yeah, well, these are my good clothes. I guess you can say that I don't just play tennis at the park's public courts. I live in the park too."

"I'm sorry I said that," Max said. "So, you're homeless and live in the park?"

"Yeah, I do. It's OK. I make do. I get some help. I have some regular guys who keep me going."

"Regular guys?"

"Yeah, it's how I heard that you like men. That's what I do to get by. I take care of the needs of men. They pay me for sex. I probably shouldn't say that in public, but you bein' gay yourself and all . . ."

"I see. So, stopping by this bench . . ."

"Yeah, I thought maybe we could do a deal. It's suppertime, and I heard—"

"You thought I might pay for your supper in exchange for a blow job?"

"Yeah. Like this bench, you know, is a favorite place for . . . you know."

"Yes, I know," Max said, thinking about the first time he'd hooked up with Neal. Neal had given him a blow job over in those bushes over there. He'd taken Neal home then and never let him go again. "I'm afraid I'm a bit too old for all of that now."

"You don't look too old to me. But, if you're not interested . . ." Jamie started to rise.

"I'm a bit lonely this evening—interests aside," Max said. "Tell you what. Since you still are playing tennis despite the difficulty of your living arrangements and remember an old tennis player like me, I'd be happy to take you to dinner for the conversation, no strings attached."

"I wouldn't mind the strings attached," Jamie said, "with you."

"Let's just say dinner, shall we?"

"If you don't want it. But just whistle if you do. You look fine to me. It would be a gas to do a tennis legend."

Rain was threatening, so Max took Jamie to a small restaurant nearby rather than into the historical area of town. They had a pleasant hour of eating and chatting, with Max discovering that Jamie was, indeed, well versed in both the playing and history of tennis. It was sprinkling when they exited the restaurant.

"I enjoyed it, Jamie," Max said. "I guess I needed company this evening and I've enjoyed talking with you about tennis."

"Thanks for dinner," Jamie answered. "And if you want, I'll come home with you and you can fuck me."

"It's tempting, Jamie. But I'm an old man and beyond that, I think."

"You think or you know?" Jamie asked. "It isn't just the dinner. I like older men and you turn me on. It would be OK, if you're worried, if, you know, you couldn't perform to the end. I do old guys; I'd help you along."

"I don't think I want to know the answer whether I could perform to the end, Jamie. But thanks, you've made me feel twenty years younger—and if I was twenty years younger, I'd still be twice your age. Thanks again for the company." And, with that, Max launched himself into the falling raindrops and hurried back to his house.

The rain picked up and had become a deluge when, while locking up before going to bed, dressed in his sleeping shorts and a silk robe, Max found Jamie huddled in the shelter of his front porch.

"Jamie," he said, turning on the porch light, and opening the door. "What are you doing there."

"There's nowhere in the park to shelter from rain like this," Jamie said, "and they've put up a metal fence closing off the church porch I usually go to. Please, just let me sleep here until the rain stops. This isn't the first time I've slept here. You just haven't noticed."

The "you just haven't noticed" stung Max, especially now that he'd met the young man. How often had he seen him and just looked through him? "No. Come on in. I have plenty of bedrooms. There's no reason for you to have to sleep out here."

"OK, thanks. And if you want to—"

"Just come in out of the rain until it stops," Max said.

Max woke to a thunderclap and a flash of light at the windows of the master bedroom. That may not have been what woke him up, though. He was on his back, his legs spread, and Jamie was lying between his legs, holding Max's cock up with a fist wrapped around the base, and Jamie had his mouth on Max's cock, sucking his cock head. Max had no idea how long this had been going on before he came fully awake, but he was in erection and was holding Jamie's head between his hands.

He was with a young man and he was maintaining an erection.

"Ummm, ummm," Jamie murmured and took his mouth off Max's cock long enough to look up into Max's face, both of their faces illuminated by another flash of lightning, and mutter, "Didn't know you'd be hung like this. I thought maybe you were worried that you couldn't get it up any more. There's no reason to worry about that, though, is there? You're huge . . . . and hard as granite."

Yes, he'd been worried about that; no, clearly there was no reason for him to be worried. He let the young man have his way as he rose up Max's body, settling himself in place straddling the older man's hips, positioned the cock head at his hole, and slowly sank on it. The two men groaned and moaned in harmony, as Jamie rode Max's cock to a very satisfying mutual ejaculation.

After coming, Jamie lowered his chest onto Max's and the two dozed. Forty-five minutes later, with the storm still raging outside, Jamie was on his back on the bed, fisting his ankles and raising and spreading his legs, while Max knelt

252

between them and fucked the young man in long, initially slow, but increasingly rapid thrusts of his cock, ending in Jamie crying out the stroke-off of his own cock with his hand and Max filling the bulb of a condom with a strong shot of cum.

Toward morning, all quiet outside now, Jamie was on his side, his buttocks cuddled into Max's crotch and Max holding Jamie's leg up while he mined the young man's ass with his miraculously rehardened shaft. The two men were panting in coordinated sighs and whispering to each other about pulling the greatest satisfaction in the fuck out of each other. Jamie had already agreed not to be homeless any more.

There no longer was any question of whether Max could still get it up and keep it up for another man.

* * * *

"So, are these your tennis buddies?" Max asked as he returned from an evening run around Forsyth Park and entered the house. He had the urge to add, and is that my beer? But he knew it was. The four young men were sprawled around the living room.

"This is them, yes," Jamie said, and he introduced the other three in the room, not showing the least bit of embarrassment that he'd brought his friends into the house. There was no point in telling them to make themselves comfortable, as they seemed to be quite at home on his expensive furniture, some of it antiques that he'd acquired during his travels abroad. Two of the young men were sitting yoga style on an Oriental carpet and obviously were being intimate with each other when they'd heard Max enter the house.

"I guess I'll go up and shower," Max said. "It was a sauna out there tonight."

"Would you like company?" Jamie asked. "Todd here is skeptical about you."

"Skeptical about me?"

"Yes, he doubts what I've told him about how hung you are."

253

Terrific, Max thought. He's sharing our sex life with his friends. "I don't think I need help showering, Jamie," he said, with a bit of pique and turned and climbed the stairs.

The door to one of the guest rooms on the floor above was open, and it was obvious to Max what was going on in there. Two more of Jamie's friends were on the bed, one on top of the other, both naked. They were, of course, fucking. Max paused and watched for a moment, in shock that it was happening in his house and knowing he should break it up, but also aroused—and feeling the arousal—which, he couldn't help appreciating, was gratifying. No, he wasn't over the hill in the ability to be aroused, to get hard from it, and to steam on to an ejaculation. This presence of Jamie and his assumptions and not recognizing boundaries couldn't go on, of course, but, dammit, it was taking years off of Max's life.

It was probably this confusion in how to react to this sexual invasion of his house and life that slowed Max's reactions and permitted desire to overwhelm him when he came out of the shower into his bedroom to find Jamie and his well-muscled black friend, Todd, standing inside the bedroom door.

"Drop the towel and show Todd how hung you are, Max," Jamie said.

To his credit, Max didn't drop the towel. To his debit, though, he permitted Jamie to walk over and pull the towel off him—and then to allow Todd to touch him, and both of the young men to suck it, and then for the young men to push him onto his back on the bed and, one after the other, to mount his hips, bury their channels on his cock, and ride him to ejaculations.

Later, after they'd dozed, Max lying between them, he took it on himself, moving in one direction and then the other, to cover the young men and fuck each of them again. This wasn't his first threesome—not by any shot. His years on the pro tennis circuit had been wild years. But it was the first time he'd had two men in his bed, fucking them both, in over twenty-five years.

He wasn't immune to the delight that he wasn't as far gone as he feared he was—that he could still perform.

They were all still there the next morning—the two young men in Max's bed, two young men each in the guest rooms, and another one dead drunk snoring on the living room floor, a wine stain on the Oriental carpet there.

"If you don't mind, we'll be camping out here for a few days," Jamie said. "You have such a big, empty house."

Possibly because Max was mounted on Todd's ass in the bed and doing pushups on him led him to just grunt, which Jamie took as assent and Max didn't countermand later.

* * * *

"There you are, hiding out in my back yard, in the dark. Can I bring you a beer?" Walker had seen the glow of a lighted cigarette on his back terrace from his second-floor breakfast room and had come to investigate.

"A beer would be nice," Max answered. He waited, quietly, thinking over his life, as Walker brought the beer back.

"It's been quiet over at your place for a couple of nights," Walker said, as he settled in a patio chair next to Max. "I would have thought you would have come over at the height of the partying rather than now. Did you tucker all of the youngsters out?"

"They've moved on. It helped that I didn't replenish the snack cupboard and drinks frig."

"You wanted them to move on?"

"Yes, I think so. It was fun for a few days—and informative—but we obviously weren't in the same generation. Jamie warned me early that they wouldn't be staying long. I wouldn't have panicked those last couple of days if I'd known he was serious."

"And Jamie? Are you glad he has left? Or hasn't he left?"

"Yes, he's gone. I'm grateful to him—for so many reasons—but he's too young for me. I arranged for him to be in a halfway house—and his friends too. The program there specializes in developing tennis talent. I'm embarrassed to say that I leaned on the program directors by using my background shamelessly."

"Grateful for him? And you said he and the other guys taught you something?" Walker stretched his forearm out on the arm of his chair. Almost absentmindedly—perhaps unconsciously—Max covered it with his forearm and took Walker's hand in his. A little chill went up Walker's spine. Could he hope?

"Yes, Jamie solved the question of whether I still could perform as I had in my thirties and forties."

"And?"

"I can, at least for now."

"Ah, good. I could tell that that bothered you."

"It scared the hell of out me. But he also helped me see that there was just too big a divide between his generation and mine—that I was more in the mood for slow and easy. Something more sunset than sunrise. I think the colors of a sunset can be just as vibrant as those of a sunrise."

"Slow and easy is good," Walker said. "That's more for someone my age, I think. You know I went to Club One that night I invited you to go with me, and I found that crowd was too young for me. I think someone a bit older than me would be more my style. Of course it would be nice if he were hung and still could keep it up."

"You think?" Max asked. "That was a nice thing I found out with Jamie and his friends—that I still could get it up and keep it up." There was a slight pause before Max added, "You know I've been sitting here thinking about what would be the perfect age in a partner myself. A lot older than Jamie and his crowd. Maybe someone in his fifties. Of course, he'd have to be a bottom."

"Yes, that's so important, isn't it? I'd have to partner with a top myself."

"And he'd have to be a real looker."

"Yes, that would be important. A real looker like me, right?" Walker laughed at his own self-depreciating joke.

"Yes, like you," Max said, without laughing.

They went silent. Walker's sensations went to his forearm stretched out on the arm of the patio chair. Max was stroking it lightly now. Walker had gone hard from that. He wondered if maybe Max was hard too. He looked down at Max's lap. The man was in athletic shorts and even in the dim light, Walker could tell that he was erect—and hung.

"Have you ever seen how I've decorated my bedroom?" Walker asked in a quiet voice.

"Why, no, I don't think I have," Max answered.

"Would you like to see it?"

"I think I would, yes."

"Would now be a good time?"

"Perfect."

About the Author

Habu is one of the pen names of a former supersonic spy jet pilot, intelligence agent, male model, movie actor, and diplomat. A wild youth in Southeast Asia was spent enjoying whatever sexual opportunities came his way, and much of his gay male writing is about recalling incidents from those days and inventing ones he'd perhaps have liked to experience. He now leads a very quiet and ordinary happily married family life.

An American, he is a published mainstream novelist and short story writer under another name and in another dimension of his life. He has written or cowritten (with Sabb) approaching 1,000 published short stories and over 100 published erotica e-books, primarily of gay fiction but also memoir, straight fiction and ménage fiction. His hand and creative writing can be seen in stories and books by habu, sr71plt, Dirk Hessian, Shabbu, and Stephen Kessel—among unrevealed others that might surprise readers. The fictionalized GM memoir *Flying High, Diving Deep* is loosely based on his life experiences. He can be found at the adults only gay male site BarbarianSpy, which he shares with Sabb and Dirk Hessian.

You can send feedback about this e-book directly to habu, or send general feedback on this e-book to BarbarianSpy. Our authors always like to receive feedback, and appreciate it when readers post reviews at distributors and other sites.

FOR LITERARY HEAT

BarbarianSpy Books

Not all books listed below may currently be on release.
* indicates the book is available in paperback and e-book.

BOOKS BY CHRIS CROSS

Multisexual Adult Romance

Pulaski Square
Chocolate in Vanilla (MF)2
Christmas with Chris (MMF) (MM) (MF)

BOOKS BY ALEX LOCKHEED

Transgender Romance

Meeting Jenna

Transgender Other

Being Sarah

BOOKS BY DIRK HESSIAN

Xtreme Historical Erotica

Dirk's Ancient Times Collection (Print only Bundle)*
The King's Men
Shores of Tripoli*
Prophecy of Noto
Pretender's Fate

General Historical Erotic Romance

Dirk's America's Founding Collection (Print only Bundle)*
Soldier,Spy
Ridden West
Deliver a Virgin
Clouds and Rain
Confederate Gold
Puttin on the Ritz
To the Hessian Hills
Fire Down the Valley*
Constantinople*
The Beautiful Way*
Blue and Gray
Colonel's Treasure
Beginning of Time
Labyrinth
Big Sky Country

BOOKS BY HABU

Gay Erotica
Memoir Faction
Flying High, Diving Deep*
Xtreme Erotica
Fist of Gold
Liaisons
Chain Gang Banged (Short Story)
Tramp Steaming*
Escape to Girne
Silas' Choice*
Last Call
Choke Hold
Apyko: The Greek Pimp
Visits of the Schlange
Second Coming: Emile La Cour Unleashed*
Vortex: Sacrificed by Curiosity*
Dark Angel Sounding *(in e-book & included in Sounding:Ultimate Control paperback)**
Sounding: Ultimate Control *(Print Only)**
Sounding Five *(in e-book & included in Sounding:Ultimate Control paperback)**
Romance
Gift from the Sea
Shore Leave
The Aviators
Poison Pen
Need to be Needed
Key Westing (short)
Finding a New Sam
Bangkok Summer Seduction
The Photograph
Inevitable Case
Turn to Love
Rain Check
Built for Pleasure (Sci Fi)
Danny's Choice*
Pull of the Groove
Sugar n Spice Christmas
Friday Nights with Lenny (Christmas Romance)
Snowy, Snowy Nights (Christmas Romance)
Tank n Bull
Sail to the Sun
War Letters
Ravens Roost
Caribbean Cruise Top to Bottom
Arena Stage

Trading Partners (Valentine's Day)
Four Coins
Lower Than the Heart (Valentine's Day)
Brambleton
Finding Amnad
Platres Conclave
Different Strokes
Other Novels/Novellas
Also Want to Thank
Ranger Guided
Key Westing
Syrian Ram
Temptation's Clutches*
Descent into Chaos
Escape to Girne
Journey Through Abilene
Harmony and Dissonance
Stallion Station
Racing With the Devil (espionage suspense)
Prepared in Cape Verdi
Gilded Cage
House on Park*
Anything for Ambition
Dance of the Ravishers
Hard Knocks U*
My Neighbor's Spa*
Man's Man: Tales of a High Priced Gay Hooker*
Trip Money
The Indian Doctor
Sailorboy
Home to Fire Island
Switching Sides*
Murder Mysteries
Retribution (Hardesty)
Snitches (Hardesty
Gotta Keep Trying (Hardesty)
All Fools Day Foolery (Mike Kavanagh)
Inevitable Case (Mike Kavanagh)
Vanishing Laura
Death on a Ping Pong Table
Clint Folsom Mysteries Compendium Volume 1*
Death to Blonds - Stolen Judgment (Clint Folsom Mystery)*
Clint Folsom Mysteries Compendium Volume 2*
Gay Erotica Anthologies
A Hell of a War*
Earth Cry*

263

Luther*
The Indian Prince*
BOOKS BY SABB
Spanish Lovers
Driver Reliever
Hiring in Hollywood
The Legend of Holleystone Grange
Surprise Encounters*
She is He
Wrong Man
Loyal to his King
Barbarian Tales - Book One - Traveler's Tales*
Barbarian Tales - Book Two - Journeys Begin*
Barbarian Tales - Book Three - The Inheritance*
Barbarian Tales - Book Four - Road to Persepolis*
BOOKS BY SHABBU
A Season in Galicia*
Blind Dates*
Velvet Interrogation
Finding Jason
Dirty Pool
Operation Black Jade
Cigars!*
Angel in the Barn
Gayly Complicated*
Despoiling David
The Tree of Idleness*
I Met a Man
Rough Road to Happiness
BOOKS BY STEPHEN KESSEL
Gay Romance
The Forever Man
Two Chances
BOOKS BY KIM BLACK
Lesbian Romance
Transfixed on Tammie (F/T lesbian)